Praise for the first Inspector Terry Mystery
The Rhythm of Revenge

"THE RHYTHM OF REVENGE is carefully choreographed and the atmosphere and setting are fine-tuned for maximum effect. Spindler's writing style literally transports readers to another place with descriptions so vivid it's as though we all become part of the performing cast."
—Patti Nunn, *The Charlotte Austin Review*

"This is a book to read at least twice, once to race to the end to solve the mystery, and then again for the beauty of language."
—Bea Sheftel, *Romance Communications*

"Christine Spindler provides the audience with a powerful psychological drama that will leave readers avidly awaiting her next tale."
—Harriet Klausner, *Painted Rock*

"Anyone who has read P.D. James will recognize the modern gentleman inspector."
—Kelly Muzyczka, *Bella Online*

"This is a well-written, thrilling first book with a hero who is sure to keep readers coming back for more. Ms Spindler and Inspector Terry kept me up long past my bedtime last night as I reached a point of no return in the book. I can't wait for the next installment of this promising series. "
—Jani Brooks, *Romance Reviews Today*

"Spindler offers one of the most sensitive, low-key portrayals of a gay man to come along."
—Melanie C. Duncan, *The Bookdragon Review*

"This book is wonderfully paced and all the character—even secondary characters— are fresh and lively. Though at first I wanted to strangle the heroine Jessica, by the end of the book I was cheering for her."
—Carol Lynn Stewart, *Under The Covers Book Reviews*

"Well plotted and incredibly involving. Expect to race towards the end!"
—Kimberly Campbell, *Scribes World*

"This book is certainly for the discriminating reader. It is first class and I recommend it to anyone who enjoys a good mystery."
—Ariana Overton, *Sharpwriter*

"With all the attention the author gives to characterization and the complexities of personal relationships, THE RHYTHM OF REVENGE is above all a novel of suspense. Elegantly written, it satisfies on many levels."
—Ilene Sirocca, *The RunningRiver Reader*

"The characters are splendid; they are beyond a doubt as realistic as characters can get with their passions, obsessions and faults. A great debut!"

–Brenda Weeaks, My Shelf

"Inspector Terry seems to be able to effortlessly get people to say much more than they intend to, and goes above and beyond the call of duty when dealing with some of the victims of circumstance."

–Erika A. Lockhart, Fiatgirl Recommends Books

"THE RHYTHM OF REVENGE touched me in ways that startled me. Detective Terry is warm, human, fascinating and would make for an excellent lead character in a television series."

–Leann Arndt, Buzz review news

"Fun to read."

–Cynthia S. Arbuthnot, Inscriptions Magazine

"Don't put this one down for a second, as you may miss something! Inspector Terry has won my heart as a sensitive, yet human character that has a lot to offer. A mysterious, spellbinding novel."

–Jeri Sax, Midnight Scribe Reviews

"This is a fast-paced book that will leave you breathless and with plenty of goose bumps as Inspector Terry unravels a terrifying tapestry of secrets and misunderstandings."

–Kathy Thomason, The Butler County Post

"An excellent book, filled with obsession, secrets, passions, lies, joys, and suspense"

–Lorie Ham, author of "Murder In Four Part Harmony"

"THE RHYTHM OF REVENGE presents a suspenseful tale filled with non-stop action that kept my attention throughout the novel. This is an excellent read for fans of psychological drama and mystery, and highly recommended. I can't wait to read her next, FACES OF FEAR."

–Cindy Penn, Word Weaving

Faces of Fear

An Inspector Terry Mystery

Christine Spindler

published by Avid Press, LLC

Avid Press, LLC
5470 Red Fox Drive
Brighton, MI 48114-9079
1-888-AVIDBKS
http://www.avidpress.com

Faces of Fear
© 2001 Christine Spindler

Hardcover ISBN: 1-929613-83-0
Publication Date: June 1, 2001

TO JOACHIM, MY FEARLESS HUSBAND

My heartfelt thanks to
Mark Harries, Albany Street Police Station, London
Dave Jackson, Lesbian and Gay Police Association, London
Treyce, The Handwriting Company, Olivia, MN
Jan and Bev Ewen-Smith, COAA, Portugal
Olwen Parma, my bilingual proofreader
Janice Wagner, Teisha Strelow and Pam King, my medical advisors
Gaby Smolarczyk, Raffaella Rossato and Becky Anne Anderson, my supportive friends
and Mrs. Forderer, the therapist who cured me from lepidopterophobia

CHAPTER ONE
MONDAY, 15 MARCH

PATRICIA ONLY CAUGHT the last words of what Daniel said. "…circumstances, touch it."

He normally left for work when she was still asleep and never cared to kiss her goodbye. She opened her eyes to a slit and found that he looked absolutely edible in a blue suit and a fresh white shirt. She stretched out a hand and drowsily ran it over his stomach.

He whacked her hand away. "Trish, did you hear what I said?"

"Something about touching you."

"Not me. The telescope."

She blinked.

"Air humidity was high last night. When I came home, the telescope was misted-up. I couldn't store it away. It's in the living room and—"

"When it was misted-up, why didn't you just wipe it dry?"

"Trish," he said with forced forbearance.

Years ago, on a starlit night, when he had impressed her by identifying every visible object in the sky, she had pointed out that she didn't like to be called Trish because it rhymed with fish and squish. "And Patty rhymes with fatty and tatty," he had remarked dryly and had continued to outline stellar constellations—and to call her Trish.

"You can't wipe a telescope. The coating of the optics would…. Look, I have no time for explanations. It has to dry and acclimatize slowly and you will not, under any circumstances, touch it. Give it a wide berth. And don't turn up the heating too high."

"What if I play the piano? Could the resonance break the optic?"

Irony was lost on him. "I don't think so. Promise not to go near it."

The door fell to with a soft click. As on so many previous occasions, Danny had run roughshod over her affection.

Don't touch the telescope. That was the clincher. Patty jammed her feet into the carpet, tugged at her pajama top and trudged into the living room.

Their two-bedroom flat was above a vegetarian restaurant in a quiet corner of

London. Patty used the second bedroom as her study, a bright room, decorated in a light color scheme, furnished with a yellow pull-out sofa, a pine bookshelf and bureau, and a white piano.

The living room was Danny's realm. The wallpaper disappeared under blow-ups of stars, galaxies and nebulae. The coffee table was laden with astronomic magazines. The shelves sagged under volumes of reference books. And now the not-to-be-touched telescope stood there, too, drying after a clear but humid night, mounted on a tripod: a black tube, almost as thick as a drum but twice as high, black as the nights when Danny packed it into the boot of his car, drove 20 miles to the north and spent hour after hour taking pictures—the same hours that Patty spent alone in bed longing for a loving touch.

"Now it's just you and me," she said to the black monstrosity that towered between Danny's desk and the kitchen door. "It's your fault I have to wither away in a sterile marriage, where sexual satisfaction exhausts itself in fantasies about versatile lovers who can't tell a supernova from lightning. In short: this house ain't big enough for the two of us." Ye Gods, if Danny could see her now, muttering empty threats at his defenseless telescope. Defiantly, she stabbed the tube with a fingertip and turned towards the kitchen to switch on the coffee machine.

Suddenly, there was a sharp pain in her right foot. Shrieking, she pulled it back. Her heel got caught under one of the legs of the tripod. Patty lost her balance, reached out for support and found herself holding onto the very object that had toppled her. There was a moment of suspended gravity, then the telescope banged against the desk and Patty hit her head on the metal fork that held the tube. Cursing and trembling, she struggled back to her feet. She just couldn't believe what had happened. Don't touch the telescope. Not only had she touched it, she had crashed into it. Would Danny believe that it had been an accident, that she hadn't done it on purpose?

After the initial moment of shock, the stinging pain in her right foot returned with a vengeance. She lifted it and winced when she saw a glass splinter sticking out between her toes. With a determined tug, she removed it and limped into the kitchen to fix a Band-Aid over the bleeding cut.

Patty returned to the living room and inspected the mess with a thumping heart. She didn't want to cause any further damage. Gingerly, she tried to put the object of Danny's devotion back in an upright position. It was heavier than she had expected. "God, you must weigh a ton." With her feet, she secured the legs of the tripod so that they wouldn't fold up, and pulled at the fork.

Finally it was back where it belonged, standing securely and looking all right. But what did she know about its inner life, the little motors, mirrors and lenses? If anything was broken, Danny would be inconsolable. He had a mellow temperament, he wouldn't get abusive, but drift into a sullen state of silent suffering.

There was an easy way out: not to tell him about her mishap. It would be days, maybe weeks before he left on an excursion again, depending on the weather. When he found something was wrong, he would most likely attribute it to a bump in the road or material fatigue.

Patty pressed a palm against the throbbing bruise on her temple. Shirking was cowardly and unfair towards Danny. There was no choice, she would have to face the music.

ALISON DALE-FROST WAS THE LAST PERSON Shirley Ryan was keen to see on a Monday morning. Or on any other day, come to that. Clad in a leather jacket, a sleazy black mini dress and platform boots, Alison barged into the anteroom of Dr. Canova's office.

"I've gotta see Canova."

Disapprovingly Shirley eyed the girl, whom she had found obnoxious from the day when she had come for her first appointment. As if a dubious character wasn't enough, she insulted everyone with her looks: hair dyed Technicolor, nose studded, eyebrows pierced and a skull tattooed on her left cheekbone. Why did she have phobia treatment anyway? It was those who had to endure her presence who needed therapy.

"Dr. Canova," Shirley answered pointedly, "will be in at nine. If you have an urgent reason to see her, she'll have a minute to spare for you."

"You don't twig it, eh? This is a matter of life'n death."

Shirley was staggered. "Wait over there," she said in a peremptory tone. The girl flipped through the magazines and catalogues which Shirley fanned out lovingly on the smoked glass table every morning. When she had created a mess, her defiance returned and she stared at Shirley, who found it increasingly difficult to pretend she wasn't noticing, especially when Alison produced a package of gum, put a piece into her mouth and chewed provocatively.

"Ah, damn it all to hell. I've gotta talk to her now. If I snuff it, you're to blame because you wouldn't let me see her. I got this nasty letter." She took a manila envelope from her tattered tote bag and flapped it like a one-winged bird.

Shirley went on typing data into her computer. She had switched from the astrology program to the clients' files. Alison would have no scruples reporting to Dr. Canova that her secretary pursued her hobby during working hours.

"Hey, you're gone deaf or what?"

"Shut up," Shirley snapped and bounced from the chair. "If you can't wait for an hour, then you might as well leave and come back another time."

"Ta muchly. Don't be difficult and call Canova down for me."

Shirley shuddered with disgust as Alison spat the gum into the hollow of her hand. "The doctor is having breakfast." She hadn't the foggiest idea about her employer's morning routine, but that was none of this punk's business.

Alison thumbed the gum down on Shirley's desk and left. The shock cost Shirley precious seconds. As she stared dumbfounded at the gum, she heard a stampeding sound. Alison was on her way up to Dr. Canova's flat.

JOY CANOVA WAS IN HER FRAGILE MONDAY-MORNING MOOD. There were basically two ways for her to spend a weekend. She would either have a migraine attack or a one-night-stand.

The migraine attacks would invariably start on Saturday morning with blue and yellow flashes in her outer field of vision. This forewarning gave Joy just enough time to activate the answering machine, draw all the curtains and fold down on her bed. The pain was so fierce that it made her cry. Later it became more dull, interspersed with waves of nausea. The best thing that could happen was that she would sleep through the attack.

When Saturday morning passed without the dreaded warning signals, she would make plans for the evening. Distinguished clubs were her hunting ground. Men were easy prey for her. She didn't seek commitment, but short, pleasure-oriented encounters. The complex nature of human relationships had never held any appeal for Joy. Instead, she was intrigued by the histrionics of a troubled mind. Being racked with hydrophobia herself, she knew what she wanted to achieve professionally. Not for her the counseling of divorced women, or of men condemned to life-long failure by over-demanding fathers, but the delving into the depth of tortured, frightened souls.

Standing under the power shower, Joy inhaled deeply and pushed back from the checkered tiles. Two minutes of terror injected with triumph each morning, with the water all over her head. She gasped, turned off the faucet and opened the shower curtain. The next moment she cried out in shock, suppressed the impulse to cover her nakedness with a towel and to blurt out, "God, you've scared me." Both would undermine her authority.

"Out," she ordered tautly. She had been patient and understanding with Alison, but intrusion into her privacy was intolerable. Joy toweled her skin fiercely. When Alison's affluent father had insisted that she treat his daughter she hadn't known what awaited her. Alison didn't want therapy and she made that clear from the start. It was okay to be afraid of bridges, she had said, picking dirt from under her fingernails, there were ways to avoid them, weren't there? Joy doubted whether Alison should be treated outside a clinic. She was a borderline case of manic-depressive cycling, with a history of drug abuse, two abortions and a previous conviction.

Joy dressed, wrapped a towel around her head and went into the living room where she found Alison pacing up and down, absent-mindedly touching the porcelain miniatures on the mantelpiece. "You don't mind I had a gander at you when you were starkers, do you? If it had been your secretary under the shower, I would have had a seizure. She's a bit of a fright."

"Please come to the point."

"I got a letter. Scares me to death, y'know." She held out a brown envelope on which ALISON had been written in capital letters.

"Who's the sender?"

"How should I bloody know? The guy's barking mad, that's for sure."

Square block letters filled the page, spaced with elaborate regularity—and they were familiar like the pattern on the tiles in her shower. Joy's well-trained self-control stopped her from crying out in pained surprise. Then slowly, like someone walking over a mine-field, she allowed her eyes to travel over the lines.

ALISON, MY SWEET GIRL

FEAR IS A UNIQUE SENSATION
SO ALIVE, SO FIERCE, SO INTIMATE
CAN YOU FEEL HOW I TAKE YOUR FEAR AND RUN MY MEN-
TAL FINGERS AROUND IT? WITH WORDS I CAN MODEL IT INTO
PERFECTION.

PICTURE YOURSELF STANDING AT ONE END OF A BRIDGE
FEEL THE DANGEROUS MAGNETISM.

YOU ARE SO PARALYZED BY FEAR THAT YOUR FEET ARE
SAFELY GLUED TO THE GROUND, BUT YOU CAN'T STOP YOUR
EYES FROM GAZING AT THAT THREATENING CONSTRUCTION.
WHAT DO YOU CARE ABOUT PIERS SUPPORTING THE BRIDGE
WHEN ALL YOU ARE ABLE TO SEE IS A ROAD SUSPENDED IN
THE AIR? AND WHEN THE WIND BLOWS, THE BRIDGE
ACQUIRES A CONSCIOUSNESS OF ITS OWN. IT WHISPERS:
"COME, ALISON, STEP CLOSER."

OH, WHAT WAS THAT? DID THE RAILING GIVE WAY A LIT-
TLE? DID IT MOVE?

AND WHAT'S THAT ROARING NOISE? A TRAIN THUNDER-
ING THROUGH UNDERNEATH YOUR FEET. ANY SECOND NOW
THE BRIDGE WILL COLLAPSE AND YOUR SCREAM WILL MIX
WITH THE RATTLING OF THE TRAIN, THE HOWLING OF THE
WIND. AND I WILL BE THERE, INVISIBLE, AND MAKE YOU LOSE
YOUR BALANCE.

FEARFULLY YOURS,
SHADOE

The writer had captured the essence of Alison's fear. "What a cruel and twisted mind."

"Spooky, isn't it?"

"I'm glad you came to see me." It was so much better than getting drunk or
stoned, which was Alison's usual reaction to stress. "Shadoe. Do you know anyone by that name?"

Alison ran her palms down the sides of her dress that was wrapped around
her skinny body like Clingfilm. "He means to kill me, doesn't he?"

"There is no direct threat."

"I'm sure he's stalking me."

"You should show this to your parents."

"And end up grounded for two weeks? They treat me like a bloody teenager."

"Then I'd suggest you go to the police. Maybe other women have received
similar letters."

"Oh, I knew you couldn't help me." Alison yanked the letter from Joy's hand
and tore it up. "There," she spat. "This pompous ass can go to blazes." She
grabbed her bag and scurried downstairs.

Joy shook her head so hard the towel-turban came loose. "All in vain," she
murmured and tore up the envelope Alison had left on the table.

PATTY SPENT THE DAY IN GROWING TREPIDATION. Between piano lessons, she
limped into the living room and studied the telescope from a safe distance. If
only she had the means to test its functionality.

When Danny came home she was so highly-strung she almost fell over him
with the bad news. "Danny, I'm so sorry, I had an accident."

He frowned at her. "Anything serious?"

"Just a cut and a headache, but that's not the problem. The telescope was involved."

He brushed past her into the living room.

Patty showed him the dent on the edge of his desk and began to explain, putting great emphasis on her woes. "You can't imagine how tender a foot is. Hurts like one of those mean paper cuts. And my head...I thought I had a concussion." Attempting to put at least a part of the guilt on him, she elaborated that the splinter must have come from Danny's desk light that had exploded yesterday. Obviously he hadn't vacuumed the carpet thoroughly enough.

He answered with a series of grunts and inspected the apparatus, moved the tube on its fork, switched on little motors and studied LCD displays. Patty watched with ragged breath. It was like waiting for a biopsy result.

"Nothing is broken, as far as I can tell."

"Oh, thank God. I got such a shock."

"That will teach you to pay more attention in future. Repairs would have been expensive."

"Thanks for your concern. If the tripod had folded the other way, it would have landed on me. Your love of astronomy is bordering on obsession."

Danny ran a finger along the dent in the desk. "Every man needs a hobby."

"But you live for your hobby. I can't remember the last time we did something together."

He dismounted the telescope and stowed it in its container. "I was actually going to surprise you with a holiday I booked today."

She was too stunned to feel angry that he hadn't asked her before he made the decision. It would be their first trip since the disastrous honeymoon in Paris. "When?"

"Half term, end of May."

"Great. Where are we going?"

"The seaside."

"Cornwall? The Lake District?"

"Portugal," he said over his shoulder and closed the container.

"Portugal?" She wouldn't let on that she was wary of flying. It was the first time Danny had shown any initiative that included her and she didn't want to dampen his enthusiasm. "How long is the flight?" she asked casually.

"Just a few hours. Look, Trish, why don't you start laying the table?"

"Where in Portugal?"

He straightened his back. "The Algarve. There's a beautiful beach close by. They serve great seafood."

"Fish?" Was he mocking her? He couldn't have forgotten that she hated fish. "Did I mention the wild flowers?"

That was too much. "Wild flowers? But Danny, there will be butterflies."

"I know they make you nervous."

Was it possible that what she had taken for gallant acceptance of her phobia was in fact another symptom of Danny's complete disinterest in any aspect of her personality? If the telescope had still been standing there she would have banged his head against it.

"I'm scared to death of butterflies."

"I'm sure they're not going to hurt you. Nice harmless little things."

She was tired of being ribbed for her peculiarity. "I know they are harmless. I can't control my fear." And she couldn't control her voice any longer, either. "How could you?"

Danny shrugged. "If you keep to the beach you're going to be all right."

"We can't go to Portugal," she decided. "I can't. And I won't."

MONDAY, 22 MARCH

JOY ROSE FROM THE SWIVEL CHAIR, stretched and took her notes over to Shirley's desk. Shirley had already left for her lunch break, and so Joy answered the phone when it rang.

"Alison won't be coming for any more therapy sessions," someone said without introduction.

"Mr. Dale-Frost?" After the fuss about the letter, Alison hadn't shown up for her last session, so this was no surprise. "What a pity. We were making good progress." It was a string of lies. If there had been any change, it had been regress rather than progress. And Joy certainly wasn't sad to lose an uncooperative client.

"She is dead," Dale-Frost said with a voice like a steel trap.

"I am sorry," Joy said automatically. An overdose. She had seen it coming.

"She was run over by a train."

Joy stared blankly at the opposite wall.

"In Oxford," he added in answer to her silence.

"Oxford? What was she doing there?"

"Did you tell her to go there?"

"Me? Why should I?"

"She was under a railway bridge. The Devil's Backbone." He hung up.

The air around Joy thickened with terror. There could be no doubt. Shadoe had killed Alison. Joy had a copy of the letter Alison had shown her. After Alison had left, Joy had written it all down. She had a photographic memory and remembered the letter word for word. It was in her own handwriting, not as it had originally been written, in those familiar, thick block letters that looked like her father's hand. But how could Victor have found out all those details about Alison's phobia?

She had filed it away as a coincidence. There are only so many variants of handwriting, and block letters are often used in anonymous letters. But now Alison had been killed under The Devil's Backbone, the railway bridge connecting South Hinksey to South Oxford, just a stone's throw from Joy's family home.

On the other hand, if Shadoe knew so much about Alison, he might be familiar with the Canovas as well. He might have killed Alison under this bridge on purpose, just as he had willfully copied Victor's handwriting.

Joy hadn't asked her father about the letter, although she was closer to him since her mother's death. He had published a self-help book she had written, *Many Ways Out*. Now, Canova Press was editing *The Immune System of the Psyche*. The old tension was gone, probably because she was grown up and able to cope with his personality shifts. From a psychological viewpoint, he made an interesting person to study, more so than many of her clients.

Joy's recollection of her mother, Faith, who had died after a massive stroke three years ago, was starting to fade. Faith had always been busy, regrouping furniture, renewing decor. She was constantly moving house inside the house, changing the library into the lounge, the guest room into Gloria's room. She had a wall torn down between bathroom and laundry room and two walls erected in a corner of the kitchen to create a larder.

It had to be in the genes. Gloria, Joy's elder sister, smoothly joined Faith in her hyperactivity and extended it into the garden. Passers-by might get the impression of plants on legs, with chrysanthemums blossoming in the evening where tulips had grown in the morning. Not even the goldfish pond was spared. Only the birches and maples, heavy and deep-rooted, remained in their places, overlooking the scene with frowning disapproval.

As long as Faith lived, the house, fluctuating and scintillating, appeared more alive than Faith, who had been invariably dressed in a brown twin-set and skirt. Her hair never seemed to grow, her moods never to change. In this peripatetic microcosm, only Joy's room and her father's study always stayed the same. They were off limits, universes of tranquility and settling dust. But Victor was shifting inwardly, as if tiny craftsmen in his brain were incessantly rearranging neurons and synapses. What his employees at Canova Press labeled mercurial intelligence, was, for Joy, a nightmare of unpredictability. His voice spanned all the registers from baritone to falsetto. Some of his reactions were fierce, aggressive. Then again he'd be laid-back and nonchalant. His square handwriting would sometimes change to elongated or roundish script.

Often, Joy would lie awake at night and stare at the cupboard, afraid that it might start migrating together with the chair, the desk and the bookshelves. Shadows crept out from under her bed. Could the Casa Canova tolerate a room like hers? Or would it take control?

One of the reasons why she had become a psychiatrist was her wish to understand the histrionics of her dysfunctional family. It gave her immense pleasure to diagnose Faith as suffering from obsessive-compulsive disorder, aggravated by a traumatic loss, the crib death of her third daughter. Victor was more difficult to tackle. The closest she had come to labeling his demeanor was Tourette's Syndrome.

No, Joy decided, Victor couldn't possibly have killed Alison. His nature made it impossible for him to carry out such an undertaking. Halfway between picking up Alison and taking her to the bridge, he would have changed his mind and invited her to a Pizza Hut instead.

God, why was she so sure someone had killed the girl? If only Alison hadn't torn up the letter, then Joy could have taken it to the police. It was no use showing them the copy. On the contrary, it looked contrived, as if she had made it up.

Maybe it was an accident. She meant to find out.

DETECTIVE INSPECTOR CLEN SMITHHAVEN sat opposite Joy in his neat office at St. Aldates Police Station in Oxford. He was dressed with casual elegance in a gray suit. Everything about him was unostentatious, his movements, his manner of speaking, the scent of his cologne, the way he rolled up his tie with his index fingers. Although he wasn't campy or effeminate, it was clear enough to Joy that he was gay. Hundreds of Saturday nights spent in bars and clubs had provided her with a fine-tuned mental gauge for a person's sexual identity.

"Thank you for coming, Dr. Canova. I understand you were Alison Dale-Frost's therapist. Her father was very upset that the papers reported his daughter's accident as a suicide. Would you think that possible?"

"She was manic-depressive, but she'd rather have killed herself with an overdose than by getting herself run over by a train. Did her father say what I treated Alison for?"

"No, he didn't."

"Gephyrophobia. It means that Alison was scared of bridges. Not scared in the common or garden sense of the word. A phobia is rooted so deep in a person's mind that avoiding what triggers the fear becomes an obsession. There's no way she'd go near a bridge. Railway bridges were the ones that frightened her most. Not only would she refuse to walk over a railway bridge, she wouldn't want to stand underneath one, either."

Smithhaven let go of his tie. "Odd. How long had she been your client?"

"For six months."

"And were you able to help her?"

"She made two steps forward, three steps back. I came to the conclusion that she needed her phobia. It protected her from facing some other, deeper fear. I don't analyze my clients. I don't think that digging for the reason of a phobia necessarily helps to overcome it. The danger is that during analysis the patient might start to reinvent her childhood, just to please the therapist, often without being aware of it. My approach is that of gentle desensitization, careful exposure in tiny steps. I had got as far as showing Alison photos of bridges. I have brought them along."

He took the photos and studied them at length. "These are all local railway bridges, here in Oxford. Aristotle Lane, Walton Well Road, The Devil's Backbone. This is where she died. Did you take the photos yourself?"

"I did. And if you're surprised that I didn't pick bridges in London—I grew up in Oxford, I know my way around here better than in London."

"When did you take them?"

"End of October last year, shortly after Alison became my client." She couldn't recall taking the photo of The Devil's Backbone. It had been the last bridge on her round. What had she done afterwards? Had she driven straight home? Ah, yes, she had stopped for a pint and then—

"Is anything bothering you?"

"I was wondering if..." Her true thoughts were none of his business. "...if Alison came here because I showed her these pictures," she extemporized.

"You mean, if they triggered suicidal fantasies, which she then carried out here?"

"Alison didn't have any fantasies. She wasn't very bright. I once told her that the meaning of life is to find the ultimate truth: that life has no meaning. She didn't even see the paradox in that."

"Not a very sensible thing to say to someone who is depressive."

"It was meant as a provocation."

Smithhaven nodded solemnly. "Do you think she came to the bridge to test her phobic threshold or whatever you would call it in your jargon?"

"Unlikely. She had no wish to test herself or to improve her current state.

She only came to see me because her father insisted."

"If she had no motivation to go to a bridge, why did she do it? Did you tell Alison where those bridges were?"

"Well, actually not. Which makes it even more difficult to explain why she ended up there. Couldn't someone…?" Joy spread her hands.

"We're looking into this possibility. Someone might have pushed her in front of the approaching train. Where were you on the night of Saturday to Sunday?"

Joy's eyes trailed over the bookcase behind him. She had never seen books so perfectly aligned. "I was at home." Looking back at him, she added, "Alone."

"Did Alison mention that she was scared of someone?"

It suddenly struck her, that in all likelihood Alison had written the letter herself. She could have seen Victor's handwriting on a piece of paper on Joy's desk. Yes, that explained it all. The girl had planned to kill herself with some special effects thrown in. "She was always scared in one way or another. She was her own worst enemy."

"Unfortunately the weather has been dry for a week. We couldn't trace any footprints leading to the railway lines, not even Alison's own. Which could also imply that she jumped from the bridge."

"Never."

"Not even under the influence of drugs? The post-mortem revealed that Alison had sniffed three or four lines of cocaine and had drunk beer and whisky."

"You should have told me that before. Of course it changes everything," Joy lied smoothly. She had seen Alison stoned, and if anything, it had made her fear worse. Fear is a unique sensation. So alive, so fierce, so intimate. These had been Shadoe's lyric notions. No, Alison couldn't have written the letter herself because she didn't have the imagination necessary to form such sentences.

Smithhaven adjusted the cuff links on his sleeves. "It explains her going near a bridge but it makes it even more difficult to imagine how she got there. No one noticed her. We found no taxi or bus driver who remembered her. No one came forward who had given her a ride. At ten thirty she was last seen in a bar in Camden. Three hours later she was run over by a train in Oxford. How did she get from A to B? How did she plan this outing in a state of heavy intoxication?"

"It wasn't necessarily planned. Maybe the result of an erratic course." She was tired now of discussing Alison's death. "It would have suited her unpredictable lifestyle."

Smithhaven thanked her. "If you can think of anything else," he said while seeing her to the door.

"Then I'll be in touch." Another lie. Smithhaven would never hear from her again.

CHAPTER TWO
SATURDAY, 29 MAY

DURING THE JOURNEY FROM Faro Airport to Poio, Patty sat with a map and a description of the route on her lap and from time to time told Danny which turn to take. She had enjoyed the flight and was quite proud that she hadn't been a chicken, after all. She had just felt a little dizzy during take-off. Seeing London rapidly get smaller below her, she had been amazed that such a huge, heavy thing like a plane could possibly gain height so quickly, let alone lift up into the air in the first place. She made the mistake of mentioning this and Danny launched into a boring dissertation about aerodynamics.

Patty was still pretty much in the dark as to why Danny had booked this trip. He had warded off all her questions with monosyllabic responses. They bypassed Portimão and crossed the suspension bridge over the Arade river. The setting sun glimmered a bright orange between the girders.

"We must follow the sign to Lagos. And here's the road to Torre Alcalar." She forbore to comment on the fact that it was a right turn, away from the sea. Hadn't he said something about beaches?

Danny drove slowly now. They had set the air conditioning to maximum and Patty began to shiver. She bent to switch it off and almost missed the next landmark, a white-painted roadside shrine.

"Sorry," she said, when Danny had to brake and reverse a few yards. He was always taciturn, but even more so today.

The last bit was a bumpy narrow road. "COAA" read the sign in blue-on-white ceramic tiles on the low wall enclosing a garden and a neat, white house that was overgrown with violet bougainvillea.

"So, here we are." Danny looked both pleased and anxious.

The road went down steeply and ended at a small car park opposite four white canvas hemispheres mounted on round concrete blocks. It took Patty a moment to understand what she saw. "What exactly does COAA stand for?"

"Centro de Observação Astronómica no Algarve. Why?"

"You told me it was a holiday center," she said evenly. It was no good starting a war of nerves with a man whose apathy would make her look like a hysterical bitch in comparison.

"Oh, it is a holiday center all right," he answered placidly. "For hobby astronomers and their families."

"You lied to me." She couldn't help the wounded tone.

"You'll hardly notice the telescope domes are there. I'll be out watching stars for two hours each night, that's all. You can have a peek through a telescope, too."

Why did she feel as if she was fighting a rearguard action? "Don't pretend you want to share your interest with me all of a sudden."

Danny got out of the car and she followed. After the air-conditioned drive, the heat hit her like a wall and a volcano in her belly bubbled dangerously.

"Shouldn't we go inside and slake our thirst?" Danny proposed, his stilted tones annoying her all the more.

She tried to find something to say that would put Danny in the wrong. "You lied to me because you knew I wouldn't come with you if you told me that this wasn't supposed to be a holiday but a prolonged astronomic excursion. All the visitors here will be clones of you, rhapsodizing about the stars all day, waxing enthusiastic about their field flatteners and focal reflectors or whatever it is that gives them a hard-on."

"Your pettiness will not be conducive to a restful stay, Trish," he said unassailably.

"For heaven's sake, stop calling me Trish."

Ignoring her, Danny opened the trunk and removed their luggage. Patty saw him smile and abstained from further reproaches. She knew he was happy at this place so far away from the unreliable weather in London. This was a paradise for astronomers, and nothing she could say would alter his mood.

Not just his fibbing hurt, but his complete negligence of her. He didn't even bother to cover up his total disinterest in her feelings. It was time she found herself a lover, then Danny would have to show his true colors. Why not start right here? Aw, no, the guests in this place would hardly be any better than Danny. No more star-watchers, please. But once back in London she would find herself a caring, horny lover, and to hell with fidelity.

BEV AND JAN, THE HOSTS, WERE SO NICE AND WELCOMING that Patty's grudging mood had no chance to persist. The tail-wagging family dog and the deaf cat trailed them upstairs to their suite when they carried up their luggage. She decided to put her marital troubles on the back burner and make the most of this holiday.

After a shower, they went down again and onto the terrace, where they met Jeremy, a man in his thirties, small and lean, his dark blond hair cropped short. Within minutes, Danny was deeply engrossed in a discussion about the astronomical facilities.

Another man joined them. "Reginald Baker," he bellowed and gripped Patty's hand so firmly it hurt. The lines on his face were not horizontal creases of age but vertical lines of bad humor. His gaunt face and grouchy manner intimidated Patty. She was terrified when everybody shuffled into the dining room and she found herself sitting next to him at the table.

"Where are you from?" he asked her.

"London."

"So am I. But let me tell you, England is no place for astrophotography." Reginald looked at Patty as if she was to blame for it. "Too lit up. I have traveled the world, to all those dark and lonely places where you can do serious astrophotography."

This turned out to be the prelude to a long-winded soliloquy that made it clear that he had an axe to grind with anyone who was careless enough to seek his company.

"To me, any odd star is just another friendly, bright spot in the sky," someone behind Patty said cheerfully and came around the table. The woman wore pink sling-backs and a floral caftan that swung with her swift movements. "Hi, I'm Misty," she chirped.

"This is Patricia," Reginald introduced her. "Meet my wife."

"Has Reg bored you with one of his diatribes?"

Patty didn't know what to answer without offending either of them. She couldn't believe they were a couple. Misty had hazel eyes with a perpetual impish expression imprinted in the thin lines around them. An outgrown haircut of unruly brown curls framed her pretty face.

"How's the food tonight?" she asked, prodding at the mushroom pie. Answering her own question, she gave a delighted sigh. She stretched out a hand and wriggled her pink-nailed fingers. Right on cue, the deaf cat shot out from under a chair and chased the flitting shadows Misty made on the floor. "Cute, isn't she? Jan says she loves shadow-hunting."

The next moment, Patty's blood froze. There were shadows on the wall, too, fluttering, sweeping. On the flower print of the tablecloth a swallowtail had landed, its wings closing and opening like eyelids.

Patty screamed and ran for her life. She came to her senses the moment the bedroom door banged shut behind her. She stood panting and shaking, her mind soaked in terror and humiliation. She had done it again. She had allowed herself to lose control. But how could she prevent it from happening when her body's reaction was quicker than a thought? Drunken with defeat she slumped down on the bed and began to sob uncontrollably in the aftermath of her shock.

It was only when Misty touched her that she became aware of her soft voice. "There, there. It's all right. It's gone. I caught it and let it out. You can come back now. No need to worry."

Slowly, Patty turned around. Not even her mother had spoken to her in these tones, soothing and understanding.

"You didn't hurt it, did you?" She remembered with unparalleled horror how her father had once smashed one of those fragile creatures in his big palm. Don't hurt it, Dad, please. Just take it out.

"Surely not. I'd never hurt an animal. Are you better?"

Patty sat up, rubbed the back of her hands across her cheeks and tucked the strands of her straight fair hair behind her ears. "Much better, thank you. How did you reckon what I was screaming about? Did Danny explain it?"

"Not a word. But I saw what you were staring at."

"You must think I'm nuts to get so worked up over a butterfly."

"Not at all. It's weird, sure, but so is being scared of spiders, when you come to think of it. Who are we to judge upon the beauty or hideousness of animals? Just take my Aunt Charlene. She's not very partial to spiders, to put it mildly. Once as she sat on the loo and tugged at the toilet paper, a two-inch spider with thick hairy legs was pulled forward, riding on top of the tissue like on an escalator. According to my uncle, Charlene's cry is still reverberating in the bathroom."

Patty laughed.

"Ah, that's better. Come, let's go back before the pie gets cold."

"Oh, I think I'd rather stay away from the others. I don't want to hear their badinage. They'll stare at me."

"All they can think about is staring at the sky, so don't worry."

Hesitantly, Patty followed, looking around to scan the walls, as if anytime they might breed more butterflies.

Danny arched an eyebrow. "You okay, Trish?"

"The reaction you just displayed," Reg said with disdain, "was a most un–"

"Most unfeeling," Misty fell in. "And I mean you, Reg."

MONDAY, 31 MAY

LYING LANGUIDLY ON A TOWEL UNDER an umbrella, her skin shining with sun-milk, the wind combing her hair, Patty looked out on the wide, blue sea, filled with a deep sense of happiness that rolled inside her like the waves around her feet.

Danny and Jeremy were walking on the wet sand. During breakfast they had started talking eagerly about something mysteriously called Messier Marathon, which, Patty was sure, had nothing to do with long-distance running. She didn't bother to ask. She had had her share of lofty oh-you-ignorant-creature stares. Once, Danny had taken her along to an astronomers' convention. Innocently, she had asked some basic questions, like: "How does a lunar eclipse happen?" or "What will you do when you are through with those thousand or so objects?" Millions, she was corrected sternly, billions of objects were waiting to be observed.

Waiting, for God's sake. Posing, huh? Next they'd have a centerfold in their magazines with the Nebula of the Month.

Watching her husband against the backdrop of high cliffs, she felt an over-whelming sense of pointlessness. There was little she could do about it, and there was nothing left she was motivated to do about it. The crisis was creeping silent-ly, filling her with stultifying boredom, a sentiment she couldn't stand for the rest of her life. The only thing that kept her stuck in this flimsy marriage was the fact that she had nowhere else to go with her piano.

Misty wasn't at the beach this morning. Yesterday they had collected shells, comparing their pickings with the serious airs of little girls. Today, she had driven to Portimão to do some shopping.

Reginald stood on the shore, shouting after two boys about the perils of undertows. Patty smiled. There now was a man who had found his true calling, which was making others feel incompetent. And yet, Misty seemed to be happy with him. Theirs was not a dead marriage.

The boys out of hearing distance, Reg shifted his attention to Patty.

"You'll get sunburn. What protection factor do you use?" He picked up her bottle of sun lotion. "Thirty. So, let's see. Skin type Nordic. Means five minutes on the first days. That's two and a half hours with protection."

"I'm not sitting in the sun."

"You have to take into account the reflection of UV rays from the sand and the water, and the hole in the ozone layer."

Patty squinted up at the sky as if checking it for holes. "Just imagine," she mused, "if there was a hole through all layers of the atmosphere, a cylindrical vacuum, reminding us of our vulnerability."

To her surprise, Reg didn't ridicule her this time. "Well, it's all about vulnerability, isn't it?" he said with a sigh and left her wondering which magic button she had pressed.

PATTY HAD TAKEN A LUKEWARM SHOWER and was now gently creaming her skin with cooling gel. Reg had been right to warn her about UV rays. Misty came in with the cat in her arms. "Full clearance," she said.

Patty reached for her dress. "Full clearance for what?"

"No butterflies in the house, no moths, no nothing to scare you. I've come to give you safe passage to the living room."

Patty had so often been the target of silly jokes that she grew angry on reflex. "Oh, don't you start."

"Sorry. I'm really trying to help you. I've never been scared of anything, but that doesn't mean I'm incapable of sympathy."

Patty searched Misty's smile for irony and drew a blank. "Well, thank you." She buttoned her dress. "Ouch. Looks like I'll have to stay in tomorrow."

"You'll not be alone. We're going to have a lot of fun. Would you like to be my tailor dummy?" Misty was going to open a boutique in Primrose Village, just around the corner from where Patty lived. "We'll go through my spoils. Fringed shawls, silky fabrics, batik, beads. What I have in mind for my shop is a hyper-gypsy look, something between second-hand and tailored. Old dresses with new fluffy, glitzy or lacy stuff to enhance the effect. I'll be the Vivienne Westwood of rags."

"Reminds me of how I cook three-course menus with leftovers."

"I can't cook at all. But Reg's good at it."

"Sorry for saying this, but it's beyond me how someone so full of the joys of life can marry a misanthrope." She repeated her short exchange with Reg.

"Reg is just a hard crust over a soft filling," Misty explained. "He likes to play with other people's vulnerabilities to veil his own. How about you? Are you afraid of butterflies because they are vulnerable?"

Patty was intrigued. "I can't analyze the fear. It doesn't even seem to belong to me. It's like an invasion."

"You've probably been too busy analyzing your marriage," Misty said with surprising insight. "Now let's go down. The dish tonight is lamb Algarve-style and lemon syllabub. I'm glad I can sew. Two weeks of Jan's cooking, and I'll have to let out my skirts."

AFTER DINNER, WHEN DANNY WAS GETTING READY for the night in one of the domes, Patty decided to give him a last chance to show that he cared.

"Danny, I was thinking about the atmosphere."

He folded up a star chart. "Perfectly clear tonight. Bev will show us his CCD camera."

"Just imagine," she went on unperturbed, "if there was a hole through all layers of the atmosphere, a cylindrical vacuum, reminding us of our vulnerability."

He frowned pensively, then came to a conclusion. "Trish, you've got sunstroke."

"Oh, Danny, please, don't treat me like an idiot. Can't you talk about anything else but Cefirelli variables and—"

"Cepheid variables."

"Who cares? I'm a human being. I'm not millions of light-years away. I want to be talked to, kissed, cuddled. I am your wife, whether you like it or not."

The way he looked at her, silent and withdrawn, she knew that he was too detached to take up the gauntlet.

"Our marriage is based on a misunderstanding. You only proposed to me because I thought I was pregnant."

During their honeymoon in Paris, Patty had been running a fever. From the narrow, sagging bed in the attic room a friend of his used as a painter's studio, Daniel watched the moon through the glass roof. When she said, "Danny, I feel sick," he reluctantly put the binoculars aside and looked at her, his eye focus still set to infinity. "They say it gets better after the third month." But her condition worsened and he had to take her to a clinic. Her presumed pregnancy turned out to be an inflammation of the ovaries. No baby for them. Unless you counted Danny's precious baby, his touch-me-not telescope.

Danny glanced at his watch. "Jeremy's waiting."

"You didn't answer my question."

"You didn't ask one."

"I want to know why you married me."

"It was an act of chivalry."

"Chivalry? If you had been more careful—"

"Trish, we always had safe sex."

"What are you implying?"

"That you were pregnant by someone else."

Patty gasped. "That's what you thought? But that's complete nonsense. I had broken up with Roy months before I met you."

Suddenly, Danny was no longer in a hurry to leave. He reached for Patty's hand. Was this the break-through? Now that the misunderstanding had been cleared up, would he be able to love her? Patty smiled at him. But he didn't smile back. His face was pale and serious.

"You mean you were pregnant by me? Oh my God."

What was wrong now? "Danny, I wasn't pregnant at all."

He swallowed, shook his head and made a funny sound, like the cicadas she had heard all day. "Of course. For a moment I thought.... Forget it. Must have had a bit too much sun today, too. Sleep well, Trish."

CHAPTER THREE
FRIDAY, 11 JUNE

ONLY ONCE IN HER LIFE HAD Joy Canova broken her long-standing habit of avoiding commitment. Ambling down Rosslyn Hill on this sunny morning, Joy's eidetic memory came up with the trivial fact that it had been exactly two years ago that she had met Leo Croft at the chiller at Budgens, where she was heading right now. The chiller is a wonderful invention for people with a sudden thirst for champagne or fortified wine. You put a bottle into one of the five cylindrical holes, press a button, wait four minutes and take it out ice-cool. On that memorable day, Joy had bought scampi salad for her dinner and was waiting for a bottle of Pale Cream to chill.

"Man is the only animal that blushes. Or needs to," a sonorous voice had intoned behind her.

She had turned and blushed. "What?"

"Mark Twain said that. And wasn't he right?"

Later, celebrating Leo's birthday, they had shared the scampi salad and the white wine in his bedroom, the only room with furniture, since he had just moved in after leaving his family. Against her better judgment, Joy began to date Leo on a regular basis. Men of his charisma and sexual energy were rare. The trouble set in when Lydia, Leo's soon to be ex-wife, came to drown him in litanies about the wrongs he had done her or to beseech him to come back.

Joy tried not to interfere, although she knew what she would do if she were Leo. He could easily have blackmailed Lydia into more civilized behavior by withholding one of his generous payments.

Then, on a Sunday morning early in September, Lydia burst in while they were having breakfast. She was out of breath and not as immaculately made-up as usual. Their son Cameron had disappeared the night before, leaving a letter that put the blame for his ruined life on his parents. Joy retreated into the bathroom to get dressed, but couldn't help overhearing the altercation in the dining room.

"If you had stayed with us, this wouldn't have happened," Lydia hurled at Leo.

"You had a choice and you made the wrong one. No further discussion of that. And I left you, not our son. He's welcome in my house any time."

"Be careful what you say. No cheap tricks. If you try to get custody of him, I'll tell him the truth about you."

"It was a mistake to let him grow up with a lie. Now it's too late to confront him with the truth. It's bad enough that he has to put up with a mother who can't get her life under control."

"Oh, now it's my fault. As if I hadn't suffered enough. You didn't have to live with a guilty conscience for thirteen years. Maybe telling Cameron everything will solve my drinking problem. Have you considered this?"

"You can't take away his last refuge. And no, I won't fight for custody, so let's drop the matter."

Twisting her logic around in a way that had Joy cringing, Lydia carped, "Now we know what kind of a father you are. Walking out on us, leaving me with the burden of an uncontrollable teenager, refusing to take responsibility."

Joy flung her toilet items into her handbag and, on passing the dining room, said, "Goodbye forever, Leo. Don't call me. I mean it."

Since she had split up with Leo, Joy shopped for groceries early in the morning when Leo would be working. She didn't want to run into him by chance. Pushing her trolley down the aisle, she decided that bachelorhood was the only lifestyle suitable for her. Sure, sometimes it would help to have someone to talk to, like three months ago, when Alison had been run over by a train, leaving Joy with a feeling of guilt that wouldn't respond to reason or rationality.

"Always expect the unexpected."

Startled, Joy dropped a package of Chinese noodles and turned on her heel. Leo was grinning at her. This time she managed not to blush or to scream with surprise.

"Happy birthday, Leo," she said calmly.

"Eidetic memory, eh? You're not angry I never called, are you?"

"I said a final goodbye and I like to be taken seriously." She was still trying not to break into a broad smile, but it was getting difficult. She had simply forgotten what a fetching grin he had.

"How about a night out? I've got tickets for Wigmore Hall."

"I've got a meeting with my producer at the BBC that will last all afternoon."

"I can't see you in a daily soap," he mocked.

"We're planning a weekly series, Defeat Your Fear or something along those lines." Then, before she could stop herself from showing a trace of vindictiveness, she said, "Why don't you take your lovely family to the concerto?"

A WEEK AFTER THEIR RETURN FROM PORTUGAL, Patty still had difficulties settling in. The COAA had felt like a home to her. She had enjoyed the days of oblivion on the Praia. Thank God, her friendship with Misty was something she had been able to take back with her to London.

Perched on the edge of the counter in La Strada, as Misty had christened her venture that would have its grand opening tomorrow, Patty sipped a bitter infusion. It tasted like Reg's scornful expression in liquid state.

Her unruly curls tucked behind her ears, Misty knelt on the floor in a frothy mess of fabrics and frills that were waiting to be turned into a window decoration. She was in a perpetual quest for beauty, and quite successfully so. She could put anything anywhere and it would look startling.

"I wish I could come with you tonight," Misty said, her mouth full of pins as if she had kissed a hedgehog. "It's a shame you have to go alone."

"I'll remind Danny shortly before we have to get ready. It wouldn't be the first time for Danny to prefer an excursion to a cultural outing. He's been planning for days to drive to Marlow this weekend to see Jeremy."

"I'm sure you'll enjoy yourself better without him," Misty said, draping a dummy in golden net fabric.

"That's so true. When we went to see *Men in Black* he kept pointing out flaws in the plot, as if it was a flaming instruction movie." Patty listlessly nipped at her mug. "Do you think he'll give me a present?"

"Hey, I almost forgot," Misty exclaimed and nipped into the changing cubicle. She emerged with a dress over her arm. "Many happy returns, darling."

"Thank you, it's lovely." Patty put on the dress, that had the color of Cerenkov radiation in a reactor pool, and twirled in front of the mirror. "I think I'll have a blue strand dyed into my hair. But I doubt the Solo Cello concerto will be appealing enough to lure Danny away from his eyepiece."

"Preen yourself and chat up a yummy guy. And tomorrow you'll come to my opening and tell me all the juicy details."

ANGUS FENNING, JUNIOR EDITOR AT CANOVA PRESS, hoped that Cecilia Terry would be early for their meeting so that he could instruct her how to handle

Victor Canova. His boss was a difficult person, unpredictably shifting between sharp-witted, whimsical and mellow moods. Cecilia would not have been the first aspiring writer to smash her career during the decisive five seconds before Victor Canova signed a contract. It had almost happened to Angus himself during his job interview. It took a while to get used to Canova's limited attention span. That Angus had a stammer hadn't made it easier.

Angus was curious to see what Cecilia Terry looked like. From her CV, he knew that she was twenty-three years old and had studied media sciences and journalism at London University. Angus had fallen in love with her when he read her manuscript, an engaging story about a man who has traveled the world and, full of memories, returns to his home town to reunite with Timotree, an oak-tree his father had planted when his twin brother Timothy died, so that the boy would have a soul mate to replace his dead brother. He discovers that all his adventures have left an impact on the tree, changing its growth, the structure of its bark, the shape of its leaves. Over four decades the tree has turned into an abstract image of the man's life.

Timotree was the stuff that might be shortlisted for the Booker Prize. If only Cecilia behaved properly during the negotiations.

"Hello, you must be Angus." A woman had come through his open office door, petite, fairy-like with long red curls and freckles. She was dressed in a white sleeveless blouse and trousers the same dark green as her eyes.

Angus got up, shot out his hand and tried to say hello, but his voice failed him.

"I'm Cece." She grabbed his hand and shook it heftily. "Ooh, I'm so excited."

"S-s-so am I," he managed to say. "S-s-sit down p-please." Only five minutes to go and he had so much to say. Blast the ol' stammer. "I th-th—"

"I know a trick. Imagine your vocal chords are the London Symphony Orchestra and you are Sir Colin Davis. I know someone who swears by it."

He had no chance to try it out because Canova peered in, saw Cecilia and switched on his charm. "Miss Terry? Let's go straight to my office."

As they went through the clauses of the contract, Cecilia behaved as if she didn't notice Canova's mood swings. Then came the moment to discuss the advance.

"I can offer you five thousand," Canova said.

Angus smiled at Cecilia to signal this was more than she could have expected as a first time writer, but she didn't look his way. "How long can I take to decide whether to accept your offer?"

"Meaning what?" Canova asked sharply.

"Is it like: 'You've got 5 minutes to sign the deal, otherwise get lost,' or more like: 'Let's start haggling.'"

"Have you come to sell your book or to play poker?"

"I'm more a chess person."

Canova leaned forward with his forearms pressed on the glass of the table. Angus thought he heard it crack. "Bad move, young lady. I was under the impression that you had sent us your material for an exclusive read. If you wanted publishers to bid for your manuscript you should have secured yourself an agent who knows how to handle this tricky business."

Angus closed his eyes. No contract, no best-seller, no Booker Prize.

"Sorry, sir. I was really overstepping my competence. To tell the truth, I have received so many rejections that I feared I might need your daughter's services because I was beginning to show symptoms of letter-opening-phobia."

Angus looked at Cecilia's cute grin when a strange sound filled the room. It was Victor Canova's barking laughter.

CECE CROSSED HOLYWELL STREET AND RAN through St. Helen's Passage with her heart pumping and her head spinning. She couldn't wait to break the news to Uncle Rick, who had driven her to Oxford this afternoon and was waiting for her at the Turf Tavern. She wouldn't have succeeded without his help. A gazillion times he had cheered her up by praising her manuscript, never had he tired of going through plot lines and discussing character development. Only after sharing her exultation with him would her achievement feel real.

The Turf Tavern lay in a quaint courtyard, accessed through a cobbled lane. She found Rick in the beer garden, sitting on a bench under a cherry tree, and paused in loving contemplation. Chocolate bar wrappers lay crumpled on the thick wooden table, against which he was leaning a book. He looked a good ten years younger in summer, which she attributed to his tan, the sun-bleached blond of his graying hair, and the polo-shirt and jeans he wore.

He looked up as if he had sensed her presence. "Cece? How was it?"

"Oh, Rick." She threw herself into his arms as he rose from the bench. "Guess how much I got as an advance!" Ever since she was a kid she had made him guess things, and in contrast to other grown-ups he had good-naturedly played along.

"One thousand," he said and pressed her down on the bench beside him.

Cece shook her head.

"Two?"

She tossed her hair around her shoulders.

"Five?"

She bit her lower lip to stop herself from blurting it out. That was what the game was all about, getting worked up with excitement until you were ready to explode.

"Ten?"

She tapped her feet to signal that he was getting warmer.

"Fifteen, my last offer."

Her moment of triumph. "TWENTY!"

"You've made it. I'm so happy for you."

She raised his glass. "Shall I propose a toast? To Frederick Terry, the best uncle in the known universe."

He ruffled her curls. "I ordered vegetable lasagna for you. I'll go and collect it and then you must tell me all."

When he returned with a plate and a pint, Cece began to speak while stuffing herself with pasta. "My editor is a nice young man with a stammer and hair that refuses to comply with a side parting. Victor Canova is creepy, though. He looks like Count Dracula and he sort of changes…. You know, those things they do on computers, transforming one photo into another."

"Morphing."

"Yes. You can't relate to him. Could be a nice set-out for a new novel. The Unrelated Man."

Rick grinned. "Nothing's lost on a writer."

Cece made an important face. "And this explains his handwriting." She had received a couple of letters from Canova Press. On all of them, Victor Canova had added some personal notes in a different style of handwriting, but all signed by him. "He just can't help it, I'd say. His personality is scattered all over the place."

Cece drank from Rick's pint and wiped the froth from her upper lip with the back of her hand. "I'm glad you prepared me for this. I followed all the advice you gave me. But then I almost lost everything with a silly remark. What saved me was Canova's sudden outbreak of humor. I wonder what it's like to be his kid. Next time this Joy Canova person is on a talk show I'll look for signs of mental disturbance. Can't be healthy never to know if you're going to be punished or praised. My Da' was always reliably strict." Brian Terry, Rick's elder brother, was a man without tenderness. "I wish you were my father." She mopped up the rest of the sauce on the plate with her forefinger.

"I'm glad I'm not. I would have to teach you manners."

"I'll throw a big party tomorrow and we'll celebrate all night. You must come, too."

"Thanks, but I'm not exactly fond of Nirvana and Foo Fingers—"

"Fighters," she corrected him. "It's Foo Fighters."

"—especially at the volume you always play them. Apart from that, I already have a date."

"Is he nice?"

"It's not a he. It's a whole troupe."

"An orgy? At your age?"

"Eileen invited me to the summer fête at The Caesar."

Cece had met Eileen when she had moved in with Rick for two weeks because she needed his Jacuzzi to replace the massages her physiotherapist Simon had given her. This was before she left for her treatment and surgery in the States. A few days ago, Eileen had returned from her long stay in the Johnson Clinic.

Gay or not, Rick was smitten with Eileen.

"Kiss her for me. Right on the mouth if you like."

"Cece, it's no use playing matchmaker."

"You would have kissed her anyway, wouldn't you?"

PATTY HAD FOND MEMORIES OF HER FIRST NIGHT AT WIGMORE HALL. It had been her seventh birthday. It was a family custom to celebrate anniversaries with treats, a posh five-course meal for her father, an outing to Cornwall for her mother, a visit to the zoo for her little sister, and a concerto for Patty.

After marrying Danny, Patty had stuck to her beloved habit of going to concertos on her birthday. Danny had stuck to his habit of ignoring her birthday.

She had told Misty she would drag Danny along tonight, but changed her mind when he came home, dumped his attaché case on the desk, mumbled something about not needing dinner and gathered his astronomic equipment. Patty just stayed out of his way and when he had left, the car with him, she looked up bus routes, dressed herself up to the nines with the new blue dress, squeezed her feet into suede stilettos and was ready for the big adventure. If feeling nervous, self-conscious and squeamish could be considered being ready. On the bus, she did some propaganda for the cause by telling herself that Danny had no feelings for her that were in danger of being hurt and that sexual frustration was the major origin for many a psychosomatic disease.

When she walked into Wigmore Hall she had to shed a feeling that she was manipulating herself into doing something she didn't want. Two deep breaths helped, as did looking at the paintings displayed in the entrance hall, because it kept her from scanning the foyer for solitary men. She had this silly notion that she was setting herself up for a fall.

The gong reverberated. Patty collected her ticket and took her aisle seat in the third row. Mellow light filtered through an oblong window in the rounded roof. The cello soloist entered the semi-round of the stage, gingerly carrying his instrument. A festive mood enveloped Patty, but was interrupted when she had to stand up for three latecomers. The first was a teenage boy, who stepped on her toes with his thick-soled trainers, then a woman so heavily perfumed that Patty held her breath, and finally a man in his forties, good-looking in a rough way, with a face dented like the surface of the moon. The wool of his suit brushed her naked arm and he stopped close to her, studying her face. Patty recognized the cold, surgical way he looked at her.

"Patricia," he said, making it sound like a diagnosis. He was Lionel Croft, usually called Leo.

Only half listening to the first piece, a Bach prelude, Patty glanced at Leo. He had changed since she had last seen him, six or seven years ago. His hair was shorter and shot through with gray. During her student years at the Academy for Music, Patty had made her living by sitting for art students. Leo had been the teacher of a sculpting class. She remembered lying naked on her belly, while he ran his hand down her spine to direct his student's attention to the alignment of her vertebrae.

She suddenly felt hot. The music floated past her unnoticed while she realized that Lionel Croft had been the role model for all her fantasy lovers.

During the break, Patty rushed to the ice-cream counter and secured herself a tub of Loseley. Licking the ice from the little plastic spoon she smiled in nostalgic delight.

Leo and his family were standing by the stairs down to the bar. His wife was of the type on whom every effort is wasted. A forgotten beauty was buried in her sallow complexion that wasn't helped by a thick layer of make-up. Their son was a scrawny youth whose blond hair had black roots. His teeth could have done with braces. The three of them seemed to be having an unfriendly discussion, ending suddenly when Mrs. Croft headed downstairs.

Leo stepped in Patty's direction. On reflex, Patty retreated until the back of her knees touched the broad leather sofa next to the ice-cream counter. She stared at the clock above the double-winged doors to the audience. So much for being a nymphomaniac on the loose.

His hand touched her arm. "There are more things that frighten us than injure us, and we suffer more in imagination than in reality."

She flung her head towards him. "Sorry?"

"A Seneca quote. This dress," he began and Patty felt unsettled, reminded of

Reg's nagging. What was wrong with her dress?

"It looks lovely on you. The color highlights the tints in your eyes."

She thanked him and hoped he wouldn't tell her that the blue strand in her hair was a terrible mistake.

"How are you faring?"

"I give piano lessons," she said. "I've never been concert hall material."

"But great modeling material."

"Thanks. I...I enjoyed sitting for you." She spooned up the cool, creamy substance and gazed past him towards his son and his wife, who had returned with two glasses of champagne.

"My son Cameron. And my ex-wife Lydia. I shouldn't have invited them to join me. It's just that today is my birthday—"

"Mine too," Patty broke in, happy that she had found something to contribute to the conversation.

"And you're all on your own? It's a shame. We should celebrate together." Without waiting for her response, he drifted back to his family. Patty was both annoyed and excited. Had he been flirting with her? Impossible, he hadn't even smiled. And there was his family, after all.

The gong sounded and she returned to her seat. Again, he brushed past her. What had he meant by "celebrate together"? She glanced sideways, but he was engrossed in listening to the Sarabande, his hands clasped in his lap. Strong hands, that had once touched her. Leo's professional touches had been more enticing than Danny's intimate ones.

This was getting out of control. Patty was forcing herself to listen to the music when she suddenly felt his hand on hers on the armrest. She tried to jerk away, but he was pressing down strongly. She struggled with the impulse to say, "Remove your hand or I'll scream." Instead, she relaxed, and in response he stopped pressing. Now his touch was soft and warm. She began to slide her hand back. Immediately, he grabbed her again. What kind of game was he playing?

The piece of music was over. Everybody clapped, and so did he, thus freeing her hand. Afterwards he pointedly placed his hand on the armrest. My turn, it crossed her mind. With a triumphant inward smile, she put her hand over his. His wrist turned so quickly she had no time to react as he clamped her tiny hand with his strong fingers.

"I'm not toying with you," he breathed into her ear.

"Then what are you doing?" she asked, causing a ripple of shushing sounds behind her.

"I am trapping you." He let go of her hand.

Suddenly, she knew she couldn't stand it a minute longer. She left, fleeing like a hunted animal. She was at the door leading into Wigmore Street when she heard him behind her.

"Where shall we go?" he asked lightly.

"You don't think I'll go anywhere with you, do you? Not after this episode."

Somewhat reluctantly, Patty walked on. He had a mesmerizing quality she found darkly attractive.

"I suggest we go to my place." His velvet voice again, unmistakable.

She turned. His family was nowhere to be seen. "Is there no way to get rid of you, for God's sake?"

"No," he said matter-of-factly. "There are two great restaurants down the street. One Indonesian, the other Italian. Let's see if we can get a table." He took her elbow and led her, looking up at the clear sky. "The stars are so huge and far away. They distort my sense of proportion. I prefer what is near and tangible."

"I hate them. I'm married to a hobby astronomer who's so callous he doesn't even care to go out with me on my birthday."

"So that in your despair you must put up with a creep like me. Under this light I might find affection for the stars after all."

The Indonesian restaurant was full, but they managed to get a seat at The Purple Sage. She asked him to order for her and he did so in fluent Italian.

"I want to inform you," he said solemnly, "that there are three things I prefer to do in silence. One of them is eating."

Patty found a crumb on the table of consuming interest.

"The others," he went on, "are driving and working. Not what you thought."

"What you wanted me to think."

The dangerous glimmer in his eyes gave way to a warm, friendly glint. There was a whole galaxy of expressions gyrating inside his pupils. Despite her qualms, she was implacably drawn to him.

Patty was glad when the food was served, which spared her further attempts at conversation. After all, he wanted to eat in silence. She forked marinated duck into her mouth and found the dish as prickly as the situation.

When the waiter had removed their plates, Leo leaned closer and plaited her hair with a practiced hand. Getting used to his invasive manner, she held still.

"Are you really going to come with me? I might turn out to be a dangerous psychopath."

"Are you playing mind-games now? Oh, I forgot, you're not toying, you're trapping me."

He smiled gently, for the first time that evening, and it caused a little explosion of heat in her solar plexus.

"What has become of your family?"

"Lydia broke a rule tonight. She knows I only endure her as long as she stays sober."

"How charming. So you're a rule-maker, a man obsessed with controlling others," she said provocatively.

"This is the only way to get what you want in life. You know, breaking a rule is the prerogative of the person who made the rule in the first place."

"What does that mean in terms of lovemaking?"

"Nothing. Sex is the only activity that lies outside any rules, which is what makes it so interesting to explore."

Patty gave up trying to get any useful statement from him. "I'll come with you, but only because you're so nicely dressed. I have a weak spot for three-piece-suits."

Leo kissed her temple. "And I have a weak spot for weakness."

When they were pulling up in the taxi, a tinge of stage fright knotted her stomach. He lived in Hampstead, in a low-built, contemporary style house in Pilgrim's Lane. Leo led her upstairs and flicked on the light.

"I moved in two years ago when Lydia and I split up. It's lovely here. In the morning, there are squirrels in the trees."

The large, loft-like living room was furnished with a confusion of new and old; metallic designer pieces were grouped with sumptuous divans. She was looking around, taking in the ingenious blend of styles, when he opened a drawer, took out a package of Durex and dispensed them all over the place.

"Are we going to use them all?"

"Sure," he said from the other side of the room. "Come, take off your kit."

She stood stock-still.

"What's the problem?"

"I'm shy."

"I've seen you naked before. But you can undress in the bathroom if you prefer. It's over there."

As she took a step in the direction indicated, she saw a small showcase that had been hidden from her view by a pillar. Her breathing stopped, her body turned cold. A panic attack was only a heartbeat away.

CAMERON, HIS HEAD BURIED IN HIS HANDS, sat on the low sofa in the living room. "Look, Ma, he warned you, didn't he?"

Lydia didn't answer. She threw back cognac as if it was table water.

"He said, don't get drunk or—"

"Oh, shut up, you fuckin' idiot. Men are all the same. They see a bit of fluff and think with their testicles. Leo's a perverse ol' git. We'll have a great evening, he says. Come and enjoy yourselves, he says. No hard feelings, he says. Words, words, words. Unreliable sonofabitch. He almost bonked the floozie right there on the red velvet seats."

"Button it, Ma. You downed a whole battery of champagne glasses during the interval. What did you expect?"

"Oh yeah, stick by him. But when the truth is known you only go to see him when you think he'll cough up some shekels. You know sod-all about Leo. You don't know a thing about despair, do ya? When problems get too big you do a runner. I wish I could run away and leave it to Leo to bring you up. But I can't. I'm your mother." Tears streaked down her face, darkening her make-up. "Will you find out for me who she is?"

"Tough shit. What are you up to now?"

"I must know if I've lost him for good."

She had lost him a long time ago. "Yeah, if it helps you."

"Attaboy." She smiled lugubriously and the crow's feet around her eyes spread all over her cheeks. Cam couldn't stand the sight of her any longer. He locked himself in his room and collapsed onto the lumpy mattress.

He knew all about despair, but he wouldn't tell her. She couldn't even deal with her own problems, real or imagined. He wouldn't tell his father either. No one cared for him. No one knew about the man behind King's Cross.

The man had been thirtyish, handsome. Some of the boys eyed him hopefully, others were too blotto to notice there was a prospective customer. A boy with a shaved head cornered Cam. He had escaped the bullies at school only to end up in this place stinking of piss, attacked by this brute whom one could smell a mile off.

"Get 'e hell outta here," Shaved Head said. "There ain't no place for your bum round here."

Cam, gauche in his best moments, held his trembling hands in front of him as if trying to push more air between them. His palms were sweating. "Only this once. I won't be coming back. I promise." He needed money. Not to buy booze, he could have plenty of that at home. Just for something to stuff his mouth.

The handsome man's attention was drawn to Cam's whining voice. "Leave him alone."

Shaved Head frowned at him. "Are you the fuzz? Or's he your boy? Take better care of him, then." He strode away.

"Thank you, sir," Cam said.

"I'll take you home. The car's over there."

He trudged along, wondering which address to give. He hadn't been home for two weeks. He'd rather die than go back. "It isn't far, I can walk, really," he lied.

The man held the passenger door open. They were at the dark end of the passage. He waited for Cam to get in, closed the door and went over to the other side. As soon as he was in the car he opened his trousers. Disgust transformed into fear.

"You a virgin? Don't worry. I've brought some lube. I'm not going to hurt you." The man was all calmness and confidence. Cam unzipped his jeans, bent over the seat as he was instructed and bit his lower lip.

"Relax a little. Good boy."

It seemed to last forever. The pain came in nauseating waves. The final thrust seemed to tear him open.

"Shit."

He didn't dare turn and look.

"The rubber broke. And you're bleeding. You should've told me you're so narrow."

Cam started to sob.

"Get dressed, for heaven's sake."

With stiff hands, Cam hitched up his trousers. All he wanted was to go home.

"Are you all right?" He scrunched some bills in Cam's clutched palms. "Now off you go."

Cam shoved the money inside his pockets without counting it. He didn't return to his shake-down but began to walk northwards, feeling sick and wonky on his legs.

He woke up in a hospital bed with Lydia and Leo sitting by his side. A month later he had a follow-up examination, and shortly afterwards a social worker phoned and asked him to come and bring his parents. Cam had gone alone. If Lydia ever learned about the man she would drink herself into a delirium. He wasn't too young to carry the burden alone. During the two weeks in the streets something sad inside him had become irrevocably grown up.

PATRICIA'S PALE FACE LOOKED WHITE against the redness around her. Her closed eyelids gave her an air of tranquility, her fine hair was soaked with sweat and tears. Leo found her heartrendingly lovely. He embraced her tenderly. She stirred, whispered his name and smiled, half-asleep with exhaustion. Her eyes fluttered open for a short moment. Wonderful intensely blue eyes. Blue satin sheets for her next time, he decided.

She had been willing and hungry like no woman he had had before. Not even Joy Canova, who considered herself London's most sophisticated nymphomaniac, had abandoned herself so completely to lust.

Leo propped himself up on an elbow and studied Patricia's small nose and fine-drawn lips. In the seven years since he had last seen her, she had grown from a promising young woman to a ripe beauty. He had not desired her then; now he wanted to devour her.

"Look at me," he said, kissing her eyebrows.

"Let me sleep, Leo."

He tucked the sheets in around her, feeling overwhelmed by the wish to protect her. That she was terrified by butterflies of all things.

"Take them away," she had screamed. "The butterflies," she had managed to say between suffocating sobs, pointing at Lydia's wedding gift, a showcase with six exotic butterflies pinned on black cardboard. It was now safely stowed away in the cellar. After much stroking and kissing, Patricia had calmed down. Incredible that a woman's soul could be so tender that she was afraid of something so tiny and soft. Leo couldn't wait to take her to her limits.

CHAPTER FOUR
SATURDAY, 12 JUNE

J OY AWOKE WITH A SCREAM that reverberated in her skull as if her head was a cavity, dark and hollow. For a second, there was recognition. A hand was pressing down on her chest, she couldn't breathe. Then the moment was gone, and she couldn't remember the nightmare, as if someone else had dreamt it. Those nightmares had started when she was a child, shortly after her little sister's crib death.

Shivering, she got up and opened the curtains. The sun was already high, warming her, but not reaching the well of coldness that kept freezing the inside of her mind. The sensations of cold and heat clashed when she stood under the shower, making the water as hot as her skin could stand it, to sweep out one terror by another.

After breakfast, Joy went downstairs to her office. The practicalities of life were her only remedy. Get busy, stay busy, stop brooding over nightmares. The BBC wanted her to come up with living examples of her therapy concept. She planned to go through her files to see whose story was suitable for a presentation on TV. It would be most effective if they made their own statements for the camera, the producer had said. First-hand experiences sold best.

The phone rang as she was busy writing a list of names.

"I tried your flat first, but you weren't there. I'm so glad I caught you in your office," someone said without preamble. Joy identified the breathless voice as belonging to Maureen Gordon.

"Good morning, Maureen. What's the problem?"

"I'm so scared. I found a letter. I don't know what to do."

Joy tensed. "What kind of letter?" she asked.

"A murder threat. It's signed Shadoe. I don't know anyone of that name."

"Please come round," Joy responded in a measured voice. "And don't forget to bring the letter."

She expelled her breath, feeling sick, replaced the receiver very slowly and dropped the pencil. She massaged her temples with her fingertips. In the months that had passed since Alison's death, Joy had managed to convince herself that it had been an accident, just as the police and the Dale-Frosts had believed. The case was closed. Alison was buried. Shadoe had ceased to exist.

The doorbell startled Joy. Maureen Gordon was as meticulously coifed, primly dressed and bejeweled as always. No one would have thought that anything could scare her. She lived alone in a house close to the Heath, and designed brooches and bracelets that sold at high prices. But she was a lonesome person. Her fear wouldn't allow her to attend the get-togethers and high-society parties of her clientele. Sometimes she drove the short distance to East Heath Parking Place and went to sit by the pond.

This morning, her movements were agitated and her gaze restless. Normally, she was a person of great self-control. Right from the start of the treatment Joy had wondered how Maureen managed to live a more or less normal life despite the never-ending onrush of fear.

Joy led her to the chair opposite her desk and took the letter Maureen removed from her purse. Sitting securely in her swivel chair, Joy ventured to take the letter from its envelope. It was a manila envelope of the same size as the one Alison had received. She unfolded the sheet and gave a gasp.

The handwriting was different, but that only made it worse. The elongated script was the second set of handwriting her father used. The block letters in Alison's letter could have been dismissed as a coincidental likeness, but not this.

"Do you know my father, Victor Canova?" she asked Maureen.

"No, why?"

"Please stop fidgeting with your purse."

"Sorry."

"It's all right, I was just getting nervous myself."

Dear Maureen,

Forgive me the intimate salutation
I know you so well
Like you, I am a recluse
Living a lonely, invisible life far from the joys of company
Bereft of the intimacy of love

But one act of love will be granted to us
We will share the fear, your beautiful, unique fear

There is your throat—delicate, tender, oh so vulnerable. And I will touch it.

What you have never allowed anyone to do in your whole life, I will do it. I will touch your most sensitive spot.

Can you see the paradox in your fear: you can't protect your throat because you won't let anything near it, not even a collar or scarf. This stretch of skin is always naked, prone to attack. You spend your life in a vicious circle of petrifying proportions.

I will break the circle by strangling you. Shouldn't you be grateful? No, frankly, you have no reason for that. It won't be over in a minute. Your death throes will last for hours. You think you have already had all the nightmares imaginable—I will take you to a new dimension.

I will show you the eternal grandeur of your fear.

Fearfully yours,
Shadoe

Joy felt like doing what Alison had done: tearing up the letter, shredding it to bits. Maureen was looking at her expectantly. Joy put on her professional face to hide her agitation and said levelly, "Do you have any idea who might have written this?"

"I'm afraid not."

"Who knows about your fear?"

"Well, a dozen people or so. As you advised me, I began to talk about it so as to feel less secluded from the rest of humanity."

It had been an important step forward. As a consequence Maureen had begun to date a man, the first in her life. "How about Hector Kelby? Would you think him capable—"

"He's such a fine man, very understanding. He hasn't even tried to kiss me yet."

"Could you get out of London for a while?"

"You think this threat is serious? I hoped so much you would tell me I was overreacting."

"I'm afraid this is so serious you should show it to the police and ask for protection." Joy hated to say this, but for her there was no mistaking the letter for a hoax.

Maureen looked unconvinced. "How can I explain why I'm so scared of having my throat touched? The police will laugh at me. They don't do much about anonymous letters, we all know that."

"They'll check it for fingerprints and compare them to those of people you suspect of having written the letter."

"But I don't suspect anyone. They won't protect me as long as no one attacks me bodily."

"It would be safer to treat this as a warning and react accordingly. You shouldn't be alone. How about staying at your sister's for a while?"

"I can't leave my cats behind. I could ask Hector to stay with me for a few days. Although I'm not sure…I don't trust anyone any longer."

"But you certainly trust your sister. She could come and stay with you."

"She's allergic to cats."

They were getting nowhere. "In that case, I advise you to return home, lock yourself in your house, activate the burglar alarm and not to let anyone in this weekend. No one at all, you understand? I will make a copy of this letter. I will analyze it carefully and prepare a watertight line of reasoning that will prove your need for protection. On Monday morning we'll go to the police together. I will insist on talking to a senior officer. Is it all right for me to pick you up at eight?"

Maureen, struggling to look dignified, nodded slowly.

Joy went to the anteroom and ran the letter through the copy machine. When she returned, Maureen was playing with the clasp of her purse again.

"Just follow my instructions and you'll be safe. Of course we could go to the police straight away, if you prefer that."

"No, I don't feel I'm up to it. You know, what really upsets me is to think that whoever wrote the letter delivered it straight to my house. There's no stamp on it."

Maureen wouldn't allow anyone into her private space, and her house was part of that space. She lived inside a bubble of fear.

"When do you think the letter was delivered? Last night? The police could make house-to-house inquiries to find a witness who saw someone drop the letter in the slit."

"That's no use. The letter wasn't on the hall carpet with the other mail. It had somehow slipped underneath. I should have a letter-tray fixed to the door. As it is, I found the letter by chance when Snow, my white angora cat, played with the fringes this morning. It could have been lying there for a long time already. The last time I checked for mail under the carpet was a month or so ago."

Joy would have loved to tell Maureen that this meant the danger wasn't acute. But in Alison's case five days had passed between the delivery of the letter and her death. "Are you sure you don't want us to go straight away?"

"The weekend staff at the station won't be very helpful," she said evasively as she collected the letter and envelope and got up.

Joy saw her out, then returned to her desk. With this new piece of handwriting turning up, she had no choice but to talk to Victor. She would call him and arrange to meet him for lunch to show him the copy of the letter.

The phone rang again. "What the hell." She pressed the receiver to her ear. "Yes?"

"You sound angry," a velvet voice said.

"Leo? Sorry, I'm uptight. Why are you calling?"

"I bet you've never come across someone who's afraid of butterflies. She's so phobic she can't even stand the sight of dead butterflies. Would you like to treat her?"

"I'll put her on my waiting list."

"Can't you squeeze her in sooner?"

Under different circumstances she would have been happy to try her skills on this off-beat phobia. Just today, with Maureen on her mind, she couldn't warm to the idea. If Shadoe killed a second time, if the whole thing became public—well, then her waiting list wouldn't be worth the computer disc it was stored on. Who wanted to be treated by a therapist who was stalked by a psychopath? It was this line of thought that prodded Joy into agreeing. Maybe soon she'd be grateful for every new client.

"I could see her on Monday at eleven thirty."

"Swell. I knew you would do it for me. Her name is Patricia Miles."

Joy grinned despite herself. He was as conceited as she remembered him. Was he also still as unpredictable and insatiable? She would have loved to find out. Maybe one day, when she had her life back under control.... It took a lot of self-control to deal with a man of Leo's caliber.

Only seconds after she had said goodbye to him, blue flashes filled her field of vision. Her neck stiffened and the pain rose like hot, fluid metal. She had a list to prepare for the BBC and had to find a strategy how to help Maureen whilst not getting her father and herself into trouble. There was so much to do, but it would all have to wait until the migraine had passed and she was herself again.

THE COOLNESS OF THE SATIN SHEETS reminded Patty of where she was. She heard Leo's voice coming from the living room. Who was he talking to? Patty sat up to listen.

"Can't you squeeze her in sooner?" Then silence before he spoke again. So he was on the phone.

Patty went to the bathroom. When she returned, Leo was back in the bedroom, propping up pillows. He had put on a dark blue dressing gown and Patty was delicately aware of her nudity.

"Morning, my love," he said and reached out to touch her hips. "I've rustled up some breakfast. Shall I feed you?"

"Who were you talking to?"

"Joy Canova. She's been on TV several times. Ever heard of her?"

"No." Somehow, she felt on the defensive without understanding why. Had it become a reflex during her marriage?

"She's a therapist, the best for phobia treatment. I made an appointment for you. Monday morning, half past eleven. Hope that suits you."

"Leo, you should have asked me whether I wanted treatment at all," she said quietly enough, but prepared to throw a tantrum if the situation required it.

"I didn't ask you because I knew you would bristle. I suppose facing that terror is a huge step for you. You must have played avoidance games all your life. The fear is probably so strongly interwoven with your nature that removing it will feel like unraveling your personality. Only a specialist like Joy can handle this. So I made the decision for you."

Had she misread him completely? He had really tried to understand what was going on inside her, quite unlike Danny? "Well, Leo, em, thank you."

"I have a hidden agenda," he said. "I want you to come back to me very often and you would be scared if—"

"You're not going to put the showcase back into the living room, are you? It's bad enough for me to know it's in the same house."

"Of course not, my love. But my neighbor has a collection of ceramic butterflies in his backyard. We returned in the dark last night, so you didn't see them. They look very real."

Nervously, Patty looked at the window. "We'll keep the curtains closed, okay?"

"Sure. So you're not miffed that I made an appointment for you, Patricia, are you?"

She shook her head and kissed the pocked skin of his cheek. He dipped a finger of toast into the fried eggs and held it out for her to take a bite.

She chewed, swallowed, then said: "I like it when you call me by my full name."

"It's a beautiful name. Tell me something about you. All I know so far is that you're married, childless and subject to psychotic episodes when a butterfly crosses your path. And you were one of the few models who could sit still for hours without falling asleep."

"I have the hots for you, that's all you need to know." She licked a bit of yolk from his calloused fingers. "Are you still teaching?"

"I stopped when my sculptures became all the rage and I couldn't keep up with the demand. My workshop's in the garden flat. I can show you later. I have small-scale models of the various postures I make. My clients bring along their wives, mistresses or lovers, choose a model and the women sit for me."

"What do you do when a woman is ugly?"

"Depends. Some want a true-to-life sculpture, others want improvements built into my work. Actually, it is more tricky when a woman is very good-looking. Recently, I had an Asian woman sitting for me who was so abnormally beautiful that I was afraid I couldn't do her justice in my work. There is no way to exaggerate her looks."

"Wasn't she tempting?"

"Imperfection is far more enticing. Your breasts, for instance, are not symmetrical."

She bit his fingers as he held out another piece of toast. He rolled over, buried her under his weight, pinned her hands on the sheets above her head and kissed her. "I will invent a new posture for you and I'll call it Chastity. You're so innocent, I bet you can use dirty words without sounding obscene."

She laughed. "I never use dirty words, you sodding old wanker."

His grip tightened. "You're really asking for it, sweetheart."

"Asking for what?"

"To be punished."

THE SUMMER FÊTE THAT TOOK PLACE in the auditorium of The Caesar was in full swing. The chairs had been stacked away or placed around bistro tables. A buffet had been sat up on the stage. From up there, eating antipasti, Rick Terry watched Eileen and her husband join the dancers.

"Can't take my eyes off them, either," someone said into his ear.

Terry turned. "Hello, Alan." Alan, the owner of The Caesar, was good-looking and, if Eileen had informed him correctly, worked both ways.

"Isn't it magic to see Eileen dance?"

"Uh-huh."

"How about us?" Alan asked. "Shall we dance?"

Frantically, Terry thought of something to say to defuse the situation. He hadn't had a partner since Michael's death. "Look, Alan, I don't think this is such a good idea."

"You're right. We had better get out of sight. I'll be waiting for you in my flat."

Terry was irritated that Alan took it for a fait accompli that they would end up in bed together. The mood ebbed away when he looked down at Eileen again. She had made it against all the odds. Why was he still allowing the odds to dictate his life? And what was so dreadful about having a one-night-stand with a handsome dancer? Would anyone see him following Alan? Surely not. There were at least two hundred people here tonight.

He was already at the door to the hall when doubts came rushing back. He needed someone's permission, a friendly pat on the shoulder, some kind of go-ahead. He wished Cece had come with him. She would have given him the thumbs-up and he would have felt embarrassed but encouraged.

"You're a disgrace to the family. I'm glad your father didn't live to hear this." These had been the last words his mother had said to him, three years before she died, refusing to see him again, even when she knew she was terminally ill. Terry had let her down for the second time. The first time had been when he had given up his scholarship at the Royal Academy of Music.

"Rick?" Eileen opened the door to her office and motioned him inside. "I know what Alan's up to."

Terry contemplated the edge of the desk.

"You're like a swan, aren't you? Loyal beyond death. If you had been the one to die of lung cancer, would you have wanted Michael to mourn for the rest of his life?" She edged in between him and the desk.

"No, of course not," he said, his eyes still lowered. He took her in a firm embrace. "I've got a melancholy streak, I'm afraid. Too many traumatic memories."

"You're not the only one with a trauma, and sex can be healing. Has it occurred to you that Alan isn't looking for an adventure? He hasn't had a lover since ... you know .... He's probably as impotent at present as you fear to be and he's looking for a way back before it's too late."

Terry cleared his throat. "I'll go and, er, talk to him."

Alan's flat was on the second floor. Terry went up hesitantly. Alan stood by the volière where his parrots resided, Ginger and Fred.

"*Hasta la vista*, baby," Ginger croaked her customary greeting.

Terry grinned. "You should teach her a new line."

"I did, just for you. Hey, Ginger, be a good bird. What's the inspector gotta do?"

"Round up the usual suspects," the parrot croaked obligingly.

Alan began to pull up Terry's polo shirt. "It's a pity you're a detective. I'm sure you looked great in uniform." He ran a hand over his stomach. "Nice and flat. Do you work out?"

"Not if I can help it. Lucky genes. We're a family of beanpoles. Could you please let me do the undressing myself? And in the bathroom, preferably."

He knew the way. The last time he had been here, Alan's flat had been an SOC. He peeled off his jeans and rejoined Alan, who was lying on the counterpane, alarmingly young-looking with his smooth skin taut over firm muscles.

Terry lay down next to Alan and asked if they could switch off the light.

Alan dimmed it a little. "There's no reason to feel embarrassed."

"I don't need a reason. Embarrassment comes naturally to me."

"Nobody's watching."

"I'm watching myself."

"That's neurotic."

"I was born with an audience in my mind."

Alan grinned, reached for the micro system by the bed and switched on the CD player. "I hope you like Leonard Cohen."

Terry closed his eyes and felt his mind rock gently with the mellow guitar chords. Alan put a hand around his waist.... *Take this longing from my tongue*...he wondered briefly if his body remembered how to react to tenderness...*and all the useless things my hands have done*...their lips met...*Untie for me your hired blue gown*...their bodies touched..*like you would do*...their breath mingled..*for one you love*...tears ran salty down his cheeks..*like you would do*...into his mouth..*for one you love*...and he had no idea if they were his own tears or Alan's.

SUNDAY, 13 JUNE

TERRY DIDN'T KNOW what to do with himself. He had returned from the party in the small hours and had slept until noon. Now he ambled through the house, tidied up the kitchen, ate a bagel and drank coffee standing in his pajamas by the sink. He showered, dressed, prowled around, realigned the books on the shelves, played two Beethoven sonatas on his grand piano, remembered that he hadn't shaved and returned to the bathroom, sorted the dirty laundry and stuffed it into the washing machine. It was no use, he couldn't dodge last night's memories any longer.

It had been his first one-night-stand. Only Alan's complete lack of embarrassment had made the whole procedure possible. He wished he had someone to talk to, someone like Michael. But if Michael were still alive, he wouldn't need anyone to discuss the matter with because it wouldn't have happened in the first place.

The doorbell extricated him from his rumination. That would be Cece. Inspiration had struck and she wanted to work at his computer. On weekdays she'd let herself in with her own key, but when she knew Terry was at home she respected his privacy. Terry pressed the buzzer for the front door and opened the door of his flat, then went to play a triumphal march on the piano, a musical red carpet for the future best-selling author. When he heard the door being shut he improvised a transition and continued with Rachmaninov's second piano concerto.

"Sumptuous." Dressed in a white T-shirt and Levi 501's with a button-fly, Alan looked like a young god. He swung a hamper. "I haven't pictured you in such surroundings, although Eileen dropped some hints."

"You shouldn't have come."

"But you're glad I'm here, right?"

"Yes, I'm not good at organizing my weekends."

Alan dumped the hamper and came over. "Why didn't you do anything with your musical talent?"

Terry played a dissonant chord. "What is stage fright like for you?" he asked back.

"I feel like the Titanic shortly before it hit the iceberg."

"And I feel like the iceberg."

Alan picked up the framed photograph that showed Michael and Terry, young, happy, healthy and convinced that they would be together until they were grumpy old men. "He was older than you."

"Eight years."

"I wonder which is worse, the sudden shock of losing someone through an accident or the long process of relinquishing hope when you see a beloved one die of a wasting disease." He put the photo back. "Of course, the worst thing of all is witnessing someone get killed."

Terry got up and ran a hand through Alan's thick, black hair. He longed to kiss him, but he felt vulnerable in his longing. "What's in the hamper?"

"I packed the leftovers from the buffet."

He broke the touch. "Fine. Let's go out and have a picnic. I don't want to be alone with you and temptation."

Alan grinned. "Yeah. Just you wait and see what I'm gonna do when we return."

JOY CAME ROUND WITH A CRAMPED, SORE FEELING. The headache was gone. She opened her eyes and saw a slit of light between the drawn curtains. The atmosphere in the room was sultry. The green LCD of the alarm clock showed 3pm. She tapped a switch to see what day it was. Sunday. Thirty hours of uninterrupted sleep. She had hurried upstairs from her office on Saturday morning, drawn the curtains, and thrown herself onto the bed before the pain in her head had stalled all her movements.

A little shaky, Joy went to the window, pulled back the curtains and shielded her eyes from the light that seemed to sting her. She opened the window. Another sunny weekend lost. She stepped into the shower. The jet of water was like a cruel caress. Joy shampooed her hair and held her head under the shower, gasped and shook her head like a wet dog. She finished with a cold shower to stimulate blood circulation, then reached for the towel. For a chilling moment she thought she saw someone standing there, dressed in black like Alison the last time she had seen her, but it was only her jeans on the towel rack.

Maureen Gordon! She had completely forgotten her.

Still dripping wet, she went through to the living room and dialed her number. Maureen's answering machine was on. Maybe she was sitting by the pond on the Heath. You couldn't blame her on such a fine day. She was probably safer outside than at home.

Swilling back a glass of milk, Joy pondered what to do with what was left of the weekend. She had to talk to her father. Why not get it over and done with right now? She dialed his number and was informed by Blanche, Victor's live-in housekeeper, that he was out until dinner.

An hour later, Joy was parking her Saab in front of her parents' house. After Faith's death, time seemed to have come to a standstill here. The opening for a planned dormer window remained covered with tarpaulin; half of the window frames had been painted pink, the others were still green. No one had cared to finish what Faith had started.

Blanche led her into the drawing room. The portrait of an unknown farmer, that had been taken off the wall in order to be placed elsewhere, still stood leaning against the fireplace. Joy surmised that, had the house been in the midst of an explosion the moment her mother died, the debris would have stopped flying around, suspended in mid-air, not daring to move without stage directions from Faith. Joy asked Blanche to help her put the heavy picture back above the mantelpiece, where the orphaned nail had been rusting patiently all the time.

"I haven't had anything decent to eat since breakfast yesterday."

"Everything's ready, Miss Joy."

While she ate, only half noticing the crisp potatoes, the perfectly roasted lamb chops and the beans so tender they melted in her mouth, she experimented with ways to tackle the subject of the letter. The problem was that she was never quite at ease in Victor's presence. This had nothing to do with his fluctuating personality, to which she had grown accustomed in the same way one gets used to the smell of one's own house. The problem went deeper, and the more they both pretended it wasn't there, the more it became evident. She couldn't put a tag to it. It had been there as far as she could remember. Maybe it was normal.

Raising children and making choices about their lives was invasive, even when done with the best intentions.

Victor came home as she was licking the last spoonful of lavender scented rice pudding. He joined her at the table, ate what Blanche served and offered Joy more wine. He was at his jovial best.

"What brought you here?"

"A letter," Joy answered vaguely.

"Details, my dear, details."

"One of my clients received a letter in your handwriting."

"Is she a writer? Did I reject her manuscript?"

"She's phobic and the letter was an anonymous threat."

"So I'm into anonymous threats now. There's always a first time."

Joy wished he wouldn't excel in cynicism right now. She opened her purse and handed Victor the copy of the letter. He read it halfway through.

"What a charming piece of poetry, indeed. But the forging is amateurish. And what is more, I don't think I ever managed to finish a letter without switching between two or three styles."

"Do you know someone who's made it a sport to forge your writing?"

Victor mulled it over. "No, I'm sorry. Why don't you just take the letter to the police and let them handle it as they see fit?"

"That's what I plan to do, I just wanted to make sure you have no objections." After a short silence, Joy asked, "Can I stay the night? Between us we have killed two bottles of Pinot Grigio."

Despite having slept through almost two days, Joy was unbearably tired and excused herself. She gave the small guest room a quick glance. She hadn't stayed in her parents' house for years. The wine heavy on her senses, Joy switched on the light in the bathroom next door. A shock wave hit her without warning. There stood the green enameled clawfoot tub she had long forgotten—or thought she had forgotten. It was inside this tub that Joy had developed hydrophobia. Memories swelled in her mind. The water rushing in from the golden faucet, her panic rising, a stifling sensation that would only ebb away hours afterwards. She recalled now that it hadn't been Faith but Victor who had bathed her. Maybe Faith wasn't up to it, her motherly instincts being too strong to allow her to force a struggling child into the water. Joy remembered with amazing clarity how Victor had comforted her and hugged her with a fluffy towel. How often had this drama happened until they saw it wasn't a temporary disturbance?

Staring at the scene of past horrors, Joy wondered if she had just found the simple explanation for the unease she felt in her father's presence.

"SHE'S A BITCH. A worthless, ugly, husband-stealing whore." It went on and on.

"Please, stop it, Ma," he implored. "And don't drink any more. You've had enough."

"Don't you dare tell me when I've had fuckin' enough. I could kill that whore."

Lydia hadn't rested until Cameron had agreed to go and see Leo and find out what had become of this blond-with-a-blue-streak woman he had chatted up. Cameron had run this kind of errand for Lydia countless times and he was tired of it to such a degree that he hated both of them: his meek mother, who kept blaming Leo for everything, and his selfish father, who had given him up easily.

He was also tired of telling his mum that it had been her fault Leo had left them. After her third therapy, Leo had simply said: "I catch you drinking just one more time and we're divorced." Cameron could hear those words ringing in his ears whenever he felt like getting bloody depressed. Only twelve years old then, he had already understood this was the death verdict for his parents' marriage.

And when Leo had done exactly what he had threatened to do, Lydia had found only one refuge: to create the myth of Leo's adultery. Cameron had no idea if Lydia's drinking was the reason or the consequence of Leo's infidelity, and he didn't care. He had run the pointless errand once again this afternoon, just to please his mum, who wouldn't stop nagging.

Leo had been stacking glasses and dirty dishes on a tray when Cam came in. "Want some garlic bread?" he had asked on the way to the kitchen. "I can heat it up for you."

"It wasn't fair to leave us behind on Friday night."

"I'm sorry. But Lydia sucked up champagne like a sponge."

Yep. Ma drinks—Dad backs out. Cause and effect. And they lived happily ever after.

Cam looked around. No blond-blue bitch anywhere. He detected an empty spot on the wall. "Where's the showcase?"

"I had to take it down." Leo brought a plate with steaming slices of garlic bread. "Patricia is phobic, so I took it into the cellar. I'll put it back when she's had therapy."

"Phobic about what? And who is she?"

"Butterflies. Patricia Miles, the woman who sat next to us during the concerto."

Bingo. Mission accomplished.

What was his reward? A sermon of swearing and abuse from his mother; nothing he couldn't have foreseen.

"I won't get your dad back as long as this strumpet's throwing herself at him."

As if anything would win him back. As if anything mattered. Cam stopped listening. It was all small-fry compared to his real troubles.

Chapter Five
Monday, 14 June

JOY THOUGHT HER TENSENESS was due to her being late for her appointment with Maureen. The traffic was slowing down the closer she got to London, and it was already ten to eight. She punched Maureen's phone number into the car phone. The answering machine was on.

This morning, after another rotten nightmare, she had woken up with that lingering sense of horror that pushed from deep inside her head and that she couldn't shed. With the memory of the dream beyond her grasp, she was unable to analyze the underlying problem. She was like a dentist who couldn't extract his own foul tooth. She spared herself another look into the bathroom with the loathed bathtub, threw on her clothes and rushed downstairs. Her father wasn't up yet.

As she drove she was nagged by the wish to look over her shoulder. At a red traffic light, she scrutinized the back seat. Of course it was empty. What had she expected? She was quite a psychiatrist, racked with an entire manual of neurotic symptoms herself: nymphomania, ablutophobia, hydrophobia; and now she was starting to show symptoms of paranoia, too. Okay, maybe she was just a psychological hypochondriac.

She still felt observed and uneasy when she parked in front of Maureen's garage at a quarter past eight. The house was a semi-detached. It sported a conservatory that looked like a section of a glass pyramid. Joy rang the bell and waited. After a while she gave up. Alone in her huge house, Maureen must have read the letter over and over again, getting so worked up that she knew she couldn't stand it anymore. She had probably gone to her sister, leaving the cats alone with a generous supply of dried food. In her confusion, she had forgotten her appointment with Joy. Or she had planned to be back on Monday morning and had got stuck in the traffic as well.

Joy was too practiced a psychologist to overlook that she was constructing this theory to blot out the fear.

In the office, Shirley Ryan gave her the inevitable meddlesome once-over.

"Morning," Joy said curtly. "Has Maureen Gordon called?"

"No. Were you expecting her to phone?"

Lord, grant me patience. "Sure, or I wouldn't have asked. Try to reach her and when you have her on the line, put her through, please."

Between two sessions, Shirley informed Joy that she had left a string of messages on Maureen's answering machine. "Shall I try once more?"

"Three messages will do," Joy said testily. Shirley loved answering machines. She had one at home and she liked to call her own number to leave a message to herself so she could replay her dulcet tones in the evening.

The last client this morning was Leo's latest conquest. Patricia Miles was delicate and cute. Her straight blond hair, highlighted with a blue strand, was tied back with a blue ribbon. Her features were so finely chiseled, her movements so coy and graceful that she looked like a butterfly, the very creatures she feared. How long would it take Patricia to discover that she was no match for Leo? His generosity and vigor might mislead her to assume he was caring and protective.

"Hello, Mrs. Miles." She moved her to the comfortable armchair.

"Thank you for giving me an appointment, Dr. Canova."

Joy went around the desk and said her standard opening line. "How do you label your fear?"

"I don't know a technical term for it, I just say I'm scared of butterflies, although it's the understatement of the year."

"But you have no inhibitions talking about it, have you? What kind of reactions do you get?"

Patricia gave her an unassuming smile. "Oh, they run the whole gamut from scorn to derision."

Joy nodded. "It's the classic problem of phobic people that they are not taken seriously. Except when it comes to spiders. That's so wide-spread it's almost a must."

Patricia's smile brightened. "I can touch spiders with my bare hands. But nobody thinks I'm heroic, just that I'm freakish."

During this short exchange, Joy had already learned that her new client was intelligent, humorous, and basically mentally sane. "I will give you a technical term. Lepidopterophobia, a variant of entomophobia." She handed Patricia a yellow Post-it on which she had written these words.

"Oh, thanks. Sounds impressive. Lepidopterae is Latin for butterflies, isn't it?"

"Uhm-hm. Entomophobia is fear of insects. Do you fear any other animals apart from butterflies? Wasps, hornets, ants?"

"I don't like to be stung, of course, but I'm not afraid of wasps. And bumblebees are cute, aren't they? Like tiny teddy bears in striped pajamas."

"So insects are not the problem. Would you please give me a short description of your daily life."

"I'm a piano teacher. Daniel, my husband, teaches science at Hatch End High School in Harrow. He's also an astronomer. More of an astronomer than a hubby, to tell the truth. When I told him I was going to have my phobia treated, I could see by his confused stare that he had no idea what I was referring to. And," she added with a slight blush, "we lead separate sex lives. That is, he leads no sex life at all, unless you count schlepping tons of astronomical equipment a form of satisfaction."

"Are you jealous of his hobby?"

"Jealous is too strong a word. Slightly vexed sometimes about his detachedness when his mind is in the stars where I can't reach him. Have you seen *Men in Black*?"

"Just the trailer."

"My favorite film. At one point Agent K says something like," she shifted her vocal register down, "'We are the FBI, ma'am. We have no sense of humor we're aware of.' Danny is all the FBI's lack of humor clustered in one human being."

Joy liked Patricia more by the minute.

"He came home yesterday as I was peeling potatoes for a stew. He had been to see a friend. Well, he had an expression on his face, like a sitting duck. I thought it was because he hadn't been at home on my birthday, but when I said I had had a great time, he just nodded absent-mindedly. Then I asked how he would feel about not having sex any longer, and he looked alert. If I didn't know he didn't have it in him, I would say he was having an affair. Then I told him I was going to have therapy and I could see that he was racking his brain as to what I was talking about. Sorry, that was off topic. I didn't mean to ramble."

"That's all right. When did you have your first butterfly episode?"

"Oh, way back, as a baby. I must have been born with it. It took a while until my mother divined why I screamed whenever she sat me down in the grass."

"How does your panic manifest itself?"

"I get paralyzed or run for my life, and I yell. I beat all the screamers in horror movies."

Joy got up and took a book from the shelf, an animal lexicon. She put it on the table, opened the B section and found a photo of a small tortoiseshell.

Patricia recoiled. "Take it away."

"What do you feel?"

"I wouldn't call it a feeling, it's too intense. Like an orgasm of terror. I'm scared to death."

Joy closed the book and waited. She knew Patricia was about to wrap it all up in one short statement.

"If I could see them as harmless, endearing creatures I would be cured in an instant. It's so irrational." She looked at Joy gravely. "For me, butterflies are demons, heralds of death."

Joy handed Patricia a sheet of paper and a pen. "Write that down in huge letters."

And Patricia wrote in a surprisingly strong, expressive hand: Butterflies are heralds of death.

"Give me a spontaneous answer to the following question. What is the opposite to heralds of death?"

"Guardian angels," Patricia said promptly.

"Good. Now write underneath: Butterflies are guardian angels. We have a starting point and a destination. Now we'll set off, in small, well-controlled steps."

Patricia smiled demurely. "In the meantime, could you please return the book to the shelf?"

TERRY HAD BEEN SUMMONED to a homicide investigation, but his mind was elsewhere. Driving towards Hampstead Village, he wondered what had got into him that he had started an affair with a man twelve years younger than he was. A man with a studded belly button and a crazy attitude. A man so painfully good-looking that Terry's throat tightened at the memory of their torrid lovemaking. He had left Alan sleeping in his bed this morning. Terry's mood was as untidy as his office. Mixed emotions wherever he looked. He should end it before he got too involved.

What was happening to him? Was he falling in love? He remembered how it had been with Michael and decided that love had felt different. Then why was he longing for Alan in every waking hour? It had nothing to do with Alan as a person. It was the closeness he had missed so much since Michael's death, the strength of a male body, the warmth of skin, the outline of muscles, the tastes and smells, all those heady elements of intimacy. The healthy, normal longing for another person had been blurred by grief for a long time, now it was back in clear sharpness. He should be grateful, not bewildered.

He parked between two panda cars, got out and looked around. All he knew was that a woman had been found strangulated.

"Who was the first on scene?" he asked the constable who stood by the front door and entered Terry in the crime scene log.

"That was me, sir. We received a call from the neighbor, Mrs. Endover. Sally Young, the cleaning woman, came this morning at eleven as every Monday. Ms. Gordon didn't open the door. Mrs. Young talked to Mrs. Endover. They heard a pitiful mew and saw a cat standing on the roof of the garage, desperately trying to get in through the back door. Mrs. Endover called us at eleven thirty. I came over from Hampstead station together with WPC Smith. I rang repeatedly, then opened the lock with a skeleton key."

"Did you have a reason to assume that something had happened? I mean, Ms. Gordon might just have gone out."

"Sally Young assured us that for one thing Ms. Gordon had always been there when she came for her weekly cleaning, and that furthermore she never let her cats out. She assumed that Ms. Gordon had had an accident in the house."

"Okay, so you forced the lock. Did you check it for scratch marks first?"

"Sure enough, sir. Actually, the killer can't have entered that way. I triggered the burglar alarm when I got in. It had been activated and not tampered with. I switched it off and called. There was no answer. Smith secured the door and I went in, straight into the living room. And that's where I found her, tied to a chair and strangulated. I backtracked to the door so as not to cause further destruction to footprint evidence, and called the SOCOs and the murder squad. The scene has been roped off, stabilized, and the team is waiting for you to start the initial walk-through. I sent Mrs. Young and the neighbor home after Smith had taken their statements. We did not tell them what had happened, just that Ms. Gordon is dead. No information has leaked so far."

"Well done. Very methodical."

Terry consulted with the leading forensic officer. They surveyed the scene of the crime, going from room to room and recording their impressions on a Dictaphone. The search pattern was determined and the officers started to mark and collect evidence.

The living room was elegantly and expensively furnished, but it lacked a personal note. It looked as if the owner had walked into a furniture shop, pointed at a window and said: "Give me all the things in there."

Like a still life, several dead cats lay in a heap on an ottoman.

At last, he gave the victim a long, thoughtful stare. She was a woman in the ageless forties, dressed in a white V-neck sweater and skirt. The skirt was stained in the lap area, showing that she had lost bladder and bowel control. Her hands and feet, tied to the arms and legs of a high-backed chair, were swollen, and under the transparent tape that had been used, the skin of her wrists and ankles was black and blue. The strangulation marks on her neck showed great variety both in depth and width. There were also welts at the sides of her neck, as if she had been hit.

Sand-colored hair set in stiff curls framed her face. The look on this face was a study in horror. Beady, sapphire blue eyes stared as if they had seen something worse than hell and demons. Tampons had been pushed up high in each of her nostrils and a piece of salmon-colored underwear hung out of her mouth. He assumed that she had been gagged with it and in her final fit of despair had managed to push it halfway out.

The tidy, immaculate surroundings made the victim look all the more gruesome. The contrast would have been moderated if the intruder had wreaked havoc on the furniture.

"Jesus," Blockley said, who had just arrived together with constable Brick. Brick was two heads taller than Terry. He was two heads taller than anyone. Normally, Terry craned his neck to look him in the eye when they talked. This time, he kept his head low and studied the items on the floor while Brick read the initial report he had just been given by the forensic team.

"Maureen Gordon, forty-eight years old, jewelry designer, is the owner and only resident in the house. There are no signs of forced entry, either at the front or back door, but they couldn't check the windows yet because the fingerprint troop is working on them. Mrs. Young told WPC Smith that Maureen Gordon had seven cats. Six of them had their necks broken, the seventh was in the garden."

Terry looked at the selection of belts lying on the Turkish carpet. During the walk-through he had seen that the doors to a closet stood open and a drawer with belts had been drawn out. None of the rooms had been ransacked. "Nothing seems to be missing," Brick went on, "which is strange considering that there's jewelry worth approximately one hundred thousand pounds in the safe, some pieces also lying around in the conservatory, where she used to work. Raw and polished gems, gold chains, everything handy, easy to nick. It doesn't look like a robbing job, more like a ritual killing."

"Torture," Blockley said gravely.

Terry nodded slowly. "Who are her next of kin?" he asked Brick.

"According to Mrs. Young, the only relative is an unmarried sister, Brenna Gordon, who lives in St. Albans. I called the local station and asked someone to inform her and bring her over."

"Thank you. Where is Gould?"

"He won't make it. He's at a meeting with his new team at the Yard. Sir, if I may...."

"Yes?"

"I would like to take the angora cat with me. The sole survivor. It has already been combed for fibers." Brick, an animal lover, was probably more upset about the slaughtered pets than their murdered owner.

"Go on, then."

"Hello, Terry. Never saw anything that looked less like a suicide." The droning voice belonged to Jed O'Leary, a police surgeon with dreadful scene-of-crime manners.

Terry put on a pair of disposable gloves and reached for a green Fortnum & Mason plastic bag that lay on the table. Peering inside, he found smears of lipstick matching in color the traces of lipstick around Maureen's mouth. "He didn't leave out anything, gagging, strangulation, suffocation. He must be an asphyxiation-fetishist. Give me the time of death."

O'Leary had developed an infallible instinct and the post-mortem more often than not proved him right to the minute. He conducted a preliminary examination. "She has been dead for at least thirty hours. I will need the setting of the timer for the central heating. If the temperature was set low at night, which is likely, then it could be more than thirty-five hours. An educated guess for the TOD would be Saturday night, between one and two a.m. Hullo. There's an inconsistency here."

Terry stepped closer. "Mm?"

"Look at her upper arms. No bruises at all. It's very difficult for one person alone to tie someone to a chair against her will. So there were probably two intruders, one of whom held a gun or knife to keep her in check."

"Or it was done by someone she trusted," Blockley suggested.

"Or else she had been sedated," Terry finished for him.

"I can tell you after the PM. I'll do it this afternoon, at four."

"She doesn't look sedated to me," Blockley remarked.

O'Leary scratched his ear. "It was either a sex game gone out of hand or a bestial execution."

Brick handed Terry a piece of evidence that had been sealed in a plastic cover. "Sir, you should have a look at this before it's taken to the lab."

It was a sheet of paper, with a text on one side, written in elongated script.

"It is not the victim's handwriting," Brick said. "They have already compared it to the script in her address book."

Terry read it aloud. When he had finished, there was an intense silence in the room. "What worries me most," Terry said, "is that the point was not to kill the victim but to watch her dying. That smacks of a killing spree in the making."

PATTY TAPPED HER FOOT. Misty's customer took forever to make up her mind between a red leather skirt and a green slip dress. In the end, she bought both and then took another eternity to decide whether to pay in cash or by credit card.

Misty practically shoved her out of the door, then slung her arms around Patty. "Where were you during my opening?" She smacked a kiss on her cheek. "The only excuse I'm prepared to accept is that you met a man who tied you to his bed."

"More or less."

"Really? Gosh. Tell me about him. I got sushi for my lunch break. Want some?"

"I hate fish. I'm not hungry anyway."

She followed Misty into the tiny backroom with a kitchenette and two pink plush chairs that had seen better days. "Guess where I've just come from?"

"A weekend trip to Rome?"

"A psychologist. Dr. Canova. Leo says she's a celebrity."

"Canova? Talk-show stardom. I've seen her. Young, vigorous, confident. 'Overcoming fear is a process of personal growth, a liberating experience that heightens the sense of self-worth.' New age stuff. But if she cures you, I'll find you a butterfly print for a dress to wear as a sign of triumph. Now tell me about him." Misty threw herself in the other chair, a Pret A Manger tray on her lap.

Patty clasped her hands over her stomach and directed a satisfied smile at the ceiling. "Leo Croft. He's a sculptor. I sat for him a few times when I needed money during my student years."

"Was he one of those who made a pass at you as soon as he dropped his chisel?"

"No, he was one of those who intimidated me with his clinical coldness. I hadn't seen him in years. I met him at Wigmore Hall. We ate together, we talked little, we had sex like I've never had sex before. Do you think I made it too easy for him?"

"I'm glad you found someone who made it easy for you. All the thrills and frills of life have bypassed you."

"Yeah, I've tasted the real thing now. If only...."

Misty cocked her head. "If only what?"

"I don't think I can tell you." Patty gnawed the side of her thumb. "You would be shocked."

Misty threw back her head and laughed. "You're like a little girl with a big secret, who thinks it's enormous and she can't tell her Ma, and when she does, her Ma can't see the enormity of it."

"That's sounds as if, in terms of sexuality, I was still a toddler."

"Did Leo really tie you to the bed? Tell me your adventure warts and all. Or should I say whips and all?"

Heat rose to Patty's cheeks. "He scares me," she said evasively. She had been so volatile with lust she hadn't even felt any pain when Leo had spanked her.

"I bet you like being scared of him. Look Patty, the risk it not to shock me but to bore me. You've often wondered what I saw in Reg, haven't you? The secret is, we are master and slave."

Patty's thumb dropped out of her mouth. In her mind a picture gelled, showing Misty reduced to tears by a hovering Reg, who wielded a whip as implacably as he usually wielded his sharp tongue. She wished she had been spared the revelation. But then, she could understand the chemistry of a master/slave relationship. Leo's little cruelties had shifted her to a level of lust that had been like a slow, deep breath in every cell of her body.

"Now you've shocked me. Not only do you put up with Reg's haranguing, you also let him humiliate you."

Misty carried the tray back to the kitchenette, and, leaning over the counter, said with a wicked grin, "I should have said mistress and slave."

"You mean it's the other way round?" She could live with that.

"Coffee?"

Patty glanced at her watch. "No, I must go in a minute. What shall I do? I've completely fallen for that manipulative bastard. Why do I have to go from one extreme to the other, from a man who thinks libido is the name of a star cluster to another who makes me see stars?"

"Don't analyze it, enjoy it. When will you see him again?"

"I'm not sure if I should. He's so intense."

"Then ask him to be a bit more gentle next time. Or test him. I think I've got something for you." She rummaged around in a stack of magazines on a side table. "It's a list with rules for masters. You can show it to Leo and see how he reacts."

"I don't think I—"

"Ah, here it is." She tore a page from a magazine, folded it and gave it to Patty. "You don't want to end up in a dysfunctional relationship, do you?"

JOY HAD A WHOLE SET OF PERSONAE at her disposal. With her clients, she was the supportive, affirmative therapist. With Shirley, she was the stern, impatient employer. With her lovers, she was whatever she felt like being at any given moment. Alone with herself, Joy sometimes didn't know who she was. I am the one who doesn't know who I am. Was that deep or dumb?

In the critical years of adolescence, she had often slipped into fantasies where she made believe that she was an alien lying dormant in a human body. From time to time, her true self would wake up and look at the world as something to explore, at the human species as something to study and at her body as a vehicle for her brilliant, superior mind. She was originally from a planet with two suns in the center of the galaxy, called Valanna. There was no water on Valanna. The ocean was of liquid silk, sweet and soothing. She had often been so absorbed in her imagined world that she had lost orientation.

Today, Joy would have been happy to be able to return to Valanna in her imagination. Shirley had gone for her lunch break and, left alone, Joy stared reproachfully at the phone on her desk. Maureen was still incommunicado. The more Joy allowed her mind to linger on the problem, the more she was convinced that Shadoe had carried out his threat. She heard a voice inside her head that kept telling her that Maureen was dead.

"Nonsense," Joy said aloud. "Her house is as safe as a fortress. And I told her not to let anyone in."

She decided to walk over to check the situation. She moved so briskly that she neither noticed the heavy traffic as she crossed Rosslyn Hill, nor the fact that she passed Leo's house in Pilgrim's Lane. Her mind was a step ahead. The moment she turned into Well's Road, she jerked to a sudden halt. An array of police cars blocked the street. With all her will-power, Joy disconnected her consciousness from the onrush of reproaches, because the presence of the police could only mean one thing: that she was too late.

Her ratio took over smoothly, and, with detached interest, she watched the coming and going of uniformed and plain-clothes policemen. Chain-smoking cigarettes, she tried to make up her mind if she should tell the police about the connection with Alison. There were several disincentives.

First of all, anyone who didn't know from one's own experience how a migraine could knock you out wouldn't understand how crippling the pain was, both to physical and mental powers. The police would ask her why she hadn't reacted appropriately after Maureen had shown her Shadoe's letter, when she knew that Alison had died after receiving a similar letter.

Secondly, it would throw a very bad light on her father if two threatening letters were connected to his handwriting. In the case of the first letter, there wasn't even a way to prove that the writing had been faked, because Alison had torn up the letter. Assuming that the handwriting in the second letter could be clearly identified as a fake, the police might still ask if Victor, unstable character that he was, had faked his own handwriting while he was in a state where he normally wrote in one of his two other styles. The best move would probably be not to tell them at all that she had recognized the writing.

The third reason for keeping this case separate from the first one was that everything she had worked for would be lost if a press release went out letting all the world know that a psychopath was singling out her patients and torturing them to death. She would soon be the focus of a sick, sensation-craving interest.

From the corner of her eyes she saw a lean man in a beige linen suit leave the house and look at her. He opened a mobile phone, spoke, closed the phone and passed on instructions. She took an instant liking to his quiet, calm bearing and the smooth efficiency of his performance. He had hair the color of a dun horse, a long face with deep-set, dark eyes and full lips. Although he was talking in a low tone and she couldn't understand his words, the quality of his voice carried—a raspy, voluminous bass. When he walked over to her, she straightened her shoulders, dropped the last cigarette and crushed it with her heel. She was Valannian from head to toe. Calm, remote, disinterested.

"Hello, ma'am. I'm Detective Inspector Terry. My constable said you have been watching us intently. Are you a friend of Maureen Gordon's?"

"I'm her therapist, Joy Canova. I was about to make a…a house call. What's going on?"

"Ms. Gordon is dead."

"Dead." The word held no meaning. Weren't all humans mortal?

"She was strangulated."

What was she supposed to say? How did it happen? Did she suffer? She knew all the answers already.

"What have you been treating Maureen for?"

"Aphenphosmphobia. She is…she was scared of having her throat touched."

His eyebrows dipped. "Is there a place where we can talk?"

"This way." Joy led Inspector Terry into her office, past a puzzled-looking Shirley.

With a casual glance, he took in the bright room, dominated by a cherry oak desk. His eyes trailed over the bookshelves and the potted yuccas before he sat down, took out a notebook and favored her with a beatific smile. Joy wondered why she felt like a visitor in her own office. He was obviously intent on creating a relaxed atmosphere.

"Wouldn't it be easier if we taped the interview?" She had a tape recorder on her desk. Her clients soon forgot about its presence, whereas taking notes kept them aware that they were being evaluated.

"Good idea. I'm not a good note-taker."

Joy put in a new cassette and started it. The inspector made some preliminary remarks: time, location, persons present.

"How long has Maureen Gordon been your patient?"

"Client. I refer to them as clients. Two years."

"Could you please repeat what you told me about her phobia?"

"She couldn't stand anything or anyone close to her throat. This variant of aphenphosmphobia often goes with pnigophobia, fear of choking. In her case, the fear had acquired such intensity over the years that she cut herself off from society."

"What kind of progress was she making?"

"Small steps concerning some of the secondary aspects of her fear."

"You treated her with desensitization?"

"I have developed an advanced form of desensitization. The idea is that a phobia changes a person over the years, creating secondary aspects of the condition, often experienced as idiosyncrasies. I start out by tackling the secondary aspects. It's a slow learning process, during which the motivation to overcome the primary fear grows with the confidence that the goal can eventually be achieved."

"What were those secondary aspects in Maureen's case?"

Did detectives always get on first-name terms with the victims so quickly? "She had no friends when she started to see me. Everything she did was organized around avoiding human contact. Narrow, stuffy rooms frightened her as much as large rooms with lots of people in them or open spaces where someone might come too close to her. Under my guidance, Maureen began to lead a social life."

"Did she tell you about the friends she made?"

"The most recent one was Hector Kelby, a gentleman in his seventies. Maureen once brought him along to a session. He didn't make the mistake of assuming that a phobia means that someone is trying to get attention. You wouldn't believe how often the sentence 'Don't make a fuss' is the response of even the most loving people to their phobic partners. Kelby quickly grasped that a phobia is a deep-rooted condition that can't be talked away. It has to be lived away. It is not like being a bit disgusted by spiders as many people are. Only those who have been through the purgatory of phobic terror can understand it."

"I understand only too well. Who were her other friends?"

She would have loved to ask him about his personal fears, but refrained. It might have made him even more personable. "Three women she met to play Bridge, and a jeweler who regularly bought her work, Arlo McCready. They had tea at Fortnum & Mason every now and then."

"Maureen received a threatening letter. It has been taken to the lab. As soon as I have a copy, I would like to discuss it with you."

"I have my own copy of it. On Saturday, Maureen came to my office at ten in the morning. She said she had found a letter under the rug in her hall when one of her cats was playing with the fringes. Oh, that reminds me, what will happen to the cats?" Joy didn't care for pets, but she cared for Maureen's love of her pets.

"Only one survived and it is in good hands."

"The cats were killed? Sad. Well, Maureen had no idea who might have written the letter or how and when it was delivered. I advised her to show it to the police."

"She didn't. Could I please see your copy?"

Joy opened her purse and handed Terry the copy she had shown Victor the night before. "I copied the letter myself. My fingerprints will be on the original."

"Would you please come over to the police station later this afternoon to have your prints taken?"

"Sure."

As Terry unfolded the sheet, Joy took a pencil, tapped it on the desk, turned it around, tapped the other end and went on doing this. She wanted to see if he was easily irritated.

"The writer gives away a lot about himself, if he is telling the truth. 'Like you, I am a recluse, living a lonely life far from the joys of company, bereft of the intimacy of love.'"

"Someone is trying to sound very sophisticated and lyrical, I'd say. A bit sententious, too."

Tap, went the pencil, tap, tap.

"And it's obvious that Maureen is known to him. She wasn't a random victim. 'But one act of love will be granted to us. We will share the fear, your fear, your beautiful, unique fear.' Beautiful is a strange adjective to describe fear."

"Absolutely." Tap, tap-e-di-tap. "Fear is ugly and woeful. But there's a pureness in fear sometimes, for outsiders, not for those who have to live with it, mind you."

He bent over, unceremoniously slid the pencil from her hand and went on reading. "'There is your throat, delicate, tender, oh so vulnerable. And I will touch it. What you have never allowed anyone to do in your whole life, I will do it. I will touch your most sensitive spot.' This is consistent with what you told me about her fear. 'Can you see the paradox in your fear: you can't protect your throat because you won't let anything near it, not even a collar or scarf. This stretch of skin is always naked, prone to attack—because you fear its being attacked. You spend your life in a vicious circle of petrifying proportions.'"

"That's an interesting point," Joy cut in. "Being afraid of snakes, for instance, isn't a threat in day-to-day life. In Maureen's case, the fear was constantly present, chronic and yet acute. What kept her together was her very robust health. She told me she had never needed a doctor, not even a dentist. Not that she would have let one close to her. She also had amazing self-discipline. Otherwise, she would have fallen apart long ago and you'd find her lolling and slobbering in an asylum."

"You don't seem to take her death very hard. After over two years of therapy sessions a bond should evolve, bordering on friendship."

"I will grieve privately. At the moment, I'm in a dissociated state which I generated willfully in order to be of use in furthering the search for her murderer." Joy noticed how stilted this sounded and reverently cleared her throat.

"Now we come to the important part. 'I will break the circle by strangling you.' And later: 'Your death throes will last for hours.' From what I saw at the scene he held his promise."

"You mean, Maureen wasn't just strangulated and it was over?"

"She was tortured."

"Good God."

"'Fearfully yours, Shadoe.' Is this a female or male name? It's probably supposed to sound like 'shadow,' conveying a sense of darkness and danger. In any case, it's certainly not the killer's real name."

"But I'm sure you'll have to look into this possibility, too."

"Yes, and it means a tremendous amount of paperwork and legwork. Who had access to information about Maureen Gordon, apart from the people she trusted, like her sister and Hector Kelby? Did you give patient data to a third party?"

"Never."

"But you keep files."

"Well, of course."

"Has your office been broken into lately?"

"Neither lately, nor at any time at all."

"Who comes and goes in this building? Friends, clients, a cleaning woman?"

"It looks like I have to write a list for you." She reached for the pencil and scribbled on her desk pad. "I have no friends and I don't entertain in my house. There's Shirley Ryan, of course, my secretary. Sally Young—"

"You and Ms. Gordon have the same cleaning woman?"

"I recommended Sally to Maureen. Sally has a simple mind, she wouldn't be able to formulate concepts like a 'vicious circle of petrifying proportions.'"

"She might have copied data from your files for someone else. She might have been bribed or blackmailed into doing it. Now, how about your clients? Are they left alone in your office sometimes?"

"Normally not, but it happens. Never for longer than a minute or two, though."

"I must ask you to write me a detailed list of all your clients, their addresses, since when you have been treating them, their phobia and a short description of their overall mental health. We are looking for a psychopath, it seems."

"I don't have to tell you about the doctor/client privilege, Inspector."

"I can easily obtain a subpoena. All your clients are prospective suspects."

How did this man manage to talk kindly and yet authoritatively? Joy weighed the options for a moment, then said: "You'll get the list."

"Thank you. I'll also need a copy of your appointment calendar."

"Anything else?" she said, making a movement with her hand to indicate her office was his.

He smiled. "That will do for the moment. It seems that Maureen didn't put up a fight. Did she have a masochistic streak?"

"She came across as a very forceful woman. And she wouldn't have acquiesced to …. But wait, there could be an explanation. I hypnotized her regularly, which was surprisingly easy, as if something inside her longed to let go of the tension. Of course, not just anybody could hypnotize her. It would have to be someone she trusted absolutely."

"Which narrows down the range of suspects considerably, to one person in fact."

It hadn't occurred to Joy that she was a suspect. She decided to play along. "You mean me? You're right. I think I was her confidante, the only person fighting with her side by side against the darkness of fear. Do you want my alibi?"

"Go ahead."

"For what period of time?" She wasn't easily trapped.

"Saturday evening to Sunday morning."

Shadoe had come by night. A Saturday night. A migraine night, just as in Alison's case. As if Shadoe knew when she wouldn't be around to stop him, to—

"Dr. Canova?"

"Oh, I had a migraine that weekend. It started shortly after Maureen had left on Saturday morning. My migraines are knock-outs. The pain almost kills me. I went to bed and didn't get up until Sunday afternoon. Not much of an alibi." She shrugged.

"When did Maureen usually go to bed?"

"That's a weird question."

"I always have a reason for my questions, even the weird ones."

Joy loved to flaunt her deductive powers. "I bet she was found in her day clothes, but the time of death was late at night, right? Well, she suffered from insomnia. She often stayed up until the small hours, reading or sketching designs."

"Would she have answered the door at such a time?"

"She never answered the door to anyone who came unannounced. She would talk to people over the intercom."

"So she wouldn't have let a stranger in."

"No way." Especially since she herself had advised her not to let anyone in.

Inspector Terry got up and handed her his card. "In case you think of anything else."

She clicked the eject button, gave him the tape and saw him to the door. Back in her office, Joy collapsed into her chair, put her head in her hands and sobbed for as long as it took to get the worst out of her system. Then she dried her face, blew her nose and tried to get back into the dissociated state. She would live through the shock in tiny portions.

After pressing certain Shiatsu points on her wrists, she felt better and capable of writing the list Inspector Terry needed. She would have written it down anyway, but for a different reason. In her eyes, every client was a prospective victim, not a suspect. The latest entry in her files was Patricia Miles. Well, you can't kill someone with butterflies, can you?

Then there was Emma Little, who was scared of blood. That was dangerous. Warning Emma had priority.

Claire Windover. Shadows. Goodness, that was eerie.

She had a client afraid of childbirth—no risk. Clouds—no risk. Mirrors—difficult to assess. Dolls—quite harmless. Fire—very dangerous.

Joy sat back and rubbed her eyes. How about herself? Would Shadoe's killing career culminate in water-torturing her? Joy's body began to shake. She was looking at a tsunami inside her head. The ocean had been tilted by 90 degrees and was racing towards her. In the outsized wave she could discern the shape of a hand.

Joy wasn't aware of the gurgling scream she gave until Shirley's voice came through to her.

"Can I bring you a glass of water, Dr. Canova?"

"Water, oh, no, no. I'm all right. I've had a shock. Maureen has been killed."

"Killed? How terrible."

Pulling herself together before Shirley could ask for details, Joy quickly went on in a business-like tone: "Clear my diary for this afternoon. Afterwards you may go home. And don't talk to anyone. We'll be in a hotbed of rumors soon enough."

DETECTIVE CHIEF INSPECTOR GOULD was leaving this week for a new assignment at Scotland Yard, the big career move he had dreamt of. Terry would lead the investigation until the new DCI arrived, Clen Smithhaven, currently DI at the Thames Valley Police.

In the incident room, which had been set up on the empty first floor at Albany Street Police Station, Terry had replayed his talk with Dr. Canova to his team.

He said, "It's too early to say whether this is a one-off murder or the beginning of a series. The letter has a ritualistic undertone and could suggest a psychopathic pattern. On the other hand, Shadoe knew Maureen so well that a personal motive is just as likely. We'll split the investigation into two main lines." He looked at DS Norman Parker. "You'll lead the team for the door-to-door inquiries."

Parker said, "The Hampstead guys have placed two Operation Eagle sandwich boards—in Well Road and near the Heath."

"I suggest that I check the database for previous cases with a similar MOP," PS Dwight Osborn cut in eagerly. He was young, black and quick. He was said to type faster than the computer could process data.

"Good," Terry affirmed. "You'll also ensure that all evidence is fed into the computer for cross-checks. Blockley, I want you and your team to talk to the people relevant in Maureen's life, except for Hector Kelby. I'll go and see him myself tomorrow morning. Has Maureen's sister already been contacted?"

"One of the local blokes from St. Albans drove her over. She identified the body, rampaged like a hooligan and had a fit of hysterics. She's being treated at the Royal Free. The doctor says she can't be interviewed before tomorrow."

"Right, I'll talk to her tomorrow, then. Now, what have we got so far?"

Blockley flipped through a stack of papers. "A preliminary report from the coroner. There are no further injuries on Maureen's body apart from the strangulation marks on her throat and the bruises on her wrists and ankles. She was not sexually assaulted. What is more, she was still a virgin."

"At almost fifty?" Parker snorted. "She took her phobic fear to extremes, huh?"

Blockley ignored him. "Then we've got a memo from the graphologist. He is sure the handwriting in the letter has been forged. The downstrokes are too much alike and the spacing too regular. A person normally writes the same letter in different ways, depending on what precedes and what follows."

"Anything else?"

"Ms. Gordon kept a very neat notebook on her sales of jewelry and purchases of material. I'm about to compare this to the list of items found in her house to see if anything is missing."

"Excellent. I have written a press release, but I withheld information about the threatening letter. We don't want to attract copy-cats and hoaxes. Any further ideas?"

"How about getting a psychological profile?" Parker asked.

"I'll ask Gould to file a request."

A veneer of urgency lay over his words, but Terry knew that during the coming weeks of collecting evidence, transcribing hundreds of interviews and looking for the tiniest of clues, the pace of the investigation would wear down as masses of details cluttered the apparatus. He needed someone able to keep an open mind for the overall picture. His eyes fell on WPC Janice Lake, a tall, spiky-haired blonde, who had joined them two months before.

"Janice."

"Sir?" She looked at him with admiration.

"We need an element of freshness. You have a good mix of intuition and curiosity. I want you to keep an eye on everything and report back to me when a detail strikes you as important, no matter how minuscule it seems. Talk to the others about their hunches, gut feelings and wayward theories. We are dealing with a killer who planned and carried out his deed like a theatre production."

Janice beamed. "With pleasure, sir."

"I'm off to the post-mortem. Brick, you'll join me." Brick's tall, friendly presence had something reassuring about it in a morgue.

As they walked to the car park, Brick informed Terry that the cat was fine. It took Terry a moment to understand what he was talking about.

PATTY STOOD ON THE OPPOSITE SIDE of narrow Pilgrim's Lane and looked at Leo's house. She hadn't called Leo to tell him that Danny had gone out again, so he wasn't expecting her and she still had a chance to return home where she would be safe. In the setting darkness, she couldn't make out the ceramic butterflies Leo had mentioned. Were they really there or had he just been playing with her fear when he told her about them? In a gift shop in Alvor she had seen ceramic butterflies, a popular motif of Portuguese handicraft. She had managed to flee without breaking anything in the shop.

Patty crossed the street and peered over the gate. There were dark shadows on the wall, shaped like triangular wings. Patty stood back and found herself again in her watching position.

Danny's peculiar behavior that evening still preoccupied her. All through dinner she had feared he would ask her whether she was having an affair. She had been prepared to shun his questions, but was unbalanced by his resigned silence. Although the sky was clouding over, he had left for Marlow, saying that he would drive to school directly from Jeremy's place tomorrow morning, as if he couldn't stand being around her. "We've got to prepare the filters for the eclipse," he had explained. "And to program Jeremy's laptop with a sequence of coordinates. We'll also go through long-term weather data, to see where we have the best chance to have a clear sky in August."

There seemed to be a lot of preparation required for an eclipse. Amazing that the sun had been able to do it all on its own for so long. She wouldn't see much of Danny until after the eleventh of August. It was her chance to enjoy a lot of good sex with Leo, although it felt more like a risk than a chance. She had the list in her purse, the one Misty had torn from an obscure bondage magazine.

At that moment, the front door opened. "There are no trapdoors in my garden path," Leo said and leaned against the door frame. A warm light from the hall formed a halo around his silhouette.

Hesitantly, she walked over.

"I wanted to show you a list," she said as she came within touching distance. She fingered the piece of paper from her purse, unfolded it and held it out like a shield. She wouldn't let him get too close until he had outlined the true nature of his intentions. He took the list, pocketed it without looking at it, took Patty by the shoulders and covered her face with kisses. She pulled away.

Slowly his strong hands released her. "Patricia, sorry. What's wrong?"

"I'm scared of you."

"Because of a passionate kiss? You liked being kissed like that on Friday night."

Appeased by his smile, she followed him upstairs to the large living room and glanced around the pillar. The empty spot on the wall gave her a feeling of great relief.

"The showcase is in the cellar and that's where it will remain until Joy has cured you. How was your first appointment? She didn't warn you about me, did she?"

"Would she have a reason to warn me?" Patty sat on a chair. She didn't want him beside her. She couldn't control her own streak of furious desire when he came too close.

He went over to the bar. "Something to drink?"

"No, thanks. Read the list and tell me what you think. I have a friend who is a...a dominatrix. I told her you spanked me and she...well, it's all a bit extreme, those items on the list. I don't want to put ideas in your head, but—"

"Hey, all right. I don't think you're scared of me, but of your own imaginings of what I might do with you. Remember what I told you when we met?"

"The Seneca quote? Yes, I do. We suffer more in imagination. A most unsettling pick-up line."

He poured himself a scotch and then turned to her and lifted his glass. "Here's to a girl's frenzy of erotic fantasies."

"I didn't imagine the spanking."

"And you didn't fake the orgasms you had before, during and afterwards." He put his glass down on the coffee table and took the list from the rear pocket of his trousers. "'The Nuts and Bolts of Trustworthy Sadism,'" he read aloud. "Um. This is the real stuff, it seems. Not fancy-spanky land, but lick-my-feet-unworthy-slave country."

He read the rest in silence. When he had finished, he put the list on the table, and looked at Patty with a flicker of amusement.

"Come over here, Patricia." Hypnotized by his calmness, she complied.

"Point one," he said, referring to the list. "Safewords. What do we need safewords for?"

"So that I can always stop you when you go too far."

"If you want me to stop, just say so."

"Misty told me that in S/M-speak 'no' means 'yes' and 'stop' means 'go on forever.'"

"S/M-speak, my eye. All I want is sex with a kinky edge. Mostly harmless. It's this silly list that scares you. You are easy to impress."

"What do you expect from a woman whose husband thinks steamy sex means doing it in a sauna? Danny once caught me playing with a vibrator and was very displeased because I had used up the batteries for the focusing motor of his telescope."

She waited until he had stopped laughing. "And you did hit me." She snatched up the list. "How can I know how far you will go? Listen to this: 'When a master slaps a slave he has to make sure that the impact only goes to the cheek and doesn't hurt ears, eyes or nose. It is also advisable to hold the slave's head with the other hand, so that it isn't hurled sideways, which might cause slingshot trauma.'"

"I didn't write this silly list. Here, look." He held out his right hand with his palm several inches from her cheek. A big, strong hand, callused from working with chisels and soldering-irons. "How could I hit your lovely face with such a rough hand?"

When he moved it closer, she jerked her head away in a reflex. He brought it back, closed his fingers around her neck and lifted her chin with his thumbs. A constricted feeling arose in her throat as he kissed her. Misty was right. She enjoyed being scared of him.

TERRY CAME HOME LATE, utterly whacked and drained, dropped his briefcase, went straight into the living room, opened the lid of the grand piano and played the *37th Song Without Words* by Mendelssohn, a simple melody accompanied by triads. It relaxed him a little. Had it only been this morning that he had kissed Alan goodbye?

He was into the first bars of *The Rustle of Spring*, when a memory caught up with him. Joy Canova's remarks on the nature of phobias had brought it forward.

It was more than thirty years ago, long before the term "panic attack" had been coined, so he didn't even have the benefit of understanding what was happening to him. He was due to play to an audience for the first time. From the day his mother had announced that she had enrolled him for the Young Genius competition, his intestines had begun to ice over. Two days before the competition he had stopped eating. The night before he couldn't sleep. In his chest, a pulse clanked against his ribs. On the evening of the competition, his body was rigid, his brain a useless block of cement. "Look at the others, they're nervous too," his mother said, patting his arm excitedly. Rick stood motionless, packed tightly in a glacial straightjacket of horror.

"Forget about the jurors. Pretend they're not there. Play as you play at home. You're so good, boy, you're better than all of them. You're not practicing five hours a day for nothing."

He didn't care about the competition. It didn't matter to him if he won or not. He was dying.

Then it was his turn and his mother nudged him on. His feet stayed put and he almost fell over. A man, the patron of the competition probably, grabbed him. Rick's feet, those traitors, stumbled forward. He was pressed down on the piano stool in front of the grand piano. He had no choice. He started to play, sure that his stiff hands wouldn't obey him. But they were traitors, too. *The Rustle of Spring* bubbled over the keys as if a faucet had been turned on, and slowly his inside thawed. Like meltwater, cold sweat trickled down his face.

When he had finished, he dashed backstage and his father drove him home. He missed the award ceremony and his mother received the first prize in his stead.

Yes, he knew all about phobias. Maureen's eyes had seen the same chilling, merciless death he had seen many times. If only he hadn't won the competition, then maybe his mother would have left him alone. "It's just a bit of stage fright. You'll get used to it," she had said, over and over again. And he had looked death in the face, over and over again, and he had never got used to it. Maybe if someone like Joy Canova had been there, who understood the nature of his problem, who could have helped him out of the debilitating terror.... As it was, he had at some point been grown-up and self-assured enough to tell his parents that he wasn't going to be a concert pianist.

"Rick?" Cece had come in.

"Hello, darling, how was your day?"

"Fine." Her voice sounded lame.

"What's the matter? Your contract hasn't been revoked, has it?"

She came over to the piano and shook her head, but didn't look at him. She wasn't her quicksilver self this evening.

"Then what?" He reached for her hand, but she withdrew it immediately.

"Don't touch me. You'll regret it," she said somberly. Now Terry was genuinely worried. But he knew better than to bother her with questions. He lowered the lid of the piano and waited.

"I'm not sure I can tell you," she began. "It's too...too embarrassing." Suddenly she broke into sobs. "You'll hate me for the rest of your life."

"Cece," Terry said calmly, "I spent the day investigating an abominable homicide. That puts everything into perspective."

"You have no idea. It's worse, it's got to do with the most sinful of all sins."

"What could be worse than homicide?"

Cece looked away. "Incest."

"Cece!" Terry exclaimed, "I never did anything incestuous to you, did I?"

"It's not something *you* did."

Amusement mixed with his concern. "I would know if you had done something incestuous to me, wouldn't I?"

"I didn't do it to you directly."

"Cece, this is not a good moment for guessing games." Then it dawned on him. His forehead creased in perplexity. "Alan?"

Cece nodded, her eyes downcast.

"You met him this morning, I suppose, when you came to write," Terry said cautiously to make the confession easier for her.

"I heard someone warbling *I Feel Pretty* in a kind of falsetto. He was in the bedroom, dancing in front of the mirror, with a pair of your boxers on."

Terry felt a grin tug at the sides of his mouth.

Cece remained dead serious. "He was so...so irresistible. You mustn't blame him, though. I took the initiative. Oh, Rick, I stole your lover." And she wept again.

"Not many girls can say that: 'I stole my uncle's lover.'" His attempt to cheer her up failed. Terry fished in his trouser pocket for a handkerchief and pressed it on her wet cheeks. "Hey, Cece, I don't hate you. I'm not even angry. Please, stop crying and look at me."

She was inconsolable. "How could I do something so dreadful? I can't forgive myself. You have been so lonely all these years since Michael's death...and then I come along and ruin your new love. You wouldn't want him back, would you?"

"Surely not. It would feel, well, incestuous."

"See? I'm so ashamed. I've hurt your feelings. It's the last thing I wanted to do, to hurt you." She now wore this deer-caught-in-the-headlights look, which showed she was in urgent need of consolation.

"Actually, you haven't. Look, I'm not in love with Alan. It wasn't meant to last."

"No?" Hope glimmered in her eyes.

"You could call it a one-night-stand with a sequel. He's far too young for me." He smiled encouragingly. "You can keep him if you want."

"Oh, no. I couldn't. I'd always think that you had him first."

"That's how it feels at present, but emotions have a tendency to simmer down after a while. Alan is a nice guy. Honestly, Cece, I wouldn't mind being best man at your and Alan's wedding one day."

Cece threw her arms around him and covered his face with salty kisses. "You're too good to be true, Rick. He's really nice. Afterwards, he helped me change the sheets."

"You did it in my bed?" He pushed her from his lap. "IN MY BED?"

CHAPTER SIX
TUESDAY, 15 JUNE

LEO LOVED TO WORK RIGHT after getting up, when dream images were still so palpable he could feel their shape in his palms. Patricia inspired him, gave his work a fresh angle. He would sculpture butterflies with female, sensual bodies and fine-boned faces, the body a carving in wood, the wings made of silk stretched on a metal skeleton. Could he persuade Patricia to sit for him? Would the idea of being transformed into a butterfly horrify her?

She was lying on her stomach. He pushed back the sheets and kissed her spine, vertebra by vertebra. Educated in anatomy, he saw a beauty that would escape the untrained eye, Patricia's harmonious bone structure and well-balanced muscle/fat ratio. Seven pale red lines ran in perfect parallel across her butt. As he had expected, she had quickly learned to relish the anticipation and the helplessness when he had caned her last night.

"I love you, Patricia," he said.

"Do you really?" She looked at him with one sleepy eye. "Would you allow me to cane you?"

"Better not. Your friend, the dominatrix, might give you another list: 'Twelve Ways to Torture Your Male Slave.' But if you need it as proof of my sincerity, yeah, go ahead."

"It's only to make sure you know how it hurts."

"I do know. Once, I was hit so hard I couldn't sit for a week." He wouldn't tell Patricia that it had been Joy's doing, with a riding crop he had removed from his arsenal afterwards.

"Poor Leo. Come, make love to me."

"I wanted to take you to my workshop."

"I prefer a warm, soft bed."

"Not for love-making. To draw some sketches of you. I have something in mind."

She stretched out her arms, yawned and shook her head. "You can draw here as well."

"Considering that you were scared of me last night, you are pretty insubordinate this morning."

She grinned. "You just said you loved me. I feel safe with you now."

He kissed the side of her nose. He had studied her so closely he could draw her from memory.

Later, after she had dressed and was ready to leave, Patricia stood at the window looking over the garden. The ceramic butterflies on the white plaster glittered in the sun.

"Yesterday, just knowing that they were there made me nervous."

Leo, who was standing behind her, put his right hand on her belly. "I wish I knew what you feel."

"I need time."

"Not what you feel for me. I mean the butterflies."

"You should be glad you don't know the feeling. It's gruesome." She glanced at her watch. "My first student is coming in an hour."

"I'll drive you home."

"I'll take the bus to Adelaide Road and walk the rest of the way. I want to pop in at La Strada to tell Misty what you said about her list."

"What is La Strada? A shop selling whips and chains?"

Patty laughed. "We're talking about Primrose Village, not Soho. It's a boutique. Will you come down with me and help me to get past the butterflies?"

"My lovely, I would fight dragons to protect you."

"I wouldn't mind dragons. They're cute," she teased him. "A bit unpredictable, like you. I never know when you'll breathe fire."

He walked her to the corner of Rosslyn Hill. Looking at her gently rocking behind as she strode away from him, he knew he would have to get inside her fear. He would take the butterflies up from the cellar and look at them, trying to see them as she saw them. He would open the case and touch their wings, imagining they were the ultimate menace, the darkest power in the universe.

Leo was about to turn when he saw Cameron coming from the bus stop. Cameron did a double take when he passed Patty, then shrugged and drew level with Leo.

"Hi, Dad. Perfect timing, eh?"

"Shouldn't you be at school?"

"I feel a bit under the weather. Haven't had breakfast."

Leo looked at the lanky boy, who had outgrown all the care his parents could give him; who wasn't loved by anyone, because he rejected every emotion offered him; who wouldn't run away again because he could have all the desolation of the streets in his own home. "How about a mushroom omelet, son?"

DESPITE A BAD NIGHT WITH FITFUL SLEEP, Joy soldiered on. She was not going to give this Shadoe person the satisfaction of forcing her to cancel appointments. She was sure he was watching her. Last night she had drawn the curtains and searched her flat and office for bugs or hidden cameras, all the time reassuring herself that this was not a dead give-away for a paranoiac episode.

Before breakfast, she had driven to the police station to hand over the lists. On her way back, she had bought a stack of tabloids. The headlines were screaming off the pages—bloodthirsty, but of little informational value. Plenty of speculation spiced with grisly details. Tampons had been pushed up Maureen's nostrils. Joy had twenty-two clients at present. Who would Shadoe pick for his next session? Selina Prigett, who was afraid of heat? Instead of tampons, would he push burning cigarettes up her nose?

When Shirley came, Joy gave her the papers. Shirley, who must have had her share of morning literature, enjoyed the sensations. Joy saw fit to make sure Shirley wouldn't run around gossiping and giving interviews.

"My name is not mentioned in the articles. I hope I can keep the lid on it as long as possible."

Shirley gave a conspiratorial nod. "You can rely on my discretion, Dr. Canova."

"Of course, the press will soon find out I was treating Maureen. We'll fob them off with a statement I've composed." She pointed at a sheet on the desk. "Don't make any extra comments."

Joy's first client this morning was Emma Little, who told her about a dream where it had rained blood. Instead of listening, Joy tried to come up with a strategy to warn Emma without scaring her. Emma, an actress, wouldn't know about Maureen. She never read papers anymore since one of her plays had been slated by the critics.

"... because I'm getting so many letters lately. My agent said I'll need a secretary and...."

Joy intercepted before Emma could wander on to other topics. "Do you open your fan letters yourself?"

"Yes."

"And you read and answer all of them?"

"I send autographs, that's what they all want anyway."

"Do you ever get nasty letters, threats and the like?"

"No. I'm not famous enough for that."

"Emma, this may sound strange, but if you get a threatening letter, would you please call me straight away?"

"Do you think it would upset me so much?"

"It could interfere with our therapy," Joy said vaguely. Sooner or later the police would turn up on Emma's doorstep. Joy knew she was shoving her problem ahead of her, but couldn't bring herself to tell Emma the unbridled truth.

She saw Emma to the door. It had started to rain—a warm, soft summer rain.

Emma grinned as she opened her umbrella. "I'm glad this is not a dream. There's something so reliable about reality. You just know it's never going to rain blood."

THE SCENE-OF-CRIME SHOTS had been pinned all over the walls. The desks in the incident room were overflowing with files. Terry had come in early this morning and tried to read as much as he could. It was mostly the usual heap of trivia, the invariable by-product of an investigation.

Dwight Osborn had printed out a list of unsolved homicides, covering ten years. The list included every case with the slightest resemblance to their current investigation. Someone would have the arduous task of getting all the files from the archives and sifting through them.

The forensic report on the six dead cats revealed Shadoe's cruel, swift efficiency. None of the pets had traces of blood on their claws.

Blockley joined Terry an hour later, balancing two cups of tea on another stack of paper. "Here are the transcripts of the phone calls to the special unit. Four hundred eleven and still counting."

"Thank you," Terry said as he took one of the cups. He grimaced at the files. "Looks as if it's time for me to go and get some interviews done."

"I talked to several people yesterday," Blockley took up the thread. "Mrs. Endover, the neighbor, saw and heard nothing. On Saturday night her teenage daughter was throwing a party. Brick phoned all of the guests to ask if they had noticed anything as they arrived or left. Zilch. I tried the acoustic situation. I went around the house, while WPC Smith stood in Maureen's living room and screamed at the top of her voice. Unless you put an ear directly on a window pane, you don't hear anything. It's all triple glazing, even the conservatory."

"More a fortress than a house. There was really no other way for Shadoe to get in than through the front door. Which brings us back to the question why Maureen opened it for her killer."

"Maybe he was disguised as a policeman."

"Maybe he was a policeman. He left no traces, no evidence at all. He must have known exactly what we would be looking for."

Brick came in. "I've thought about Snow."

"Snow? In June?"

"Snow is the angora cat Shadoe didn't kill but let out, as if he wanted someone to notice her, so that his victim would be found in due time. Why else should he have let her escape?"

"Maybe she was in the garden all along," Terry argued.

"Ah, no," Brick said expertly. "Maureen's cats were over-sensitive pedigrees, definitely not made for catching mice and sharpening their claws on bark."

Blockley nodded. "That's what Sally Young said. She told us that Maureen never let her cats out. She was organized to the point of being pedantic. She had done the housework herself for many years because she didn't trust anyone. Sally had been instructed by Joy never to get close to Maureen and not to talk unless she was asked a question."

"Like a flunky," Terry remarked.

"Most importantly, she was not to spread rumors about Maureen's eccentric ways and the valuables lying around, so as not to attract thieves. Sally said she kept strictly to those rules. She had a reputation to lose, after all, she told me. I had the impression she was sincere in everything she said. She's a widow with four grown-up children who are all financially secure. There's nothing to follow up there."

"Did you ask her about visitors Maureen had?"

"Sally was very reticent about this. I had to remind her three times that we are looking for a murderer and not collecting material for a gossip column. She finally mentioned that she saw Hector Kelby twice. Some time before that, in spring last year, Maureen had a male visitor, a man Sally hadn't met before. He and Maureen were in the conservatory, talking. He left shortly afterwards. He had dark hair, streaked with gray, and bad skin."

"What's that supposed to mean?" Terry asked.

Blockley consulted his notebook for the verbatim quote. "'He had a face like a dry sponge.'"

AFTER LISTENING TO THE TAPED INTERVIEW, Blockley had formed a picture in his mind of a middle-aged woman with angular features and short-cropped hair. He was mildly surprised when Joy Canova turned out to be young and attractive.

"I was expecting you," she said. "Inspector Terry called. Why don't we go upstairs?"

Blockley, still suspicious, wondered if there was something or someone in her office she didn't want him to see. He followed her into a spacious living room with an open-plan kitchen.

She led him to a chair, poured out coffee at the kitchen counter, and joined him, smiling warmly. "It is kind of you to come so that I have a chance to talk to you before you go to see my clients. Some of them are prone to severe social anxiety or live on the brink of clinical depression. A sudden intrusion of the police into their lives would be harmful."

Then, as if she suddenly became aware that her gleeful mood was out of place, she put down the cup, folded her hands in her lap and gave him a long, mournful stare. "Maureen used to be my second client on Tuesday mornings. This is the hour I would normally have spent with her."

Blockley sipped his coffee, strong and delicious, then opened the folder he had brought along. "When I studied your list, I couldn't help but wonder if some people are really scared of mirrors, clouds or butterflies. Maybe Freud was right when he coined the term hysteria. Or did he?" He looked up to see how she was taking the challenge. When she showed no reaction, he went on. "And all those fancy names, like maleusiophobia for fear of childbirth. If I were a woman, I'd be afraid of giving birth, too, and I wouldn't care how they termed it in professional circles."

"You're right. Words mean nothing. Take hippopotomonstroesquippedaliophobia," she offered. "What do you think it signifies?"

"Fear of hippopotamuses?" he tried.

"No. It means fear of long words."

"You're pulling my leg."

"Not at all. But, as you said, it's just a word. The condition is the trouble. People are afraid of the most absurd things and animals. My clients live on the far end of the scale, where such simple conditions as claustrophobia seem like heaven in comparison."

"Did Maureen socialize with some of your other clients?"

"I don't do group therapy."

"Did Maureen sometimes meet the clients who came before or after her?"

"They passed each other at the door every now and then. Emma Little is my first visitor on Tuesday mornings. I never saw her exchange more than a cursory glance with Maureen. The client who comes next today is Claire Windover."

"The one who is afraid of shadows," Blockley said, consulting the list.

"She'll be here in a few minutes. You can talk to her then, if you think it necessary," Joy said defiantly. "Claire and Maureen said hello a few times, but as far as I know that's all they ever got to see of each other."

"That's all that is needed." An interesting scenario crossed Blockley's mind. "Let's assume that Claire is our poison pen. Her phobia has taken her beyond the borders of mental sanity. You said that some of your clients were endangered in this respect. Trying to compensate for her fear, Claire begins to identify with the feared object, namely shadows. Feelings of power follow. Dark fantasies. She writes Maureen the death threat, signing as Shadoe, thus forming a bond with the devils that haunt her. On Sunday evening she calls her, telling her that she has just been to see you because she got an anonymous letter and that you informed her that Maureen had received a similar letter. They talk and decide to compare the letters and then to go to the police. Claire comes over. Maureen would be totally unsuspecting in these circumstances. Then Claire hypnotizes Maureen—and we know the rest. Did you ever hypnotize Claire?"

"Ye-ss."

"So Claire knows your method and was able to use it on Maureen."

"I'm sure I would have noticed if Claire had undergone the dramatic change you suggest."

Setting off on a different course, Blockley asked, "Would you notice if a client faked a phobia?"

"Are you insinuating that Shadoe has been using me? That he or she infiltrated my world by pretending to suffer from a phobia?"

"He might not have intended it from the outset. He was probably getting a kick out of telling you about his invented panic attacks. Then he began to see the options opening up to him. A fear fetishist's treasure trove." Blockley was pleased with the psychological profile he had extemporized. But Joy didn't share his enthusiasm.

"It would take a brilliant actor to pull this off."

"Emma Little is an actress."

Joy lifted her hands, palm upwards, a gesture of mock defeat, underscored by an ironic grin. "Next you'll tell me that Claire and Emma were in this together. Sergeant, if one of my clients was a sociopath of such proportions, do you really think I wouldn't have noticed?"

"Does one of your clients have a history of participating in a satanic cult?"

"Actually, Claire was the victim of a satanic ritual as a very young child, hence her sciophobia. She was taken into a cellar that was lit by candles. The first thing she saw when her torturers came were their shadows on the wall. Luckily for her, the abuse lasted only a very short time span, until the leader of the sect committed suicide. I would appreciate it if you didn't mention any of this to her. Victims of child abuse are very fragile. I don't think you've got the sensitivity to handle the interviews with my clients. I wish Inspector Terry had sent someone with psychological training."

After this rebuff, Blockley said with a fair amount of complacency, "I've also come to check your alibi."

"There is no way to check it. I don't invite friends to watch over me when I have a migraine attack."

"The name of your GP would be helpful, so that he can endorse your claim to suffer from migraines."

"I don't have a GP. Over the years, I have tried everything modern medicine has to offer. I gave up, eventually. I haven't seen a doctor for ages."

Blockley heard a voice at the front door.

"My secretary," Joy explained. "I asked her to bring Claire upstairs."

Claire Windover was the picture of fragility. She gave Blockley a limp hand and sank into a chair, where she sat with her head lowered. A colorless, wispy fringe fell over her hooded eyes.

"I won't take much of your time," Blockley said. "You've probably heard about Maureen Gordon's death."

"I read about it in the papers." As if she needed a backing for even this simple statement, Claire glanced up at Joy, who stood leaning against the mantelpiece.

"You met her sometimes, didn't you, when you came for an appointment with Dr. Canova."

"Two or three times, I'd say. I found her scary. I don't mean to say anything bad about her. She just…. She was intimidating." Her palms rubbed against each other in an uncontrolled manner.

Blockley thought that for Claire probably everyone was intimidating. After all, every human being casts a shadow.

"Please don't be upset about my next question. It's pure routine and I'm not insinuating anything. Where were you this weekend?"

"At home, with my aunt. She's my surrogate mother. My parents are dead."

Blockley wondered if Claire's father had been the suicidal sect leader Joy had mentioned. "You and your aunt were alone?"

"Some friends came on Saturday evening and played chess. My aunt organizes private tournaments. I serve them drinks and sandwiches. I don't like chess.

Black and white, it's darkly foreboding." She said it without inflection and Blockley felt that, although Claire had the mental disturbance necessary to write twisted death threats, she lacked the moxie to do anything that required forward planning and physical effort.

"That's all, then. Thank you for your cooperation."

Joy led him downstairs. "You saw for yourself that Claire is a person living at the breaking point. Many of my clients are. I wish you would stay away from them. If anything, you should protect them rather than suspect them."

"GOD ALMIGHTY," JANICE SAID when they entered the hospital room. Terry wasn't sure if she was referring to Brenna Gordon's looks or to her demeanor. It was as if Maureen had returned to the living. Sitting straight as a ramrod in her bed, her hair in disarray, Brenna was shouting abuse at a nurse in a most unholy fashion, reminding Terry of Gould's eruptions whenever he had read one of Terry's flowery reports.

"I refuse to pee into a potty or to take any of those pink pills. You can tell the quack in charge I'm tranquil enough. And no messing around with needles. It's outrageous how I'm being treated here—as if I weren't able to make my own decisions."

"You're in a state of shock," the nurse pointed out, her voice as starched as her coat.

"And I'm not going to get out of this state as long as my personal rights are being violated. Is this an asylum or what?"

"It's the Royal Free Hos—"

"Free. There. Now that's a word to my taste. I herewith discharge myself." Brenna swung her legs over the edge of the bed.

"Doctor Maven will be very angry."

"Then he had better take those tranquilizers. And who the hell is this?" She waved her hand towards the door. "Your bodyguard?"

"Detective Inspector Terry," Terry said. "I've come to talk to you."

"You've got a nerve, I must say. If the police didn't handle death threats in this slapdash way, Maureen would still be alive."

The nurse used the shift in Brenna's attention to leave the room.

"Your sister didn't show us the letter," Terry said calmly.

"Because she knew you wouldn't take her seriously. She was always being ridiculed by the authorities. Now go out and let me change into something decent, will you."

"What was that?" Janice asked when they were in the corridor.

"The most vituperative variant of shock reaction I've ever seen. We can consider ourselves fortunate that she didn't throw an oxygen cylinder after us."

"Osborn didn't mention they were twins."

"Twin or no twin, if Maureen had been half as furious, she'd have bitten off Shadoe's fingers when he tried to gag her."

The door exploded outwards and Brenna appeared, dressed in a blue pleated skirt and a creased blouse. "I hate wearing yesterday's clothes. It's all your fault. There was no need to hospitalize me. I didn't have anything remotely like a nervous breakdown, let me tell you that. I was infuriated by the insensitivity of the officer who took me to the morgue. My goldfish have higher IQs than your people. This man just opened the body bag and said: 'Is this your sister Maureen?' Can you imagine what it's like to know this is how you're going to look when you're dead? It was a completely normal reaction that I began to shake and scream."

"You hit the morgue attendant," Terry reminded her.

"Now did I? Must have been a reflex. Anyway, instead of abducting me to this hideous place, they should have given me a cognac. There's no common sense among young people today."

The nurse came back, carrying a hypodermic syringe in a kidney bowl. Before the doctor, who accompanied her, had a chance to say anything, Brenna warned: "Don't you hassle me." With a roguish smile, she added, "I've just been arrested by the inspector." Shouldering her handbag, she sauntered down the corridor.

"I hate hospitals," Brenna announced when they caught up with her in the street.

"I twigged that."

"You're not as obtuse as your colleague in the morgue."

Janice, who had gone over to the panda car and rummaged around in the boot, came back with two small bottles of whisky.

"How did you wangle that?" Brenna asked.

"It's for emergencies."

"So consider me an emergency." Her head thrown back, she downed the contents in one huge gulp. "Not bad. You can drive me home and on the way there you can grill me with questions, how's that?"

They sat in the back seat and Terry handed Brenna a copy of the threatening letter. She read it with growing fury. "All you would have had to do was wait outside Maureen's house and catch him. This is a matter of gross negligence."

"We found the letter in her desk. I told you she didn't show it to the police. Did she call you and tell you about it?"

Brenna flipped the letter back at him. "The last time we talked on the phone was two weeks ago. We didn't have much contact. And I was away over the weekend. A hunting trip to Exmoor."

Janice turned her head and asked: "You were twins, weren't you?"

"Sure enough. And we were two sweet li'l girls. During puberty Maureen began to develop neurotic traits." Brenna had finished off the second bottle of whisky and was eyeing it woefully. "My parents told her to get a grip, but her condition just got worse and worse. Whenever we thought that she had reached the peak and could only get better, she'd find a new twist. Not that she did it on purpose, but it was so totally out of character. She was so forceful, self-assured and equipped with a ribald humor—just like me." She winked at Terry. "She hated our local community. She said she felt like a monstrosity because of her eccentric ways."

"So everybody in St. Albans knew about her phobia?"

"Sure enough. That was why she moved to London, where she would have anonymity."

"When was that?"

"A few weeks after my wedding. We were twenty-two. I was engaged to the most good-looking, charming man. Now, what was his name? Eric Eastwood? No, Eric Eastman. I remember it as if it was yesterday." She giggled behind her hand. "We stood in front of the vicar, me in a frilly white satin dress, he in a black suit, and the vicar asked perfunctorily if there was anyone who had any objections to our getting married, and Maureen rose from her seat in the last row and enumerated Eric's previous convictions, business frauds and marriage swindles. I never found out how she had unearthed all that."

"Couldn't she have told you before, in private?"

"Of course, but think of the complications. Calling off the marriage, writing excuses to all the guests. It was easier like that, with everyone hearing what she had to say. And she had a sense for drama, hadn't she? I didn't believe a word of it until I saw Eric's face. Maureen had got him sussed all right. I freaked out, grabbed the vicar's Bible and aimed it at Eric, but it only hit his shoulder because he was dashing down the aisle to go for Maureen's throat."

"Good heavens."

"Not to worry. My father knew some effective judo throws. In the end, Eric lay on the floor with a bleeding nose."

"Weren't you angry that she turned your wedding into a public humiliation?"

"The twerp was after my money and she had spared me a far greater humiliation."

"What became of Eric?"

"He married an addle-headed, rich heiress. I haven't heard from him in years."

"What happened after Maureen's move to London?"

"She became more and more of a hermit. The last time I went to see her was four years ago after she had bought the house in Hampstead. She had just acquired her first cat. I suffer from allergic asthma, so I only stayed in her house for half an hour or so. I was shocked about the state she was in—outwardly very controlled, but I could read the agitation in her eyes. And she wouldn't even let me hug her. I think she was relieved when I left."

"Then you never met Hector Kelby."

"No. She mentioned him on the phone. It was a step forward in her therapy, but I felt she was more inclined to step further and further backwards, to return into a mental womb and hang herself on her umbilical cord, metaphorically speaking. She was dead, an empty shell, immobilized by fear. Some autonomous reflexes kept her going, that was all."

"She designed beautiful jewelry," Janice said. "Creativity requires a good deal of energy."

"Or boredom. I've been everything from a hobby ornithologist to an antiques expert. I painted oils, made floral arrangements and designed underwear. Maureen was like that, too. She just kept busy. Creativity is a side-effect of ennui. All you need is a little talent and a lot of time to kill. Oh, would you mind stopping at that pub? I have to get myself another emergency dram."

"THIS IS IN TOTAL CONTRADICTION to what Joy Canova said about Maureen," Janice commented as they drove back to London. "She said Maureen was improving steadily, whereas Brenna described her condition as deteriorating. Maybe it's because they weren't meeting up personally any longer. She didn't have the full picture, just her sister's voice on the phone."

"I tend to believe her, rather than Joy Canova," Terry said. "Twins have a deep insight into each other's psyche, even when they're apart."

"That's a myth. And they weren't very much alike, anyway. Maureen was psychotic, Brenna is stable."

"That's what she seems to be. But take a closer look. Brenna suffers from allergic asthma. That's a psychosomatic manifestation of fearing suffocation. And they were both unmarried. We should have a closer look at Eric Eastman—soon."

"I called Osborn when you were seeing Brenna into the house. He'll look Eastman up in the database."

Terry smiled. "It's really a pleasure working with you."

"Thank you, sir. I also had a short talk with Parker. Arlo McCready came to the station this morning to give his statement. He said he and Maureen used to meet every now and then for tea at Fortnum & Mason, but he had given it up. Maureen was getting more and more uptight and nervous and he saw no point in forcing this activity on her, just because her therapist thought it was a good idea. So Brenna might be right. Arlo also said he didn't understand why Maureen refused to take tranquilizers. Even people with harmless neurotic derangements consume them all the time."

"Maybe Brenna's fit of rage at the hospital was chicanery to cover her medication phobia, if such a condition exists. I must ask Joy Canova about it. If one twin has it, the other is likely to have it, too."

"And they both drink whisky. Maureen had a large stock of Glenfiddich."

"Closet alcoholics. Well, if it helped Maureen to cope...."

Janice looked grimly through the windscreen. "I hate it when people hide their weaknesses. I bet Brenna is going to have her nervous breakdown right now, when nobody is watching. Losing a twin must be like losing one half of yourself."

A twin, Terry thought, a half of oneself. Now what did that remind him of?

SHIRLEY RYAN STOOD IN FRONT of Joy's desk with her arms akimbo. "I feel left out of things. The police come and go, but no one cares to ask me any questions."

"They have filed you away as harmless."

"And so they should," said Shirley, ignoring the sarcastic undertone. "I have an airtight alibi—all my activities during the weekend listed with time, location and witnesses."

"Good for you."

"But they didn't even begin to suspect me. If this is how the police handle a homicide—"

"Let them do their job the way they see fit." Joy was tired of discussing this crime. Really tired.

"You're more stand-offish than the conjunction of your ruling planets might excuse."

"That's enough." Joy swung around in her swivel chair, turning her back on

Shirley. Alison was right, she looked a bit of a fright. "I won't need you for the rest of the week."

Shirley gasped. "Those are the vagaries of life."

Joy wondered if she ever talked like a normal person. "Sure, you're a reliable secretary," she said to the window pane.

"And that's why you can't dismiss me like this. I'm tempted to call *The Sun* or *The Mirror*. They would pay well for an exclusive interview."

"Yes, you can tell them that it was all in Maureen's horoscope."

She heard the door bang. Glad to be rid of her nosy secretary, Joy breathed in a slow, controlled manner. Her stress level had been rising by the minute this morning. She was walking on thin ice. The police would find out about Alison and would ask her why she had hampered the investigation. Maybe she could plead insanity. She could tell them she was an extraterrestrial, that would do.

Joy mounted the stairs to her flat, walked round the kitchen counter, opened the fridge, took out a bottle of beer and drank it down in huge gulps. Just to be on the safe side, she sank another bottle and then shambled to the living room and slumped back onto the sofa. That should help. Although she held the professional opinion that a crisis should be faced in an observant state, she noted that she was presently going through a denial phase. In hindsight it almost seemed to her as if she had been in a denial phase all her life. Those repressed nightmares, the migraines, the hydrophobia, the feeling of being watched. Her symptoms screamed post-traumatic stress syndrome.

The ringing of the phone startled her.

"Yesss," she hissed into the receiver.

"Hello, sweetheart," a schmaltzy voice said. "Guess who this is?"

Her eidetic memory immediately fed her the necessary data. Only two men had called her sweetheart and one of them was a heavy smoker with a rough voice. So this had to be the foot fetishist she had met sometime in April. "Still alive and licking?"

"I bet I am the hero of your masturbation fantasies."

"Sorry, but you have been demoted. Now you are the hero of my castration fantasies."

He sniggered. "Sweetheart, I can't get your beautiful feet out of my head, figuratively speaking, and I was wondering if I could take some photos of them. I've got an assignment and we could share the fee. And of course I'd also like to—"

"No," she cut him short. "I've got myself a dog and its tongue is longer then yours."

She dropped the receiver and grinned maliciously. "Prat," she said aloud. "I'm fed up with perverts, psychotics and phobics. I'm fed up with all of them.

I've had my share of loonies."

What was she scared of anyway? Her producer at the BBC would be happy about her involvement in Maureen's death because it would boost the ratings for her show. What did she need clients for? She could make money with books and lectures. Her job hadn't given her much delight lately. It had been different at the beginning. Not every quirk is a mental illness. She had healed many clients, often in a matter of months. Somehow, the difficult cases had accumulated over the years, and now she was left to deal with the hopeless and lost, the obstreperous freaks with debilitating phobias. When gradually exposed to their fear they didn't develop coping skills but evolved improved avoidance techniques.

Patricia Miles was a pleasant exception. Joy's instincts told her that Patricia had a lot of untapped potential. She was a candidate for an almost instant healing. All she needed was the right mix of succor and prodding.

When the phone rang again, Joy thought that some men just couldn't take no for an answer.

"I've also got athlete's foot," she fibbed moodily.

"S-s-sorry to hear that."

She had never heard this voice before. Could it be Shadoe? "Who are you?" she inquired sharply.

"Angus F-f-fenning, ma'am. Canova Press. The il-l-lustrations for your book are r-r-ready."

Joy squeezed her eyes shut. "Oh, I see. I normally talk to Mr. Norton."

"He's on a h-h-holiday. He asked me to disc-c-cuss the illustrations with you as s-s-s-soon as they arrived from the p-p-printers. When would it s-s-suit you?"

"You can come straight away, if you want." She hoped he wouldn't insist on her driving to Oxford.

"That's f-f-fine with me. S-s-see you in t-t-two hours."

Joy went to get herself another beer. Angus Fenning, what a name. She figured he was bandy-legged, with a scrubbed pink complexion and a clammy handshake. Not to mention the stammer. I'm attracting losers wherever I go, she thought.

"I CHECKED EASTMAN'S RECORDS," Osborn said when Terry and Janice came into the incident room. "A dead end, literally. He died after a massive heart attack two years ago. The only news at the moment is the report from the medical lab. Maureen's blood analysis is negative on all known drugs and sedatives. Alcohol level at 0.4."

Parker said: "The tampons and the sticky tape are of makes you can buy anywhere. Same for the manila envelope and the Xerox paper. No way to trace any of these things to a specific shop. And no DNA from licking the flap. It's a self-adhesive envelope."

Janice, who had begun to water her potted plants, held out the watering-can like a flag. "I wonder if a man would think of using tampons. It's not a part of his universe. Could Shadoe be a woman?"

"Sure," Parker said. "Or we are dealing with a mixed sex team."

"Who's that?" Terry asked and snatched the photo Blockley was waving at him. It showed a man with features so unremarkable that it was difficult to remember what he looked like even while looking at him.

"It's the new guv."

"Smithhaven?" Terry put on his reading glasses and eyed the photo again. High forehead, gray eyes under thin brows, dark brown, graying hair, neatly parted. "What do we know about him?"

Blockley shrugged. "Not much."

"He's obsessively tidy, I've heard," Parker volunteered.

Terry swallowed. "And I thought Gould was a pest."

A silence fell.

"He's due to arrive on Thursday, isn't he?" Terry asked conversationally.

"I had better catch up with my backlog of reports," Blockley mumbled. Terry knew he never had a backlog. He stood, the photo still in his hand, and felt that something was wrong with the new DCI.

JOY OPENED THE DOOR OF HER FLAT and waited for Angus Fenning to come into view. She was agreeably surprised. He had an instantly likeable face with well-cut features. He won her heart fully when he gave her a strong handshake, accompanied by an enchanting smile.

"H-h-hi, I'm Angus. I h-h-hope I'm not disrupting any of your p-p-plans."

"Call me Joy. I'm free on Tuesday afternoons. Come in and have tea with me. Or would you prefer coffee?"

She had turned her back on him to switch on the gas under the pot, and was baffled when he answered fluently.

"Tea is just fine. Two sugars, please. This is a lovely place to live in. And so close to the Heath."

Goosebumps rose on her arm. Had she let in Shadoe in disguise? She whipped round and caught the last movements of Fenning's hands. It looked as if he was conducting a miniature orchestra. With a relieved little laugh she asked: "Is this how you control your stammer?"

"Ingenious, isn't it? One of our authors told me the trick just a few days ago. It's like a miracle. It only works when I use both hands, that's why it's no help on the phone. And it looks a bit foolish, I'm afraid. But for me, it's a great achievement."

Spellbound, she watched the loops he made in front of his chest. His inflection had taken on a certain musicality, a gently rocking rhythm. "Not at all," she assured him. "It's smooth and elegant."

When the tea was ready, Joy stacked cups on a tray which she carried to the marble table, where he had already begun to lay out the illustrations. "We had better spread them out on the floor." She put the tray on a little side table. "If you help me move this to the wall, then we will have enough room."

"Sorry, but I can't lift anything heavy. I've got a hernia."

She looked him up and down. "Where?"

"In the abdominal wall."

"Sheesh. When will you have it operated on?"

"I've had it for two years and it doesn't hurt at all."

She was all clinical interest now. "Hernias don't repair themselves. The tissue gives way slowly, the bulge gets bigger."

"I know, but I don't like the idea of an operation."

"Nobody likes that. But the longer you wait the greater the risk."

"It's not the risk I'm afraid of." He reached for the illustrations. "C-c-could we n-n-now—"

"What's the trouble? The scalpel or the general anesthetic?" she persisted.

He dropped the photos to have his hands free for smoothing his talk. "The scalpel. I don't like to imagine how I'm being cut open."

Was he phobic or just a sissy? Joy said, "Excuse me a moment," went into the bathroom and fetched the scalpel which she used to remove callused skin. Angus was filling the teacups when she returned. He shot up immediately when he saw the scalpel. The china rattled.

"Here. Want to hold it?"

"Just p-p-put it away, okay?"

"It's just a blade in a shaft."

"It's sharp."

"There we are, Angus. You're tomophobic. I could treat you."

"Are you f-f-fishing for clients?" His laugh rang hollow.

"What if the hernia strangulates? That's a surgical emergency. And what if you have an accident? Or a serious illness? You can't run away from surgery for the rest of your life. Think about it. I'll treat you for free."

Distressed, Angus ran his fingers through his hair. "Is there n-n-no other w-w-way?"

Joy placed the scalpel out of sight and he relaxed instantly. "The problem is taking the first step. When someone is afraid of heights, to take a common example, his initial aim would be to overcome the fear in order to live without it, not in order to go bungee jumping. This changes as the secondary aspects of the fear are overcome. You will need some time to get used to the idea of really having an operation. When you feel that you are ready to face the possibility, give me a call."

She expected him to nod in the fashion people do when they mean, "No way," but don't want to disappoint you. But again, he surprised her.

"Thank you for the offer. The concept of therapy will take a few days to sink in, but you will hear from me. After all, I have nothing to lose."

Joy's heart sank. By enrolling Angus as a client, she had put him in the line of danger.

JANICE LAKE WAS TAKING A LATE LUNCH of cheese sandwiches and coke in the station car park, leaning against the bonnet of the panda car on which she had spread out her uniform jacket. She crumpled up the sandwich wrapper and stood to attention when Terry sprinted across the car park.

"Sorry you had to wait," he said.

"We hadn't fixed a time, sir."

"The address is…oh, well I'm sure you've memorized all the addresses we need."

They got into the car. He was a wonderful co-driver. She had a wide experience in this field, ranging from the self-appointed driving instructor to the nervous type who brakes in unison with the driver. Norman Parker was an insufferable mix of both. On their last patrol he had shouted "Look out" whenever she changed lanes and had given her a briefing on the use of the gear lever. She had filed him away as a misogynist.

Terry would sit in easy silence, following his own line of thoughts and giving her the impression that he had complete confidence in her driving skills.

He pointed out a parking space as they rounded the corner into Hyde Park Street where Mr. Kelby lived in a block of serviced apartments.

"An off-white carpet in the lift, I ask you," Janice sneered, as they rode up, then bit her tongue as she remembered that Terry lived in an interior decorated extravaganza in St. John's Wood.

"I would have chosen light brown. You needn't clean it so often," Terry said practically.

The door to Hector Kelby's flat was opened by a man servant.

"Another twin?" Terry said with mock astonishment. The servant, tall and black, was the spitting image of Dwight Osborn.

"In here, sir, ma'am," said the doppelganger of the station's computer geek.

Entering the reception room, Janice felt as if she was walking into Africa. Leopard-skin-covered Rattan sofas, a jungle drum as a coffee table, ebony masks and spears on the walls. Kelby, wearing an ill-fitting tropical suit and smoking a long pipe, got up and offered Terry an age-speckled hand. He was tall, corpulent and aged, with veiled eyes under bushy brows and a colossal walrus moustache. He waddled back to the sofa, incessantly sucking his pipe.

"Jabu, the port, please," he addressed his servant. Then, to Terry, "Don't ask me about Africa. My heart is bleeding. I'm no longer fit for travel in the tropics. And don't ask me about Maureen, either," he added gloomily.

Terry seemed absorbed in taking in the details of a chess board with ivory carvings of lions, gazelles and elephants serving as chess men. He took up one of the chess men. "To what animal could one compare Maureen?" he said, more to himself.

"A swan," Kelby prompted. "Elegant, calm, but paddling frantically underneath the surface."

"A double-glazed personality," mused Terry, leaving Janice at a loss what to write in her notebook. "Too proud, I should say, to call you on Saturday, after she found the letter."

"Oh, she did call, late in the evening, when her nerves were getting the better of her. I insisted on going over, but she would have none of that. So I did what I had planned to do and went to see a friend in Dover." With a wily look at Janice, he dictated his friend's name and address. "And the last time I saw Maureen in person was on Wednesday last week. We sat on a bench by the pond, her favorite spot apart from the security of her own house."

The pipe made gurgling noises and went out. Rapt in memories, Kelby sucked on regardless.

Terry opened his briefcase and gave him a copy of Shadoe's letter. "Did she read the letter to you over the phone?"

"Three times or more. The way she read it, her voice high and quavering, it sounded absurd. In hindsight, of course...."

"The handwriting doesn't by any chance look familiar to you?"

Terry held out the letter and Kelby gave it his furrowed-brow scrutiny, then shook his head so hard the mouthpiece of the pipe clanged against his teeth. "Take it away. And take yourselves away, as well. I'm an old man, tired and world-weary."

Terry refilled his glass from the decanter and stared through the maroon liquid. "I think you are just impolite," he said, not unfriendly.

Kelby finally parted from his pipe and upended it into an ashtray that looked as if it had been made of a lion's paw. "You're wasting your time, Inspector. I didn't kill Maureen and I don't know who did. I knew none of her friends apart from the man who introduced us."

"The man who introduced you?"

"A friend of my great-niece Marusha. I went to see her in her gallery last summer when I returned from Kenya. Sculptissimo. That's the name of the gallery. Marusha was wearing a beautiful, expensive brooch and I asked her where she had bought it. You see, I'm not one to buy real estate or shares when I have money to invest. I prefer jewelry and foreign art. Marusha told me it was a present from an artist whose exhibition she had hosted. I called him and he offered to introduce me to the designer of the brooch. We met by the pond, Croft and me on one bench, Maureen on the other."

Janice's jaw dropped. "Croft?"

Kelby turned his watery eyes on her. "Lionel Croft," he said. "Shall I spell it, dear?"

Janice tried to attract Terry's attention, but he was oblivious of her excitement. Was it possible that he hadn't read the files thoroughly? Then this was her time to shine.

"Could you describe him?"

"In his forties, tall, strong-boned, dark hair, pitted skin."

"What was Maureen's exact relationship with Mr. Croft?" Terry asked.

"Pond-sitting, as you may call it, that was all. Maureen didn't warm to people." Dolefully, he eyed the pipe in the ashtray.

Terry rose. "Thanks for the port, sir."

"Jabu will see you out."

When they were walking to the white-carpeted lift, Janice said, "Maureen's pond-sitting acquaintance isn't unknown to us."

"He could be the man Sally Young saw in Maureen's living room."

"It's not just that," Janice exulted. "We have his name in the files."

Terry gaped at the parting lift doors. "We have?"

"He's on Dr. Canova's list." She paused to watch his eyebrows rise. "Her ex-lover."

"*Caramba.*"

PATTY'S WHITE PIANO TOOK ON a special shine when Caroline's long, spidery fingers danced over the keys. Patty closed her eyes so that the intense music filled all of her mind. Within just three weeks Caroline had mastered Brahms' second rhapsody. What a child prodigy. It wouldn't be long before she had nothing left to teach Caroline. The girl would soon need more sophisticated tuition. Patty sighed in orgiastic pleasure as the last note died away.

"I'm lost for words, Caroline. I think we can tackle Liszt's—"

She was interrupted by two insistent chimes of the doorbell. "Excuse me a moment." She picked up the intercom in the hall. "Yes?"

"Cameron Croft. I wanted to ask about piano lessons."

Incredulously she stared at the handset. Leo's son? What the hell.... "All right, come on up." In the study, Caroline had begun to try out La Campanella. God, the girl could sight-read. At her age, Patty had had to count the ledger lines to find the deeper notes.

Cameron had mounted the stairs and now stuck out a filthy hand. Patty ignored it. "Hello," she said in a gruff tone. "I'm just giving a lesson."

"I'll wait." He went into the study and catcalled at the sight of the piano. "Blimey, cost a shekel or two, eh?" He shed a grubby jacket on the bureau.

"Sit down," Patty hissed. "Sorry for the interruption, Caroline."

"No problem." Caroline stood up so that Patty could sit on the piano stool and play the new piece for her. Patty felt uncomfortable and had to start again because her hands wouldn't find the right notes. Forcing her concentration back to the music, she played, all the time irritated by Cameron's goggle-eyed stare. Eventually, he got up and desultorily began to touch things, as if to scent-mark the room. Could she fall in love with a man who had produced such offspring? As soon as she had finished the piece, she got up and wrung the precious pan-pipes from Cameron's hands.

"You either sit still or you leave," she said to put him in his place.

He chucked himself back into the chair. "Keep your hair on, lady."

Patty resumed the lesson. She penciled the fingering onto the sheet music. Cameron took out cigarette paper and a pack of tobacco from his back pocket.

"No smoking in here," she said austerely.

"My giddy aunt." He began to scratch his crotch.

She should have thrown him out right away. Or better still, she shouldn't have allowed him in at all. She would give Leo a good piece of her mind.

"I'll let myself out," Caroline said. "See you next week, Mrs. Miles. Bye, eh—"

"Cameron."

Caroline's piano lesson was the highlight of every week, and this insolent bastard had spoiled it for her. "So Leo wants you to take piano lessons. Well, he didn't say anything to me."

"Must be because I said I didn't want any. But then I thought, why not give it a whirl?"

"The prerequisite is a love for classical music. I don't think—"

"Ah, I'm an opera-buff and all that. I was at the violin concerto, too, wasn't I?"

"It was a cello concerto and you looked as bored as Danny always is on such outings."

"Danny?"

"My husband."

His answering smirk almost cracked her composure, then the realization hit her full force. He had come to spy on her, probably sent by his mother. What a fool she had been.

"Well, Leo will have to find you another piano teacher. I'm not taking on new students at present." She got up brusquely and waited for him to collect his jacket and follow her out. They were halfway down the short corridor when Patty heard the rattle of a key. The door opened and Danny appeared.

"Evening, Trish," he said and pulled the key out of the lock. Suddenly, an expression of utter disbelief breezed over his face. He stood stock-still, his right hand holding the key in mid-air, his left dropping the briefcase. All color drained from his face. He was gawking at Cameron.

Almighty, he couldn't possibly think that Cameron was her lover, could he? Even if he had been a good-looking boy, he was more than ten years younger. But one never knew what was going on inside a man's head.

Cameron jostled Danny aside and charged down the stairs.

"Who was that? What was he doing here?" Danny's voice had an edge of panic.

"He came to ask for piano lessons," Patty said, closed the door, took the keys and the briefcase, and pecked Danny's cheek. "He's just a kid, so don't be stupid."

Danny still didn't budge. He looked like a sickly pale moon.

"Nothing doing, he hasn't got any talent at all," she gabbled on. "So we won't have to see his ugly face again. And he smelled." Giving up her efforts to tear Danny from his numbness, she went to air the study.

LIONEL CROFT HAD A MOST REMARKABLE FACE, strong-featured and cratered with acne scars. Apprehensively, he looked from Terry to Janice in her uniform. "Don't tell me my son has done a bunk again."

"Can we come in?"

"Of course." He shepherded them upstairs. "Find yourself someplace to sit." He masked his anxiety with a wry grin. "Before I launch into further speculation, could you please impart some facts to me?"

"We've come to talk about Maureen Gordon."

He looked surprised, but not appalled. "Yes, what about her?"

"Didn't you read the morning papers? Maureen Gordon is dead."

"Oh, come on now. She was in perfect health."

"She was killed."

"Killed. You mean murdered, actually murdered? How could that happen? I've never met anyone as careful as her."

"She was found strangulated in her home yesterday morning. We are interviewing all her friends. Routine inquiries."

"Very unsettling. Not the inquiries, but the crime."

"When did you last see Ms. Gordon?"

"I dunno. Two or three weeks ago. We met by chance."

"At the pond?"

"The pond, as usual. Who told you?"

"Hector Kelby."

"Oh."

Terry saw that it was impossible to prod Croft into verbiage. "Why don't you tell us the whole story of your acquaintance with Ms. Gordon right from the start?"

"I moved into this house two years ago after I had split up with Lydia, my ex-wife. Our son Cameron was causing trouble. I started the habit of walking over the Heath to soothe my nerves. And one day when I sat down on a bench, she came up to me and asked if I minded vacating the bench for her, said she needed to be on her own. So I sat on the other bench where a young couple was holding hands. They left a few minutes later and she began talking to me. That's how it started. We just sat there and talked. The vibes between us were right. Two troubled minds. My concerns were acute, her problems chronic, but still we found some common ground. We met again by coincidence, or maybe we homed in on each other's routine, I don't know. I always respected her reservedness."

"So she trusted you?"

"I don't think Maureen ever trusted anyone except herself and her cats."

"We know that she invited you to her house."

"Only once, and that was more than a year ago."

"Could you please tell us about this visit in greater detail?"

"Sure. Let me think. She rang me up."

"Your phone number was not in her notebook."

"I'm listed in the directory. She said that a kitchen cupboard had come down. She hated having strangers in her house and she couldn't fix it herself. So rather than call a craftsman, she wanted me to put it back up. I took my toolbox and walked over. I had to ring in a certain pattern, long, short, short, long. Inside, she immediately had me take off my shoes. She was persnickety about dirt."

That could explain the absence of footprints at the scene of the crime. Maureen must indeed have been completely unsuspecting when she asked her killer to take off his shoes.

"There were some cats around," Leo said. "I wanted to bend down and stroke one but she wouldn't let me touch them. I did the job in the kitchen, a matter of minutes, just a loose hook. I think she felt she had to compensate for her lack of hospitality and asked me if I wanted to see her jewelry, since I was an artist too. I was so impressed that I bought a brooch. We stood several meters apart all the time and talked in hushed voices. I was glad when I could leave. I took the brooch right with me and paid for it by money transfer later."

"You gave it to Marusha Kelby."

"I see you've done your homework. Marusha's great uncle called me sometime early last summer and said he wanted to know where I had bought the brooch. I arranged a meeting by the pond. It was the only way. Maureen wouldn't let strangers into her house. She leads a life of vicarious satisfaction. She led a life, I should say. I haven't quite taken in the fact of her death yet. Did it happen on the Heath?"

"In her house. And it was not broken in."

"This is odd. I mean, her house was very secure. You'd need a jimmy to get in, and that would set off the burglar alarm."

"It's especially odd when you take into account that she had received a threat and was on her guard." Terry slipped the copy from his briefcase and handed it over. He watched Croft's face as he read it and saw him struggle for composure. "This is terrible, awful. I'm looking for a stronger word, but nothing comes to mind. And you know, the handwriting looks somewhat familiar."

Terry's skin prickled. "You recognize it?"

"Yes and no. I can't place it, but I must have seen it before." He looked up. "Can I keep the copy?"

"Sure. It would be very helpful if you could identify the writing."

"I'll do my best. Sometimes a photographic memory would come in handy. I know someone who...well, you must have talked to Joy Canova. She is...I mean she was Maureen's therapist."

"Did you recommend her? We know you had an affair with her. That must have been shortly before you met Maureen."

Croft smiled. "If you go ahead at this pace you'll have the case solved by sunset. Yes, I told Maureen about Joy and advised her to make an appointment."

"Do you think the therapy helped?"

"Frankly, no. But don't tell Joy I said that. There was more fear in Maureen than anything else put together. In a way, she was her fear, and I think that's what made it possible for her to live with it without losing her mind."

"Canova said Maureen had made progress."

The phone on the coffee table rang. Croft ignored it. "Show me a therapist who would admit defeat." He grinned. "It's not easy to resist a ringing phone." He picked it up. "Yes? ...Look, love, I'm.... Sure, sure you can come." He fingered the flex. "Just why do you sound so angry?" Perplexed, he looked at the receiver. "She hung up."

"You could tell us about the last time you saw Maureen."

"Oh, when was that? February? March? The pond was iced over. Maureen had changed, she was—how shall I put it? You know, when someone has been injured in an avalanche and after hours of exposure to the cold is brought back to safety, he has to be frozen out very slowly and carefully. If the colder blood at the periphery mixes with the warmer blood in the body core too suddenly the result is shock and death. I think Joy tried to defrost Maureen too briskly."

Terry was amazed by Croft's interpretation. So far, he had heard disconnected statements about Maureen that hadn't contributed much to an overall picture. "You must have known her very well. You are the first person to make sense of Maureen's incoherent nature. What did you do last weekend?"

"On Saturday, my girlfriend stayed with me. I drove her home in the afternoon, did some shopping on my way back, worked on a sculpture, watched the late night news on TV and went to bed. On Sunday morning I went for a walk and then worked a bit more."

"So you were alone on Saturday night?"

"All on my own. I'll go through my correspondence to see if there's a letter in this handwriting."

"Thank you, Mr. Croft." He handed him his card. "By the way, did Joy ever hypnotize you?" he asked on his way to the door.

"Yes, why?"

They left and Terry stopped to inhale the mild evening air. A taxi halted and a young woman got out. She paid, then called, "Excuse me, please," from the other side of the road.

"Yes, ma'am?"

"Would you mind standing in front of that car, the one over there?" She pointed at a red Fiat in an off-street parking space.

"Sure," Terry said.

She rang at Croft's house. Terry waited until she was inside. "Must be his girlfriend. Is she scared of red cars?"

"No, sir. Butterflies. Look." Janice pointed at the garden wall behind the gate.

Terry laughed. "We are seeing phobics everywhere these days, aren't we?"

"I'm serious, sir." She frowned in concentration. "I'll take every bet that this is Patricia Miles, piano teacher, aged twenty-seven, married, no kids, suffering from lepidopterophobia."

Terry was most impressed. Then he inferred, "She's another one of Canova's clients, isn't she. Is Croft collecting them?" He decided he had to ask Joy Canova some more questions. They crossed Rosslyn Hill.

Joy greeted them with a grunted, "What is it again?"

Terry lifted an eyebrow. "Again?"

"Haven't you already interfered enough? You have disrupted my clients' peace and privacy."

"Aren't you interested in new developments?"

"I'm only interested in news about arrests and confessions." Suddenly, she laughed. "God, you must think I'm on the defensive because I act as if I had something to hide. Do come in."

She waved them over to her office and flopped into the swivel chair. "So, what is this news you have?"

"Maureen Gordon was a virgin."

"I know. She was proud of it. Haven't you got anything better?"

"She was friendly with one of your ex-lovers."

Joy shook a cigarette from the package and rolled it between her fingers before she lit it with a match. "Impossible. I was in the picture about all her social contacts."

"Including Lionel Croft?"

She prodded a stub in the ashtray with the match. "You're joking."

"I'm not. They met on the Heath by the pond."

"Once?"

"Many times. As I said, they were friends."

Joy shook her head. "And I was so sure she told me everything. I can't believe she had secrets."

"She didn't tell you that Croft had recommended you to her?"

"Says who?"

"Croft himself. Did he also make your appointment with Patricia Miles?"

"You're stunning," Joy mocked. "You've figured this all out in such a short time."

"How often did he come to your house?"

"Leo? Not once, meaning he didn't have the opportunity to sneak into my office and it wouldn't have been of any use to him. Maureen wasn't my client at the time I dated Leo. She had her first appointment with me in September of that year. And I never saw Leo again after we split up. You seem to suspect him."

"Do you suspect him?"

Joy screwed up her face. "Freudian analysts do exactly this. They take your statement and turn it into a question. You can play at this game for hours."

"A homicide investigation isn't a game. I would like to have your impression of Croft."

"He's very intense, he fumes sexual energy. He's irresistible." She looked at Janice. "I'm sure you noticed that, too, dear."

Janice's head perked up. "He's not my type."

"Really? I thought his appeal was universal. Maybe that's why Maureen didn't talk about him. She fancied him and was ashamed of it. Yes, that would explain it. More than that, she was in all likelihood embarrassed because she knew Leo and I had been lovers."

"I met Maureen's twin this morning, Brenna Gordon. She seems to suffer from a sort of medicinophobia."

"Pharmacophobia. Just like Maureen. It made treating her very difficult. You see, I'm not disinclined to use psychotropic drugs. Like a plaster-cast immobilizing a broken bone, they help to get the mind straight so that it has a mold into which it can heal. I wrote a chapter about this in my new book, *The Immune System of the Psyche.*"

Twins, the immune system, a new book. Something trapped in Terry's subconscious was trying to come forward.

When Terry remained silent for a while, Janice asked the next question. "Dr. Canova, how often have you been at Maureen's place?"

Good girl, Terry thought. No fingerprints matching Joy's had been found in Maureen's house.

Joy frowned. "Me? Never."

"On Monday you said you had come for a house call," Terry reminded her.

"House calls? I'm not a GP. That was just an off-the-cuff remark."

"So why did you go over to Maureen's house on Monday?"

"Do I have to explain even the most obvious facts? You know pretty well why I was there. Maureen had shown me the letter on Saturday and I had advised her to take it to the police. On Monday, I wanted to ask what had come of it. When I couldn't get her on the phone I was worried." She started her pencil tap-and-turn routine, while she went on smoking and rolling her cigarette between two fingers of the other hand. Terry guessed it was her variant of nervous fidgeting.

"So you didn't have an appointment with Maureen on Monday."

"She used to come on Tuesdays."

"I mean, an appointment to see her on this specific Monday."

"No."

"We have been informed by everybody who knew Maureen that she never let in uninvited visitors."

"With her not answering the phone, I couldn't announce myself, could I? She might have had a nervous breakdown. I just had to check. Somehow."

"Maureen Gordon bought everything by mail-order, even her furniture. She had her food brought to her house. She wouldn't have gone to the police station all on her own and you knew it."

Joy snapped the pencil across the desk. "We had an appointment to go to the police station," she said blandly.

"Why not on Saturday?"

"I wanted to. But she stalled. So we agreed on Monday at eight."

"You were a bit late, weren't you?"

"I was there shortly after eight, but she didn't answer the door. We had discussed the option of her going to stay at her sister's over the weekend, therefore I wasn't worried, but it nagged me all morning and this is why I walked over to check. I wish I had taken the threat more seriously." She crushed the cigarette into the ashtray. "I want to get Shadoe out of my life."

Terry saw something cold and deep shift in Joy's eyes as she said this.

PATTY, PACKED WITH PENT-UP ANGER, pushed past Leo into the hall. "We have to talk."

Leo followed her upstairs and grabbed her waist as she reached the landing. He turned her around, his head on a level with hers. "What is it this time? Another list? A marriage crisis?"

"Your gorgeous son Cameron harassed me. Did you give him my address?"

Leo let go of her and mounted the last two steps. "No, but I think I mentioned that you're a piano teacher. Maybe he found you in the Yellow Pages. What did he want?"

Patty plopped down onto the sofa and puffed a scatter cushion. "Piano lessons."

"You're kidding."

"That was the pretext. Of course he came to spy on me. I'm not going to have any of this."

"Lydia must have sent him. It's her way of tormenting herself."

"Fine. As long as she doesn't expect anyone else to join the fun. You must tell her this has to stop."

"I don't think that would be of any use. She never listens to anything I say. Never did. She's difficult to deal with." He sat with his neck bent back. "I wonder what I ever saw in her."

Patty watched his Adam's apple move. "My lovely, I would fight dragons to protect you." That's what he had said when she had left him this morning after their second night together. Why had she ever thought he was dangerous? She kissed the side of his throat. "Did you love her?"

"Sure. She was beautiful, witty, sexy. A little unstable, but aren't we all when we're young?"

"Tell me more."

"She changed when she got pregnant, she became sulky and introverted." It didn't get better after Cam was born, he told her. Lydia said he had nudged her into getting pregnant. All he remembered having said was, "Yes, sure," when she asked if he wanted children. "I'm good with children. I can build amazing brick castles. Still, I don't know how Lydia got the idea that I wanted children so badly that I emotionally blackmailed her into a pregnancy. She called it subtle manipulation."

"You? Subtle?"

It was getting more and more difficult for him to understand how Lydia ticked. And then he discovered that she was an alcoholic. After withdrawal therapy she was sober for a year. What he had overlooked was that the problem was still there, her insecurity and possessiveness. She was abusive, accused him of having a lover, or a series of lovers, or several lovers at the same time.

"Well, did you?" Patty asked.

"No." She had developed clinical jealousy. He couldn't use the pronoun 'she' without raising a firework of suspicion in her eyes. One day he caught her as she was opening a bottle of cognac. The evening before she had gone into another frenzy of reproaches, and this was her way of alleviating the emotional pressure. He snatched the bottle from her and threw it against the wall. She crept over and began to lick the stuff from the floor. He dragged her out of the room, she screeched. He said: "Please stop or our son will hear you." At which she laughed hysterically. "He's not your son, you silly fool."

"What?"

"At first I thought she was just trying to hurt me. Then she told me that when she didn't get pregnant within a year of going off the pill she was convinced it was my fault. Her brainwave was to answer an ad in the lonely hearts section of a paper. She had an affair."

Patty was glad to hear that Cameron was not a product of Leo's genes, but she knew better than to bring this up now. "She was probably looking anxiously to see whether you noticed dissimilarities between you and the boy."

"She lived in a self-made hell. Her grasp of reality was distorted. I put the blame on myself which only made it worse in the long run. She was back on the booze in no time and I couldn't stop her."

"Does Cam know you're not his real father?"

"I wanted to tell him—carefully of course, because he was only eight then." But Lydia didn't want it. She had another withdrawal therapy and all was well until Cam began to cause trouble. He was bullied by classmates, his grades went down, he played truant and disappeared for a few days every now and then. Lydia's self-control was on the slip, and so Leo did what the family counselor had told him to do. "As long as alcoholics think they can rely on family support, they'll inevitably go back to their drinking habits when times get rough. If I threatened to leave her, it would ram home the message that she wouldn't get another chance."

It was growing dark, but neither of them cared to get up to switch on a light.

"We had sexual problems at that time, too. She was still suffering bouts of unfounded jealousy. When I began to take sexual themes into my sculpting, she was over the top. With her constant carping about my alleged affairs she finally drove me to do exactly that: to find myself a lover. I made sure she never learned of my extramarital affairs. Lydia seemed to do well until Cameron was caught shoplifting." Leo blinked. "I had threatened to leave her, and I did."

"And why didn't you take Cameron with you?"

"That's what I wanted to do. I knew Lydia couldn't cope. But whenever I brought up the matter, she warned me she would tell Cameron about my 'dark secret,' which was in fact her own secret. How can I be held responsible for her getting pregnant by another man? Not on the grounds that I'm infertile, to be sure. Lydia always managed to make it look that way. I'm sure she believes in her version of the truth. And since I'm not Cam's biological father I had no chance to get custody of him."

"This makes it more difficult for me to understand why you took them out to Wigmore Hall."

"A wave of nostalgia. I thought the cold war was over."

They were sitting in total darkness now, except for the street light. When a breeze moved the leaves on the tree in front of Leo's house, Patty felt reminded of fluttering wings and quickly leaned over to switch on a table lamp. "Could you draw the curtains? I'm never quite at ease in your house. Those butterflies in your cellar are a threat even when they're out of sight. Last night I dreamt they came flying up the stairs."

Leo got up to close the curtains. "I heard you moan in your sleep. I thought you were lusting for me."

"Right now I'm lusting for something to eat. If you cook me something yummy, I'll stay the night."

The thick brown velvet curtains were all drawn. "Now you're safe, like inside a cocoon."

She sped after him into the kitchen and pinched his behind. "Hey, you, that's not the best metaphor to use with someone who's scared of butterflies."

TERRY WAS GREETED BY A SMELL of garlic and thyme, of veal sizzling in olive oil, and a whiff of ripe tomatoes. He found Cece in his kitchen, stirring meat and onions in a pan while shaking a colander with lettuce with her free hand.

Terry dipped a finger into the salad dressing. "Are we having guests?"

Cece dropped the colander into the sink and the mixing spoon into the pan. Her face was hot from the summer heat, the cooking and something else, a blend of embarrassment and excitement.

"Only one guest. Alan. I thought it best to get over the dreaded moment as soon as possible. You and he have to meet under the new terms of your, er, relationship. You're not cheesed off, are you?"

Terry was used to Cece's surprise parties, and of course she was right: the longer they waited, the more they'd feel mortified.

"You're burning your veal." He went over to the cooker and resumed the stirring for Cece, while she tossed the salad and opened the oven to poke a needle into the roasted potatoes.

The doorbell rang and Terry went to answer it. "You and Alan could lay the table," she called after him.

He let Alan in. "Cece wants us to lay the table."

Being the father of a seven-year-old girl, Alan saw through the pedagogic motive of Cece's order. "As if we were two boys she wants to keep from monkey business," he said with a grin and followed him into the living room.

"Look," he began, as Terry pressed the cutlery into his hands, "I know that what I did was the most indecent thing I could possibly do. The only excuse I have is that I fell in love with Cece the moment I heard her giggle. Did she tell you about the boxer shorts?"

"*I Feel Pretty*, my eye." Terry fumbled with the handle of the china cabinet.

"That's how you made me feel. I wish Cece had let me do the confession. I'm sure it wasn't easy for her, your being her uncle and all."

"It wasn't that bad. You know, we share a special sense of humor."

"And now the two of you will share me?"

"You'd like that, uh? No way. It's either Cece or none of us. The Terrys are a family of strict moral values and high-held principles."

Alan grinned. "And the Widmarks are a bunch of bawdy, barbarian nitwits. That makes for an interesting gene-pool."

"We had better stop talking about it, or the whole setup isn't going to work." Terry turned around, three plates on his palms.

Alan put the forks and knives down, took the plates from Terry, set them on the table and embraced him in a firm full-body hug. Terry felt light-headed, but the moment passed.

"You and Cece are so alike," Alan said as they drew apart.

Terry laughed. "She's a head smaller, with red curls, freckles and a very tiny nose."

"I mean, in character."

"Couldn't be more different. Really. That's why we get along so well."

"Just take away everything that's Irish about her and she's you as a young girl."

CHAPTER SEVEN
WEDNESDAY, 16 JUNE

Joy looked around in amazement. To her left, the sun stood low, bathing the sky in shades of red which reflected on the pearly white of the ocean. Like a sheet billowing in a breeze, liquid silk swept over fine yellow sand and licked at her toes. The sky was cloudless and so densely sprinkled with stars that night would never fall. She was back on Valanna, her home planet in the center of the galaxy. The sun touched the horizon and as it began to sink, Joy saw a second sun rise to her right. Those were twin suns of Valanna.

She stepped towards the sea. The liquid silk was cool and fresh, but preserved the body heat. With a shudder Joy thought of the draining coldness of water, then dived into the silk. She could breathe under the surface. The oceans of Valanna were no menace.

When Joy awoke from her lucid dream, she thought that maybe the afterlife was shaped according to our own imagery, and that the last conscious moment determined what we experience as eternity. Joy carried Valanna inside her. Dying would mean coming home.

The mood swept away like retreating waves. Half awake now, she preferred not to think this theory through to the end, to what it would have meant for Maureen, who had died in extreme agony.

She yearned to return to her planet of never-ending daylight. Why was she stuck on Earth? Why had she come here in the first place? Joy let go of her fantasy with a sigh, grateful that she had had this hideaway inside her mind throughout her stressful childhood. A darkly confused childhood. Her sister Hope's burial was the prominent memory.

She hardly noticed that she was falling asleep again, returning to the pivotal point of her youth, when she had been six years old. Tombstones threw slanting shadows on the path. Polished shoes reflected the light. Around her were lowered, solemn faces. Gloria held her hand and wept silently. Joy felt guilty, but couldn't tell why. Was it because she was alive and Hope was dead? Was it because she hadn't liked the baby that now lay inside a coffin that was as small as a doll house?

Dad's scowling look searched her face. He was so tall and dark. His shadow fell on her as he reached out to pick her up. She shrank back. Suddenly, water rose around her. It spilled from a brass faucet. A hand pressed on her face.

When she awoke the second time this morning, Joy knew she had had her nightmare again, the one she never remembered because it belonged to somebody else.

DCI DEREK GOULD USED the briefing meeting to hold his farewell speech. He ended on a personal note. "Terry, it was an interesting experience to work with you. Keep up the good work, keep your reports to the point, your notes legible and your office tidy."

With a royal wave of his hand, Gould walked out. Terry intercepted him at the door. "Did you have any success with your request for a profiler, sir?"

"Dr. Vandyke will be put on the case as soon as he returns from a conference in Utrecht."

"When is that?"

"Friday next week." He placed a jovial paw on Terry's shoulder. "With luck, you'll have the case solved by then."

Terry slipped his reading glasses into his shirt pocket and followed Blockley into the incident room. "More reports?" he asked when he saw a new pile of paper on a chair.

"This is what we have on Joy's clients. I talked to nine of them yesterday and got handwriting samples, which I passed on to Forensic Graphology for comparison."

"What's your impression of the clients?"

"They range from batty to completely off the crumpet, but I wouldn't classify any one of them as psychotic. Parker is having their alibis checked. And Osborn has gone to some trouble to feed the data into a program which produces all kinds of statistics and tables. But I think we're wasting our time on Joy's clients."

"You've got a hunch?"

"Sort of."

"Let's have it, then."

"The complete absence of sexual interference could hint at a woman. I'm very suspicious of Joy Canova. She's so unpredictable. Like someone with an ace up her sleeve."

"Or a surplus shadow in the cellar. Come on, Blockley, you can do better than that."

"The most simple explanation is often also the right one. Maureen Gordon knew and trusted her killer. The only person Maureen trusted completely was her therapist. What Maureen and Alison had in common was that they made no progress whatsoever. Like a quack, Canova might be burying her failures. And isn't there a saying that shrinks often have a screw loose? I think we should extend the house-to-house interviews to Thurlow Road, to check what's going on in Joy's house on weekends when she claims to be having a migraine attack."

"I'll see if I can get some more men from Hampstead Station," Terry promised. "I'm currently trying to think in terms of investigative psychology. What comes to mind is one recurring feature. Control. Shadoe showed a particular delight in controlling his victim. And he also controlled himself very efficiently. No fingerprints, no fiber transference, nothing. He has great forensic awareness. What could be at the root of this wish to control? Is he himself racked by a fear which he can't control?"

"You're playing into my hands, sir. It's Joy's profession to help people control their fears. With Maureen she had little or no success."

"And so she took therapy to extremes? Doesn't make sense to me. I've read the death threat so often I'm beginning to feel I wrote it myself, but have found no access to the person who wrote it. Whichever way Shadoe ticks, it's far, far away from all we can possibly fathom. He is someone who lives outside society."

"A hermit in London?"

Terry scratched his head. "I mean he doesn't function in everyday life. I feel I'm very close. All I need is a missing link. It's as if I have seen the handwriting before. The more I try to dredge it up from my mind the more it slips away."

"What's the association?" Blockley asked.

"Twins. Another recurring theme."

"Recurring? We've had Brenna and Maureen and that was it. Maybe you've proofread Cece's manuscript too often. It was about a man and his twin-tree, right?"

Terry smote his forehead. "Rick, you're a right eejit. That's what Cece would say right now."

PATTY'S FEELINGS FOR LEO CHANGED all the time. Sitting for him as a student, she had been intrigued and intimidated by his cold, surgical touches. During their wild lovemaking, she had been swept away by his intensity and heat. In the days that had passed since this fierce encounter, she had gone through a whole range of contradicting sensations. She was scared, beguiled, bewildered, doubtful—but never bored or embarrassed.

She let him do things to her that would have been impossible with Danny, not only because he wouldn't have done them in the first place, but because it would have felt unnatural, if not highly awkward.

Her hands tied to the bedpost, Patty was kneeling on the dark blue sheets, bathed in the morning sun. Methodically, Leo chose a whip. She eyed him defiantly as he rolled up his sleeves. He looked divine. Or devilish? A bit of both. If only she knew how far she could trust him.

"Leo," she said calmly as he was about to raise the arm that held the whip. "This looks mean."

"It's made of soft deerskin. It will hurt just enough to make you feel weak with lust. And you know I will stop as soon as you ask me to."

That was the cue she needed to stage a little test. "But how do you expect me to build up anticipation and arousal when I know that I'm always in control? How can you ever take me to my limits? How can I feel you're my master when you don't have the power to—"

"Patricia," Leo interrupted patiently, "we're not master and slave. I thought I had made that clear."

"You could gag me."

"That's enough," he warned.

"Leo, I'm just trying to—"

He dropped the whip on to the bed and opened the snap hooks of the leather bracelets.

"What are you doing?"

"If you want to bicker and tussle you should have your hands free."

Her hands sank into her lap. "I interrupted the foreplay, didn't I? When all I wanted was to further things a little." She found that she was playing her part well.

"I'd say that things have gone far enough already."

"So we will be master and slave one day, when you feel the time has come?"

"That's crap. I could really do without this discussion."

Patty smiled at him. "I'm glad you said that. I thought—"

"What?"

She could see anger rise to his eyes, so quickly and hotly, that she backed away to bring a safe distance between them.

He edged closer. "You tested me."

"Yes. I'm sorry, I know it wasn't fair."

"No, it sure wasn't. I've been married to a fickle woman for sixteen years. I hate being manipulated."

"Please, don't compare me to Lydia. I promise I won't do it again."

"Maybe it's my fault. I started all this too suddenly. I wish I had taken my time. I've made a bad habit of taking women to bed without much ado. I've completely forgotten how lovely it is to begin with a slow prelude."

"I didn't put up much resistance, did I? Can we go on now?"

"Patricia, you don't come here only to make love, do you? Just because your hormones are roaring—"

"I admit that I have a deficit and I'm still catching up. You should be glad you've found a woman who doesn't care you treat her as a sex object."

"I wonder which of us is the sex object here," Leo said, still containing his fury.

"Stop being so openly self-controlled. You can shout at me as much as you want."

"If I shout, you'll start crying. Lydia—"

"Forget her. I'm different. Maybe I'll cry, maybe I'll shout back, maybe I'll give you a pasting with the handle of the whip. I've lived in a marriage of such tepidness that I haven't even had the opportunity to find out how I react to being shouted at. So give me a chance, will ya?"

"It's difficult to be angry with someone as sweet as you, my love." He kissed her fingertips. "I'd love to hear you play the piano."

"Then you must come to my place."

"Why don't you forsake Danny and move in with me, piano and all?"

She grinned. "You'd regret it. Danny is away all day, he doesn't have to listen to my students playing the same Etude over and over again."

"I'll chisel along in my workshop while you're teaching."

"I'm not sure if I have the guts to give up the security of my present life."

"Do you mean financial security? I'm pretty well off."

"Leo, you're not my husband. I'd feel like I was exploiting you."

"So marriage is an excuse for exploitation. Very interesting."

She played with the black hairs on his lower arms. "Of course not. But if I leave Danny then I'll want to start a serious relationship, a family."

"You want children and I've already proven my infertility. Is that it? You only need me until you have found a man worthy to share—"

"Leo, don't vent your bitterness on me."

"I'm not bitter. I'm desperate. I love you." He held her head so that she couldn't avert her eyes. "And I want you, Patricia, I want you all for myself."

The whip forgotten, they made love with great tenderness.

Patty returned home, still caught in an orgiastic trance. When she found Danny in the living room, ducked behind a copy of Astronomy Now, she gave a tiny scream of surprise. "Didn't you go to work today?"

"I wouldn't be here if I had, would I?"

"Are you ill?"

"Not really."

"I'm sorry I stayed away over night. I hope you weren't worried."

He lowered the magazine. "I like sleeping alone. Would you mind moving out of the bedroom?"

What a cheap act of revenge. If he went on like this she'd soon be prepared to move in with Leo. "You mean I have to sleep on the hop-out sofa in my study?"

Danny smiled generously. "Except the nights when I'm away, of course."

CECE STEPPED INTO EILEEN'S OFFICE. "I know what you feel for him."

Eileen, engrossed in a stack of registration forms, gave a short, welcoming grunt.

"You're in love with him," Cece tried again.

"Sure, I'm in love with Simon, or I wouldn't have married him."

That was better. "I'm talking about Rick."

Eileen grinned. "You're only slagging me," she said in a mock lilt. Eileen had Irish grandparents, but neither her looks nor her speech showed any trace of her ancestry.

"And Rick's in love with you, too," Cece carried on regardless. "And since right now there's an emotional void in his life—"

"— you thought you could recruit me to fill it."

"You're always so quick on the uptake. I don't exactly expect you to replace Alan, but you could look after Rick a little, take him to concerts, invite him to lunch on weekends, and just be around when he needs company."

"Which is what I intend to do anyway."

"Then do more of it."

"Cece, you have a guilty conscience."

One couldn't fool Eileen. "Rick is playing it cool," Cece conceded. "He's too considerate to show I hurt his feelings."

"Actually, I don't think you have."

"Hey, who has known him longer?" But Cece felt a surge of hope. Eileen's insights were always brilliant.

"He's twice your age. Things look mighty different from his perspective. But I'll go and see him tonight, if that puts your mind at rest."

"It sure does. You're a darling, Eileen. Now, where's my avid dancer?"

"In Studio 4, rehearsing with the boys."

Cece blew Eileen a kiss and nipped upstairs. The boys looked very macho in their black track-suit bottoms and sweaty T-shirts. Cece slid away from the mirror and posted herself near the hi-fi tower. They repeated the same two or three bars over and over again until all four of them were synchronous, then they danced the whole piece in one go.

"You're in pretty good shape for your age," Cece teased when Alan switched off the music.

"Michael Flatley is also coming up to forty, I've heard."

"Yeah, and Fred Astaire would have turned one hundred this year. I hope you're not too tired for a bit of the other."

He laughed. "As a writer, you should be able to come up with a more subtly worded invitation." He picked her up, a nice way to show he wasn't fatigued, and carried her up the stairs to his flat.

"Hi, Ginger," she said as he put her down in front of the parrot cage. "Any bars?"

"Round up the usual suspects," the parrot squawked.

"That was for Rick," Alan explained. "I'll have to teach her a new welcome line for you." He made for the bathroom. "I need a shower."

She was straight behind him, tore the T-shirt off him and blocked his way. "You smell just fine. Didn't I read somewhere that physical exercise raises the testosterone level?" She pushed him into the bedroom, where he let himself fall spread-eagled onto the bed.

"Have mercy."

A beeped Für Elise startled Cece. It was her mobile phone. She cursed and took it from her purse. "Yes? ...Oh. Sure, I'm on my way."

If that was Rick's belated revenge, it was perfectly timed.

AT LUNCHTIME, JOY CLOSED the office and ambled over to Leo's house. When he opened the door she was overwhelmed by the intensity of his presence. He wore tight black jeans and a black silk shirt with rolled up sleeves and looked like a very sexy Lucifer.

"Hi, Leo. Can I come in?"

"I'm alone. Have you come to talk about Maureen?"

She hadn't. Her mind had been elsewhere, in fantasized silky oceans and the real-life equivalent, Leo's bed. Now she saw that she had chosen a bad time for a reunion, but she followed him into the living room. You never knew your luck.

Leo had been busy with some files, which he now closed and put on a side table. "Anything to drink?"

"A beer, thank you." Looking at his firm butt as he went into the kitchen, she regretted that she had walked out of his life in a snap decision. All those meaningless flings she had had since then had only served to highlight Leo's qualities. He returned with a can and a glass. "I was shocked."

"So was I," said Joy.

He sat down on the couch opposite her. "Are you plagued by the media?"

"Not yet. They have kept my name out of the case for the moment. Leo, what's that business between you and Maureen? What was going on?"

"Going on? Well, nothing. We met on the Heath when we happened to be by the pond at the same time. We talked."

"She never talked to strangers. And you don't look very trustworthy."

"Yeah, Patricia says I have a dangerous glimmer in my eyes." He laughed.

"Is Lydia's war of attrition finally over?"

"The canons still roar, but the powder is wet. Look, why exactly have you come?"

"A fit of nostalgia. And curiosity. Did you kill Maureen?"

Leo narrowed his eyebrows until they formed a straight line. "Did I what?"

"Do you have an alibi?"

"No, I don't have an alibi, but neither do I have the psychopathic potential to commit such a gruesome crime."

"We both know that, but the police might think otherwise. It's pure conjecture, but I had the impression that you are a suspect. Take it as a well-meant warning."

He flapped open one of the files. "They gave me a copy of the death threat. The handwriting looked familiar. I'm just going through my correspondence."

Joy's head came up sharply. "But that's great," she said, masking her shock with excitement. "I could help you." Where had Leo seen Victor's handwriting?

"Well, I can't let you see my business letters, that's all confidential. But you can help me with this one." He handed her a file labeled MISC.

Joy opened it and began to sift through the pages. She imagined what would happen if Leo's correspondence yielded a letter in Victor's hand. She couldn't very well exclaim, "I never noticed my father's writing looked like that. What a fool I've been, ha ha."

Halfway through the file, she hit home. She turned the page quickly, then said: "You know what, I'm getting peckish."

Leo was already on his feet. "Sorry, I should have offered you something. How about egg-and-cress sandwiches?"

"Just fine." When he was in the kitchen, she turned back the page, opened the bracket, removed the letter and skimmed the typed rejection slip, with two sentences added—one in elongated script and the other in a roundish hand, but not the square block letters Shadoe had used in his threat to Alison. Joy folded the letter and shoved it into her purse. She quickly thumbed through the rest of the file, but it contained no further correspondence with Canova Press. She found the query letter to which Victor's rejection belonged. Leo had tried to publish a book with photos of his sculptures. He had sent the submission to eight publishers and had received rejections from each of them. All this had happened over a short period in spring last year. Joy was sure Leo wouldn't notice the missing letter.

"Want another beer?" Leo called from the kitchen.

"Yes, thanks." Joy looked at her hands. They were trembling, but just slightly. Now she wasn't only withholding evidence, she was deliberately destroying it. She was out of her depth. What was going on? Why was she doing all these bizarre things? It complicated matters, it was dangerous, illegal, and in the long run it would all come out anyway.

Leo brought the sandwiches. "You look pretty frazzled. When he killed Maureen, this crazy bloke violated you as well, didn't he? You must feel like a man whose wife has been raped."

"Don't be silly," Joy said briskly. She drank the second beer straight from the can, took a sandwich and got up. "I'll let myself out."

"What's the rush?"

In an attempt to compensate for her guilty conscience, she offered, "When you see Patricia, tell her I can squeeze her in tomorrow at ten, if she likes."

"Joy, are you sure everything is all right? You are—"

"I'm on my way. Almost forgot an appointment. Sorry. We must have a drink sometime."

The door fell to behind her. Jesus Christ. She had almost had a panic attack, just because of Victor's letter in her purse. She controlled her breathing. What was so incriminating about Shadoe's letters? Or had it been what Leo had said, that Shadoe had violated her. Yes, he had raped her psyche. And he had already done it twice. He would do it again. She wished she would get a chance to meet him face to face and mind to mind.

Two letters lay side by side on the overhead projector: the death threat Maureen had received and a letter Victor Canova had written to Cece when he offered her a contract for Timotree.

What the expert who had come over from Forensic Graphology explained at length, was easily spotted even by the untrained eyes of the officers in the incident room: Shadoe had forged Victor Canova's handwriting, and not very skillfully.

Terry asked if it was possible that Victor Canova had written the death threat, disguising his own writing. The expert's answer, larded with lingo—upstrokes, connectors, loops and flying starts—took all of five minutes and amounted to a clear and unambiguous no. "Of course this is just a preliminary and rough impression. I'll send you a detailed report tomorrow."

Terry thanked the graphologist for his assistance.

After remembering where he had seen Shadoe's handwriting before, Terry had called Cece to ask her to bring Canova's letters to the station. Then he had decided that Smithhaven, who was still in Oxford, would be the right man to interview Victor Canova and had faxed him all the necessary reports.

Smithhaven called back half an hour after the graphologist had left.

"Let me see if I've got this right," he began. "Maureen Gordon received a really grisly letter, closed herself hermetically into her house—and then this scared mouse of a woman opens the door for her killer. And all we've got is a collection of negative evidence. No signs of forced entry. No signs of a struggle. No suspect with a motive."

"That's the gist of it."

"What did the graphologist say?"

Terry gave him a short summary.

"I see. So it's mostly a question of finding out who knew Mr. Canova's handwriting. I hope he's more cooperative than his daughter seems to be."

Terry said, "We'll bring her in for questioning. Did you read the transcript of my first interview with her? She was eloquent about her therapy methods, the nature of phobias and all that, but she left out everything of real interest."

"I went through it. It struck me that she didn't mention the letter. It was only when you said that you had found it that she admitted she had a copy. Wouldn't it have been a natural reaction to blurt out: 'What a terrible crime. And that so shortly after Maureen got a threatening letter. Did you find it?' Something like that. She must have recognized the handwriting. I'm not surprised that she didn't mention Alison Dale-Frost."

Terry heard the name for the first time and told Smithhaven so.

"A woman of twenty-one, a former client of Dr. Canova's. She was run over by a train here in Oxford in March this year. We identified her with the help of a London Transport season ticket with a photocard. Alison lived with her parents in Hampstead Village. We never found out what she was doing in Oxford. The girl was on a high dose of cocaine. According to some of Alison's pals she got the stuff in one of the clubs in Camden where she used to hang out. Nobody knew what she was doing in Oxford, under a railway bridge of all places. She was afraid of bridges."

Terry drew a sharp breath. "Did anyone mention a death threat?"

"No. But there's still a lot of coincidence to be accounted for. Like Maureen, Alison was a client of Joy Canova's. She died at a place she would have avoided at all costs. I'll bring the complete file on Alison with me tomorrow. The inquest ruled accident under the influence of drugs. Officially, the case is closed. We'll reopen it."

"You said Canova was Alison's therapist. Did you ever talk to her?"

"That's why I saw the connection. Canova made a statement, said she was confused by the circumstances of Alison's death, but that didn't help us much."

Terry was shaking his head at the door in front of him. "Two of her clients die in a similar way, by exposure to their fear. The only excuse for her not telling me about Alison would be that she didn't want the press to get wind of this. Nobody wants to be treated by a psychologist whose clients are in danger of getting themselves killed instead of cured."

JANICE WAS LEANING AGAINST the wall by the door when Terry came into the interview room. Joy, elegant and calm, was smoking without signs of nervousness. The light blue of her blouse and skirt didn't suit her complexion, but they underscored her cool attitude.

Terry sat down, placed a green folder on the table between them and said: "Why didn't you tell me about Alison Dale-Frost?"

She showed no surprise, but she puffed a little harder at her cigarette, then crushed it into the ashtray. "I could tell you about her now, but since you mention her name I suppose you have her files, including my statement. I have nothing to add to that."

"When did you last see her?"

She lit another cigarette and blew the smoke sideways. "That must have been when she came for her last session. Or rather, the one a week before. She didn't turn up for her last session. It was insignificant at that time, because it happened quite often."

"Her death must have come as a complete surprise to you."

"Not her death as such. We are all mortal, aren't we? But the circumstances surprised me. Not that Alison wasn't suicidal. She had a destructive streak. But she wouldn't have chosen to die under a bridge by night. Of that I was sure. So I went to the police and told them."

"Why did you bother to drive to Oxford to make your statement?"

"I grew up in Oxford and return there very often to see my family and some old friends, so it wasn't really a bother. I also hoped to learn a little more than the papers would reveal. The inspector told me that she had been under the influence of drugs and alcohol. Intoxication must have led her to believe she could face her fear."

"Doesn't it strike you as a strange coincidence that two of your clients have died in similar circumstances?"

Her eyes followed the smoke rising from her cigarette. "I've seen stranger coincidences in my life."

Watching her closely, Terry shot the crucial question. "Did Alison feel threatened?"

Joy stared back unblinking. "Not as far as I can recall."

"Did she get a letter similar to Maureen's?" This question insinuated that Joy had held back information and he expected her to show anger.

Joy wrinkled her brow as if in concentration. "I would remember if she had said anything about a letter."

"The case will be reopened."

A muscle in Joy's temple twitched. She flicked the cigarette stub in the ashtray.

"Was your father acquainted with Alison Dale-Frost?"

Her cool composure was cracking. "My father? Are you kidding? What's he got to do with it? Just because he lives near the bridge? Lots of people do. And hadn't you better solve Maureen's death?"

"Let me rephrase then. Did your father know Maureen?"

"Well, of course not. He knew neither of them."

From the green folder in front of him, Terry took out one of the letters Cece had received from Victor Canova. It almost hurt him when Joy rudely tore the document from his hands.

"Jesus Christ," she said. "Who is Cecilia Terry? Your daughter? Not very likely."

"My niece." He waited. "You can't have failed to recognize your father's handwriting. Why didn't you tell us?"

"I don't know why…. It wasn't my intention to obstruct the law…I was just scared." She was very pale.

"Let's get this straight. You recognized the likeness to your father's hand-writing the moment Maureen showed you the letter."

"Yes, it was a shock." She shifted in the chair. "As if the letter held a sub-liminal second threat, directed at me. 'I'm going to get you.' I felt like—you know…. When I was a child I had this silly fear that there was something living under my bed, a dark, evil creature. If I dared to stretch out a foot over the edge of the bed it would grasp me, it would draw me underneath and eat me. So I lay there, with my legs and arms tightly crossed, and afraid to fall sleep and be easy prey."

"Most children have scary fantasies. I had a wolf in my cupboard. Sometimes I even heard it scratching against the door from inside. And Cece was afraid of sharks in the bathtub. All highly irrational, but it can't be helped."

Joy's face went even paler. "So, you see, it was that kind of uncontrollable fear that made me ignore the handwriting. I was mentally crossing my arms over my belly, fearing to move so as not to stir the evil. I'm sorry."

"I'm not interested in your repentance. Did you talk to your father about the letter?"

"He said it was an obvious fake and I should show it to the police. That was on Sunday, but at that time I didn't know Maureen was already dead."

"Is there anything else you would like to tell me right now?"

Joy Canova blinked ruefully. "I'm not hiding Shadoe under my bed."

SMITHHAVEN CALLED LATER IN THE AFTERNOON. "Victor Canova is a funny bird."

"That's what Cece said," Terry remembered.

"I caught him completely by surprise. Joy hadn't told her Dad about the murder. She had shown him the letter on Sunday. He said the imitation of his handwriting was a shoddy effort. Hundreds of people know about his habit of writing in different ways. Which means huge amounts of work for us. I have a box full of copies from Victor's files and logs about his employees, his family and friends, the authors he contracted and all the authors he ever rejected. He likes to add a personal touch to rejection slips. I hope you have the manpower to deal with it."

Terry grinned. "We have Dwight Osborn."

"Should I have heard of him?"

"You'll get to know him tomorrow. Does Victor have an alibi?"

"Not a good one. He was in his office all Saturday, then drove home, had dinner, read a book and went to bed early. The name Dale-Frost didn't mean anything to him. I'm good at detecting a lie, but it's impossible with a man whose moods are so volatile. But I really think I surprised him completely when I told him that Alison had been one of his daughter's clients. Joy will have a lot to answer for the next time she sees her father. She doesn't seem to be very communicative, does she?"

"She opened up a bit and told me about scary childhood fantasies. But I think it was to distract us from the fact that she hadn't informed us about Alison. She said she was scared but couldn't explain why."

"Tell me the rest tomorrow. I'm packing up here now."

"Do you need help with the move?" Terry asked. "Wouldn't you prefer to take a day off?"

"I have plenty of friends doing most of the heavy work for me. When I drive down to London I'll stop by at the gallery, Sculptissimo. Croft seems a very interesting candidate in our shadow hunt, excuse the pun. I want to know more about him, and this seems a good place to start."

A tad annoyed, Terry gave him the address. He had planned to talk to Kelby's great-niece the next morning. Smithhaven was poaching in his preserve, but he was his superior now and had every right to do so. Gould had preferred to be the mastermind behind the scenes and had left the legwork to Terry.

TERRY SWIRLED THE WINE AROUND in his glass and blinked moodily at the russet liquid. With Eileen in his arms, her head nuzzled against his chest, everything was all right and the world was a perfect place. He had given up analyzing his feelings for her, and now his mind opened into a wide expanse of delight. He was more at home in his own house when she was with him.

He asked idly, "Wouldn't Simon mind, seeing you here like this?" Eileen had bathed in his Jacuzzi, and now she was naked under his silk gown, into which she had wrapped herself, because it was more comfortable than putting her clothes back on.

"I think if I told him something like, 'Hey, guess what, I've had it off with Rick on top of his grand piano,' he'd just ask if it hadn't been too hard for me to lie on."

Terry gently pinched her cheek. "Anywhere but on the piano. I've just had it tuned." He would have liked her to stay all night. He played with the soft hair at the back of her neck.

She looked up at him. "I love you dearly, Rick. I wish I could stay with you all night, cuddled up to your warm body."

He laughed and kissed the top of her head.

"How did you meet Michael?" she wanted to know. "I mean, a policeman and an interior decorator, that's an extraordinary combination."

"That was quite an adventure. I almost lost my job over it."

"I thought nobody knew you had a male lover."

"It wasn't that. It had to do with Portia. The story earned me Brick's undying devotion."

"Who's Brick?"

"Our resident Animal Rights Campaigner. You see, Portia was a cat, Michael's cat. I saved her life."

Eileen took a sip from his wine glass. "How was that?"

"I was a sergeant when it happened. A PC and I were speeding through St. John's Wood to a house where the burglar alarm had gone off. Suddenly I heard a thud and told the constable to stop. He didn't. You don't stop when you have the sirens wailing. I pulled rank and ordered him to reverse the car. So he did. I got out and told him to drive on and said I'd take care of the cat he had injured. It howled when I tried to lift it up. I rang at the nearest house, which was this one, and Michael opened the door. It turned out to be his cat, Portia. We took her to the vet, who wanted to put her to sleep because her sacrum was broken. We protested in unison, took her home and spent the rest of the day feeding her milk through a pipette. My superior wasn't pleased, I can tell you."

"And the burglary?"

"False alarm, which is why I was able to keep my job. I came back every day to see how Portia was doing. Her hind legs were paralyzed, but they slowly recovered. Then it was only her tail, hanging down limply, but that healed, too. In the end, just the last 3 inches of her tail remained numb. She lived a long and happy feline life."

"Like me. You saved my life, too, when I was alone, desperate and hurting. And later you helped me to get through one of the toughest experiences of my life, my third operation in the States. It was done with a local anesthetic because that was better for my kidney. I was given a sedative and I couldn't see what was going on because there was a screen over my chest, but I heard Johnson's comments to his assistants and that gave me a very graphic idea of what they were doing inside my leg. And I heard those dreadful sounds that only an opened body part can produce. You can't imagine—"

"I think I can. I've been to several post-mortems."

"Oh, must you? The operation was a nightmare of sounds, Simon's visualization techniques didn't help me. Then I remembered how you had sung lullabies for me. That saw me through. Can you sing and accompany yourself on the piano?"

"Sure."

"How about *Bridge Over Troubled Water*? It's one of my favorites."

Terry sighed from the bottom of his heart. "I'd really prefer lyrics with no bridges in them."

CHAPTER EIGHT
THURSDAY, 17 JUNE

TERRY WAS OPTIMISTIC THAT, if he had a chance to work undisturbed, he'd muster the energy and determination to do what he had put off for weeks.

At five in the morning, he was at the police station and opened the door to his office. Although he knew what awaited him he saw it with different eyes today, those of an obsessively tidy person. Standing with one hand on the handle, he glanced around the crammed room. A helluva mess, and that was an understatement. His last try to tidy up had been cut short by an outing to Hampstead Cemetery two weeks ago, on the day Eileen had returned from the States. The neat stacks of folders he had piled on the floor were now lopsided, some had been pushed over by Brick, who was too tall to notice things at ground level. No two books on the shelves stood in line. The desk was cluttered with circulation files, maps, computer printouts, files, photos, notepads with doodled stick-figures and wrappers of chocolate bars. On the window ledge, a pile of forms was held down by a stained tea cup.

It would take years to wade through all this, make sense of it, give it its proper place. He should have brought Cece along. She always made a marvelous job of realigning the books in his library. Clen-obsessively-tidy-Smithhaven would have a coronary. Terry should put a warning sign on the door, as Gould had once suggested. If he just patted the papers into neat piles…

"Got some letter bombs lately?" someone asked and made Terry turn.

Smithhaven looked a good ten years younger than on the photo. His gray eyes twinkled.

"Just the odd whirlwind, sir," Terry said with a sheepish smile. He felt an impulse to close the door and make for the canteen before Smithhaven could see the full extent of the chaos. The new guv placed his attaché case on the floor and stretched out a hand.

"You must be Terry. Call me Clen, please. Or whatever nickname you come up with. Back in Oxford they used to call me Lassie."

"Like the dog in the TV series?" Terry asked, overwhelmed by Smithhaven's dynamism.

"No," Smithhaven laughed. "More like Scottish for girl. You see, I'm a member of the LAPGA."

LAPGA was the acronym for the Lesbian And Gay Police Association, a group Terry had never felt it necessary to join, deep in the closet as he considered himself to be. And here now was a man who made no big show of being homosexual and didn't care about the nicknames they gave him and the jokes they certainly made at his expense. Maybe he even invented the best jokes himself. Terry suddenly felt deeply inadequate.

Smithhaven passed him and pivoted, giving the room the once-over.

"I'm sorry," Terry said with a defensive shrug. "I hoped to be able to organize my office a bit before you arrived."

"Great idea. Let's get to work on that landfill." Smithhaven shed his jacket and hung it neatly over the back of a chair.

"Well, sir, er, Clen, it's is very kind of you to offer to help me, but—"

"Bring us two cups of tea, kiddo. No sugar for me. And a chocolate bar for you, right?"

Terry raised a quizzical eyebrow.

"I heard they call you the Camden Dipper."

"I wonder what else you've heard."

"Gould filled me in about all your little vices. Doodling on notes, embroidering reports, and, worst of all—" He paused for effect and Terry felt a cold shiver run down his spine. Smithhaven bent forward and said conspiratorially, "Putting shoes on your desk. Gould never got over that one." He rolled up his sleeves.

Terry exhaled in relief. Since there was no stopping Smithhaven, Terry mumbled he'd get the tea. When he returned with two steaming cups, he found Smithhaven sitting on the floor, flinging folders here and there. Terry watched him for a few minutes, not knowing how to help. After a while, Smithhaven got up.

"Thanks." He sipped leisurely. "I'm a tea-oholic. Bags or loose, Earl Grey or Assam, makes no difference to me as long as it's hot."

Terry dipped his chocolate bar into the other cup. "Shouldn't I lend a hand? It's my office, after all."

Smithhaven, who had returned to sit cross-legged on the floor, looked up. "Oh, I'm sorry. It didn't occur to me that I was intruding onto your territory. It's so irresistible."

"I don't care about my territory. I just have a bad conscience at seeing you do my dirty work. Em, what do you mean by irresistible?"

"The greater the mess, the happier I am to clear it." He started whistling and tossing paper around like a juggler. The jumble grew to frightening dimensions. Terry went to get more tea. When he returned, Smithhaven had extended his activities to the desk. Terry began to feel seasick.

"Circulation files," Smithhaven sighed blissfully, folded a yellow sheet of paper and ran his thumbnail along the fold. "Letter-opener," he said, holding out his palm like a surgeon waiting for the scalpel. Terry found one in a drawer and smacked it into his palm. Smithhaven parted the paper in one neat slash and made a paper-boat with one half. Then he halved the remaining bit of paper and folded a boat half the size of the first one. After finishing his seventh boat, tiny as a fingernail clipping, Smithhaven gave up.

"In my old days I managed eight." He whisked the boats into the wastepaper-basket and gave Terry a thoughtful look. "What got me off the promotion fast-track, origami or homosexuality? I once had a superintendent who thought those were synonyms."

He sent Terry on errands to empty the wastepaper-basket or take files back to the filing-room. Patterns began to emerge from the chaos, like galaxies forming after the Big Bang. Fascinated, Terry watched Smithhaven work with relaxed concentration. Every now and then he would look up, smile or scratch his ear and resume whistling.

The fact that Blockley had not dared to tell him that the new guv was gay could only signify that everybody knew that he was gay as well. No one had ever asked him personal questions and he hadn't volunteered details about his lifestyle, as if an unspoken agreement of silence had been made. With a DCI who was openly homosexual, Terry saw trouble ahead and braced himself. It couldn't get worse than losing your lover to your niece, could it?

Two hours after he had started, Smithhaven brushed some dust from his trousers, picked up a stray paper snippet from the floor and announced, "Finito."

Terry was awestruck. Very much the proud owner of a flawless office, he sat down behind his desk, pulled out the top drawer and found its contents arranged like the display in a stationery shop. He opened the file that lay on the middle of the desk, and handed Smithhaven a photo, the full frontal of Maureen tied to the chair.

Smithhaven gave it close scrutiny. "Asphyxiation, administered the slow way. How many men were needed to tie her? One to hold her, one to attach the sticky tape."

Terry, who had been doodling on a phone message pad, dropped the pencil.

"There were no subcutaneous bruising on her upper arms where you'd expect it if she had been held; no abrasions on her toes that would signify she had been kicking. It was as if she had just sat down quietly and waited to be tied up. No drugs were found in her blood."

Smithhaven began to roll up his striped tie with his index fingers. "What was going on there?"

"The most likely explanation is that Maureen held still because she had been hypnotized."

"So we are looking for someone who knew Maureen and her weird ways, who knew how to hypnotize her, and who is antisocial enough to enjoy torturing her to death. There is Lionel Croft. What struck me first was that he has been hypnotized by Joy. He knew Maureen. But it doesn't end there." Smithhaven winked. "Don't ask me how, but I made Marusha Kelby talk about her love-life. Croft is a pervert. Don't think I'm old-fashioned. I know that playing with whips and chains is en vogue. What interested me was the strong element of dominance in his work, or rather the air of submission shown in his statues of subdued women."

"But we can't suspect Croft on the grounds that he plays dominance games with his women."

"Actually, it's exactly because he plays those games that we have to give him the benefit of the doubt. Rapists and psychopathic killers suffer from repressed sexuality. Judging from Marusha's hints, there is nothing repressed about Croft." Smithhaven took a folder from his attaché case. "Let's move on to Joy Canova. Maureen would have opened the door for her. And she failed to inform you about the Dale-Frost girl."

"I asked Joy why she drove to Oxford to make her statement. Her answer was evasive."

"Yes, and all she had to say when she talked to me amounted to 'Alison was afraid of bridges, so see if you can find evidence of a homicide.' She could have phoned to get that message across. It's as if she didn't want the police to come to her office. We were sending round someone from the station in Hampstead Heath."

"And she beat you to it."

"Not quite. A constable walked over." Smithhaven sifted through the papers in his attaché case and produced a handwritten note. "The shorthand is hardly decipherable. I've never been good at that." He handed over the note.

Terry put on his reading glasses. "He writes that Shirley Ryan, Canova's secretary, said: 'I'm afraid you've come in vain. Dr. Canova drove out to talk to the police in Oxford.' The PC asked when she had last seen Alison Dale-Frost. Mrs.

Ryan: 'She didn't come for her session on Thursday. She often forgot. Well, as long as her father paid, who cares? The last time I saw her was last Monday morning. Alison stormed into my office ranting about a letter. I couldn't stop her from going up to Dr. Canova's flat.' End of note."

Terry slipped off his glasses. "Goodness gracious."

"Ranting about a letter." Smithhaven rubbed his hands. "What kind of letter would one rant about? A really nasty one. A threatening letter. Oh, my."

"It's not too far-fetched to assume she had received a threat, went to see Dr. Canova, stormed into her flat and showed her the letter. Most natural thing to do. Everything that has to do with your phobia has to be discussed with your therapist."

"I'm sure she would," Smithhaven agreed. "She had no one else to confide in. Alison's parents were more on bellowing than on speaking terms with their offspring."

Terry scratched his temples. "When I talked to her yesterday, Joy said the last time she had seen Alison was during a therapy session, and she maintained that Alison never mentioned a letter."

"So we'll question her again. I wonder which of us should talk to her. Who has the better chance to shake her composure? You see, the two of us being on the wrong side of sexual proclivity...."

Terry understood. He tried to say something, but nothing came to mind.

"Now I've spilled the beans," Smithhaven said evenly.

"Gould told you that as well?"

Smithhaven nodded.

"I'd never have expected him to be so broadminded. I hope that doesn't signify that everybody knows. I always thought, or deceived myself into thinking, that I was sort of invisible."

"Oh, you were. Gould took you for a loner. But when your friend died and you broke down completely, Gould understood the full extent of your loss."

For a whole year after Michael's death, Gould hadn't complained about his flowery reports. That must have been his way of showing compassion.

DR. CANOVA'S VOICE FADED INTO THE BACKGROUND, then was filtered out completely. All was calm.

With her hands around her knees, Patty sat at a seashore that looked like the Praia do Alvor. Then, slowly, the craggy rocks smoothed away, the sand turned from ochre to yellow and the water from blue to a pearly white. The sun was low, the air a soft, warm breeze. Her breathing came and went with the waves. The sun set, and another sun rose.

Lowering her head she saw that a butterfly had landed on her toe where it sat balancing with gracefully unfolded wings of pure white. She could make out the tiny, furry rump. A lovely creature, a living being, not a symbol of death. Patty smiled and watched it fly away. There was a voice. Someone was talking to her.

"Stretch your arms and legs."

The sand felt like the leather of a chair.

"Your energy flows harmoniously. You feel fine and comfortable."

The rising sun was just the daylight shining through her eyelids.

"You are back in the here and now. Open your eyes."

Patty blinked.

"How do you feel?" Dr. Canova asked after a while. "Did you see the butterfly?"

"Yes, it was cute. It didn't scare me."

"You're amazing. You don't cling to your fear. You're already letting go. I've got some homework for you. Next time you see Leo, have a closer look at the ceramic butterflies in his neighbor's backyard. When you are frightened, just think of your little friend from Valanna."

"Valanna?"

"That's the name of the place I showed you. It is the planet where I come from."

Patty grinned. "Oh, and I thought you were an Arquillian."

"Sorry?"

"Never mind. I saw *Men in Black* once too often."

WHEN TERRY ENTERED THE INCIDENT ROOM, closely followed by Smithhaven, he was aware of everyone staring curiously in their direction. Dwight Osborn hadn't noticed them, because he was telling Janice a joke. "His hand caught fire."

Smithhaven joined in immediately. "Oh, I know that one. The question is: How did Pinocchio find out he was made of wood?"

Janice's face reddened. Osborn looked admiringly at his new chief.

Thus encouraged, Smithhaven offered to tell them his favorite joke. "What do you get when you cross a gay Eskimo with a black?" Expectant silence. "A snow blower that doesn't work."

Osborn doubled over. Blockley looked apologetically at Terry. You could rely on Brick to find a zoological metaphor. "The cat's out of the bag," he said.

After a general round of introductions, Smithhaven said, "I suppose Terry has already informed you about a seemingly related case, that of Alison Dale-Frost. We have reason to believe that Alison also got a letter that scared her and went to show it to Dr. Canova on Monday, March fifteenth, because Shirley Ryan told an officer that Alison stormed into her office and ranted about a letter. Canova claims that the last time she saw Alison was on Thursday the eleventh. We'll have her brought in for questioning. First, though, we have to know what happened on that crucial Monday before Alison's death. Blockley, could you talk to Shirley? There must be more she remembers about that morning. I don't understand why she hasn't been interviewed yet. She's the only person apart from Dr. Canova with access to the client data file."

When Terry started to apologize, Smithhaven raised a hand. "Next we have Victor Canova, an interesting character. A man who writes in three different kinds of handwriting and suffers from uncontrollable mood swings. I've brought along a good deal of work. There's a box with Victor's business correspondence, copies of his address book and his list of employees, including the ones that left Canova Press in the past five years. Osborn, when you feed all these names into the computer, what can you do with the data?"

Osborn grinned from ear to ear. "Anything you want. First, I'll see if I get a match with one of the names that have turned up so far."

"You mean Joy's list and Maureen's address book?"

"We also have a file with previous cases with similar MOs and phone calls to the special unit."

"Brilliant. The box is in the corridor."

Smithhaven assigned some other tasks and then left to look at Maureen's house.

Blockley followed Terry into his office. "I think we should have told you—" he began, then stared open-mouthed at the tidy room. "What happened?"

"Our new chief is a genie. He snapped his fingers and clicked his heels—and there you are."

IN HER ELATED MOOD, PATTY HOPPED ALONG Pilgrim's Lane like a kid with a skipping-rope. She would tell Leo about Valanna and her therapy breakthrough. Telling Danny would be no use. Her self-appointed expert in stellar sciences would spoil it for her. He would put on his scholarly airs and say: "A twin-star system doesn't have stable orbits for planets." Like when they had gone to see

Contact and he had pointed out didactically and loud enough for everyone in the cinema to hear: "Venus doesn't rise by night." And later: "Those asteroids are too big. Didn't they do their homework?"

Patty went past the ceramic butterflies without much ado this time. She quickened her pace a little, but she didn't have to wait for someone to stand guard. She let herself in with the key Leo had given her so that she would feel at home, not like a guest, in his house.

"Leo," she called and hurried upstairs to throw herself into his arms. "Leo?" He wasn't in. Slightly disgruntled because she longed to kiss and embrace him right now, she went into the kitchen, opened the fridge and drank milk straight out of the mouth of the carton. Danny would never let her do this because he thought it was unhygienic. Maybe he considered sex unhygienic, too. Patty wiped her mouth and looked around in Leo's house with a new perspective. Could she imagine living here? Well, it was the thing to do, wasn't it? She couldn't stay with Danny, no way. Now that she had a lover, her marriage was a struggle with mixed loyalties.

In the living room, there was plenty of space for the piano. She would also need a room for herself. Upstairs, looking for a spare bedroom where she could put her bureau and sofa, she peered into the room next to the bedroom. What she saw was such a shock, that for a moment she refused to believe it. She banged the door, jerked her hand from the handle as if it had burnt her fingers, stumbled downstairs and ran straight into Leo.

"I was in the workshop. I didn't hear you come in, love." He lifted a hand to her hair.

She pushed it away. "I hate you. Let me go."

He grabbed her around the waist, threw her over his shoulder and carried her back into the living room where he dumped her on a sofa. "What kind of game are you playing this time?"

She shot up. "You are the one who's playing games. You and your sweet talk. 'Come and live with me. I want you all for myself.' As if this had ever been an option. Just as I was beginning to warm to the idea.... How could you disappoint me like this?"

"Like what? I invited you to move in, you said no, and now I'm the bad guy because you suddenly changed your mind and then changed it back again. My offer is still valid." He pulled her on his lap and tried to kiss her fury away.

"It's not and it has never been. I just found Cameron's room. Do you really think I could live under the same roof as that dreadful boy?"

"He might be dreadful and he's not even my real son, but he's a part of my life, whether you like it or not. Didn't you say you wanted a family of your own?

Well, you should get used to the idea that your children might not turn out the way you'd like them to. What will you do then? Throw them out? Life is not all fun and good sex around the clock."

"Don't change the subject now. Why didn't you tell me about Cameron's room?"

"I assumed that you knew that Cameron stayed overnight sometimes. And of course he has a room. I won't lock him into the cellar for you as I did with the butterflies."

"You led me to believe it would be just you and me."

"I love you, Patricia, but you're a real drain on my emotional resources. I thought you needed time to find out what you feel for me. What's the sudden rush?"

Patty sighed and ran her fingers down Leo's rough cheeks. "I can't stay with Danny any longer. It's not just his infatuation with astronomy. He makes me feel like a stranger in my own home. I had to sleep in my study last night."

"I'd say it's time for a reality check. What is it that you want?"

"I want to divorce Danny."

"Good. Then do it."

"But where shall I live? I don't make enough money to pay the rent."

"Show some gumption. Find yourself a full-time job at a music school or take on a part-time job in the morning when you don't give lessons. You could help out in your friend's boutique."

"I'd rather spend my mornings in your bed."

He laughed. "Then you'll have to kill Danny and live on the pension."

SMITHHAVEN, A GYPSY AT HEART, quickly found his bearings in a new town. He made friends easily, and some enemies, too. Most of all, he had a penchant for looking at houses. When the news about his promotion and transfer to London had become official, he had called a couple of estate agents and asked for their brochures and exposés to be sent to him. He reveled in looking at ground plans. In March, when the Dale-Frost inquiry had necessitated an interview with the family of the dead girl, Smithhaven had grasped the opportunity to look at some of the houses and flats he had short-listed.

Today, as he drove to Willow Road to scrutinize the scene of Maureen's death, Smithhaven noticed that the Dale-Frosts lived pretty close. Did that imply a further link between the victims?

He preferred indoor crimes to outdoor crimes, for the simple reason that the former gave him a chance to have a really close look at a house or flat, untrammeled by the necessity to humor an estate agent.

Maureen's house looked promising. Splendid architecture. He was all the more disappointed by the interior. Uninspired, more like the showrooms in a furniture shop than a lived-in house. The only asset was the tidiness. Even the workplace in the conservatory was uncluttered. The tools and sketches for designs lay neatly arranged. Some people might say that no one could be creative in such sterile surroundings, but—a stickler for orderliness himself—Smithhaven knew better. He cooked five-course meals in a kitchen that afterwards looked none the worse. Spices and ingredients were laid out in the order in which he would use them, knives and spoons were placed as if along a grid, pans were greased beforehand. Cooking and working in a disorganized fashion was anathema to Smithhaven.

Maureen's life had been dictated by order and fear. What had her last day been like? First, she had found the death threat. After talking to her therapist and closing herself into her house, she must have re-read the letter many times with growing anguish. Like you, I am a recluse / Living a lonely, invisible life far from the joys of company / Bereft of the intimacy of love. Never before must it have been so clear to her that her life was a tedious trudge across deserts with no oasis in sight. You spend your life in a vicious circle of petrifying proportions. Maureen must have reached a state of mind where this threat would have turned into a promise of redemption. By the time her killer had come she had probably been ready to let him in, no matter who he was.

Smithhaven saw that nothing could be learned from Maureen's surroundings and walked uphill to the Dale-Frosts' double-fronted Georgian house, set in mature gardens in a quiet side street with a rural charm. He was let in by a maid and ushered into the reception room.

Isobel Dale-Frost, a buxom woman clad in a dress that was twenty years too old for her, sat on a brocade chaise lounge and waved a vague hand at him. Smithhaven told her formally that her daughter's death was again under investigation. He wasn't sure if she listened.

She stared past him. "I always thought I would be a proud, overprotective mother who doted on her child, but somehow I never managed to love Alison. Even my sorrow about her demise feels shallow."

Demise. What a peculiar word to use for your only child's violent death.

"And yet there are days when I can't stop crying. I wish I had shown more forbearance when she was uncouth. Maybe she had hidden depths. I am responsible for Alison's death because I failed as a mother."

"Mrs. Dale-Frost, please let me explain. New information has turned up.

Did you hear about the homicide in Wells Road?"

She looked at him, bleary-eyed. "Certainly."

"Like your daughter, the victim was a patient of Dr. Canova's. She received a threatening letter. Did Alison mention such a letter?"

"A letter? Well, no."

"Would you have noticed if she had received a letter in the morning mail?"

"Yes, I would, because it would have struck me as unusual. There was no one with whom she corresponded by mail."

"Can you remember what happened on Monday, the fifteenth of March?"

"Yes, I do, because it was the day after my birthday. Alison came home from her nightly jaunt," Isobel said with some bitterness. "She went up to her room, but a few minutes later, she barged down the stairs again and left. Not that I had expected her to give me a gift. But that she had been gone all Sunday, that really hurt."

"She didn't say where she was going?"

"I had long given up asking."

"Do you by any chance know someone called Lionel Croft?"

"Never heard the name. I wish George was here to answer all your questions. He's never around when I need him. When they found Alison's body he wasn't around either."

Smithhaven pricked up his ears. "Where was he?"

"I don't know. He's often away on weekends."

So Georgy-boy was having an affair and Isobel had decided to ignore it. What a sad life. Smithhaven got up.

"Could I have a look at Alison's room?"

"I'm afraid I had it cleared out completely. This house is so big. And I'm alone most of the time. I couldn't stand sharing my loneliness with the leftovers of Alison's life. If only I had helped her when she was pregnant, I could have stopped her from having an abortion. It would be lovely to have a grandchild."

Before she could embark on a cruise into the oceans of self-pity, Smithhaven asked what had become of Alison's things.

"You must ask Elsie, the cleaning lady. She's doing the bathrooms right now."

Smithhaven found Elsie upstairs, bent over a bathtub and scrubbing the pearly white enamel with a sudsy sponge. When he introduced himself, she looked up momentarily.

"Can you tell me what happened to Alison's things?"

"Threw them all out, didn't I?" she said over her shoulder. "Nothin' worth keeping, 'cept some papers and stuff. Put them in a box. It's in the storeroom."

She nodded towards a door in the hall and Smithhaven went to look for the box. It was on top of a jumble of boxes, marked 'Alison' in thick block letters. He peeled off the brown sticky tape, opened the lid, carried the box to a table on the landing and spread out its contents: a few crumpled letters, store receipts, bank account statements, a postcard from Boston, a leaflet with tour dates of a group Smithhaven had never heard of. Finally he unearthed an address book. He pocketed it, packed the other things back into the box and did his best to reattach the sticky tape before he returned it to the storeroom.

He intercepted Elsie, who passed him on her way to the next room, tugging along a trolley with brooms and detergents. "When you sorted Alison's things, did you see a manila envelope with her name in block letters on it?"

"No."

He urged her to dig deeper in her memory.

She looked at him as if she considered him pretty dumb. "Look, guv, I would surely have remembered the envelope if I had found it among Alison's things."

"Why?"

"Because I put it on her bed."

"You put the letter on her bed?" he parroted.

She sighed and dried her hands with a cloth. "Well, it was on the Sunday morning when I came in to help with the preparations for the Missus' birthday party. I found the envelope on the doormat and put it on Alison's bed. The most likely place she'd find it."

Smithhaven made a mental note to send two constables to pry into the memories of the neighbors about the night when the letter was delivered. "Was there a stamp? A sender address? Anything else?"

"No."

"Thank you very much. Did you mention the letter to Mr. or Mrs. Dale-Frost?"

"'Twas none of my business."

Smithhaven rejoined Isobel who was still reclining on the chaise lounge. He put her in the picture about the letter, but she shrugged it off.

"Police work must be awfully boring when you can get so excited about a letter. If it was a threat, I'm not surprised Alison didn't confide in me. What could I expect from a child who never wanted me to tell her bedtime stories?"

"COME IN, OFFICER. This is such a nice surprise." Shirley Ryan steered Blockley into the kitchen, crammed but tidy. "A minted milk?"

"A what?"

"Recipe of my great-aunt's. Very refreshing. You make a strong peppermint infusion, sweeten it with maple syrup and let it get cool. This you mix with milk. The hubby loves it."

"A glass of milk will do, you don't have to go to all that trouble."

"No trouble at all. I made the infusion this morning. Step aside so I can open the fridge."

With some dismay, Blockley watched as Mrs. Ryan filled two glasses with milk and the dark greenish-brown infusion. When he was retired he would write a book on the sacrifices involved in the job.

"Now you try."

It smelled like Vicks VapoRub. Blockley sipped a tiny drop. "Very, er, refreshing."

"My words." She waddled through the narrow corridor and into a dark, overstuffed room. "Our reception room," she said proudly.

Blockley sat down on a plum-colored sofa next to a huge lamp with a fringed shade. "Why are you not at work, Mrs. Ryan?"

"Dr. Canova said she wouldn't need me for a while. I suppose you've come to ask me about Maureen Gordon. I've always said that we bring about what we fear. Do you believe in collective awareness? On Monday morning, Dr. Canova had me call Maureen's number over and over again. She must have sensed that something was wrong."

"We've heard your messages on Maureen's answerphone."

"Isn't it blood-curdling? To think that she was dead already? After lunch, Dr. Canova returned with a detective but didn't bother to introduce me. She's got such an uppity way of treating me. That's so typical for a Sagittarius." She looked him up and down. "You're a Taurus, right?"

"Astounding," he said with an engaging smile. He was a Libra.

"Many people think they know all about astrology, but they're mostly dabblers. I draw star charts. It's a science."

"Do you draw star charts for Canova's clients as well?"

"Sure enough. They all have a weak Mars, hence the phobias."

"How about Alison Dale-Frost?"

"That snotty girl. She had a most unfortunate star constellation. The sun in Scorpio, the moon in opposition to Mars, and Venus in the seventh house in conjunct with Saturn and in grand square with a retrograde Pluto. You get the picture?"

"Vividly," said Blockley and turned the glass of minted milk round and round between his palms. "When was the last time you saw Alison?"

"That was on the Monday before she died. She came bursting in at around eight. I had only just switched on the computer. She said she had to see the doctor immediately, that it was a matter of life and death. I told her to sit down and wait. She messed up the magazines, began to swear and insisted on talking to Dr. Canova. She waved an envelope at me, ranted about someone wanting to kill her, and insulted me."

"Do you remember her exact words?"

"I'm a secretary not a mnemonist."

"Describe the envelope, please."

"A sort of manila envelope."

Blockley showed her the envelope Maureen had received, sealed in a plastic bag.

"Yes, exactly like this one. Same size."

"Do you have any of these envelopes in the office?"

"No, we use cream-colored DL envelopes."

"What did Alison do next?"

"She spat a gum on my desk and ran upstairs."

"At what time was that?"

"Around a quarter past eight, I'd say. A while later I heard her bolt downstairs and bang the front door."

"And Dr. Canova?"

"She was late that morning. She scolded me for letting Alison up, but she didn't tell me what it had all been about. Not that it surprised me. She's always very abrupt and impolite."

"Did she talk about it at some other time? Did she mention it after Alison's death?"

"No. I wanted to ask her about it after we learned that Alison had had this accident, but Dr. Canova has a way of cutting me short. Do you think I should look for new employment? I'm an efficient, loyal and absolutely discreet secretary. Dr. Canova never appreciated me as she should have."

"You wouldn't have passed on any details about clients to a third party, would you?"

"I'm not a gossip, sergeant. Not even the hubby knows anything." Shirley wriggled a scolding finger. "You can wire me to a lie-detector, if you have any doubts." In a tone that reminded Blockley of a torturer announcing the next level of martyrdom, she added: "Oh, I almost forgot to offer you some of my curry and garlic cookies."

For the first time in many years, Terry didn't feel the irresistible impulse to escape from his office—since it no longer looked like a war zone. For a half hour he immersed himself in paperwork, humming the tunes of the songs he had sung for Eileen, *Piano Man* and *Sisters of Mercy*.

Janice brought the copies that had been made from Victor's address book. "Osborn is through with it. I thought you might like to have a look."

Terry thanked her and continued to hum *Sisters of Mercy*. He read the entry "Gloria Anderson." Gloria was Joy's sister. Talking to her might give him a better picture of Joy and Victor Canova.

Two hours later he pulled up in front of the Anderson's house. Joy's sister lived in Summertown, a spacious, tranquil shopping area in North Oxford. As she had directed him on the phone when he announced his visit, he found her in the greenhouse, stuffing potting compost into earthenware.

She was a softened version of Joy, and highly pregnant. Her eyes had the deep blue of cornflowers. Auburn hair curled around her pretty face that was smeared with soil. She greeted him with a smile. "I'm glad you have come. I had no idea what was going on until I went to see my father yesterday evening. Blanche told me he had had a nervous breakdown. Apparently there have been two murders and he is somehow involved. What's all this about?"

Terry gave her a summary. Visibly agitated, Gloria took a pair of garden shears. "Got to trim those roses."

He followed her into the garden, a jungle of shrubs and flowers, laburnum and privet, striped petunias and red geraniums in pots all over the place. The house, where it was not overgrown with ivy, was covered by trellis-work.

"I hope my father is not a suspect."

Terry assured her that the handwriting in the death threat had clearly been identified as a fake. "Has he always had those mood shifts?"

Gloria snipped away at the roses. "They started after Hope's death. Hope was born when I was nine. Joy was a violent-tempered rascal of five or six. After Hope's arrival, Joy's tantrums became even worse. You see, Hope was a little angel. I would carry her around and show her everything, and she would make lovely gurgling sounds. When my father came home he spent the evening playing with Hope, feeding her, bathing her, singing lullabies. And my mother would sit, tired and pleased, smiling to herself. Victor had never been so crazy with me, but Joy had been his favorite daughter for a long time and so she was jealous. She would pinch Hope when she had just fallen asleep. Or she would insist on feeding her and then push the spoon far down her throat. After a while mother forbade her to go near the baby again. Well, one morning Hope lay dead in her little bed. She hadn't been ill or anything. The doctor said it was sudden infant death syndrome." Gloria placed the shears on the ground and ran her hands down her lower back, leaving a trail of mud on her green maternity dress. "Now that I have children myself I can understand how devastated my mother must have been. After Hope's death we all underwent a personality change. My father's moods veered from one extreme to the other. My mother began to rearrange the furniture over and over again. I dug tiny graves in the garden, in which I buried old toys, then I planted flowers on them. This was my way of coping. Joy, amazingly, changed into a really lovely girl. We only found out how disturbed she truly was when she began to have hysterical attacks in the bathtub. My father would bathe Joy on Saturday mornings, and she would scream and fight. After a few weeks he gave it up. My mother took over, but at that time Joy downright refused to go near the bathroom. It had turned into a serious phobia."

"Like the ones she's treating people for now."

"She was taking the bull by the horns. The other problem that started at that time was her migraine attacks. Of course, a child of six can't tell you she's having a migraine. She shrieked at the top of her voice and hit at everyone who came near her, she held her head and rocked it from side to side, and then passed out. A specialist finally came up with the right diagnosis, but none of the treatments he tried were any good. Fortunately, she slept through most of her migraines. Sometimes she sleepwalked."

"Did she remain inside the house?"

"Normally, but once, she disappeared and it was already dawn when Dad found her on the railway bridge, looking through the wire netting."

Terry lifted his head, shielded his eyes against the sun and said glumly, "The Devil's Backbone."

FOR TWO HOURS, JOY WAS KEPT WAITING in the cold interview room.

At one sharp, Sergeant Blockley had come to her office and inquired after Shirley. She had given him Shirley's home address, and after that she had known it wouldn't be long before they came to fetch her to the police station. So she had cancelled her appointments and tried to figure out what Shirley could reveal: that Alison had stormed in on that last Monday before her death and that she had gone up to Joy's apartment, a fact that belied her assertion that she hadn't seen Alison after her last session.

Joy's handwritten copy of Shadoe's first letter no longer existed. She had torn it up, first into strips, then into neat snippets, which she had flushed down the toilet, just as she had done with her father's rejection letter to Leo.

She changed from her summer dress into a pair of jeans and a T-shirt. Removing the cellophane from a packet of cigarettes, she felt as if she was preparing for an execution. If she demonstrated her wish to help, they would be less suspicious. She went down to her office, booted the computer and printed out Alison's file. Now that the case had been reopened, they would demand it anyway. Joy stapled the sheets, then retrieved the three photos of bridges from the filing cabinet and put them in a transparent cover.

The next moment, the doorbell rang and there was the tall constable she had seen in front of Maureen's house on Monday, and he asked her to come along. Her heart was hammering. She hadn't found the time yet to make up a plausible story.

As it turned out, she had more than enough time. She was taken into the interview room and told to wait. If she needed anything, she could ask the constable who was standing guard at the door. She asked for a cup of coffee, sat down, then thought better of it. Pacing up and down, she weighed possibilities and invented scenarios. In the end, she came up with a brilliant story.

When the door finally opened, she was sitting calmly at the table, drinking her third cup of coffee, smoking her fourth cigarette and bristling with confidence. Inspector Terry was not alone. Joy expressed surprise at seeing Smithhaven. He informed her curtly that he had been transferred to London.

"Sorry we kept you waiting," Terry said in his nice, rasping bass.

"I've got something for you." She pointed at the papers she had laid on the table. "Maybe you can use it. It's Alison's file."

"Thank you. Dr. Canova, we would like you to give us a detailed account of what Alison said and did when you last saw her."

"You mean her last session or the last time I met her?"

"You said yesterday that the session was the last time you met her."

"I was wrong. I'm sorry. I confused the dates. I saw her again on Monday the fifteenth. I got up at the usual time, which is seven thirty. After my morning routine—"

"Please be more precise."

"I do workouts; knee-bends, push-ups, the lot. Around a quarter to eight I prepare breakfast. I switch on the coffee machine, put toast in the toaster.... Do you really want to hear it all? My breakfast is sumptuous."

"You can skip that part."

"When everything is ready, I have a shower, get dressed, put on some lipstick and blow-dry my hair. On said Monday, when I went into the living room,

I saw Alison sitting on the bar stool at the counter, eating my breakfast. The pot in the coffee machine was empty, but the red light was still on. I went to switch it off before it overheated. The kitchen looked a mess, with crumbs everywhere. I was furious, as you can imagine. I threw her out, then I tidied up the kitchen. I know I should have reacted a bit more sensibly, because it had happened before. Alison had once come on a Sunday and then had sat on my sofa, eating all the fruit in the fruit bowl and complaining about her mother. The girl never respected people's privacy. Instead of throwing her out, I should have used the situation to explain some general rules of behavior to her. And most of all I should have made her do the tidying up."

"Why didn't you tell me all this during our last interview?" Terry asked.

"It was half-forgotten before it was over."

"But you must have remembered it on Thursday when Alison didn't come for her session."

"I think it passed through my mind that she might be afraid I would reprimand her. By the time I learned about her death, I was too shocked to give much thought to anything else. I drove to Oxford and talked to you." She inclined her head towards Smithhaven. "I must admit that it was out of curiosity. I wanted to know more details."

Joy was very pleased. She had delivered her story in an erratic manner so that it hadn't sounded rehearsed. "I was still very concerned about the bridge, though, because it was on one of the photos I had shown Alison."

"How did Alison react when you showed her the photos?"

"We talked about each bridge at length. I gave her some historical background. We discussed statistics, construction types, anything that would distract her from her fear. By the end of a session, she was ready to look at a photo for a few seconds."

"Let's return to Monday, the fifteenth. Did you ask Shirley what Alison had wanted from you?"

"No. I think I said something to her along the lines of 'Don't let this happen again.' That was all."

"Are you absolutely sure Alison didn't mention a letter?"

"Oh, that's what you're still after. Why are you so keen to have a serial killer on the loose?"

"Please answer the question," Smithhaven insisted.

"No, Alison didn't mention a letter."

"But we know that she had one with her."

Joy didn't have to fake her surprise. "What?"

"She showed it to Shirley Ryan."

Joy put her cigarette in the ashtray and folded her trembling hands in her lap. This had to be a trick. "That's the first I've heard of it."

"Alison told Mrs. Ryan that seeing you was a matter of life and death. She waved the envelope at her. It was a manila envelope, same size and color as the one Maureen received."

Joy angrily shook her head. She would fire Shirley. "Why didn't Alison say anything about the letter? All right, I was rude to her, I told her to leave straight away. But if she was so agitated.... On the other hand, there's no way of knowing if this envelope contained a letter from Shadoe."

"Did she have anything with her on Monday morning?"

"Her tattered black tote bag. I didn't ask her to empty it on the coffee table, did I? How was I supposed to know—" Joy stopped, afraid of overdoing her part.

Smithhaven tugged at his tie. "Why don't I believe you?"

Joy looked him straight in the eye and smiled. "Well, sir, I suppose this has to do with your job. You have been lied to so often that you feel safer assuming that the truth is something you don't get for free, but have to extricate."

"I didn't ask to be counseled."

"Just a professional reflex. Like your mistrust."

Smithhaven puckered his lips. "You've been giving us information in dribs and drabs. Let's go through it all again from the moment when you went into the bathroom."

"I'm not going to tell the same story twice. You can ask me all those questions over and over again, if the protocol requires you to do so, but all you'll get is silence."

"Let's move on," Terry said. "Did you see Alison again after her intrusion on Monday?"

"No."

"Did she call?"

"She didn't."

"Did she write you a letter?"

"No, and we didn't communicate by telepathy either."

Terry grinned. Joy felt a pang of guilt. It wasn't fair to lie to him. But it was too late to retreat.

"Of course we will now have to talk to your clients once more. This time it is not to check their alibis, but to warn them."

"No, please don't. It's going to disrupt their therapy progress."

"Getting killed is much more of a disruption, I'd say. We'll have to tell them about the danger they're in and discuss their safety with them. Those who live alone deserve special attention. We don't even know if Shadoe is going to announce his deed next time."

Joy held up a hand. "It won't be necessary. I've already warned them."

"You've warned them?" Smithhaven said with a sarcastic lilt. "Why did you think they needed to be warned when you didn't know that Alison had received a letter, too?"

"I wanted to be on the safe side."

"The safe side of what? You just said that warning your clients would disrupt their progress."

"I'm not going to say anything else."

Smithhaven puckered his lips. "Do you want a lawyer?"

"I don't need a lawyer. Just because you turn everything I say against me, doesn't mean I have anything to hide. I'm just confused. Therefore I won't say another word."

Terry ignored that. "On the Saturday when Alison died, where were you?"

Joy looked out of the window.

Terry followed her gaze. "I'm sure you were at home, having a migraine attack."

She studied his profile. What was he driving at?

"Tell me about your sister."

Taken by surprise, Joy fumbled the stub in the ashtray. "Gloria? What's she got to do with it?"

"I was referring to Hope."

Joy, who until this moment had considered herself in control of the situation, shrank back as if he had hit her. "But she's dead," she managed to say.

The door opened and an officer beckoned to Smithhaven. "We've hit pay dirt, sir."

IN THE CORRIDOR, SMITHHAVEN ASKED, "What have you found?"

Osborn grinned and held out a letter. Terry immediately recognized the letterhead of Canova Press. The letter was addressed to Lionel Croft and dated the first of May the previous year.

Re: "Croft's Craft—Pictures of an Exhibition"

Dear Mr. Croft:

Thank you for sending us your book proposal. With regrets, I inform you that we see no marketing potential for it. Thank you for thinking of Canova Press.

Best of luck elsewhere.

Sincerely,
Victor Canova

Below, in Victor's elongated script, he read: "Although the photos are of outstanding quality and the objects bespeak great artistic talent, the material is too salacious for our London Art imprint."

Then, in rounded handwriting: "Please, don't hesitate to get in touch when you launch a new project."

"This is the missing link," Smithhaven exclaimed. "Lionel Croft had the means to fake the handwriting."

Remembering the sinister threats Cece had uttered after each rejection she had received, this would provide a motive. But Terry couldn't share his superior's excitement. "Croft told me he had seen the handwriting before, so this isn't all that surprising. Actually, this letter exonerates him."

"Does it?"

"Look, if Croft composed the poison pen letter to Maureen, he would have expected Joy to tell us straight away that the handwriting looked like her father's. He would have been very surprised that I didn't have this information when I showed him the letter."

"I think it's time you introduced me to this kinky artist."

"Brick can bring him in after he's taken Joy Canova home," Osborn offered.

"Thanks, but I suggest that Terry and I drop in at Croft's place."

When they entered Croft's workshop half an hour later, Terry understood what Victor Canova had meant when he called the sculptures salacious. The walls were decorated with photos that would have made brilliant covers for fetish magazines.

Smithhaven, less reserved than Terry, walked around and ran his fingers over the sculptures, picked up some of the small ones and held them at different angles.

Croft, who had been working on a wire model of a butterfly wing, washed his hands at the washbasin.

"Sorry we interrupted you," Terry said. He knew how Cece hated any disturbance when she was writing. A sculptor might experience a similar creative flow.

"No problem."

Smithhaven was looking at photos and sketches. "This one is beautiful," he said, pointing at a sketch showing a young Asian woman on her knees, her palms pressed together in prayer. She had all the ingredients of perfection. The lips were full, but not overfull, the cheekbones slanted to the right degree, the almond eyes shiny, as if she was on the point of crying.

"It's called Supplication." Croft moved a stool in Terry's direction.

"I wonder," Smithhaven said, "whether heterosexual men get a kick out of looking at a woman with such a perfect face and body. Or is it more an aesthetic than an arousing experience?"

Terry began to feel uncomfortable with Smithhaven's flaunting his homosexuality.

Croft sat across the edge of a worktop. "For me, it's purely aesthetic as long as I'm not in love with a woman. But I suppose you haven't come to discuss my art."

"We've come to discuss a letter with you." Smithhaven gave Croft the copy of Canova's rejection letter.

Croft read it, frowning at first, then grinning. "Yes, of course. I knew I had seen the handwriting before." Suddenly, his expression changed back to a scowl. "Excuse me."

Croft returned after a minute, a file under his arm, which he opened on the worktop. "Here are the rejection letters I received. Canova's is missing."

"You didn't perhaps remove it? After all, it's evidence."

Croft squinted at Smithhaven. "Evidence for what?"

"For the fact that you had the means to forge the handwriting."

Terry noticed a change in Croft's big, rough face, a subtle rearrangement of the lips, and he knew that the next thing Croft said would be a lie.

"Maybe I threw it away on the day it came. After receiving all those rejections I was pretty frustrated and lost interest in the project." He closed the file.

"Maureen was tortured to death. You have a penchant for beating women, haven't you?"

Terry saw Croft relax. He seemed to be back on safe ground. "A whipping, when it's done nicely, can be terrific foreplay. Between consenting adults you can't call it torture, unless you want to offend all the real-life torture victims."

"Pain induces fear. Do you like to scare women?"

"No, frankly, I don't. But you seem to enjoy scaring law-abiding citizens."

Smithhaven indicated the room with a sweeping gesture of his hand. "Everything in here bespeaks anger, aggression, abuse."

"It also bespeaks the fact that if I harbor any of these emotions I can always find a creative outlet. There would never have been a Holocaust if Hitler had been accepted into the art school in Vienna. 'I came to the conclusion many years ago that almost all crime is due to the repressed desire for aesthetic expression.' Evelyn Waugh said that."

"Waugh, aha. Ever heard of Dale-Frost?"

Terry's mind reeled at Smithhaven's non sequitur. He preferred to follow one line of reasoning at a time.

Croft frowned. "What's a management consultancy got to do with it all?"

"So you know them?"

"I know of the firm. It's said to be one of the biggest in Europe."

"How about Alison?"

"I don't think I ever met a woman by that name."

"Alison Dale-Frost? Doesn't ring a bell? She was killed by the same man who strangulated Maureen."

"Someone else was killed? By the same man? So soon after Maureen's death?" He looked genuinely shocked.

"No, a few months ago. Have you ever been to Oxford?"

"I can't follow you. Yes, I've been there a couple of times, but what—"

"Know The Devil's Backbone?"

"Is that a pub? No. I know The Jolly Hunters, though."

Smithhaven laughed. "Touché. We'll leave you to your work, your creative outlet. Goodbye." And he strode to the door.

"What was so funny?" Terry asked when they stood in Pilgrim's Lane.

"The Jolly Hunters is a gay pub in Oxford."

"I wish you would be a bit less outgoing."

"You're right, I'm getting too old for indecency. I'll try to hold back a little. You didn't like the way I questioned Croft, did you? You think I'm jumpy and aggressive."

Terry smirked. "You mindreader."

"Did you see what he's sculpting? A butterfly. We should keep a watchful eye on Patricia Miles."

"WHAT THE HELL DID YOU think you were doing?" Leo stood in Joy's living room, arms folded in front of his chest.

Joy, displaying self-righteousness, sashayed around the sofa. "I was protecting—"

"I don't need your protection, because I haven't done anything wrong."

"Not you, my father. I was trying to keep him out of this. As a young man he had some psychotic episodes. And now that he's been drawn into the investigation, he's had a nervous breakdown, just as I feared."

"I want the letter back." It had taken Leo only a second to figure out what had happened to Victor's letter in the file. He never threw letters away, not even rejection letters.

"I haven't got it any longer. I destroyed it."

"You had no sodding right to do so."

"Yes, you're right. I've been a naughty girl." In one swift movement, she unbuckled his belt and pulled it out. "I think I deserve to be punished."

Leo snatched the belt and flung it on the sofa. "No games. You'll call the police and tell them what you did. Right now."

"That's not a good idea. Terry will believe me. But Smithhaven will make a mess of it. He'll think we're in it together. We would make perfect accomplices. I have the knowledge about my clients' dire fears, you have the perverse personality to plan the details."

"You've really lost it now."

"I'm just emulating Mr. Smithhaven's way of thinking. He's creepy."

"This entire business is creepy. I don't want to have anything to do with it."

"You should have thought about it before you befriended Maureen."

"You're still not over the fact that she didn't tell you about me. That's your possessive nature."

"Come on, I'm not jealous of a woman who's old enough to be my mother. And you didn't shag her, did you?"

All Leo could do to keep himself from slapping her was to thread the belt back into the loops with studied slowness. "I mean you're possessive about your clients' lives, not about mine. You want them to share all their secrets with you."

"Will you stay, Leo?"

"No way." He fastened the belt.

"I spend my nights gripped with anxiety."

"Then lock the doors."

"I can't lock it out." There was a change in Joy's voice that made Leo turn his head to look at her. "When I was a child there was something living under my bed, dark and dangerous, with huge black hands." She hugged him frantically. "It's back. Please Leo, stay and help me keep the shadows away."

CHAPTER NINE
FRIDAY, 18 JUNE

PATTY PACED BETWEEN the coat-stands. "I'm such a selfish bitch." She had given Misty a summary of her quarrel with Leo, but Misty, who was applying some finishing touches to a white silk jacket, failed to see the problem.

"What's wrong with being selfish? Most people are not exactly running around feeding stray cats or giving shelter to the homeless. This is a world of egoists. You're just well-adapted."

"I still feel ashamed about the things I said. You know, in a way I'm sorry for Cameron, and for Lydia, too."

"Next you'll tell me you feel sorry for Danny, as well."

"I do. I couldn't bring myself to tell him that I was going to leave him. All evening I tried to come up with the right words, but he is always evasive when I want to talk to him, and it's been worse since we returned from Portugal. "

Misty grinned. "He doesn't make it easy for you to forsake him, does he?" She began to sew on a golden button.

"I'm not sure if I'm doing the right thing. I don't like to act in a rush. I haven't even sorted out the practical aspects yet. But the situation is unbearable. Danny and I aren't really living together anymore. We exist side by side."

"Your problem isn't selfishness, it's indecisiveness. But you can't live without making choices." She held up a silver button. "I just had to make up my mind if silver or golden buttons look better on this jacket. If I had refused to choose one and discard the other, all I would have in the end is a button-less jacket. Your current situation is of no use to you, Danny or Leo."

"My life is a jacket without buttons. Very poetic. And how am I going to support myself if I decide to move out?"

"With the help of Danny's maintenance payments."

"Oh no, I want a clear cut." She fingered the collars of the coats on a rack. "God, all I wanted was an affair on the side to make my marriage more bearable, not to replace it. Leo says he loves me. And I think he really does. After all the nasty things I said yesterday, he still desired me and made love to me. Danny was reluctant to touch me even when we were newly wedded. I can't remember whether I was in love with him. I was so shocked about my pregnancy."

"You mean false pregnancy. It's beyond me how you could marry on mere suspicion. Didn't you check?"

"I did, or rather tried to. My gynecologist had this embarrassing knack of being funny at the wrong moment. And his repertoire was limited. Each time he would start by saying: 'Would her majesty please climb onto the throne.' and 'Now let's have a peep inside the jewel box.' Stop grinning, you."

Misty's head bent deep down over her sewing.

"And then there was this dreadful mobile hanging above the examination table, five witches on brooms, chasing each other in circles. Like a rattle above a cot. I felt so mortified. When I went to see him for the pregnancy test, he said, 'Would her majesty please climb onto the throne,' and I thought, 'No, her majesty would rather emasculate the court jester.' I put my feet in the stirrups and pressed my eyes closed. When he said his jewel box line, I opened my eyes to roll them in disgust. I shouldn't have done it, because—"

Misty cut the thread with her teeth. "Becosh?"

"Because my eyes fell on the mobile. He had replaced the witches with butterflies. Not real ones, but very realistic looking ones."

"And you ran for your life."

"I went ballistic. Before I knew what had happened I was standing in the anteroom, naked from the waist down, screaming at the top of my voice and making an unholy show of myself."

Laughing, Misty fell backwards onto a heap of fabric. Patty felt her stomach muscles ripple. "Yes, it was the most spectacular phobic attack I've ever had. In the end, the receptionist brought my clothes and I managed to put them on. Everyone looked at the doctor and he assured them that he hadn't done anything indecent. 'I don't know why she started screaming all of a sudden. I was just going to peep inside her jewel box.'"

Misty went completely hysterical. After a while, wiping her tears with the silk jacket, she sat up again. "That beats my Aunt Charlene's toilet spider. I suppose you never returned to this specific doctor."

"Never ever."

Still shaking her head in delight, Misty reached for the next button.

"I have to sort it out, somehow," Patty said. "I won't go to see Leo this weekend. I need time to think. I hope Danny will be away. Lately, he has been spending more time at Jeremy's than at home. And that's fine with me. When he's gone I can sleep in my own bed. Did you notice when we were in Portugal how different he was with others? He was so outgoing with Jeremy. He has never been like that with me. I can talk better with Reg than with my own husband, and I wouldn't describe Reg as charming and personable."

"You should see him when he's wearing his dog collar."

"Oh, please. You know I don't want to hear any details."

Misty slipped on the jacket and twirled in front of a mirror.

"You know what," Patty said. "The silver buttons would have looked better."

CAMERON HAD COME AROUND DAWN this morning and for hours had stood opposite Patricia's house in Erskine Road, leaning against a wall next to a window. When he had pins and needles in his legs, he strolled over and read the menu of the vegetarian restaurant. After a quick pee in an archway he returned to his post, sitting down this time, his baseball cap shielding his face.

He knew Patricia wouldn't let him in when he rang so he had to wait for her to come out. Didn't chicks go shopping all the time?

She finally appeared around ten and turned into Regents Park Road before he had a chance to call after her. With a curse, he got up to follow and saw her entering a boutique. It took her almost an hour to re-emerge. And she hadn't even bought anything. Next she went inside a deli, but this time she was quicker to reappear. When she turned back into Erskine Road, he called her name. She stopped, faced him, frowned. Cam was pleased to see a hint of shock in her eyes. Gloating over her panic he took a step forward. "Don't worry. No piano lessons today."

She took an apple from her shopping bag and held it ready to throw.

"Hey, I've come to do you a favor. You've been two-timed and I thought someone had to open your eyes."

"Leave me alone. Just leave me alone."

"You're so barmy. Don't you see I'm here to help you? You know bugger all about—"

"I don't want to hear your lies. Leo never sent you for piano lessons. You're spying for your mother. I'm sorry for her, but it's got nothing to do with Leo and me. So get the hell out of my life."

This took him into the red zone. "You silly cow. I've been freezing my butt off waiting for you."

The apple hit his cheek, bounced on the ground and rolled into the middle of the street. Before he had time to realize she had actually thrown it at him, she was already safely inside the house.

"You and your grotty piano can go to blazes," he called after the closing door. All right, she wanted it the rough way, she'd get it. He'd tell Leo. He'd show him the apple.

But nothing worked out the way he planned it. By the time he reached Leo's house, he had eaten the corpus delicti. Leo was in his workshop and didn't even look up when Cam came in. Cam felt universally hated. He went up to his room and flung himself on his bed. He was having a shit time. Everything was cocked up. How could Patricia dare to tell him to skive off? One day she'd find out the truth, and then she'd be sorry and think if only she had listened to Cameron Croft. Yep. Did she really think she looked dishy with that silly blue strand? Leo would drop her sooner or later. C'mon, who really loves a chick scared of butterflies?

Slowly, a grin spread over his face. It made his cheek hurt, but he didn't notice. He was too busy telling himself what a smart boy he was, after all.

"SORRY, NO TEA, LUV."

Janice raised her eyebrows. "No tea, Katie?"

"No." The canteen lady shook her head. "It's the new guv. Drinks it quicker than I can brew it. Have some coffee."

Janice took the cup and carried it to the table where Parker, hands clasped behind his neck, tried to rock the plastic chair. "This is never going to work. I give them half a year at the most. My bet is that Terry will be the one who'll have to leave."

Janice felt she had to come to his defense. "Nobody cares, as long as we don't make defamatory remarks and spread silly rumors. I, for one, am not homophobic."

"I wasn't talking about that, sweetheart. Eccentricity's the word. As long as Gould ran the shop, there was a compensating force. But with two loonies in charge...."

"This is disgraceful," Janice said. "They are both accomplished detectives."

"Smithhaven tries to obscure his eccentricity with joviality and jokes. How long is it going to take until the powers that be will interfere? Place your bet."

Rowlands at the next table turned his head. "What's the stake?"

Janice snorted, pushed away her cup, got up and headed downstairs to Terry's office. Terry and Smithhaven seemed to be following their own private investigation, but she was the officer in charge of keeping track of all the diverging ideas and she intended to do just that. Nobody knew what Terry was up to. He had buried himself in the library all morning and had emerged muttering under his breath, frowning, shaking his head and staring into the middle distance. Later he had blocked Osborn's computer after he had asked to be primed with the use of the internet.

Terry beckoned her in. "I think we've been looking for the wrong sort of evidence. All those allusions about twins and shadows...." His gaze went right through her.

"Sir?"

"Yes? Oh, I was just thinking that it wasn't the man who murdered, it was the tree."

"Sorry?"

"Our culprit is someone who lives and kills vicariously."

Another cryptic remark and Janice would return to the canteen to place a bet with Parker.

"I made an appointment to meet Joy Canova for a walk on Hampstead Heath. You could join us and take notes. I'll have to get her talking about private matters. I wish this profiler—"

"Professor Vandyke."

"Brilliant memory, Janice. I wish he was here. It would help to have a professional opinion. This is a sort of eerie concept I'm mulling over."

The whole undertaking seemed eerie to Janice.

Joy Canova was waiting for them at the end of Well Road, where a path with "No Cycling" signs all over it led into a thicket. As she had been instructed by Terry, Janice walked behind them. Joy and Terry were conversing in low voices and she had problems understanding what they said, let alone making sense of it.

"Let's talk about your childhood. Do you attach any traumatic memories to your little sister's death?" Terry asked Joy.

"No memories at all, I'm afraid. All I recall is her funeral, and not even with a sense of sadness and loss. What I really lost was a functional family. Everything fell to pieces. I started to hear a voice that was whispering in my ear, but I couldn't understand what it said. It could be my subconscious. I'm very tense sometimes and just block off my intuition."

"You can block off emotional pain, too, can't you? Active dissociation, in your lingo."

"Well, it's part of my identity as a psychologist. Don't you have one?"

"A professional self? I wish I had. I'm always up to my eyebrows in a case. When it's very bad, I try to escape into a world of sounds. Music helps me to forget the pictures of mutilated corpses, at least for a while. Do you have an internal world where you can hide from reality?"

"I have a planet all to myself."

Terry left the path and leaned against a tree. "I have frequent nightmares. They haunt me for the rest of the day."

"That's a blessing, believe me. I have a recurring nightmare which I can't remember. It leaves me shaken—I can't even suppress it because it doesn't belong to me."

Janice, looking up from her notebook, saw Terry grow tense. "How about bouts of depression?"

"Show me someone who's never been depressed in all her life. What are you aiming at? Are you trying to find out if I match your killer profile?"

"I want to get inside your head."

"Don't. You might get hurt."

"Because of the migraine? The painful flashbacks?"

Joy laughed. "You're a hoot. But at least you're not going totally astray. Your buddy Smithhaven suspects Leo, doesn't he? Well, I can prove that Leo's innocent. He spent last night on my sofa. If he was Shadoe he would have had the perfect opportunity to make me his next victim. As it was, he didn't even come near me, more's the pity."

TERRY MOVED A PEN FROM THE LEFT to the right, realigned the phone with the notepad and folded up the Oxford map as Smithhaven would have done. No, he couldn't think clearly in orderly surroundings. So he spilled some papers from the in-tray on his desk. That was more like it.

He was in a quagmire. If he was right, then more killings were likely to happen and he had the means to prevent them, but he would have a hell of a time trying to prove it, let alone get an arrest warrant.

"Give me a nice little post-mortem on a fresh body any time, but no more exhumations." Smithhaven had returned from the coroner's court. He closed the door behind him and sat down. "Do you know what O'Leary said when he saw Alison's corpse?"

"Looks as if she's been run over by a train," Terry ventured.

"How d'you know?" Smithhaven frowned at the shy beginnings of a new mess on Terry's desk.

"Chaos breeds inspiration." Terry shoved the papers aside. "Did anything new turn up?"

"According to O'Leary, the train only caught her upper body. Her legs and hips were fractured evenly, as if she had fallen from a considerable height, as opposed to being smashed and ground by wheels."

"You mean she was on the bridge? But Joy said that walking across a bridge was impossible for Alison."

"Which means she wasn't there of her own accord. Someone took her to this place and pushed her over the railings."

"They weren't low enough for her to fall over them by losing her balance, were they?"

"No, and they consist of a metal construction filled with meshed wire. There is no balustrade you can climb upon to stand and look down and imagine you can fly, like a person on a cocaine high might do." Smithhaven tugged at the knot of his tie. "Shadoe went to a lot of trouble to kill Alison. He found her on her nightly outing in Camden, made her get into his car with him, drove all the way to Oxford, carried or dragged her along The Devil's Backbone and heaved her over the railing."

"I don't think he planned to kill her. Writing her a threatening letter was all the fun he intended to have to start with. Somehow she played into his hands."

"Excuse my French, but that's bollocks. My theory is that Croft wasn't alone in this. Victor Canova helped him. I'll give Canova the third degree."

"You can't. He's had a nervous breakdown."

"How convenient for him."

"I think you're right insofar as there were two people involved. It's a similar problem as with Siamese twins." Terry eyed Smithhaven with the same acute attention as he did with witnesses and suspects. He feared Smithhaven would shred his theory before he had a chance to lay out all the material he had assembled over the day. "There are several indications that Shadoe is invisible, just as he wrote in his letter."

"An invisible Siamese twin? Now we're talking." Smithhaven got up and stretched like a panther. "Some people deliver their best jokes dead-pan. But can a man with such a deep, rich voice pull anyone's leg? Have you read *Wyrd Sisters* by Terry Pratchett? 'Coal ordered by this voice would become diamonds.'"

Terry decided to ignore his ramblings. Osborn came in and Terry feared a new output of data sheets, but he only brought Alison's address book.

"I checked the entries against our database. She was hanging around with drug addicts, petty dealers and ex-convicts."

"Get some men out to talk to them, although it's probably a waste of time," Smithhaven said. "The choice of words in his letters indicates that Shadoe has a posh family background."

Osborn nodded. "And then there's Mr. Dale-Frost. He's waiting outside."

"Finally someone who will show a more than fleeting interest in the exhumation."

Dale-Frost was firmly built with a full shock of gray-brown hair and dark, hooded eyes. He took the offered chair, sat with his hand-sewn shoes exactly parallel and didn't budge while Smithhaven gave him a short summary of the autopsy.

"I blame Dr. Canova," Dale-Frost said, as if this explained everything. "Had it not been for the therapy that eased her phobia, Alison wouldn't have been on those railway tracks where she got run over."

"She was actually thrown down on them, as I just tried to explain."

A short silence. "Well, does that make any difference? You should have been at the funeral. There was a horde of punks who were desecrating the ceremony by their sheer presence, let alone by their get-up. Their influence had put Alison on the wrong track."

"Mr. Dale-Frost, we are not looking for a scapegoat but for a murderer," Terry fell in. "Where were you on the weekend?"

Dale-Frost plucked at the knife-edge crease of his trousers. "You mean the weekend of Alison's death? I don't know."

Smithhaven squinted at him sideways. "I'm sure you do. According to your wife, you came home on Sunday evening and the first thing you learned was that your daughter had been run over by a train. I assume that this has ingrained a vivid memory of that particular weekend in your mind."

"What are you insinuating? That I killed her myself? This is outrageous. I shall make a complaint."

"Please yourself. During an investigation we have to check upwards of one hundred alibis. I wonder why you are so alarmed."

SATURDAY, 19 JUNE

PATTY OPENED THE SLIDING SHOWER doors and saw that Danny had already gotten up. Wearing no more than a striped pajama top, he was brushing his teeth. Quickly, she wrapped a towel around her. Although it was two days since she had been with Leo, there were still marks on her skin she didn't want Danny to see, unlikely as it was that he would notice them.

After their argument and the inevitable wild orgy on Thursday, she and Leo had agreed that she had to sort out her problems with Danny first. But she hadn't got anywhere in her attempt to have a serious talk with her husband. Danny buried himself in end of year reports.

Gently rubbing her stomach with the enveloping towel, Patty looked at her husband's soft hair, short neck and reliable shoulders, and tried to evoke some of the tenderness she must once have felt for him. Had the magic called chemistry ever existed between them? "I loved our trip to Portugal," she said tentatively. "I would like to go there again."

"That's what Jeremy and I are planning to do."

"Jeremy and you, I see. Are you going away over the weekend again?"

He spit out some foam. "No, I'm afraid I have to finish the reports."

"We have to find a moment to sit down and talk about our situation."

Danny rubbed his eyes and turned around. Patty held the towel tighter. "Trish, you don't have to stay with me. I can see it's pointless." He looked at her blandly. There was something in his eyes that scared her, an emptiness, a void big enough to house the universe. "I'll leave the logistic problems to you, if you don't mind. You know, getting a lawyer, sorting out what belongs to whom and all that." He put the shaver into the socket and switched it on.

Patty dropped the towel and hugged him from behind in a final, desperate effort to get an emotional response. He patted her hands, then unclasped them. Patty withdrew quietly and dressed.

SMITHHAVEN DROVE TO THE STATION after lunch and asked the desk sergeant to give him a tour of the building. It was time he got his bearings in the new station. They had just returned to the front desk when a woman came in, dressed in a white blouse and charcoal gray skirt and jacket. She was an Asian beauty, tall for her race, with almond-shaped eyes and long, thick hair.

Smithhaven did a double take. "I think I've seen you before."

She smiled and her beauty spread beyond belief. "I'm Kim Zhao. I'm a model. My photos were on the covers of Vogue and Elle. Not quite your kind of reading."

He didn't correct her mistake. "DCI Smithhaven. How can I help you?"

"It is about George's alibi. George Dale-Frost."

"Oh, I see."

"He was with me on the night his daughter was killed. We have a penthouse apartment in Prince Albert Road." She gave him a card with her address. "Nobody is supposed to know about it. He often spends his weekends at our place. Will that be enough to eliminate George from the investigation?"

So far, the investigation hadn't even included George Dale-Frost. He was way down on Smithhaven's list. "Was he also with you last weekend?" He had already cleared this question over the phone. Isobel Dale-Frost had told him that they had been at the theatre on Saturday night, followed by a party that lasted till long after midnight. If Kim saw a need to cover George, she would lie.

"Why do you ask?"

"The killer who did Alison in struck a second time."

"No, he wasn't with me last weekend, but his wife should be able to provide an alibi because they had an invitation."

"Good. We will need a signed statement," he said and watched Kim as she dictated it to the desk sergeant. When the statement was typed, she read and signed it, cast a regal look at the two men and was gone, leaving behind a cloud of expensive perfume, an open-mouthed sergeant and a perplexed Smithhaven. "I can't place her, but I could swear I've seen her somewhere before."

CHAPTER TEN
SUNDAY, 20 JUNE

WHEN HE HAD BEEN NEW to the job, Terry's adrenaline level had tripled within a second and made him bolt out of bed when he had a night call. Over the years, he had become inured to this sudden interruption of sleep.

But tonight was different. It was a weekend, the most likely time for Shadoe to strike again if he stuck to his modus operandi. With some difficulty, Terry had arranged an observation team for two of Joy's clients, Emma Little and Selina Prigett, who both lived alone. Blockley had volunteered to cover Joy's house.

On the first ring, Terry was wide awake. "Yes?" His first impulse had been to shout, "No!"

"We have a dead male. He has been knocked about badly," the sergeant on night duty informed him. "Primrose Hill, railway bridge."

"On my way." He was already unbuttoning his pajama top with his free hand. His thoughts were rattling away all the time as he threw on his clothes. Of course it might be pure coincidence that the killing had taken place on a bridge. Alison had been Joy's only client suffering from gephyrophobia. Also, the victim was male this time. Joy didn't have any male clients.

Terry hopped into his car and jammed in the gear. He knew the bridge well. It was a pedestrian bridge with a bicycle lane in the middle, connecting Regents Park Road with the Bridge Approach from Chalk Farm. When he had work to do in the area, he liked to take his lunch break at the Pembroke. When the weather was fine, he would sit in the beer garden, directly by the bridge. The massive concrete walls of the bridge, six feet high, had recently been painted. The left side in green, the right side with a pattern of leaves, birds, fish and flowers. Thirteen glass containers were aligned along the left wall—Terry compulsively counted them each time he crossed the bridge—followed by an Oxfam Clothing Bank and a Book Bank.

The sky had the unreal color of approaching dawn when he arrived. The area had already been cordoned off and lit. Brick came to meet him and led him to the victim, feeding him the details on the way.

"He was found by a man cycling home from late shift, a Mr. Winter. The body is lying behind the Book Bank. You can hardly see it when you walk by, but from his bike, Winter had a better vantage point. He got off his bike to take a closer look and recognized the man, a neighbor living in the flat below his." Brick pointed to the telephone booths at the near end of the bridge. "He dialed 999 at a quarter past four. I was the first on the scene, took his statement and sent him home."

They reached the place where the corpse lay alongside the wall, slumped on its right side in an uncomfortable variant of the recovery position. Terry knelt next to the body without touching it. Blood pooled around the man's head. The white shirt under the gaping coat was dirt-stained. He noticed something sticking out of the gaping mouth and bent lower to see what it was.

"Butterflies," he said, closed his eyes and pinched the bridge of his nose.

"What's a man in a Burberry doing behind an Oxfam Clothing Bank?" O'Leary was looking for a nice opening line as always.

Terry ignored him. "Brick, what's the name of the victim?"

"Daniel Miles."

Terry broke into a cold sweat. "I need Smithhaven here to take over."

"I've already called him."

"Good, we must—"

"Head injury," O'Leary said, unasked, "and probably internal bleeding. But he wasn't dead on the spot. If he had been found sooner he could have been saved. Time of death around two thirty."

"Thanks," Terry said automatically. "Brick, I have to leave the scene. Tell Smithhaven that I fear Patricia Miles is in danger."

Janice drove up as he was bending under the crime scene tape. He signaled her to stay in the car and got in at the passenger side. "Erskine Road." It was just a few hundred yards away, but he had this every-second-counts feeling. "Patricia's husband has been beaten to death. He has butterflies in his mouth."

Janice understood immediately. "You think Shadoe is torturing Patricia right now?"

He was out of the car before Janice had stopped it. He rang Winter's bell. A head poked out of a second-floor window. "Finally. I was told to stay up until–"

"Just let us in, will you?" Terry cut him short. The buzzer sounded. "Okay, what now?" Janice said, when they stood in front of Miles' flat. No sound could be heard. "Shall we ring?"

Terry hadn't thought that far. If Shadoe was in there he needed more manpower. He depressed the bell button with his elbow. They waited. Finally, a voice. "Who is it?"

"Inspector Terry, Camden CID. Are you all right, Mrs. Miles?"

"Me? Sure." The door was opened a slit.

Terry held up his warrant card. "Can we talk to you?"

She unhinged the chain and let them in. He was so relieved to see Patricia Miles in one piece, that for a moment he forgot that he had to inform her of her husband's violent death.

"Sorry for waking you up, Mrs. Miles."

"I know you, don't I? I've seen you in front of Leo's house. Has anything happened to him?"

"It's your husband," Terry said gently.

She led them into the living room, switched on some lights, then disappeared into another room, probably to put on a robe. But she returned still dressed only in a sleepshirt.

"He's not in his bed," she said with an air of confusion. "I had no idea Danny planned to go out tonight. It's overcast, isn't it? You see, he's a hobby astronomer."

Terry took off his light summer coat and wrapped it around her. "Mrs. Miles, your husband is dead."

She sank onto the sofa. "He's dead? What do you mean he's dead?"

There was no way to say it nicely. "He was killed. Your neighbor, Mr. Winter, found him on the railway bridge."

"Are you sure it's Danny?"

"I'm afraid we'll need you to identify the…him." He hated using the word "body" in this context.

She hugged herself. "Please, no, he hasn't got killed, please. I was going to be divorced, not widowed."

"When was the last time you saw your husband?"

"When I went to bed, around ten thirty. He was still working on his end of year reports. He's head of science at Hatch End High School in Harrow."

"You didn't wake up when he came to bed?"

She looked down at her hands. "We sleep separately. I told you we were on the brink of divorce. Nothing spectacular. We've just grown apart."

"Do you know if your husband was scared or felt threatened lately?"

"Not at all, no. Of course, we didn't talk very much, so I'm not sure if he would have told me."

"Did Joy Canova warn you about threatening letters?"

"My therapist? What's she got to do with it? No, she never mentioned letters. Warn me about what?"

"Two of her clients have been killed."

"I didn't know that. Who?"

"A young woman called Alison Dale-Frost. She was thrown over a bridge. And Maureen Gordon, who was found strangulated in her house in Well's Road on Monday. Both victims had received death threats. Joy Canova assured us that all her clients would be warned. My sergeant had started to talk to the clients, too, but you were way down on his list, naturally, since one can't kill anyone with butterflies."

Patricia shuddered. "You could scare me to death by closing me into a room with three or four of them. That's all it would take. I don't understand all this. Danny wasn't Joy's client and one could hardly mistake him for me."

"Maybe he intercepted the letter and tried to protect you," Terry said.

"Why do you think this is connected to those two other murders?"

"Alison and Maureen were confronted with their phobias. Now your husband, he—" Terry saw a startled expression form on Patricia Miles' face. Carefully choosing his words, he went on. "He had something pushed inside his mouth. A couple of dead butterflies."

Patricia pressed her hands over her lips. She stopped breathing and was shaking violently.

WHEN TERRY HAD MADE SURE that Patricia Miles was all right, he entrusted her to the care of Janice and went upstairs to talk to Mr. Winter.

He was a tall, sinewy man in his forties, dressed in white right down to a pair of deck shoes. He exuded an air of serenity and probity. His shoulders twitched portentously as if dancing to a slow rhythm.

Terry introduced himself, then said, "You acted very prudently. Most people would have walked by, taking the body for that of a drunkard."

"I'm a nurse, Inspector. I can tell the difference between a drunken man and a dead man." He spoke in a pouting tone. "The streets were empty like the moon. Ah, Miles would have liked the comparison, wouldn't he?" His eyes clouded with compassion, but Terry could see that he wasn't a bleeding heart.

"Where do you work, Mr. Winter?"

"Hampstead Medical Center. I checked the body for signs of life. There was no pulse, the body was cold and the blood on the ground had begun to congeal. So all I could do was to call the police, which I did." He pressed his flat hands on his trousers as if he wanted to iron out some invisible creases. "I didn't examine the body further so as not to destroy evidence. From what I saw of his head, he seemed to have been hit with a blunt instrument."

"We'll know after the post-mortem," Terry said demurely. He didn't want to alienate an attentive witness by pointing out that he had been overzealous. "Is there anything else you noticed?"

"Nothing, except that it was Daniel Miles."

"How well do you know the Miles'?"

"They are friendly and affable. Patricia asked me for my work schedule to make sure that she wouldn't wake me playing her piano. She's a music instructor. Nice and patient with the kids. Daniel was a reserved if not reticent person." A wistful sigh. "Not someone you would expect to get killed in a street robbery."

Terry nodded thoughtfully and got up. "Please let me know if anything else comes to mind."

"That goes without saying, Inspector. I know my duty and I'm always glad to be of help." With a ceremonious air, he saw Terry to the door.

JANICE STIFLED A YAWN. The complete team was assembled in the incident room. Smithhaven was the only one who didn't look as if he had slept in his suit. He opened the meeting with a brisk nod.

"The first question we have to ask ourselves is: does this killing in any way relate to Shadoe? Let's look at the cons first. The victim was not phobic, and he wasn't one of Joy's clients. And why did the culprit leave Danny behind when he was still alive? This looks more like manslaughter than premeditated homicide."

"It doesn't even look like a planned attack to me," Terry said. "More like a quarrel gone out of control. You don't plan a killing in an open space lit by street lamps and overlooked by windows. Have you sent a house-to-house patrol?"

Smithhaven grinned. "I have. After you fled from the scene. Brick said you thought Patricia Miles was in danger. Janice called in to say she was all right. It seems that Janice and I are doing your job these days." He winked at her and Janice felt like a traitor.

Terry didn't seem to notice. "I've never heard of a killer stuffing his victims with butterflies. There must be a connection with Patricia Miles' lepidoptero-phobia, it doesn't make sense in any other way. Maybe Daniel was killed because he tried to protect his wife. Shadoe wanted to lure her to the bridge, but Daniel went instead."

"We have two contradicting aspects here," Blockley said. "On the one hand, it doesn't look planned, on the other hand, if it wasn't planned, why bring along the butterflies? What were they to be used for? To scare Patricia, most likely. So Shadoe got sidetracked by Daniel somehow."

Terry shook his head. "But Patricia didn't hear her husband leave. There was no disturbance at all. Was anything found on the body?"

Smithhaven played with his tie. "You mean a letter? No. All he had on him were his house keys and a handkerchief."

"No wallet. So maybe it was a robbery, after all. Or that's what we would think if it weren't for the butterflies."

"No, sir," Janice said. "His wallet was at home. I went through Miles' belongings with his wife when she felt better. Nothing is missing."

"All right," Smithhaven resumed, "it looks like another Shadoe killing, even if the handiwork is not quite the same. It might be a copycat killing."

All morning, preliminary forensic reports came in and the team discussed every detail. Janice felt dizzy in her attempt to add this new set of data to the huge amount she had stored already.

Smithhaven had sent out interview teams. "Terry, I want you to check Joy Canova and Lionel Croft. I wish I could come with you, but I have to go to Daniel's PM. Or shall we swap?"

Terry was already heading for the door and beckoned to Janice. They went to Pilgrim's Lane first, and there Janice's patience was put to a tough test. Much as she admired Terry's calmness, she wished he would finally come to the point. For half an hour he chatted with Lionel Croft about his love life. Croft was remarkably uninhibited. Janice was sure it was due to Terry's conversational style. Most of his questions focused on Joy Canova. How had Croft met her? What had their relationship been like? Why had it ended? Janice wasn't sure if he expected her to write all that down.

"To sum it up," Terry finally said, "Joy Canova is an intermittent nymphomaniac."

Croft leered. "Very well put. She either wants no sex at all or she wants it intense, varied, long and wild."

Janice had hoped that, having cleared this up, Terry would move on to other, more acute matters. But Terry's curiosity about Joy Canova wasn't satisfied yet. Why was he so fascinated by her? Had she put a spell on him?

"Does she seem absent-minded sometimes?"

"Not more than other people. Do you suspect her?"

"I don't suspect her—not her personally."

Croft grinned, which gave his crude face a nice, boyish aspect. "I see. You suspect her shadow, right?"

Terry smiled in response. "Patricia Miles is a completely different kind of woman, isn't she? Fragile, petite, indulgent."

"What are you driving at?"

"When did you last see her?"

Croft jumped up so suddenly, that Janice dropped her pencil. "Has something happened to her?"

"Her husband was murdered."

Croft lowered himself back on his chair, his face white and tense. "Patricia's husband has been killed? When? Where? How? Why didn't you say so immediately? All this talking about Joy. Was Patricia with him when it happened?"

"He was beaten to death not far from where he lived. Patricia was at home. Her friend Misty is with her now."

Croft swallowed. "Why? Why was he killed?"

"A very good question. Where were you last night?"

"Oh, please, don't tell me I need an alibi again. I was in bed, alone."

"Let's talk about your motive."

"I don't have one. Patricia's marriage was on the point of breaking up. The problem was her husband's complete lack of interest in her."

"She told me she was going to be divorced."

Leo shrugged. "I wasn't sure if she would take the plunge."

"How long have you known Patricia?"

This was the overture to another hour of intense talking and by the time they were finished, Janice had writer's cramp and her pencil, which Croft had sharpened for her five times, was only a stub. Finally, Terry got up and thanked Croft.

They walked over to Joy's house. Janice told Terry that her notebook was full. He gave her his. "What is your gut feeling, Janice? Was Daniel killed by Shadoe? By his wife's lover? Are they one and the same?"

Weighing what little evidence they had, Janice said: "By neither of them. Shadoe wouldn't have killed without gratification by inducing fear. And Croft has no apparent motive. But that's all pure conjecture. As you said during the meeting, this looks like a killing in the heat of the moment. Daniel Miles made someone so angry or desperate that he saw red."

They had arrived in Thurlow Road. Through the opaque glass in the door they could see Joy moving towards them. She opened it and looked at them guardedly. "Leo called me and said you were coming. He didn't want to say what it's all about, though. He sounded very distressed. I hope you're not about to tell me that I've lost another client." She led them into her office.

"No, but one of your clients has lost her husband."

Joy's reaction was the exact opposite to Croft's. Visibly relaxing, she lit a cigarette. "I'm sorry. Who is it?"

"Daniel Miles. He was beaten to death."

Joy hesitated, then went around her desk and stared out of the window. "How did Patricia take it?"

"Not very well. She might need counseling."

Janice turned and scanned Terry's face for irony. "Do you want my alibi? I've been alone this weekend. I wasn't in the mood for going out and enjoying myself. I don't have an alibi, not even a migraine attack."

Well, she did have an alibi. Her house had been under observation. Terry had already changed tracks.

"You have impeded the investigation long enough now," he said. "This would be a good moment to tell me all about Alison."

"You think I was lying?"

"Yes. I think you were lying all the time without knowing why."

She looked at him for a long time, until Terry said, "Incidentally, the cigarette ash is scorching your fingers."

Joy's eyes followed Terry's down to her hands. Slowly, she pressed the stub into the ashtray and flicked the ash from her fingers.

"Do you often hurt yourself without noticing?"

"Not more often than I hurt others without noticing. Inspector, you still haven't told me what I've got to do with the death of Patricia's husband."

"His mouth was stuffed with butterflies."

Joy sank her forehead into her hands. "Does this never end? I will tell you the truth. On that Monday in March, Alison showed me the letter and I tried to calm her. In the end, she got all worked up and tore it up. That was the last time I saw her."

"Describe the letter."

"It was written in one of my father's varieties of handwriting, or rather a bad imitation of his square block letters. I know the content of the letter by heart. Do you want to hear it?"

Although it was Janice to whom she dictated the text, her eyes remained fixed on Terry all the time. When she had finished, Janice was sure that Terry would lose his temper, no matter how self-controlled or gentle he was said to be. But if anything, he grew even calmer.

"When you went to see Smithhaven in Oxford, why didn't you tell him about the letter?" he asked.

"I wish I had. I knew it was a mistake."

Still in a soft tone, Terry said, "Your so-called mistake cost Maureen her life. If we had known about the first letter, we would have immediately reacted to the second one. If you had had the common sense to inform the police about the second letter, that is."

"But I told you, I had a migraine and—"

"The migraines are your escape route, right? What happened to Hope?"

Terry had hit a nerve. Joy cringed, held her hands over her eyes and made tiny, squeaky sounds. "She's dead. We buried her. I don't know what happened. I was a kid. Please, don't torture me."

Terry stood up and gently removed her hands from her face. "Who tortured you?"

But Joy had already snapped back. "What?" she gasped. "What are you talking about?"

Yes, Janice thought, what the hell was he talking about?

TERRY DECIDED TO MAINTAIN a low profile during the afternoon meeting. He wasn't prepared to offer his hypothesis. Right now, with the Miles murder on their plate, nobody would pay attention. He had to organize all the facts and ideas he had assembled over the past few days, so that he could present them in a neat, comprehensible way.

Smithhaven returned from the morgue, rubbing his hands and beaming. "I've learned something very important during Daniel Miles' post-mortem," he said to an attentive audience. "I've learned that I prefer gay jokes to medical jokes."

Terry squirmed, half expecting Smithhaven to quote some of those jokes. But when the laughter had died down he was serious.

"Daniel Miles had a laceration at the back of his head and a concussion. He was pushed with considerable force against the railings, as we already knew after finding traces of his hair and skin on the ledge. After he had gone down, he was kicked ten to fifteen times in the ribs, the abdomen and the genital region. His spleen was torn. He died of internal bleeding. Miles had no defense injuries. He must have been talking to his killer, because the initial attack was carried out frontally. Judging from the severity of his injuries, O'Leary said the time of the attack was around half past midnight. Two hours later, Miles was dead. Blockley, you talked to the landlord of the Pembroke. What did he say?"

"He saw someone when he took out the garbage a few minutes after midnight. A young man, tall and slim, wearing a dark coat and a baseball cap. He was standing next to the Book Bank. That's all he could tell us."

Smithhaven laid out his battle plan and assigned tasks to the team. He broke up the meeting with the inevitable joke. Terry followed him to his office.

Smithhaven had installed a coffee machine which he used for making tea. He switched it on. "You were quiet the whole time. What is your view?"

"Initially, I did agree that this looks like another example of Shadoe's handiwork. But he doesn't kill with anger. He kills with relish."

"Maybe he relished in anger this time. What did Croft say?"

Janice, on cue as always, came in at this moment to bring the typed notes of this morning's interviews. Smithhaven thanked her, offered her a cup of tea, and began to read. When his eyebrows went up slowly, Terry knew he had reached the text of the letter to Alison.

"Joy fooled us all the way, but I have no idea to what end," Terry said. "And I don't think she could explain it even if she wanted to."

Smithhaven smacked the sheets on the desk. "The letter will be analyzed. It's too bad we don't have the original. Shadoe has a very elaborate modus operandi. There can be no doubt now that he killed Alison. Unless Joy made up the letter to distract from something else."

"We have Shirley's statement that Alison showed her an envelope and said it was a matter of life and death."

"Right. And the cleaning lady of the Dale-Frosts saw the envelope and the address in block letters. I sent someone over to show her the envelope of Maureen's letter. Elsie said it looked the same and the handwriting was similar, too." Smithhaven tapped the tip of his nose. "Back to Croft. He's having a steamy affair with a married woman, invites her to move in with him, and a short time later her husband is beaten to death. Although jealousy can be dismissed as a likely motive because Patricia and Daniel were on the brink of divorce, I wonder if it would work the other way round. Was Daniel holding on to Patricia? Did he initiate the meeting with Croft? Did they argue up to the point where Croft got physical and abusive?"

"Croft wouldn't have put the butterflies into Daniel's mouth, knowing that it would scare Patricia."

"If Croft is Shadoe, then he probably thinks he's doing her a favor. Near Oxford, we had a series of brutal rapes. After the fifth rape, we caught the offender. He was convinced that he was doing his victims a service. He kept telling us how they had enjoyed the experience, how he had seen in their eyes that they had multiple orgasms. So don't tell me Croft wouldn't want to scare Patricia. Even love is no argument. Psychopaths love in different ways."

Janice snapped her fingers. "I think there is a vital bit of evidence in what Joy Canova told us. She said the letter to Alison was written in block letters. The rejection slip Croft received from Canova Press had two notes by Victor, both in script. So where did Croft copy the block letters from?"

SMITHHAVEN HADN'T FORGOTTEN Kim Zhao and the penthouse apartment in Prince Albert Road. He decided to drop in on his way home. He had to find out why the woman looked so familiar. He was lucky, both Kim and George were there. She let him in with a nonchalant smile. "I thought I had already given you all the information you needed."

"Just checking on a few details. May I come in?"

Smithhaven was tempted to ask to be shown around the whole apartment. The living room was airy and large enough to house a cricket field. A balcony ran along the south and west side, permitting a panoramic view across Regent's Park. The place was decorated with what looked like the most eclectic collection of erotic art: photos, paintings, ceramics, and a sculpture that was the big version of the model he had held in his hands in Croft's workshop. Masking his excitement, he turned to George Dale-Frost, who got up from a white leather sofa, and asked casually: "This is a Croft, right?"

Kim crossed the ankle-deep carpet. "It's called Supplication."

"When was the sculpture made?"

"This winter."

"When did you sit for Croft? When was the statue delivered?"

Kim lowered her perfectly shaped chin. "If you stay for a few minutes, I can copy the dates from my diary."

"Thank you." Smithhaven sat down on another huge affair of leather and angular cushions. A room like this wasn't made for small furniture. "How did you get in touch with Croft, Mr. Dale-Frost?"

"I saw his catalogue in Dr. Canova's office when I was waiting during Alison's first session. I took down the telephone number and called him a few days later. That was all. Why is it of importance?"

Kim rejoined them and handed Smithhaven a sheet of paper on which she had noted all the dates. Her handwriting was as perfect and shapely as she was. The sculpture had been delivered on the sixth of March, two weeks before Alison's death.

"Thank you. Mr. Dale-Frost, did Lionel Croft ever meet your daughter?"

"Not as far as I know."

"Did you tell him where you had seen the catalogue? Did you tell him why you had been at Dr. Canova's place?"

"I might have mentioned it in passing. I don't see what you are getting at."

"How often did you meet Mr. Croft?"

"Just twice. When I accompanied Kim for her first appointment, and then on the day when he and two men brought the sculpture. A business transaction like any other, except that Mr. Croft was supposed to handle this with discretion."

"He did. I asked him if he knew you and he denied it. Well, Ms. Zhao, how did Croft treat you when you sat for him?"

"He is a true gentleman. He praised my body awareness, but did not say a single thing that could be taken as offensive or improper. Very professional. Almost like a surgeon."

Smithhaven opened his notebook and wrote: "Almost like a surgeon," and added an exclamation mark. "Thank you, Ms. Zhao. You have been very helpful."

MONDAY, 21 JUNE

IN TERRY'S OFFICE, SMITHHAVEN found Terry and Osborn bending over one of those never-ending printouts. "Morning, kids. One day they'll rename the HOLMES computer system and call it OSBORN, for Official Survey Brain Organization Relay Network or something."

Osborn grinned, saluted, grabbed the list and left. Smithhaven pulled out a chair. Trying not to sound too smug, he gave Terry the gen about his visit to George Dale-Frost's love nest.

"Looks like he's got a sort of erotic theme park," Terry said judiciously.

Smithhaven folded his tie into zigzags. "Croft told us he didn't know Dale-Frost. And now we learn that he has made a sculpture for him. And what is more, that sculpture was delivered shortly before Alison received the letter. We have linked Croft to all three cases. You can't dismiss this as coincidental."

"Linking Croft to all three cases only makes sense as long as we think they were all carried out by the same person. The more I look at the evidence, the more I believe we have two separate cases. I have sent Parker to talk to Daniel's colleagues at Hatch End High School, and Blockley to see his family. We must not forget the routine inquiries just because we have a suspect."

"As if I didn't know that. Yes, go ahead, go through all the trials and tribulations of a thorough investigation. This is what I expect from you. But you can't say Croft is innocent of either killing Daniel or of torturing Maureen and Alison, because if he is Shadoe, then he is also the one who stuffed Daniel's mouth with butterflies. It all hangs together."

"I don't think Croft is innocent of either the one or the other. I think he's innocent in both cases."

Smithhaven straightened his tie. "I like a good battle of minds. Give me your theory so I can smash it."

Terry shook his head. "I can't. I have to talk it through with Vandyke first."

"Then let me guess. Joy Canova?"

"Well, yes, I think Joy Canova killed Maureen and Alison. Whoever killed Daniel hated him. And he hated Patricia as well. Hence the butterflies. The idea behind it is not quite the same as Shadoe's motivation."

"You mean Joy's motivation," Smithhaven said.

"Joy has no motive. She's a victim herself."

"I can't get it into my head how you can let Croft off the hook after I've caught him out lying about his connection to Dale-Frost."

"He wasn't lying, he was protecting his customer," Terry countered smoothly. "Dale-Frost's penthouse is a secret. For Croft, a breach of confidence would be the end of his career. I am sure that many of his customers are very persnickety about discretion."

"You crafty sod. You should have been a lawyer. Then what do you make of the following? Joy Canova has lots of clients. Only three of them were known to Croft. Two of these were killed and the third lost her husband."

"Maureen and Alison were also the only ones who lived within walking distance of Joy. And we don't know for sure if Croft knew Alison. What is more, it is not a coincidence that Croft knows Dale-Frost, but a direct consequence of the fact that Croft and Joy were lovers and that she put his catalogue in her waiting room."

"Cause and effect aside, the point is not how and why he got in touch with Croft, but that he did it in the first place."

"You're running in circles."

"And you're running in squares."

Brick came through the open door, lowering his head under the frame. "Folks, there's some interesting news. The lab called. Daniel Miles was HIV positive."

"FINGERPRINTS ON BUTTERFLY WINGS, that's something I've never done before." Andrew Sedgewick, the forensic technician, pushed up his glasses. Together with Janice and Terry he was staring at the tiny creatures that had been gingerly retrieved from Daniel's mouth. The broken wings lay on the chrome table like pieces of a jigsaw puzzle. "There are six of them. Exotic species. I've sent photos over to the Butterfly House. When we know the names we can try to trace the source. Unless the killer is a private collector, he must have bought them somewhere."

Terry found himself touched as he looked at the dead creatures. "Lovely little things. So vulnerable. It's hard to imagine someone could be scared of them."

"Hm," Janice said. "Children sometimes make up stories to get their parents' attention. Maybe Patricia Miles was only faking her phobia. And when she discovered that it did the trick she played it on and on, until it was too late to give it up. And it came in handy when she wanted to get rid of her husband. It's better than an alibi."

Terry, who had been intently studying a turquoise, black-rimmed wing, looked up. "Interesting point. Maybe this is why the butterflies were put in Daniel's mouth. It wasn't meant to scare Patricia but to make sure she wouldn't be suspected."

He was discussing this possibility with Patricia half an hour later, while Janice was going through Daniel's desk.

Patricia had a washed-out look and spoke with a lifeless voice. "No, I can't imagine that Danny had an affair. Why do you ask?"

"Your husband was HIV positive. Did you know that?"

"Danny had AIDS? That's impossible."

"He didn't have AIDS yet. He just had the antibodies in his blood."

"I have no idea how he could have.... I mean, I was the first woman in his life. He never had surgery or blood transfusions or anything. And I'm sure he didn't date another woman. He had no sex drive whatsoever. I'm not even worried that he might have infected me. I'll have myself tested, just to be sure, but we had the safest sex imaginable. He hardly ever kissed me on the mouth." She rolled a handkerchief between her hands. "Maybe all his reluctance to touch me stemmed from his fear of infecting me. But why didn't he tell me? Was he afraid I would leave him? I wish he was here so I could ask him."

"Yes, that's the problem with sudden death. So many questions remain unanswered. Did he work late sometimes?"

"No, he always came home on time. Sometimes he left again later, but that was for scientific studies."

"Astronomy, I know. Did he have a companion, or was he with a group?" Terry asked.

"He always went alone, but when we were in Portugal in May, he made friends with someone from Marlow, Jeremy Beech. They went on some excursions together. I don't think Daniel used this as a cover for adultery." She shook her head and her uncombed hair fell into her eyes. Terry, a man of soft, caring impulses, raised a hand and raked it back. She didn't notice.

"It's such a stereotype," she said. "Jealousy. Revenge. No, I can't take this in."

Neither could Terry. There was a notion forming in his mind, slowly, like a galaxy forms of rotating atoms, and he didn't like it at all. "Your husband had a secret. More than one secret. It starts with the fact that he didn't tell you he was HIV positive."

"Maybe he didn't know either."

"Oh, yes he did," Janice said in a low voice, as if sensing Terry's mood. "I've found his test result. He had known since August 1995."

"He had known about it ever since we married? That doesn't make sense." Patricia banged her fists together. "Nothing makes sense any longer. I was married to a stranger. Who is this man that got killed? Who was he? Who? Can you tell me?"

Terry got up slowly. "I'll find out. I promise."

During his drive to Marlow, Terry had enough time to think his idea through and to start having some doubts. But they were dissipated the moment Jeremy Beech opened the door. He was lean and wiry, dressed in tight vinyl trousers and a muscle shirt—a former club kid type homo, grown into a boyish adult with tousled hair.

"Thanks for agreeing to see me," Terry said.

"Sure. Come in."

The living room was an incredibly stylish affair of dark blue and white, dominated by large prints of galaxies, spiral nebulae and other celestial objects.

Beech waited for Terry to choose a seat, then slumped down on the sofa. His face was a study in grief. "He meant so much to me. It was a once-in-a-lifetime thing. Or shouldn't I be telling you this? Nobody knew Danny was gay. I'll go to his funeral. I'll feel like a widow. More so than his wife."

"I know how you feel."

"No, you don't. Heteros think homosexuality is an inferior way of feeling. That it's only to do with sex."

In his line of work, Terry had often been tempted to disclose his homosexuality when confronted with a gay man. Whenever he met someone who was painstakingly arranging life to either resemble normality or to ridicule it with flippancy, he wanted to say: "Oh, it's all right. I know what it's like." But he was too reticent to ever let go—except now when he was faced with Jeremy Beech's sorrow. Or rather with his apparent need to explain his sorrow.

"Who says I'm a hetero."

Beech gave up his defensive posture. "Then I can tell you what it was like for

Danny. I have to tell someone. I don't want people to think it was easy for him to deceive his wife. He had been brought up by strict moral standards. He tried to act like a hetero. We can do that, can't we? I've done it, too. It's no fun, but it's possible."

Terry nodded, although he had no first-hand experience. He had never tried to date a woman.

"So he meets Trish and she's sweet and intelligent and he dates her a few times. She thinks she's pregnant and Danny is sure it must be from another man, because they never had unprotected sex. Not that he cares if she cuckolded him. It's his chance to settle down, to find the perfect facade. The pregnancy turns out to be some other female mystery, ovari-something, but that doesn't matter. What matters is that an ex of Danny's gets AIDS and Danny has a test and he's positive. Shit, eh? Does he tell Trish? Of course not. He's too used to living a lie. He reduces the intimacy with Trish, tells her he doesn't want children yet. He still dates men, does some cottaging, whatever he can get to relieve the craving. At the same time he is mortified by his physical needs. There he is, teaching young boys and girls, and then he goes to have a quick number with a rent boy behind King's Cross. He feels more of an hypocrite than his parents ever were. He's torn between two worlds. Living the hidden life is a double-edged knife these days when everything is so open and easy-going. I mean, there was a time when you had no choice but to hide your true sexual proclivity. But today, with all this tolerance…how I hate that word, it's so condescending, if you know what I mean."

"You can only tolerate someone when you see yourself endowed with the power to judge him."

"Right. And then he meets me and he's happy because we truly belong to each other. He was so relieved when Trish found herself a lover. If he got killed by his wife's lover, that would be the ultimate irony, wouldn't it? I mean, he wasn't in their way, was he? He had me. I told him, come and live with me. You can have your coming out and still find another job when they fire you from that prestigious school. I loved him so." With this, he began to shake silently.

"Mr. Beech, did you leave another man for Danny?"

Beech ran the fingers of both hands through his hair. "Jealousy as a motive? No. I had been single for a couple of months when I met Danny. Please tell me more about the way he died. I can't believe what it says in the papers. Butterflies in his mouth. Was it an act of homophobia?"

"I think it was." It had been on his mind all the time. "A very personal act of homophobia."

CHAPTER ELEVEN
TUESDAY, 22 JUNE

THE NEEDLE PIERCING THE CROOK of her arm caused a moment of thin, sharp pain. Instead of looking away as usual when she had her blood taken, for fear of fainting, Patty watched with fascination this time as the dark red liquid rose in the syringe. The needle was removed and a pad of disinfectant pressed onto the minute puncture in her skin.

"We'll call you when we have the results," the nurse said, stuck on a Band-Aid and dismissed Patty with brisk efficiency.

After two days in a hazy state of shock and denial, Patty felt sobered up by the mundane necessity of an AIDS test. The mist of sadness cleared. She was able to think and act again, to make decisions and come to conclusions.

She walked all around Russel Square before she went to the bus stop. She needed to get her blood circulating strongly, feeding her brain with enough oxygen to ensure that the line of thought that had opened up was not just another foggy nightmare.

Those silly words Leo had said about killing Danny had branded her with guilt. But she had the means to find out the truth, to prove his innocence and to chase away the doubts for good.

Patty boarded the bus to Hampstead Heath and checked whether the key to Leo's house was in her purse. She found it in the side compartment, where she had put it on Thursday morning, the day she discovered Cam's room; the last time she had seen, touched and kissed Leo. Now that she was unable to feel anything remotely resembling sexual lust, thinking of Leo made her aware of that other feeling that had been there all the time, concealed by desire: she was in love with him.

Everything would be fine, were it not for the butterflies. Six exotic butterflies had been found in Danny's mouth. She had seen six exotic butterflies in Leo's showcase. All she had to do was to check if they were still there. It wouldn't be easy. It wasn't just a matter of letting herself into his house, tiptoeing down to the cellar and searching for the showcase. It was a matter of getting face to face with her demon.

"SO HE WAS GAY. AREN'T WE ALL?"

Terry didn't find this funny and he told Smithhaven so.

"You're too touchy, my boy. And you're too bogged down in details. Let Blockley look into this aspect." Smithhaven went over to the coffee machine and poured two cups of tea. "You must learn to delegate minor tasks. It's our job to see the big picture."

"I don't think there's a single big picture, but two overlapping pictures. That's why we think the cases belong together."

"Here, drink and listen. Everything points to Lionel Croft. He knew the Dale-Frost family and Maureen Gordon. He's the lover of Danny's wife. You agree with me that far."

"I said overlapping pictures."

"I say one picture. And I'll show you how it looks when you're inside the picture." Smithhaven raked through is hair. "Let's assume I am Lionel Croft. What's going on in my mind? I've always been fascinated by fear and weakness in women because in their presence I feel strong and in control. A psychologist would at this point inject a nice analysis of my problematic childhood with a dominant mother."

"And a hamster that was a bedwetter."

"Will you hear me out? I—I as Leo that is—marry a wife who is a study in neuroses. I'm attracted by her vulnerability. A wonderful playground opens up. I feed her fears, watch her getting more and more out of control. Unfortunately, the game isn't as much fun when she's drunk and beyond my influence. I begin having affairs. I explore the joys of sado-masochism, expand my repertoire of cruel little games and keep up the image of being nothing but a neglected husband with a kinky edge. Just messing around. But my appetite grows. I leave my wife, who's now in the way—and meet Joy Canova. Her list of clients is like a treasure box. In my workshop, I have all the tools necessary to make a duplicate of her keys. I go to search her office when she's not in. I take along a disk, make a copy of the relevant computer files, and now I've got all I need to feed my fantasy. Because it's still all just in the mind. I'm not planning to kill yet. I return again to copy more files, but it's not as exciting an adventure as the first time round. I need a closer contact with fear. When George Dale-Frost orders one of my sculptures he mentions his daughter. I already know about her through the files. Maybe something George says triggers the wish to dominate this girl. I've probably been writing letters, never meant to be sent, to Alison and others, as a mental exercise, part of my exploration of fear.

"Why do I fake Victor Canova's handwriting? Because I know what it will do to Joy. She'll hold back information, she'll attract suspicion to herself. A bit of a punishment because she had the nerve to walk out on me. So, for the first time, I deliver a letter. Then I have to get the dope. In Camden, that's easily done. I've been watching Alison for a while to get to know her movements. I get her into my car by offering her a sniff. We arrive at the bridge, a lonely place where nobody will hear her scream. I frogwalk her up the stairs, then make her look down. Her fear is ambrosia to me. She trembles in my arms. I lift her and watch her fall, rejoicing in her terror. For a few days, I'm excited and exhilarated. I did it. The threshold has been overcome. Then a stale feeling expands. It happened too quickly. She should have suffered longer. A new idea pops up. How about Maureen? I've met her several times on the Heath. God, what a pathetic woman, who wouldn't even let me sit on the same bench. It all started out as another game when I met her for the first time. I fiddled my way into her life by playing Mr. Charming. In sexual terms, Maureen is a girl in her teens. Pubescent girls love to have secrets. To have a man interested in her, a good-looking man, is a cherished secret for Maureen. Mr. Kelby is the kind of man her mother would have chosen for her. How boring. I am a menace as well as a promise. So she plays along and agrees not to tell her therapist about our growing fondness for each other. When, on one occasion, I have a chance to get inside her house, I make sure I keep my distance, so that she never feels uncomfortable in my presence. Thus a bond of trust builds up. Then I write the letter and wait for her to work herself into a panic."

"How do you know when she's read the letter?" Terry couldn't help asking.

"Of course she phones me, just as she phoned Kelby, the other man in her life. On Saturday night I walk over. She's still awake, scared to death. She doesn't want to let me in. Later I call her and say I saw someone creeping around her house. Very suspicious person. I say I called the police and they will send someone round in half an hour. Again, I offer to come over and protect her. This time she agrees and lets me in, grateful for my concern."

"Clen, you're astounding. Are you sure it wasn't you who killed her?"

"Don't interrupt. I tell Maureen she needs to get more relaxed or the police won't believe her. With her nerves all aflutter, she won't be taken seriously. I hypnotize her. Joy once tested her method on me, so I know how it's done. Then it's time to play. I tie Maureen, then kill the cats. I close one of them in another room. I'll let it out later, when I've finished with Maureen. The mews of the cat will attract someone's attention. I want Maureen to be found. After all, I'm an artist. My work has to be exhibited. I kill Maureen with great relish. She's all mine now. We have a great time."

"This is sick."

"I'm putting myself in his shoes." Smithhaven tapped his foot against a drawer. "It's amazingly easy to profile a killer."

"Alleged killer. Lionel Croft could be as innocent as you and me. Although I wouldn't put my hand in the fire for you any longer."

"I know why you are fighting my theory. You don't want it to be Lionel Croft because of what it would mean to Patricia to learn that her lover is a dangerous killer."

"This would be a very unprofessional attitude. No, it's because I'm still of the opinion that Danny's death is completely unrelated to that of Alison's and Maureen's."

A slow smile spread over Smithhaven's face. "You haven't heard the finale yet."

"The finale," Terry echoed scornfully. "There you are. You're delivering a performance, you're construing a silly narrative as a framework to include all known clues. It's seductive, but what can you do with it? You can write a novel like my niece, but you can't get an arrest warrant."

Smithhaven swept that aside impatiently. "I'm fully aware that I have no degree in investigative psychology and that Danny's death doesn't make sense in terms of Shadoe's modus operandi. But circumstances forced the killer to change his approach. A threatening letter would ring the alarm bells immediately. So he adapts."

Terry frowned. "And kills Patricia's husband instead of her?"

"Not instead of her. Not at all. With Patricia, fate placed an irresistible opportunity into Leo's hands, but he can't write her a letter. And the letter is important. It is the foreplay. When Leo killed Daniel Miles—"

"He did it to replace the letter," Terry exclaimed in sudden recognition.

"That's it. Daniel's dead body is the letter. The butterflies in his mouth are the words. 'Look, Patty, what ghastly things I can do. It could happen to you. It will happen to you.' They have on her the same effect as the letter had on Maureen: scare her out of her wits. Who does Patty turn to in her despair? Leo, her caring, reliable lover, not knowing that she's the one who is going to die next. How's that for a silly narrative?"

Terry slung his jacket around his shoulders. "Let's go."

PATTY SCANNED THE WINDOWS to see if Leo was behind one of them. It was no use slipping into his house silently when he had already seen her. But there was no sign of him. With luck, he was out or in his workshop. The key glided in and the door opened without a click. For a minute she stood, holding her breath, in the small hall between the main staircase and the door that led to the cellar stairs. A minute was the time it took her eyes to adjust to the dimness of this window-less space, and her ears to assure her of the absence of any other sounds apart from the pulsing of her own blood and the hammering of her heart.

She had come to a crucial point in her life. Weakness wouldn't take her any further, so she had to be strong. She wasn't doing it for Danny. If this had been the case, she would have told the inspector about Leo's showcase and would have left the checking of its contents to him. She didn't do it for the sake of getting justice either, or for any other abstract concept. She had to do this for herself. What had Leo said? Show some gumption. She wanted the butterflies to be there. She was prepared to look at them and not to see them as heralds of death but as guardian angels. It would be their absence that would scare her. If she found the showcase empty, her reaction would outdo a phobic attack.

She circled the doorknob with her palm and turned. The door to the cellar opened with a slight creak. Cold air, carrying a smell of dust and clay, mixed with the warmth of the hall. Patty shivered and buttoned up the cardigan she wore over her T-shirt. She found the light switch and looked down a flight of stone steps. She closed the door behind her and instantly felt trapped, like a prisoner in a dungeon. When she reached the bottom of the stairs and looked at the short corridor to her left, she half expected to find manacles on the walls.

There were three doors, one in each wall. So far so good. Next, she had to open a door. It didn't feel like a safe thing to do, not with six exotic butterflies, albeit dead, waiting behind one of them. A vision swept over her, a room dark-ened by fluttering wings, bearing down on her like eyes without a face. Sweat prickled between her shoulder blades.

Patty, get a grip, she commanded herself and reached for the handle of the first door. She heard a remote click. Had someone turned the key and locked her into the cellar? Another click followed, this time it sounded closer. Patty glanced over her shoulder and managed to localize the third click. It came from behind the door. Butterflies don't click, you silly girl. This had to be the connecting door to the workshop. The noise indicated that Leo was in there, working.

That left her with two doors. One of them was a fire door, a clear indicator that it led to the boiler room. And so she was suddenly faced with no choice at all. The door on the far wall had to be the one.

She stepped towards it and opened it to a mere a slit, lest some butterflies should come fluttering out. Her sweaty palms slid from the handle. On tilted hinges, the door swung open as if someone had torn it from her hand. She expelled her bated breath. Her eyes darted around the darkness. When no immediate signs of danger alerted her, she switched on the light and gave the room another quick once-over. No jagged wings anywhere.

To the left, she saw a rack with wine bottles. To the right, shelves were laden with pasta and canned food. In front of her, a worktop with drawers was empty except for a wooden box. It took her a moment to take in that this was the showcase, lying upside down. Patty wetted her lips. If only she were a normal person, someone who could just go over there, pick up the box and turn it around without much ado.... But she wasn't and she couldn't. Fear pulsed through her like lava. She, who had never even touched a book with prints of butterflies; who had jumped screaming from the gynecologist's examination table when she saw the new mobile; how was she supposed to touch this case with its six lepidopterae exoticae?

She was sobbing now, weakened by the sheer effort of standing still, rather than running for her life. Patty forced her feet to step closer to the workbench, she stretched out her arms until her fingertips touched the sides of the showcase. Oh, what the hell. Feeling like a first-time parachutist going for the dive, she turned the box around. But her eyelids were firmly pressed down and she let go of the dreaded thing, making it rattle down on the worktop. She was only a heartbeat away from the truth. All she had to do to find out if Leo had killed Danny was open her eyes. Patty swallowed and prayed. She turned halfway around. She would look at it over her shoulder, knowing that once she saw the butterflies she would run. With her back to the dreaded showcase, she opened her eyes and found herself face to face with Leo.

As if in a belated reaction to having the blood sample taken, Patty lost consciousness.

THE DOOR WAS OPENED WITHIN SECONDS after Terry had pressed the bell. Lionel Croft stood there, holding a lifeless, limp bundle in his arms. In a reflex, Terry felt for the artery in Patricia's neck. Her pulse was slow but strong. Over Croft's shoulder Terry saw an open door and a narrow, lit staircase and he inferred that Croft had carried her up from the cellar. Smithhaven had inferred likewise, because he asked: "What have you been doing with her down there?"

"Nothing. I didn't even know she was here. Close both doors, will you?"

Croft carried Patricia upstairs. "And what are you doing here?"

"Oh, you know what it's like with policemen," Smithhaven chaffed. "We never run out of questions."

Croft lowered Patricia onto the sofa. She groaned and he gently rubbed her hands and arms. "I was in my workshop. I went to get a piece of wood from the boiler room where I had put it to dry. Patricia was standing with her back to me in the storeroom. I've no idea what she was up to. She turned around, saw me and collapsed."

Terry chose a place to sit, but Smithhaven paced around the sofa. Terry was sure he was dying to go and unearth any secrets the cellar might hold.

Patricia opened her eyes. "Leo," she said faintly.

"How are you feeling?"

"Just a bit shaky."

He helped her to sit up. "Oh," was what she said when she saw Terry, and then again, when Smithhaven came around the sofa and inquired if Croft had hurt her.

"Hurt? No, why? I was just—" She stopped and rubbed her palms against each other. "Just—" She gave up.

"It's all right, love. Explanations can wait. The police can wait," Croft added with a scowl at Smithhaven. "You are so thin, have you eaten anything at all since…since Sunday?"

"I don't know."

Croft got up. "I'll make you a cup of chamomile tea and buttered toast."

Before Smithhaven could shoot another question at Patricia, Terry said softly: "You have your own keys to this house?"

"Yes, I…I let myself in and…. There was something I had to see, just to make sure…."

He followed her gaze to a spot on the wall with two small hooks, about five inches apart.

Croft, having switched on the kettle and lowered the toast in the toaster, stood in the open kitchen door. His eyes narrowed, his lips thinned. He had clearly understood the significance of whatever it was Patricia had to make sure. "So you really thought I did it. Jesus, Patricia."

"But no, it's just the opposite. I wanted a proof of your innocence. I love you, Leo."

"Love and trust go together. You must have been very desperate to take this extreme step. I mean, did you really think you could look at them? Did you look at them? Is that why you fainted?"

"I was about to look when you came in."

"Look at what?" Smithhaven asked.

In the ensuing silence, Terry could hear the toast hop. Croft disappeared into the kitchen. Patricia sighed, but said nothing.

"All right, then." Smithhaven removed a pair of surgical gloves from an inner pocket of his jacket. "With your permission," he called into the kitchen, "I will have a look around your cellar, Mr. Croft."

Croft came out, a cup of tea in his hand, which he placed in front of Patricia. "You don't have my permission."

"Fair enough. Then we'll take both of you to the station where you will be detained until I have received a search warrant. And we don't offer around chamomile tea."

Terry saw through him and was puzzled. If Smithhaven wanted to unsettle Croft by threatening to detain Patricia, thus exploiting his protectiveness for the woman, how did that go with his theory that the next item on Croft's agenda was to torture Patricia to death?

"Go and look if you must," Croft said, stroking Patricia's hair. "I didn't even know Daniel. I never met the man. Why should I kill him?"

Smithhaven slipped on the gloves. "You will have to come with me. To make sure I don't plant evidence."

Patricia got up, ignoring Croft's protests. She held on to him as they descended to the cellar.

"In here," Croft said. "This is where I found Patricia. I assume she was looking for the showcase."

The case lay on a workbench.

Smithhaven studied it, with his hands on his back, blocking the view for the others. "What were you looking for, Mrs. Miles?"

Patricia averted her face. "Butterflies."

Terry edged in between Smithhaven and Croft.

All that was left was a tip of a wing against a background of black. It was turquoise with a black rim and belonged to a Peruvian morpho butterfly, as Terry had learned when he talked to the forensic biologist who had identified the six species retrieved from Daniel's mouth.

Smithhaven looked at Terry when he said: "Mr. Croft, you are arrested. You had better get yourself a lawyer because you will be charged with the murder of Daniel Miles. You are not obliged to say anything unless you wish to do so, but what you say may be put into writing and given in evidence."

WHEN TERRY CAME HOME LATE in the evening, he heard Cece typing wildly at the computer in his study.

"Do you want to set a new record?" he asked through the open door, and didn't take umbrage when she failed to answer. Her forehead was set in deep lines of concentration and her freckled nose twitched. Terry went to take a shower. When he emerged from the bathroom, Cece had prepared a late-night snack in the living room.

"Why are you so gloomy?"

He reached for a sandwich. "I made an arrest today."

"Isn't it a reason to celebrate?"

"Consider me in deep mourning. How could I have been so catastrophically wrong? I would have sworn on the success of Timotree that Croft was innocent." He gave her all the background information she needed to understand his confusion. "The noose around his neck is tightening. We've been interrogating him for hours. The poor man."

"You don't sound like a detective."

"I don't feel like a detective these days. More like an agony aunt. I treated Patricia with kid gloves and made sure Clen didn't question her too long. Janice drove her to her friend Misty's to stay the night. She refuses to believe she was in love with a monster."

"She's lost both her husband and her lover in one go. That's a tragedy I could...."

"Use in your next story? I think it's been done before." Terry took a sandwich and chewed it vigorously. "I wish I had Gould back. At least I could call him 'sir.' This made it easier to disagree while keeping up the appearance of respect."

"This sounds to me as if you are still convinced of Croft's innocence. He's been arrested, not sentenced."

"The evidence against him is overwhelming. The snip of butterfly wing fits into the one we retrieved from the victim's mouth."

"Which doesn't necessarily mean he put it there. Other people had access to the showcase as well."

"I know. Patricia Miles and Cameron Croft both have a key to Croft's house."

"What else did you find?"

"A tear-out from a magazine. 'The Nuts and Bolts of Trustworthy Sadism.'"

Cece giggled. "Is this an oxymoron or a paradox?"

"The whole thing reads like a medieval torture manual. Clen was doing a rain dance when he read the entry about asphyxiation games."

"So, that's what you found. But what did you not find?"

"Negative evidence? Good point." He ruffled her hair. "Smithhaven has this fixed idea that Croft stole client data by copying it onto a disk. But we didn't find a duplicate key for Joy Canova's house. And Croft doesn't own a computer. But this won't help Croft because it relates to the other case. He has only been accused of killing Daniel Miles. So far, I should say. Clen is working like a fiend to get him nailed on all three killings. He's combing Croft's car to find evidence that Alison was in it. He believes everything Croft's alcoholic ex-wife reveals about her screwed-up marriage. I am redundant."

"Then talk to some people you haven't thought of before. Say, Patricia's piano students. Might be a complete waste of time but it will keep you away from the interview room and your hyperactive superior."

"SIT DOWN. PLEASE," Misty urged. But Patty couldn't stand still, let alone sit. She stomped around Misty's living room.

"Like a fleeing gazelle," Reg said over the top of his copy of *Astronomy Now*.

Patty snatched the magazine from his hands and flung it under the coffee table. Reg bent to pick it up. "What was that in aid of?"

"Seeing you read this reminds me of Danny. What am I going to do with all his things?"

"Give them to Oxfam."

"What's Oxfam supposed to do with a telescope?"

"I can sell Danny's equipment for you," Reg offered. "Demand is high because of the eclipse."

"How can you say such a thing? He was looking forward so much to the eclipse, and now he's dead and he's not going to see it."

"I think you should call her therapist," Reg said to Misty. "She's going to have a shut-down any minute now."

Misty got up and put a firm hand on Patty's shoulder. "Try to calm down."

"Calm down? It was my fault they arrested Leo. I started the search for the butterflies. I wish I had never thought of it."

"You should be glad they caught him."

Patty moved away from Misty's touch. "But he's innocent."

"If you had discovered the empty showcase first, wouldn't you have been sure that Leo killed Danny? It's only because the police made the discovery that you feel protective about him."

"Leo isn't a killer."

"The correct term for the deed is manslaughter," Reg said, shaking the magazine back into shape.

"Thanks for pointing that out to me, thanks a lot." Patty needed to lock horns. Any outlet for her anger was welcome. "He lay there, bleeding to death, and nobody came to help him."

"Enough," said Misty. "Do sit down and eat something."

"Eat? I won't be able to eat for the rest of my life."

"That'll be a short life, then," Reg murmured.

"Can't you understand? I knew the butterflies they had found in Danny's mouth. I can almost feel them on my tongue. This is…it is the very center of my fear. A mouthful of broken wings. Oh my God." She sank down onto the couch and covered her face with her hands. "I can taste them. They taste like death."

"You were right," Misty said to Reg. "This is getting out of hand. I'll call Dr. Canova." She left the room.

"Here, drink this." Reg pried away her hands and held a cup to her lips. "When was the last time you had something to drink?"

"That was when Leo made me some chamomile tea. He isn't a killer."

"Sure, killers make poisoned ivy broth, not chamomile tea. Now drink."

She took a sip and spat it out. "If I swallow, the butterflies will go down my throat."

"There are no butterflies in your mouth."

"Not real ones."

Reg's voice became louder. "There are no unreal, invisible or virtual butterflies in your mouth either."

Misty came back. "Canova said you should lie down and meditate as she has taught you. Valley-something with two suns. Come on, Patty, I'll take you to bed."

"Don't call me Patty. It's a name for someone who's young and carefree."

"Well, Patricia, if you would please come now."

"That's what Leo calls me. It's only for him."

"Oh, for God's sake, Trish, be a good girl and—"

"Danny was the only one who ever called me Trish. Nobody else has the right to use the name."

Without more ado, Reg picked her up and carried her into the spare bedroom. "She doesn't need a name," he said over his shoulder. "She needs a sleeping tablet. Or a sound spanking."

Patty wanted to say that Leo was the only person allowed to spank her. When Reg lowered her onto the coverlet, she allowed exhaustion to close in on her.

Misty sat at her side and took her hand. "There, that's better. You have to relax. Shall I help you undress?"

Patty was too tired to answer.

"I think she's already asleep," she heard Reg say.

The door closed and she was alone. Alone with so much on her mind that her head threatened to cave in. Leo's incredulous face when they found the empty showcase...a snippet of a turquoise wing against black velvet...the eclipse...her mouth was so dry...like the dust on the wings of a butterfly...Danny's smile when they arrived at the COAA...the beach...wide and blue...that was better. The sun, children jumping in the waves, the smell of sand and salt, a tiny white butterfly sitting on her leg, silken ocean, Valanna. She squinted at the second sun as it rose. The vision changed. The sun was now framed by a window. Patty turned around and found herself standing in a room she had never seen before.

It was long and narrow, furnished with a cupboard and a bed with a bedside table. On the bed lay an old woman. Her emaciated body hardly made the sheets bulge. Her teeth floated in a glass on the bedside table. Her eyes, shiny like congealed eggs, had lost all their color.

A red admiral came fluttering in through the open window and sat down on the wall, its wings opening and closing in slow grace. Patty saw that bright, colorful butterflies were everywhere, but they were just a pattern on the wallpaper. She felt dizzy and suddenly found herself lying on the bed, not next to the old woman, but inside her. She could feel her tongue twitching like a charmed snake in the open cave of her mouth. The old woman was dying.

The red admiral set off on its light, erratic flight. The old woman's eyes opened wider and she saw all the other butterflies follow. One by one they lifted off the wall and soon the room was dark and quivering with the beating of their wings. She knew they had come to get her, to escort her to hell, and she wasn't able to chase them away or to shield her face with her useless hands. She tried to scream, but her throat was dry and no sound came. Her breathing failed her. The butterflies, smelling the sweet aroma of decay, began to land on her cheeks and nose. They crept into her mouth. In her last conscious moment, the old woman's entire being gave off a shrill, desperate scream.

"Patty, for God's sake, Patty, are you all right? Patty, please, come round. It's me, Misty. Everything's fine. You're safe." She stroked Patty's sweaty forehead. "She isn't breathing properly."

Patty blinked and swallowed dryly.

"Shall I call a doctor?" Reg asked from the door.

"Patty? Take a deep breath, come on."

Her fists opened, her eyes began to focus on Misty's face. "Jesus Christ," she said.

Reg said, "Must have been a nightmare."

Patty looked at him, then at Misty. Slowly, she smiled like a wise but weary Buddha. "I feel shaken. Like someone who has been weeping for hours. But I'm much better now. Much, much better. Everything is making sense. The fear never belonged to me. You see, the old woman, she was dying, the terror of her last hallucination took on a life of its own."

"What old woman?" Reg and Misty asked at the same time.

"I had a vision when I tried to do the Valanna meditation. I must have drifted into a deep trance, and then I saw…oh, it's a long story. The important bit is that everything falls into place. Why I was scared by butterflies sitting on walls, why I took them for heralds of death."

"You said 'was scared,' as if this were no longer the case."

Patty's smile broadened. "Could be."

"Let's see." Reg left and after some rustling around in the living room returned with a leaflet. "The Butterfly House in Syon Park."

Misty protested. "I don't think it's a good idea to take her there."

"I just want her to look at the photographs." He proffered the leaflet and Patty took it without hesitating and opened it.

"A clouded yellow, beautiful. A red admiral. I always feared the dark ones most." She ran a finger over the photo. "Tiny creatures. Not a pattern on the wall that comes alive." Tears streaked down her face. "They are lovely. I never knew how lovely they were."

WEDNESDAY, 23 JUNE

THE WAKEFIELDS LIVED IN a purpose-built block in Eton Road. From the living room of their top-floor flat, they had a view over the northern slope of Primrose Hill. Terry stood at the window, waiting for Caroline to return from school. He had spent the day talking to all of Patricia's piano students, which had proved a complete waste of time.

"It's such a dreadful thing to happen, isn't it?" Mrs. Wakefield said feelingly. "How is Mrs. Miles coping with her loss?"

Terry assured her that Mrs. Miles was not doing too badly. His eyes fell on the upright piano, a Gothrian-Steinweg, its timeless grace out of place in the cheaply furnished room.

Caroline arrived a few minutes later. She asked for Terry's warrant card, then turned it over in her hand.

"It's not that I want to check your identity, I've just never seen a warrant card. Hey, your name's Frederick Terry? There was a guy called Frederick Terry who won the Young Genius competition in the sixties. I know the names of all music competition winners, like some people know Nobel Prize winners or football scores. I like to know what becomes of them. How many make it to fame? How many are never heard of again? Some win a whole string of competitions." She returned the warrant card. "I thought his parents should have called him Frederic only with a C, like in Frederic Chopin, when they wanted him to become a pianist."

Terry pocketed the card. "My parents had no high-flying plans for me when I was born."

Caroline's mouth fell open. "It is you? Well, really? How come you're a detective? I hope you didn't quit playing completely."

"I wouldn't know what to do with my leisure time."

"Can you play La Campanella?"

"'Course."

"It's what I'm just practicing. I hope to win the Young Genius competition next year. I came out third this year. I had a lot of fun."

Terry played some arpeggios to get a feel for the touch of the keys, then played what she had asked for. This was his idea of fun, playing for a music-loving teenager, not an audience of grim-faced jurors.

"God, you are so talented," she enthused, which made him grin. "Mrs. Miles played it for me, too, and her play lacked intensity and brilliance. But maybe it was because of that nosy boy who had come to irritate her. His name was Cameron."

"Cameron Croft?"

She shrugged. "He came shortly before the end of my lesson. I was reluctant to leave her alone with him, but I knew her husband was due home soon. He always came around the time I left. I met him when I turned into Regents Park Road and I felt relieved that she wasn't alone with that freak. It was the last time I saw Mr. Miles. Sad, isn't it?"

"I JUS' KNEWIT, KNEWIT all the time. He's a dangerous man, Leo is." Lydia gulped down her Jim Beam and reached for the bottle on the worktop to refill the tumbler.

Cameron was quicker and emptied it into the kitchen sink. She was too far gone to fight him. "Do stop talking about Dad like that. We know he's not a killer. And the police will soon find out he's innocent."

Lydia stared at the empty tumbler as if it was the core of all her misery. "I should've divorced him long ago, when you were still young. He's ruined your life and mine."

Cameron felt as if he was going to be sick. He smashed the glass into the sink. It broke on the hard enamel. "My dad is innocent. And you didn't divorce him, he divorced you. Stop twisting the facts. If anyone has ruined my life then it is you."

Lydia slapped him without force. "This is no way to talk to your mother, my boy. You are my boy, not his. Don't try and defend him."

Bile rose in his throat. "I love him," he shouted.

Lydia gave a short ugly laugh. "Oh, stop wasting your feelings on Leo. He's not even your father. Do you hear me? I had to sleep with another man to get pregnant. There. I always wanted to tell you. Children should know the truth. All your loyalty and—"

"Ma!"

She looked at him blearily.

"Ma, does Dad know about this other man?"

"Yeah. Stealing another man's child, that's like him, innit?"

"Shut up, Ma." He opened the cabinet with her "secret" supply and unscrewed the cap of a brandy bottle. "Here's all the company you're ever going to have. First you chased Leo away and now you've lost me, too."

"But, Cam, you need me. I'm your mother."

"I'd have been better off with a drink dispenser." He motioned towards the door.

"Where you goin'?"

"None of your bloody business. Leo's going to take care of me." He kneaded the handle.

"He's in the nick, had you forgotten? Your darling dad's a killer."

What a shabby triumph. He banged the door with the sole of his shoe.

JOY NEEDED TO DO SOMETHING to occupy her hands. They had been trembling a lot lately and it got worse in the evenings, when it was dark. She longed for Valanna, her planet of never-ending daylight.

She traipsed around her flat and did all the mundane things she could think of. She descaled the coffee machine, scattered fertilizer pellets on the hydroponics and sharpened the pencil that lay by the telephone. She had unplugged the apparatus this morning after two calls from reporters who weren't put off by her huffy answers. She knew they would write eloquent diatribes, and she couldn't stop them. Psychoanalysts reinvent your past, she thought, and journalists invent your present. And Shadoe would take care of her future.

When there was nothing left to do, she went downstairs to see if her office could provide her with any activities. She was surprised to find Shirley in the anteroom, emptying the contents of a drawer into a small suitcase.

"Good evening, Dr. Canova," she said venomously. "I'm handing in my notice. It doesn't look as if you need me any longer. I've only been here for twenty minutes and in that short time four of your clients have called to cancel their appointments."

Joy clasped her hands behind her back so that Shirley wouldn't be able to see that they were trembling. She would probably think that the shock of seeing her leave made them quiver. "Did they say why?"

"They had silly excuses. Patricia Miles had the audacity to claim that she was cured. Tsk." A hairbrush was whacked into the suitcase, followed by three issues of *Astrology Monthly*.

"Don't forget to uninstall your Star Charts program from my computer."

Shirley's face turned an unbecoming shade of red, but she did as she was told. When she had everything together, Joy held out her hand. "The keys. You won't be needing them any longer." With this, Joy saw Shirley out of the house and locked the door. She checked all downstairs windows, switched off the lights and the computer. She had never felt more alone. She drew both bolts on her apartment door. She had added the second bolt after Maureen's death.

Count your blessings, she thought. At least she had got rid of Shirley.

But she felt more like counting her misfortunes. And this she did while she sorted the dirty laundry into little heaps on the bathroom floor.

One. Leo, the only man she had ever came close to loving, had been arrested. It would end with a terrible miscarriage of justice. A white blouse landed on top of a T-shirt.

Two. The exodus of her clients. A bra was flung into a corner.

Three. The press was intruding into every aspect of her life. A tea towel joined a washcloth.

Four. The BBC had backed out of their contract for her TV series. Two stockings were turned inside out.

Five. Her father had had a nervous breakdown. A dark blue sweater was wrung between her fingers.

A dark blue sweater? Joy couldn't remember wearing it in ages. She had never liked the thing. A bad buy. She held it up by the shoulder seams. It had cats' hairs on it.

Suddenly she knew it. She was the next. This was Shadoe's next threatening letter. She could read it inside her head.

Beloved Joy

I was in your house. I stole clothes from your wardrobe. I can come and go as I please. And I will return. This is the sweater I was wearing when I killed Maureen and her cats. Now what shall I put on when I come to drown you? Your wish is my command.

Fearfully yours,
Shadoe

Joy stuffed the garment back into the basket and threw everything on top of it. She didn't stop screaming when she ran into the bedroom and crouched on the coverlet, hugging her knees tightly. There it was again, the shadowy creature under her bed, whispering dark, vile threats.

CHAPTER TWELVE
THURSDAY, 24 JUNE

TERRY SAT IN HIS OFFICE, his feet resting on an open drawer, and read the notes he had made the previous day. Only one fact stood out. Croft's son Cameron had shown up during Caroline's piano lesson and had annoyed Patricia. Shortly afterwards, her husband had returned home. I met him when I turned into Regents Park Road. Terry could only make some wild guesses as to what happened then. Had Daniel had a bust-up with Cameron? Had he enraged the boy so much that he sought revenge?

Terry reached for the phone. Best thing was to ask Patricia. The phone rang as he was about to pick up the receiver.

"Terry."

He didn't understand a word at first. A voice, its pitch falling and rising oddly, screeched at him. Finally he made out some fragments. "He was here...Shadoe...a letter...on my own...please."

"Calm down and tell me—"

"Come. You must come. He could still be around."

"Come where? Who are you?"

"It's me, Joy."

"Joy Canova?" He hadn't recognized her voice, distorted as it was by hysterical sobs. "Where are you?"

"At home."

"Where at home?"

"In my office. Please—"

"Are you alone?"

"I don't know," she wailed. "I don't know."

"Have you been harmed?"

"No, no."

"What happened that upset you so?"

"I found a letter. Shadoe wrote me a letter. He wrote it on my own stationery. I just found it. In my desk. The bottom drawer. Don't you see what that means? He was here, he's probably still around."

"Stay where you are," Terry said, already standing and grabbing his jacket, "Don't touch or move anything. I'll be with you in a few minutes. I'll also send someone over from Hampstead station. They're closer."

Janice drove the panda car, lights flashing, while Terry put through the call to the SOC team. They turned into Thurlow Road with screeching tires.

An officer stood guard at the door. "She's fine," he informed Terry the moment he shot out of the car. "Just a bit strained."

"You didn't search the house, I hope."

"Of course not, sir. You told us to leave everything alone until the troops arrive."

"Good."

He found Joy sitting in the anteroom, looked after by a WPC. "Thank you, I'll take over. Please secure the place." They had never been closer to Shadoe. "Joy, are you all right?"

"I'm so glad you're here." She clung to his lapels.

"Why did you call me instead of 999?"

"I had your card. I wanted you. You would understand. I'm so scared."

"Sure, I understand. Now first of all, you must tell me exactly what happened. Start with yesterday evening."

"I went down to the office and Shirley was there. She wanted to hand in her notice."

"What time was it?"

"Around nine. After she had left, I locked the front door." The words came out jerkily as she gasped for breath.

"Was the front door locked this morning?"

"Yes, I had to unlock it to let the officers in."

"The key?"

"Was on its hook by the door."

"Who else has a key to your house?"

"Shirley had one. But she returned it before she left."

"Would she have had a chance to put the letter in the drawer last night?"

"Yes, she was already here when I came down."

They were interrupted by the arrival of the forensic team. Terry passed on his orders, then resumed the Q & A. Janice was standing by his side, taking notes.

"When was the last time you looked into this drawer?"

"I don't know, a few days ago maybe."

"So the letter could have been there for a while. What did you do after Shirley had left?"

"I checked all the downstairs windows. I've been nervous these last few days."

"Understandable. How many rooms are there on this floor?"

"This room, my office, a bathroom, a kitchen, and a large empty room. I haven't found a use for it yet."

"How about the basement flat?"

"It's empty, too. Do you think he came in through the basement?"

He gestured to the officers who had started to unpack their equipment. "This is a very efficient team. They'll clear up this question within the hour. I'm just looking for options. After checking the windows, did you go upstairs?"

"I did. There's a door to the stairway. I locked and bolted it. And I also locked and double-bolted the door to my flat. I've been doing this ever since Maureen was killed."

"Shadoe had no chance, then, to sneak upstairs."

Joy frowned, drew a sharp breath and then shook her head almost imperceptibly.

Terry was looking her straight in the eyes and saw something move inside them. The pupils contracted, and the next moment Joy was calm. Her breathing was no longer forced, her hands opened and let go of Terry's. She smiled. Terry wondered if what he had just witnessed had been the quickest conceivable process of active dissociation.

"I am sorry," Joy said, her voice warm and sincere. "I shouldn't have caused such upheaval."

"You had every reason to be scared after receiving a death threat from Shadoe."

"It isn't a death threat."

"It isn't?"

"It is more of a confession. I can show you—"

He pressed her back in the chair. "This will have to wait until the photographer has finished. Okay, so Shadoe wasn't upstairs. We won't have to waste time searching for clues there. When did you go to bed?"

"Shortly after I had locked the doors. I started sorting my laundry, but I was knock-out tired. I slept soundly until six this morning. I came down after breakfast. I had nothing specific to do, just rummaged around, looking if anything needed to be tidied. And I found the letter. Two sheets of paper. One of them in the same hand as the threat to Maureen. The other—" She paused and looked at Terry with a rueful smile. "This is what pushed all my buttons. The other is a fake of my own handwriting."

"You took the letter out of the drawer and placed it on the desk, I assume."

"Yes, I'm sorry I touched it at all. I know how keen you are not to have fin-gerprints interfered with. I put the sheets on my desk side by side, but was too shocked to take anything in. I read the message after I had called you. It didn't make sense. Why did Shadoe take such a risk just to tell me how he enjoyed killing Maureen?"

"Janice, please ask if I can see the letter now."

She went into the office and returned with two sheets, each in a separate sealed transparent cover. Both sheets bore Joy's letterhead. Janice looked over Terry's shoulder as he read.

My Sister in Fear,

I hypnotized Maureen as you would have done. When she came round, gagged and tied to the chair, she looked at me in disbelief. This time I would do it in silence. I talked too much to Alison because I was apprehensive. But now I wanted a slow swelling of anticipation.

All the Venetian blinds were down and only a small table lamp illuminated the room. Maureen's wide-eyed gaze wandered around as if she was looking for help, and she saw the cats. I had found and killed six of them, a quick death for those useless creatures. You would have been proud of Maureen. Her eyes turned liquid with tears, which she quickly blinked back. With her mouth blocked, she had to breathe through her nose.

My first move was to touch her throat with the palm of my right hand. I had to wear latex gloves. Oh, if only I could have touched her skin to skin.

I experimented with a plastic bag, but it was no use, for I couldn't see the manifestation of agony on her face. I looped a belt around her throat, I pulled then let go again. Maureen squirmed in rhythm with the tightening and loosen-ing. I decided to punish her for her lack of cooperation and stuck one of the tam pons up her nostril. Immediately, all movement stopped and her tongue pushed at the cloth in her mouth until it sagged out, wet with her saliva. I dared not push it back in, lest she might bite me.

She was fierce now. I stroked her hair, then groped for a wide belt to fix around her neck.

And so it went on and on, until I could no longer distinguish between her and myself. Her pain, her angst, all her beautiful fear was mine now. We were nearing the climax. I stood behind her, raising her head with my left hand, running the fingers of the other hand along her throat, up and down. There was no fighting power left in her. She had totally submitted to my domination.

Calmly, feeling as if I was floating underwater, I returned the knickers into her mouth. A second tampon into her other nostril followed.

At this point, she was longing for death, for what else is fear than desire in its extremity? I looked down at her and our eyes locked. I pressed the edge of my right hand against her throat, allowing her just enough air to breathe painfully through the cloth. Her chest heaved, her hands clutched at the arms of the chair. Her fear emanated from her, transformed, filled the room, filled me with life.

Yes, yes, let it come, don't hold back, give it all to me, all that beauty and perfection. Blindly I reached out for a belt and lashed it across the sides of her neck. The pain enhanced her fear, her head fell from side to side.

And then she was dead and the spell was broken.

Exhausted, peaceful and relaxed, I sat down on the floor at her feet. After a while, I heard a scratching sound at the kitchen door. In my satisfied state of mind, there was no room for further cruelty. I unbolted the back door and gently pushed the white, furry bundle out into the darkness.

Such is the sweetness of fear.

Fearfully yours,
Shadoe

Terry swallowed hard. "Joy, you have an eidetic memory. Please try to recall when you last opened the drawer."

Joy looked at the ceiling. "I hardly ever use the stationery with the letterhead. I'm not much of a letter-writer." She closed her eyes for a while, then opened them again. "I used a sheet of my stationery when I took down the details of the Valanna meditation for Patricia Miles and my notepad was full."

"Seems I need one of your lists again."

"Everyone who has been here in the meantime, right? That's not going to be a long list. I lost some clients. They are afraid to see me." She laughed. "I want to treat their fears, and now they fear me."

"And who do you fear?"

"What do you mean?"

"You were scared to death when you found the letter. Is your fear associated with anyone in particular? A client or friend? Someone who is likely to call you his soul companion, his sister in fear?"

"I wasn't scared of a person. I was scared by the idea that someone had invaded my home. It's a basic instinct to protect your territory."

"You thought Shadoe was still in your house. What did you think he might do to you?"

Joy stood up and walked to the open door of her office. For a few minutes, she watched the forensic team. "Water," she said with her back to him. "I had a vision of a hand, big enough to cover my face, pressing me under water. I held my breath until I thought I'd explode. The pain was like a dagger in my chest." She turned around. "I felt so tiny and helpless. Like a child."

"AT LEAST WE KNOW NOW why Shadoe let out the cat. I bet Brick will like that last paragraph." Smithhaven twisted his tie. "You have too much on your plate, Terry. Far too much. I should give one of your cases to another department."

"I thought you considered the Miles murder solved," Terry said tersely, staring out of the window. There were moments when he wished his office wasn't tidy. His eyes seemed to slip off the surfaces.

"Yes, but you don't, and I don't want you to waste your energy on this one, especially after this new letter turned up. It's another nail to Leo's coffin. He spent the night from Thursday to Friday last week on Joy's sofa, just inside the window of time for writing and hiding the letter. What did the graphologist say?"

"The letter was written by the same person who concocted Maureen's death threat. Joy's handwriting has obviously been faked and the chances of Joy writing the letter herself are a million to one against. Something about the flying starts being insecure and the loops too round."

"It would have been the best explanation as to why we found no signs of a break-in. But why should she have done it?"

"To release pressure, maybe. The letter is a confession of sorts. I tried the direct approach, taking it literally. Sister in fear."

"And?"

"Gloria had her baby last night."

Smithhaven laughed. "That's the nicest alibi I've ever heard of. Maybe Joy has other siblings. Did Hope really die? Was there a twin given away to another family?"

"You sound like a Gothic novel. For me, this letter is a clear proof that

Shadoe is sexually immature." Terry got up and paced in front of the window. "When normal people have a sexual desire they seek a sexual outlet, intercourse, masturbation. But some people seek a sexual outlet for a non-sexual desire, the desire to control."

"Rapists. I've been to police school, too, kiddo."

"Would you mind not calling me 'kiddo.'"

"You must learn to ease up, Terry. I should take you along to one of the LAGPA drop-ins. We have a monthly evening when we all meet in a gay bar. It's an open venue and we don't advertise that the place is full of gay police officers. It's great fun."

Terry counted to ten in his mind. "Thanks, but no thanks. Can I go on?"

Smithhaven made an appeasing gesture with his hands.

Terry sighed. "Let's talk about the real dangerous minds, those who seek a non-sexual outlet for a sexual desire. When I was a DS, I was assigned to the investigation of a series of homicides. Three prostitutes had been strangulated. The killer never touched the victims sexually. I talked to hundreds of prostitutes. Two stories caught my attention. In both cases, all the customer had wanted was to look at them as they were lying naked on the bed. He didn't touch them. He didn't want them to touch themselves. And he didn't touch himself either. He just walked around the bed, looking at the naked woman. He had an erection and in one case he ejaculated. I had this very strong gut feeling that he was our man. He wasn't impotent, so why didn't he touch the women? Why was it enough for him to look at them? What did he feel that was stronger than sheer lust? Was it the feeling of power? The knowledge that he could kill her if he wanted to?"

"And was it him?"

"Yes. We caught him and he was convicted. During an interview I asked him about the feeling of power and he said that not to kill felt even better than to kill. It made him god-like. When he ejaculated over the woman it was a baptism."

Smithhaven was silent for a while. "The cat. Shadoe spared the cat."

"Right. And he got deep satisfaction from his deed, bordering on the sexual. 'We were nearing the climax.' And later, the language gets even more explicit. 'Yes, yes, let it come, don't hold back, give it all to me, all that beauty and perfection.' Sounds like a line from a porn movie. Shadoe doesn't have a sex life. Controlling other people's fear is his substitute. He is sexually retarded. Now, would you call Lionel Croft sexually retarded?" Terry sat down, pleased with his line of argument.

"That's the psychological side," Smithhaven said. "But we have physical evidence. It's not just the empty showcase. We found a box of latex gloves in Leo's workshop. He says he needs them for working with coatings. But whatever he has them for, there they were, handy and within reach."

"We found two pairs in Joy's office, as well, in the medicine chest. She said they were for emergencies. AIDS protection."

"Granted, everybody can buy them. But then there is the beating of Maureen's throat with a belt. Shadoe knows how to land a belt where he wants to land it. Have you ever tried to hit someone on a certain spot using something as unsteady and difficult to handle as a belt?"

Terry harrumphed.

"It's not a rhetorical question. We tried, Andrew Sedgewick and I. We used a crash-test dummy and belts similar to the ones found in Maureen's living room. Most of the time we landed the darned thing on the dummy's temple or shoulder. It takes a lot of practice. And Leo has practice. You know what we found in his house. Four whips, two canes—"

The telephone rang and Terry answered it, glad about the diversion.

"Inspector? This is Theobald Winter speaking."

Terry thought he heard Winter's starched shirt crackling. "Have you remembered something?"

"That's right. On Friday morning, when I let some fresh air into the kitchen, I saw a young man leaning against a window sill on the other side of the street. I couldn't see his face, it was hidden under a black baseball cap. When I shut the window half an hour later, he was still there, sitting now. I was on late shift, so I was at home all morning. Around eleven o'clock, as I was preparing my tea, there was a commotion outside and I looked out again to see what was going on. The young man and Patricia Miles were yelling at each other. She sounded considerably frightened and I wanted to go to her assistance, but she got rid of him herself. He called her a silly cow and the next moment she threw something at him. An apple, I think. The man, or rather boy, picked up the apple and stomped away, cursing."

"Can you describe the boy?"

"He was thin, dressed in baggy black trousers and a leather jacket."

"Brilliant. Could you hear what they said?"

"Patricia screeched 'Leave me alone.' And he shouted he only wanted to help her. She said he was spying on her and something about not giving him piano lessons. She yelled at him to get the hell out of her life. Which was when I considered intervening. But then she threw the apple and it was over. The entire exchange lasted only a few seconds."

Terry thanked Winter profusely, praised his excellent memory and disconnected. Smithhaven, who had been listening over the loudspeaker and fiddling with his tie all the time, resumed his list of evidence. "Two canes, a leather paddle—"

"For God's sake, Patricia had a quarrel with a boy two days before Daniel was killed. A boy she knew. I bet it was Cameron Croft. Caroline Wakefield had seen him on Tuesday, when he came to ask for piano lessons. He was a pain in the—"

"Like father like son."

Terry, normally a soft-spoken, self-controlled man, found himself in a volatile mood. "You can go on reveling in Croft's Whips'R'Us collectibles, but I'm going to do my job. I'll interview Cameron. He has a key to his father's house, giving him access to the butterflies."

"You can save yourself the trouble. We checked his alibi. His mother said he was at home."

"His mother is an alcoholic. She wouldn't have noticed him leave at night. Anyway, first I have to know if the boy was Cameron. I'll go and see Patricia. So, if you'll excuse me." He leapt up and grabbed his jacket.

"If I didn't know for sure that it's impossible, I would say you have a crush on her."

The explosion came completely unexpectedly, even to Terry, who couldn't remember ever raising his voice above domestic level. "That does it," he shouted and banged his chair against the desk. "You silly prick. You can take your insinuations and idiotic jokes and shove them where the sun don't shine. And if I ever see you play with that tie again I'll cut it off even if it costs me my job."

He left before Smithhaven could react. Several heads appeared and were withdrawn quickly. This would go down in history as Terry's First Ever Fit of Rage. Almost as spectacular as an eclipse. He felt deeply ashamed and knew he should go back in and apologize, although that wouldn't stop Smithhaven from taking disciplinary action.

He trampled down the corridor. It took him the drive to Primrose Hill plus another five minutes walking up and down Erskine Road to get the adrenaline out of his system. After a while, Terry sat down opposite Patricia's house and found that one got cold and stiff. The boy must have had a very good reason for wanting to waylay Patricia.

Patricia didn't answer his ring, so he went around the corner to La Strada, where she had said she could be found when she wasn't at home. The boutique, a maze of fluffy and shining materials, welcomed him with an embrace of dampened music and burning incense.

"I don't think we have your size," a woman giggled.

He swept off the fringes of a shawl that had got caught in his collar. "Misty

Baker? I'm Inspector Terry. Is Patricia with you?"

"She's gone for a walk on Primrose Hill. She's looking for butterflies."

"Butterflies?"

"She had a healing experience."

Terry thanked her and walked over the hill. He didn't have to search long before he found Patricia sitting under a tree. She looked content and contemplative. Her hair had its shine back and her posture was comfortable.

"Hullo, Inspector. Lovely day. Come and sit down by me."

He complied.

"Do you believe in reincarnation?"

"I'm not sure," Terry said. "Would it help you to think that Danny will be born again?"

"It's nothing to do with Danny. I had a vision of an old woman dying in a room full of hallucinated butterflies. It would make sense if it was a flash of a memory of my death before I was born in this body. I don't understand what's happening to me. You have seen people in my situation before. Is it normal to feel happy at one moment and break into tears the next? To feel numb, barely alive and unable to taste food and then again to wake up and think, what a gorgeous morning, and feel like singing? Do you think I'm still in a state of shock?"

"I've seen crazier reactions, that's for sure. The best thing is to flow with the moods as they come."

"I feel so free." As if to prove the instability of her mental balance, she switched to gloom without transition. "Leo isn't free. I want him back. I didn't know how much I loved him until you took him away from me. I tried to see him but they wouldn't let me talk to him. It's my fault he was arrested. I shouldn't have gone looking for the butterflies. And all that fuss about the sculpture he was making. Me as a butterfly. He didn't do it to scare me."

She had told Terry all that before. "I know, and I believe you. I'm onto something and I need some background information. Tell me about Cameron."

"He's a wicked boy. But it's not his fault. His mother sent him spying on me. She can't let go of her ex. Cameron would be better off with his father."

"He interrupted one of your piano lessons, didn't he?"

"Oh, yes, that was so embarrassing. Danny came home just as I was seeing Cameron to the door. He turned pale and wide-eyed. He must have thought I was having an affair with the boy. Can you imagine that?"

"Did he say anything?"

"Danny? No. He just looked at the boy as if he had seen a ghost. I hope he believed me when I said he wasn't my lover."

"On Friday, he bothered you again, is that correct?"

"Where do you get all the info from? I don't know what he wanted. He said silly things about helping me and about wanting to tell me some truth or other. I threw an apple at him. I really lost my nerve. I felt so abashed afterwards."

Recalling Smithhaven's incredulous stare when Terry had hurled abuse at him, he knew exactly what she meant. "Did you see him again after that?"

"No."

He thanked her, returned to his car and drove to Camden. Lydia Croft's living room reeked of whiskey and sweat. Terry opened a window. "Mrs. Croft, you are in a bad state. How much have you been drinking?"

"Noddenough to kill me."

"Where is your son?"

"Where's ma precious son, eh? Gone. I told 'im the truth and now 'e's gone."

"The truth about what?"

"Leo isn't his father. He loved a man who's not 'is father. Thad'll teach him noddo trus' anybody."

"Have you any idea where he could be?"

"Nope."

"Has Cameron run away before?"

"Look iddup in yer files."

Terry took out his mobile and called an ambulance. Lydia protested but Terry knew an emergency when he saw one.

Back at the station he organized a search for Cameron. Brick passed around sandwiches for lunch. Nobody in the incident room made any allusions to Terry's outburst this morning. Only Blockley came up close and said: "Just stay clear of interview room one and you won't run into him."

Terry cast him a grateful glance.

Osborn made a eureka-sound. "I've found something. Two years ago, Cameron Croft disappeared and was found two weeks later, in the wee hours at the St. Pancras Hospital Bus Stop, halfway between King's Cross and his home, slouched on the seats, unconscious. I'll print it out."

Terry read the report and, as the truth unfolded, his stomach knotted. Another blow for Patricia. Another reason for Lydia to drink herself to death. Another life destroyed.

"We have to find the boy, and pronto. Janice. If you were Cameron, where would you hide?"

"He's a child. Children seek shelter with their parents. Even if his father's in prison, his house is still there and Cameron has got the keys."

"H-H-HELLO?"

"Hi, Angus, is that you? Why don't you hold the receiver between your ear and your shoulder? Then you've got your hands free. I can't stand hearing you stutter. Just can't stand it, sorry. I'm a bit nervous these days."

"Done. Joy, I've been to see my GP. He says you're right. The rupture is bad and I should have it fixed ASAP. Could you help me?"

"You're welcome anytime."

"Are you free on Saturday? How many sessions do you think I'll need?"

"Saturday is fine. With luck, we'll have your tomophobia fixed in a month."

"Is ten o'clock all right with you?"

"Perfect. See ya."

"HI, CECE, IT'S ANGUS. How are you?"

"Fine. How're you?"

"Splendid. Except for a conductor's elbow and a cramped neck from tucking the receiver under my chin."

"Relax your arms and stutter away. I don't mind."

"No, it's all right. I wanted to tell you that we have two sketches for the sleeve of Timotree."

"Oh, brill. When can I see them?"

"How about Saturday? I'll be in London for a therapy session. Afterwards we could have lunch."

"Suits me. I planned to go to a book signing at Waterstones in Hampstead in the morning. Looking an accomplished writer over the shoulder and all that."

"My therapist is in Hampstead, too."

"Then I'll pick you up."

"I should be ready around twelve."

"Fine. Give me the address."

JANICE WAS USED TO TERRY'S silence during car rides, but this was different. He was so engrossed in his thoughts that she didn't dare ask him what exactly he expected to unearth once he had found Cameron Croft.

She had studied all the documents in the case, had gone through a plethora of variations in her mind. Did he suspect the boy of killing Daniel Miles? What could possibly be the motive? Maybe he longed to have a family again. If his father married Patricia, he might move in with them. Cameron wants to butter her up, asks for piano lessons, claims he has something important to tell her. He's not spying, he's ingratiating himself. When he kills her husband he thinks he's smoothing the way for them. But the butterflies still needed to be explained.

Or else he hated his dad, thought him an abject liar who had made him believe he was his real father. Lydia's constant nagging had poisoned his feelings. If Lionel was convicted of murder, Lydia would give him up and they could start anew.

When they arrived at Croft's house, they found that the police seal over the lock had been broken.

"This is not going to be easy," Terry said as he fumbled with the lock. "Cameron is a very hurt and lonely boy."

Janice nodded quietly. The door swung open. From the second floor they heard a pounding rhythm. "Placebo," said Janice appreciatively. The noise grew louder when they mounted the stairs. They found Cameron on his bed, surrounded by a mess of open CD jackets, discarded clothes and half-eaten hamburgers. He lay on his side, with his eyes closed, and his hands held fetus-style in front of his chest. He looked very hurt and lonely, indeed.

Terry switched off the CD player. "Cameron?" He sat down, carefully avoiding a ketchup-stained T-shirt, and touched the boy's shoulder.

"I didn't mean to kill him," he muttered without opening his eyes. "'Twas an accident."

"I know," Terry said. "And in fact, it is the other way round. Daniel Miles killed you. Two years ago, he destroyed your future. Ain't it so?"

Cameron struggled into in a sitting position, crackling some cheese and onion chips under his butt. "Who told you?"

"A shot in the dark."

"Oh, you're not daft, eh? I thought the police were all daft and ignorant, arresting my Dad and thinking he was a serial killer. He's a good dad. He loves me, although I'm not his own son. I wish I had known before."

"Then you wouldn't have been so angry."

"Yep."

"I must caution you before you make a confession." He looked at Janice and she understood that he wanted her to take over this part. So she informed the boy of his rights, removed a headset and a Superman comic from a chair and sat down. She flipped open a new page in her notebook.

"You ran away after your parents split up," Terry began the tale for Cameron.

"I wanted to punish them. I wanted to show them what they had done to me. I had some money but it didn't last long. And I had heard about...." He stared at his bitten fingernails.

"The rentboys?"

"I didn't mean to be one of them, just try to get some dough so I wouldn't have to go home. And this punter, he...it hurt. I thought he was going to break me in two. And then the rubber burst and there was blood and I thought I was going to die."

"You were picked up that night and taken to hospital. Did you tell your parents what happened?"

"You crazy? You don't go and say: Hey, Mum, guess what, I had some anal sex with a pervert. There was a social worker who talked to me, wanted to know about my parents, and I said there's only my Mum and she's pissed all the time. Then he left me alone in his office for a moment because there was some sort of hubbub in the corridor, and I had a peek at the papers on his desk. There was a slip in it that said I was HIV positive. I snatched the folder and did a runner."

"And then, two years later, you suddenly stood in front of the man who had infected you."

At this point, Janice finally understood the connection Terry had made. She felt her pulse beat deep in her throat.

"Yep, 'twas him, coming home to his lovin' wife. Puke. I felt like taking a swipe at him right there, but I ran away. It was all coming back twice as bad, the pain and humiliation. But I'm older now, right, and I thought, okay, you're gonna get through this like a man, you're gonna bleed the bastard for money, that'll teach him. So I wrote him a letter, told him to meet me on the railway bridge. I took the letter to his place early on Friday morning, and then I thought, I just have to tell his wife. If Miles had AIDS, then his wife might have it, too, and she could infect my Dad. So I wanted to tell her, but the bitch threw fruit at me. An apple hard as stone. And I thought, I'll tell Dad about her real character and about the risk and all. But he was in his workshop and was bloody inspired and wouldn't listen to me. I just had to do something to get it out of my system. And then I remembered the showcase with the butterflies. Dad had told me he put it away because it frightened Patricia. I opened it, unpinned them and put them in an envelope."

"We didn't find your fingerprints on the glass or the hook."

"I wrapped handkerchiefs around my hands. Smart, huh? I wanted to drop the envelope into Patricia's letterbox. Just a bit of shock treatment, you know. I had it on me when I went to my appointment with Daniel."

"That was on Saturday night?"

"Midnight, yes."

"I bet he kept you waiting."

HE HAD KEPT HIM WAITING for almost twenty minutes. Cam had planned to be aloof and self-assured. He wanted to master this situation in a way that would make him proud, that would take away the feeling of shame. But after leaning against the railings for twenty minutes, he was nervous and insecure.

Miles came ambling along the road as if he had all the time in the world. He was wearing the same coat he had had on two years ago, and for a dreadful moment Cam thought he was going to be raped all over again.

"You're late," Cam said in a voice that was supposed to sound mature and dangerous. "Where's the money?"

"I'm not going to give you any money," Miles said, looking sternly past Cam.

"I'll tell your wife."

"It doesn't matter, we're going to be divorced."

"I'll tell your boss." Cam didn't even know where Miles worked.

"Good luck."

"I'm going to destroy your career."

"There isn't anything you can say that could possibly threaten me."

So, maybe he could shock him. "Tell you what, you fuckin' bugger," he spat. "You've got AIDS. You're going to die in a nasty, ugly, painful way."

Miles gave a short, cynical laugh. "That's exactly why I don't care about my career any longer. I've known it for years and it's worn me out."

Even before the message had been fully processed in his brain, Cam threw himself at Miles with all his strength. The bugger had known, he had infected him knowingly. Miles' head crashed against something and suddenly he was on the ground and Cam kept jabbing and kicking away at him while tears stung in his eyes.

It stopped as abruptly as it had started. Cam bent down. "I'm sorry. Are you all right?" He didn't move. The envelope with the butterflies slipped from Cam's jacket. Yes, that would give Miles something nice to taste when he came round. He stuffed them all in his mouth. It was like castrating him. A man with a mouthful of butterflies can't harm anyone.

Procrastination was not Terry's thing. Not even when his office had still been a mess, and had therefore offered plenty of excuses to busy himself, had he been able to postpone a dreaded encounter for longer than five minutes. So he found himself in front of Smithhaven's office at seven in the morning, feeling not much different from the petrified boy he had been when he had waited for his turn at the Young Genius competition.

He hadn't known his superior long enough to be able to foresee his next move. Would the fact that Terry had solved the case be enough to outweigh his misconduct, or would it add to his undoing because he had destroyed Smithhaven's pet theory? How much of Smithhaven's joviality was facade?

Terry knocked stiffly and entered.

Smithhaven stood by the window with his back to him. The only document on his immaculate desk was Cameron's typed confession. Terry suppressed an urge to cough politely. For a while, only the bubbling sound of the coffee machine filled the room.

"Well done," Smithhaven said in a flat voice, addressing the window pane. "We had to let Lionel Croft go. I am still convinced that he is Shadoe. I mean, there are people who knew Maureen, and people who knew Alison. We have to look for someone who knew both, which narrows down our choice to Lionel Croft and Joy Canova. Joy has been exonerated because of the letter she received." He ran a finger along the sill. "On the other hand."

He turned around and Terry saw that instead of a tie, Smithhaven was wearing a bow-tie, blue with black polka dots. The kinks in Terry's neck softened when he understood the conciliatory offering.

"On the other hand, all I can do is congratulate you on your sensitive handling of this difficult arrest. Well done, indeed." With a smile that was just a bit on the wicked side, Smithhaven settled the matter for good.

"Thank you. I'm sorry I insulted you."

"No harm done. Actually, it was exactly what we needed."

Terry gave him a questioning look.

"There won't be any rumors for a while. Did you know that they were taking bets on us? I don't know the exact nature of the bet but I mean to find out. Oh, by the way, we'll have to wait another week or two for Vandyke. He's been assigned to a different case."

"What? I mean, sorry, but I was relying on him to join the team tomorrow. I have prepared a folder with a theory I wanted to talk through with him."

"Maybe he wouldn't like your theory at all, simply because you hadn't given him a chance to come up with it himself. A few years ago, I suffered from various symptoms and after reading up on them I made my own diagnosis. I went to see a specialist and when he asked what was wrong I told him my diagnosis, complete with the tests I expected him to run and the medication I wanted him to prescribe. He was displeased and did everything in his power to prove me wrong. The next time I need a doctor I'll still read up the symptoms before I put myself into his hands, but I will fake total ignorance of anything that goes beyond taking my temperature." Smithhaven poured tea into cups. "Tell me your theory and I'll promise to consider it seriously."

Terry took his cup and sat down. "All members of the Canova family have names with a meaning. Faith, Victor as in victory, Gloria as in glory, Joy, Hope. And then there is Shadoe as in shadow. The killer we are looking for is Shadoe Canova."

"And who is he? A forgotten uncle? A son they gave away for adoption?"

"It has something to do with Hope. The balance of power changed when she was born. Before that, Joy had been her father's favorite. Hope took her place. When Hope died, everything got out of control. Joy began to suffer from migraines, somnambulism and hydrophobia. Victor started to behave in unpredictable ways, as if he was trying to outrun voices in his head caused by an extremely guilty conscience. I wondered whether Hope's death was really a case of crib death, or if she was killed. If Joy saw her father kill Hope that would have been traumatic. But I'm sure it didn't start there. Joy and Hope were probably both sexually abused by Victor."

"Wait a minute. Where are you heading with your speculations? And where does Shadoe come into this?"

"Shadoe came into being when Joy dissociated herself from the ongoing traumas she suffered. Look at Joy Canova today. A renowned psychotherapist, good-looking, healthy, successful. I scratched the surface and what I found was a deeply disturbed person. She has no sexual identity. She takes whatever she gets. She has never had a lasting relationship, except the one with Lionel Croft. She still suffers from hydrophobia, nightmares, depressive episodes. She is capable of active dissociation. With this in mind, I had another look at the letters and began to take them literally. 'Fear is such a lovely thing.' Initially, we saw this as a weird, cruel form of cynicism. But what if Shadoe really means it? 'I am invisible.' Where can a person hide? 'Like you, I am a recluse.' Something clicked into place when I read this and remembered that Joy had told me about her childhood demon, a dark creature living under her bed. Croft told me that he recently spent a night on Joy's sofa because she feared shadows under her bed."

Smithhaven found this funny. "You think Shadoe is hiding under Joy's bed?

We should have a closer look then."

"I think Shadoe is hiding inside Joy Canova. She is a split personality."

With thumb and forefinger, Smithhaven flapped the bow tie like a butter-fly. "Are we talking about the latest psychological fad here? Multiple Personality Disorder?"

"It has been renamed Dissociative Identity Disorder."

"Which doesn't make it any more real. In my eyes, MPD will end up in the trash bucket, along with frontal lobotomy and abduction by UFOs."

"I've done my homework, Clen. I know MPD is a highly controversial issue. The symptoms are often iatrogenic, meaning that the therapy causes what it sets out to cure."

"I know what iatrogenic means, kiddo. Oh, sorry, I forgot I wasn't supposed to call you kiddo."

"What I was going to say," Terry went on with studied patience, "is that even though MPD is often a misdiagnosis, it is still a mental condition which is made possible by our neurological layout. It is a self-preserving mechanism, caused by severe abuse in childhood, carried out by a person loved and trusted. Unable to deal with the horror of being tortured by a person whose role it is to protect and nurture, the child flees into a state of negation. It's like saying: 'This isn't hap-pening to me but to someone else.' The unity of consciousness is disrupted."

"Let's get this straight," Smithhaven said. "Apart from Joy, there is also Shadoe. The two of them lead separate lives, not knowing about each other."

"Not necessarily just the two of them. The longer and more varied the abuse, the more personalities appear. The most common is a split of three to five distinct personae, differing in many ways, age, sex, intelligence, religion, sexual orientation or any combination of these. One person is allergic or diabetic, the other isn't. One can be short-sighted or color-blind, while another individual in the same body sees perfectly well without glasses."

"Who can tell if these differences aren't made up? I can pretend I'm a woman any time."

Terry ignored this. "You can't fake changes in the rate of cerebral blood flow or brain electrical activity. PET Scans have demonstrated that each personality is active in different regions of the brain. MPD is a compartmentalization of the psyche."

"Let's, for the sake of discussion, take it as a given that Joy is a split person-ality," Smithhaven said. "Would this mean that she doesn't know that there is a cruel alter ego inside her?"

"Yes, in most cases the personalities are mutually excluding and amnesiac. Shadoe certainly shares some of Joy's memories, as well as her knowledge, otherwise she couldn't have called her Sister in Fear and wouldn't be able to drive a car, write letters and, most importantly, she wouldn't know about Joy's clients. The amnesia is part of the mechanism to keep the traumatic memory away from the self that can still function healthily, in most cases the birth person, the one who was there from the beginning. For Shadoe, amnesia isn't important, because the trauma is her own memory anyway. But for Joy, there exists no trauma. She doesn't know about Shadoe, at least not on a conscious level."

"And why did Shadoe start his, or should I say *her* killing spree now and not sooner?"

"Alters often lie dormant for a long time until they are triggered off by a new trauma or something that threatens to bring the memory back to the birth person. Maybe it was when Joy went to take the photo of The Devil's Backbone. I am sure something happened on this bridge, something that deepened the ridge in Joy's mind when she was a child."

Smithhaven scratched the bridge of his nose. "But why is it that Joy isn't aware of the fact that there are periods of time which she cannot account for?"

"Because she thinks she was sleeping through a migraine. Shadoe doesn't suffer from migraine. He takes over. Maybe sometimes she notices that things have been shifted in the house or that something is missing in the fridge. But a migraine attack always leaves you with a feeling of dizziness and disorientation. It's like recovering from the flu. She has more to worry about than counting the eggs in her kitchen."

"You haven't thought your theory through to the end. Joy is a psychologist. She might fake MPD symptoms to make us believe she suffers from a personality split, so that if she's found guilty, she can plead she is of unsound mind."

Terry drank the tepid tea. "But Joy can't fake her own handwriting. Only Shadoe could do that."

Smithhaven was silent for a while. Pensively, he aligned two ball-pens on his desk. "We must talk to her again, with a psychologist present. We can try to gain access to her past."

"I would prefer to talk to Victor Canova first."

Smithhaven smiled benignly. "I'll call Oxford and ask them to drive him over."

"Tomorrow morning would be better. I have to consult with a counselor. I don't think I would get anywhere with him without thorough preparation. If he abused his daughter, he's not likely to tell us. I want to make sure I get the most out of this interview."

"I trust you fully. You did a great job with Cameron."

LEO HAD THOUGHT THAT the day when the charges against him were dropped would be the happiest day of his life. It turned out to be the saddest, most stressful day he had ever had.

Lydia, as his lawyer revealed to him, had made a royal pain of herself during interviews, getting all worked up because she had been married to a psychopathic killer. Hadn't she felt all the time something was wrong with Leo? Wasn't this why she had become an alcoholic? And so forth. She showed neither relief nor remorse when his innocence was proven. Relief would have been misplaced because now her son had confessed. Remorse had never been a part of her emotional layout. In her inimitable way, she had put the blame on Leo once more: if Leo had killed Daniel Miles then Cameron wouldn't have done it.

Leo's prime concern was to make sure that Cameron was not treated as a criminal but as the confused child he was. While Leo talked to the social workers and a lawyer, Lydia became more and more hysterical and was taken back to the hospital where she had already spent the night. So he was left to deal with all the formalities alone, glad to be rid of her messy presence.

What troubled him far more was Patricia. She had abandoned him. He hadn't seen her nor heard from her since the day of his arrest. During the sleepless nights on his hard prison cell bed he had imagined how she would cry her eyes out. She was so weak, so fragile.

When he came home on this day, late in the evening, he felt that even his house had forsaken him. Everything in it had been touched by official hands. Leo showered until his skin felt as sore as his soul. He toweled his hair as if he wanted to descalp himself, then shaved fiercely as if he wanted to scrape off his skin. He threw on some clothes and went into the kitchen where he continued his rampage with the contents of the refrigerator. He dumped moldy cheese and limp lettuce into the rubbish bin. The phone rang and he barked at a reporter until long after the man had rung off.

Mumbling all the four-letter-words that came to mind, he unplugged the phone, then plugged it in again and dialed Patricia's number to say his final goodbye to her, something that was best done when anger subdued the finer nuances of his feelings. She didn't answer. At the very moment when he banged down the receiver, the doorbell rang. He knew instantly that it was her. He clomped downstairs.

"Hello, Leo." She held up a shopping bag. "I've brought you something to eat."

He slammed the door in her face. How could she dare come to him on his darkest day, looking like spring in a white dress with a blue butterfly brooch.

Baffled, he opened the door once more.

She was still standing there. "You look like a hunted animal."

"This is a butterfly." He pointed at her breast. "Made of feathers. Looks mighty real. So it was all a scam. You're an undercover agent and—"

"Leo, for Lord's sake. I'm cured, that's all. If you let me in I can make you something to eat. You look hunted and hungry."

She squeezed past him and he pushed the door shut with a sigh. Patricia made for the kitchen and unpacked the bag. She had brought all the basics, bread, butter, cheese, cucumbers, milk, orange juice. He tried not to feel too grateful and not to show it either. She spread butter on slices of bread, added cucumber and ham, and stacked the sandwiches on a plate. He grabbed the one on top and wolfed it in two bites.

"Poor Leo." She started making tea. "I wish they had let me talk to you."

The implication of her words dawned on him like a sunrise. "You mean you tried to see me?"

"*Mais oui*. I was worried and I missed you."

The china Leo had stacked on a tray rattled as he couldn't suppress the trembling of his hands. "And I thought…. Oh, I'm so sorry, Patricia. I thought just like Lydia you were sure I was guilty."

She inched closer and touched the backs of his hands over the cups. "Didn't they tell you I asked to see you? I'm going to file a complaint."

Her anger was like fresh well water on his wounded nerves. He laughed. "Never mind. Now let's get all these delicious things on the coffee table. I'm starving."

When they were seated, he apologized again. "I'm not a tad better than Smithhaven, who wanted to nail me for three murders. I had a theory about you and didn't give you the benefit of the doubt. Tell me what happened to you."

"In a nutshell: my HIV test is negative, my lepidopterophobia is a matter of the past and my feelings have crystallized. Leo, I love you."

He looked into her blue eyes and said in as steady a tone as he could muster. "It's over, Patricia. Can't you see that? My son killed your husband."

"Cam's story is all over the papers, just the kind of dirt they love to thrash. We have to stick together to get through this."

"You're so naive, darling. You think we kiss, make up and all is well."

"No, nothing is well and I know that. Try to see my side of things. My husband sodomized your son and infected him with AIDS. Who can tell which was the bigger crime?"

"With all this standing between us, we—"

"We have to make a choice or we'll end up with a jacket without buttons."

"Sorry?"

"Tailor's metaphor. Leo, I've grown up. I know Danny's death will always be part of my life. I have decided to accept it. It would be easier for both of us to start anew, with a new partner."

"That's what I'm trying to say."

"I said it would be easier, but not necessarily better." With this, she sat across his lap. Her cool fingers closed around the back of his neck.

"Patricia, what are you doing?"

She blinked away a tear. "I'm trapping you."

CHAPTER THIRTEEN
SATURDAY, 26 JUNE

THE DAY DAWNED GRAY AND WINDY. Lying motionless on her bed, Joy watched the clouds race across the sky. She hadn't drawn the curtains, she couldn't even remember going to bed. Getting up seemed pointless. What was life anyway? An erratic journey from nowhere to nowhere, surrounded by insignificant people doing trivial things in a meaningless world. Human interaction was just a long series of banalities, profanities and stereotypes. Why did she bother to cure people of their fears that were just variations of the ultimate fear, fear of death? There was no cure for mortality. The Valannians lived forever.

In an instant, she was on the shore of the iridescent ocean of silk. She plunged into the billowing waves, she swam and dived, she lay in the fine, yellow sand, warm and secure, watching the first sun set. A perfect world. Suddenly there was a small flash of blue lightning in her outer field of vision and the horizon was lit up by a ring of yellow fire. She couldn't get a migraine attack in Valanna. That would destroy the perfection, the beauty, the confidence. She slid forward on the sand until the waves were gently licking at her feet. The flashes disappeared and she saw the second sun rise. The sky had turned a cold, chrome-like gray. As the pain rose in her neck, Joy refused to believe what she was seeing. The second sun was black.

SHADOE GOT UP AND LOOKED down her front. A silky nightdress fell over her breasts. It reminded her of the night when she had been christened.

She had been her Dad's darling, she had loved and feared him. He was strong and mighty. A special bond secluded them from the rest of the family. Nobody was supposed to know about the nights when he came to kiss her. Shadoe would awake to his touch and hold still so as not to stir Joy, the other girl inside her, the one who was weak and treacherous, who wouldn't let Dad touch her and threatened to tell on him. Instinctively, Shadoe felt that this would be her end. She would no longer be needed.

But Dad protected Shadoe. He flung Joy over his shoulders. She wept and kept saying that she would tell Mummy, that Mummy wouldn't want him to do it again. Joy was so silly. She wanted her Mum to know even though Dad had told her that Mum would hate her for it, that she would send her away from home, give her up to strangers. Mum was having a new baby that would take Joy's place—Shadoe's place. Dad put a hand over her mouth and carried her out of the house and down the street to the bridge where she wasn't allowed to play because it was dangerous. He held her over the railing, told her he would throw her right down on the railway lines. "If you say a word to Mum, I'll do it. There can't be the shadow of a doubt that I love you, but I swear by God that I'll do it. It's to protect you. I would rather sacrifice you than let you ruin your life. You understand? Joy, do you understand what Daddy is saying? I'm not going to kill you. I will sacrifice you."

And Joy was gone. She was gone for a long time. Shadoe now had a name all for herself. Not the shadow of a doubt. She was in full control ... until Hope was born. Suddenly the bond was broken. Shadoe felt weaker each day. Dad no longer came to see her at night. One night, Shadoe tiptoed into Hope's room and looked at the sleeping angelic face. She covered it with a pillow. She couldn't stand the sight of Hope, knowing that all the love and fear her Dad had to give were now for little Hope. And she fetched another pillow from her room, and then her coverlet, anything she could find to blot out the angelic face.

The next morning, her Dad stood in the door, his face was white. For the first time, he looked frightened. "You did it, Joy. I know you did it. Why? Why?" And he began to throw the pillows at her, sobbing. Hope was dead.

"I saw you kiss her," Shadoe whispered. "You kissed her where Mummy wouldn't want you to." And so the bond was forged anew. He said he wouldn't tell on her if she promised not to tell on him.

But it wasn't the way it used to be. He hated her now. He wouldn't kiss her any longer, but torture her when he bathed her. He pressed her underwater. He was in total control of her fear. And one day, it was over. No more bathing, just the nightmares that remained with her and became her sanctuary.

Joy grew up. Shadoe watched her from afar, unable to take control. Alone. A recluse. Fear was her companion. Sometimes she was half aware of her surroundings, in a muffled, filtered way. But on some days she came round fully, quickly and painfully, as if falling from a great height. She would walk around, dizzy and insecure.

One day, after years with only small snippets of consciousness she suddenly found herself standing on The Devil's Backbone, the place of her christening. She held a camera in her hands. What was she doing here?

Her next memory was a young woman, looking at the photos with baited breath. Shadoe sucked up Alison's fear, fed on it, drew strength from it. It was the only emotion she knew, a strong, physical impact, like in the dreams when Dad's hand, its outlines moving like a shadow in the water above her, pressed her down, and she heard his god-like whisper: "You're a demon. You must be exorcised."

She began to use her body again. She dressed and undressed, drank and ate, left the house for nightly walks. And she played. She wrote letters, which she then burnt in the kitchen sink, poems of fear, imitating her Dad's handwriting. She just had never learned to write in a hand of her own. One letter was so beautiful she had to deliver it. She looked up the address in Joy's files and took the letter to Alison's house.

Shadoe had not meant to kill the girl. She was practically begging for it. On Saturday night, when Joy had been gone again, Alison came to her place, bedraggled and repulsive.

"Dr. Canova, thank God you're at home. I've lost my keys and I can't ring home or my parent's will make a helluva scene."

Appalled by her looks, Shadoe wanted to shut the door in her face, when she understood that Alison had followed her call. Alison, afraid of bridges, had come because she had promised to model her fear into perfection.

"I'll get the car keys," she said. "There is something I want to show you."

She had never driven a car, but it was easy. She just had to allow her body to do it. Alison babbled all the way. She was high. After a while she stopped asking where they were going. By the time they pulled up at The Devil's Backbone, she was asleep. Shadoe carried her thin body up the steps, just as Dad had done with Joy, then lifted her into a sitting position on the railings and waited for her to wake up. She couldn't throw her down in this lifeless state, or else there would be no fear they could share. No, she wasn't going to kill her. She was going to sacrifice her.

When Terry had talked to her on Friday evening, Nicole Clark, the police counselor, had given him a set of instructions which he was determined to follow implicitly.

"Choose a room where you and Mr. Canova can sit comfortably and in daylight. An interview room would be giving the wrong signals. Mr. Canova must not feel like someone who is being interrogated but like a partner in a conversation."

Terry scanned his office. Even in its new orderliness it didn't give a sense of comfort. After peeking through every door he could open without a key, he settled for Smithhaven's office. Its furniture in dark, mellow woods was cozy enough for the purpose.

"Make sure that there will be no interruptions. Get an ample supply of what you and he will need to drink or smoke. If he agrees to have the conversation taped, then get a tape that runs two hours, so that you won't remind Mr. Canova of the tape's presence when you turn it over."

A tape recorder was plugged in, a choice of drinks, cigars and cigarettes was put on the desk.

"Keep in mind that it is not your aim to find Canova guilty of child abuse. You and he together will establish if there is a trauma in Joy's past that could have initiated a dissociative disorder. Don't ask him any questions. Questions tend to put people on the defensive. Make statements, so that he is forced to agree or disagree. Canova is not a mentally healthy man. Even if you are shocked about the things he might reveal, don't show any signs of disgust."

Terry sat down behind Smithhaven's desk and practiced a benevolent smile towards the empty visitor chair.

"Most of all you must not forget that Victor Canova is a psychologically challenged person. He has a history of personality shifts. He is recovering from a nervous breakdown. Treat him like a criminal and he'll balk. Treat him like a raw egg and there is a slim chance that he'll cooperate. Concentrate on everything he says in a relaxed way. No distractions."

Terry put all papers and pencils out of reach. No doodling. And then he waited.

THE MEMORY OF ALISON'S FLAILING ARMS as she fell onto the railway line was not enough to keep Shadoe happy. Even Maureen, her perfect partner in pain, couldn't satisfy her. She was living through a crescendo of beauty, but she knew there had to be a finale.

Dressed in her favorite sweater, which she had unearthed from the laundry basket, Shadoe sat down at Joy's desk. A third letter had to be delivered. Tonight. Emma Little was the next person on her list.

Dear Emma,

Has it ever occurred to you that blood is circulating inside you all the time? Ten pints of it. There, under your skin. How can you live with that?

Ladies and Gentlemen, Shadoe proudly presents: the ultimate lesson in fear, tailor-made to fit the astounding actress Emma Little.

It's raining blood
You see it, feel it, taste it, smell it
And finally you will drown in it. What a kinescope death. Worthy of an Academy Award—not for you, I'm afraid, but for me in the Special Effects Section.

Since you will not live to see the photo of your blood-stained corpse go round the world, relish in the concept right now.

Fearfully yours,
Shadoe

She sat back, pleased with herself. But not for long. Where would she get the blood from? There was a scalpel in Joy's bathroom. She could cut Emma, catch the drops in a glass. Mixed with water to increase the quantity, the blood would still look scary enough.

The scalpel reminded her of something. Oh, yes, sure. Angus, the stutterer, who was so beautifully afraid of being cut. Angus was coming today. Shadoe would get all the blood she needed. But what would she do with the body? Things were getting out of hand. But Joy would take care of it. She would know what to do. She had lied for her. Maybe she would remove the evidence when she came round on Sunday morning.

IT HADN'T BEEN A GOOD IDEA, and Angus knew it. It was almost as bad as the time when, as a boy, he had been forced to see a string of speech therapists. Only the prospect of meeting Cece for lunch would see him through this morning. Maybe he should have asked her for help instead of Joy. Cece had healed his stutter, hadn't she?

By the time he turned into Thurlow Road, Angus was convinced this wasn't going to be a happy morning.

He was a little reassured by the fact that Joy was quite businesslike when she opened the door and led him into her office. She was dressed in a baggy sweater and wore no make-up. Her hair was combed back in a tight pony-tail. Recent events had taken their toll. At Canova Press, Victor Canova's nervous breakdown was the talk of the day.

"Before we start, I want you to describe your fear to me."

Before they started what? Wasn't talking about a phobia part of the therapy? "It's just the idea of having my skin cut."

"Did you know that a surgeon opens the skin in separate layers?"

Angus was vaguely disturbed. "No, I didn't know and I wish you hadn't told me."

"Are you squeamish when you're preparing a meal and have to dice the meat?"

"I'm a vegetarian."

"Neat."

She went on asking him all kinds of outrageous questions and told him stories full of gory details.

"What potential," she said in the end. "I am so glad you came to me. You're tense. It's time to make you relax. Hypnosis is the fast lane to healing. Let us see how suggestible you are."

Angus was prepared to do anything, just to get this over with. His eyelids dropped and he was lulled by her soporific tones. At one point it felt as if something closed around his wrists, but he was too far inside himself to worry.

She addressed him harshly. "Open your eyes and look at me."

His eyes flashed open. Joy towered over him, balancing a scalpel on her open palm.

"I'm sorry I couldn't write you a letter. I usually do so before I share the beauty of fear."

Angus tried to move and found his hands fixed to the armrests with scotch tape. "Wh-wh-wh—"

"Whatever it takes to show you perfection."

"THANK YOU FOR COMING," Terry greeted Victor Canova.

Canova, who looked jaded and emaciated, said in a faint, colorless tone, "Did I have a choice?"

"Yes, you did, and I'm glad you chose to help us." No, that wouldn't do. Flannelling Canova wasn't the right approach, no matter what Nicole Clark had hammered into him. Terry brought his vocal register down and wiped the phony smile off his face.

"Mr. Canova, Joy is suspected of having killed two of her clients. I want to make sure that she won't be treated like a common criminal because I don't think she even knows she committed these murders. I know it will be a shock for you to be confronted with the fact that your child is a double murderer."

"I must correct you," Canova said stiffly. He looked straight into Terry's eyes. "My dear daughter Joy is not a double murderer."

Denial, Nicole Clark had assured him, was to be expected. Best way to deal with it was to make concessions on minor points. Terry was looking for a reassuring answer, when Canova went on.

"She is a triple murderer."

Before he had time to think, the name was out of Terry's mouth. "Hope."

He could see Canova's relief at letting go, of no longer holding back what had bothered him for years. "Joy hated Hope. She was her rival." And with this, Canova broke down completely. Covering his face with his trembling hands, he sobbed. "She didn't love me any longer...Hope...tiny...soft.... That would teach Joy not to reject me again...did it all wrong. She was just a kid. How could I torture her? I turned her into a monster. I am responsible. Don't arrest Joy. Arrest me, Inspector."

It was no use asking him questions about details now. "Maybe it would make you feel better if you had a chance to apologize."

Canova looked up. "I tried to. After Faith's death. But Joy didn't understand what I meant. I think she has forgotten it all."

"But Shadoe hasn't forgotten. We believe that your daughter suffers from a split personality. Shadoe is the one you tortured." And turned into a monster, he added in his thoughts. "I would like to confront Joy with some facts about her childhood to see if I can provoke Shadoe. Would you be willing to help me?"

"No. All I want to tell her is I'm sorry. And that I love her. I never meant to harm my little girl."

Terry hadn't expected this sudden development. "I will call our counselor and see if she can come with us."

"I don't want anyone with me when I talk to my girl. Where is she? Have you put her in a cell?"

"She hasn't been charged. I presume she's at home."

"Then let's drive over. I want this to end."

FOUR PARALLEL CUTS RAN DOWN from Angus' shoulder to his elbow. Shadoe made sure that she didn't cut too deep. She didn't want her victim to fall unconscious too soon. Angus made low, whining sounds.

"Does it hurt? I am sorry. I don't mean to cause you pain. Fear is all I want you to feel." She held the scalpel up close to Angus' face and was rewarded with a stammered "Please don't."

"We will need a mirror. I want you to see how the blade cuts into your cheeks. I'll be back in a minute."

She was passing the door on her way to the stairs when the bell rang. She wanted to ignore the interruption, but then she realized that, just as she could see the visitor as a blurred dark shape, so could the visitor see her through the translucent glass.

"Just a second." She went to close the doors to the office and the anteroom, then opened the front door. A young woman, petite, freckled and red-haired, grinned at her.

"Hi, I'm Cece. Angus said I should pick him up here."

"He has already left."

"Oh. I can't imagine he forgot we were going to have lunch. When did he leave?"

"A few minutes ago."

She looked at her watch. "I'm not late. Why didn't he wait for me? Did he leave a message for Cecilia Terry?"

Terry. Cecilia Terry. Shadoe remembered a scene in the interview room. Joy had been smoking, playing it cool. They had shown her a letter to Cecilia Terry. "Your daughter? Not very likely."

"My niece."

Her visitor was Inspector Terry's niece. What could that mean? Was it a trap?

The young red-head cast her a strange look and Shadoe said quickly, "No message, no."

"Okay, thanks. I'll just walk around a little. Maybe he'll come back."

"It's drizzling. You can wait inside. I have a client at the moment."

"Thank you." Cece snuggled into a seat.

This wasn't too bad, when she came to think of it. Sliding into the office, Shadoe began to see the possibilities presenting themselves to her.

"My dear Angus, I must ask you not to make a sound. Unless of course you would like to watch someone die. Someone you know. Cecilia Terry."

"P-p-please," he whispered. "L-l-let h—"

"Shhh. Let her go? I'll let her go in a few minutes. She's just waiting, she thinks you forgot her. She doesn't know you're here. If you make a sound loud enough for her to hear, I'll go and get her and tie her to the other chair. And then you will have the pleasure of watching me doing a vivisection."

Angus made a gagging sound. His fear was stronger than his pain now. Shadoe reached for the scalpel. Angus couldn't know that the door's thick padding would swallow most of his screams. He would fight to hold back, afraid of endangering Cece. That was better than a mirror.

JANICE SWERVED INTO A PARKING SPACE in Thurlow Road. Terry got out and held the door open for Victor. He stepped onto the pavement and pointed at the car in front of them. "This is Fenning's car. I recognize the bumper sticker. 'I Brake for Stutterers.'"

Terry was beginning to feel uneasy, but he couldn't pin it down. "Cece's editor? What's he doing here?"

"He's in charge of Joy's next book, so probably they had something to discuss. I don't know, I haven't been at work all week."

The little group climbed the steps to the front door. Terry's index finger was already near the buzzer when he heard a familiar voice.

"What kind of mass gathering's this?"

Terry turned around. "Alan?"

"I've come to fetch Cece."

Ever so slowly, Terry moved his finger away from the buzzer. There was a faint ringing of warning bells in his head. "Cece?"

"She went to a book signing. Afterwards, she had an appointment with her editor. When she came to fetch him, Dr. Canova told her he had left. Cece called me and asked if I could come round."

"You mean, she's inside?"

"Yes, waiting for me. What's wrong?"

"Did she call you using Dr. Canova's phone or did she use her mobile?"

"How would I know? But I've never seen her without her mobile, so.... She said she was sitting in the anteroom. Canova is seeing a client."

Victor attempted to ring the bell, but Terry intercepted his hand. "Wait. We don't know who is in there. It's Saturday. Migraine day. It could be Joy, but it could just as well be her psychopathic alter ego."

Janice stood between Victor and the door. "And why was she lying about Fenning? His car is still parked here."

"Maybe he went on foot to meet Cece and they missed each other," Alan suggested.

"Please, shut up all of you. Sorry, but I have to think." Terry switched on his mobile phone. "I'm calling Cece." He dialed. "Cece? It's Rick. Don't say a word. Just listen and do what I tell you. Is Joy in her office? Good. You'll come over to the front door and open it for me. Yes, I'm here in Thurlow Road in front of the house. Got it? Good." There was a moment of tense silence.

"LOOKS LIKE CROSS-STITCH." Shadoe admired the pattern she had scratched on Angus' cheek. The fear emanating from the young man was like a halo. "I suppose Cecilia will leave soon. Then you can scream all you want. Just hold out a little longer. We could advance to amputation now."

Angus wriggled, his head moved from side to side.

"We'll start with a tiny bit of the earlobe. Hold still, dear. It hurts more when you fight. I might cut off the complete auricle if we're not careful."

As she was bending over, pain flared up in her ankle. Angus had managed to free a leg. Shadoe stumbled and cut a finger on the tip of the scalpel. She hit Angus across the face. "Now you'll get what you asked for. You'll see your girlfriend die."

She flung open the door and saw Cecilia walk to the front door. Shadoe was behind her before she could reach out for the handle.

THE SILENCE WAS BROKEN by a commotion behind the frosted glass. Terry heard a scream. His hand closed into a fist, shot through the glass, got hold of the handle. The door swung open. He saw Cece being pulled away from him. She struggled wildly. Terry ran. He bounded into the anteroom and reached the door to Joy's office a fraction of a second too late. It shut in his face. What's happening to Cece? What the hell had he learned about hostage situations?

He opened the door and froze. He was aware of many things simultaneously, as if his brain cells had recruited in groups with different responsibilities.

Joy Canova, a wild look in her eyes, was holding a scalpel to Cece's throat.

Alan's hand gripped Terry's wrist like a steel clamp. Did he think he would risk Cece's life by throwing himself onto Joy—or rather Shadoe? Or did Alan need the support to stop himself from doing just that?

Victor Canova, a ticking time bomb in a situation where one wrong move could prove fatal, stood stock-still, but for how long?

Angus Fenning was tied to a chair. Blood oozed from numerous cuts that formed a pattern on his cheeks. Sweat mingled with the blood, giving it an unreal shine, like drops of water-color in a glass jar.

Janice, as good a police officer as he had ever met, had not joined the storm troops. She had stayed behind to call reinforcements, as he would have ordered her to do if he had had the time to think.

Most of all, he was aware of Cece and the acuteness of her fright. His eyes were glued to the hand with the scalpel. It was Joy's hand, cramped into a tight grip by Shadoe's mind, steadily nearing Cece's throat.

"Nobody move," Terry said.

"I'm sorry, Joy," Victor blurted out. "Please, Joy, don't do anything you might regret."

Terry stopped him with an instinctively outstretched arm. "I said, nobody move. I'm in charge."

"She's my daughter. Only I can talk her out of this."

"This isn't Joy," Terry postulated. "You are Shadoe, aren't you?"

He saw a minute change in Joy's posture when he said her name. The knuckles of her hand had relaxed long enough to allow the blood to run back. When Terry mentioned Shadoe, they turned white with tension again. She was there. Joy was somewhere in there. Victor Canova was right, they should let him talk to her. When Joy took control, Cece would be safe.

"Talk to her, but don't move."

Canova, tears in his eyes, muttered incomprehensibly. "Joy? My girl. I am sorry."

When the scalpel touched her neck, Cece produced a gurgling sob and Terry thought his mind was being torn apart.

JOY WASN'T SURE ABOUT THE REALITY of the situation. Pain filled her brain like liquid lead. Fragments of visions swam before her eyes. A pillow dropped over Hope's tiny body. Alison fell without a scream. Maureen fought for breath, the muscles in her arms were hard as iron from the futile reflex of trying to protect her throat. Angus was slapped across his bleeding face.

Where was she? Who was she? Why was she holding a scalpel in her hand? Whom was she pressing against her chest? And why couldn't she let go? She had to stop this.

She felt a stirring inside her, the headache retreated. A second pair of eyes opened inside her head, a mind within her mind.

The shadow under her bed had found its way into her. There was only one way to stop it. Just one way. She struggled not to think of what she planned to do, lest the shadow could read her mind. She thought of Valanna. That's where she would soon return. She would dive into the silky ocean, she would swim, float, breathe in the open sea.

A SCREAM, SHORT, FAINT AND GHASTLY, escaped from Shadoe's mouth. The blood flowed back into her knuckles. If only Terry knew how long it would last, then he'd take the plunge, wring the scalpel from her hand and free Cece. He wished he could change places with her. He had to distract Shadoe and give Joy a chance to take control.

"I offer you safe transport to the airport, from where a jet that will take you anywhere you wish."

Shadoe's brows dipped in a frown. "Safe transport?"

"It's better than going to jail, I'd say."

"You can't put Joy in prison," Canova erupted. "She's innocent."

There were too many people involved. Victor Canova was the dangerous party here. Alan was admirably self-controlled. Cece, his lively little girl, was still as a rock. "How much money will you need?" Terry asked.

"Money?" Shadoe wasn't taking the bait.

"You'll need another hostage," Alan said. "You can take me. Rick, have you brought your handcuffs?"

Terry drew them from a pocket in slow motion. Shadoe watched with mounting confusion. "What's all this about?"

"I'm handcuffing this young man, so you have a second hostage. We're just trying to be cooperative, aren't we, Joy?"

That was the moment Terry had been waiting for. Shadoe had been dazzled by the unexpected turn of events and Joy had heard her name. He could see the change in composure and the sudden pained grimace on Joy Canova's face, bespeaking her migraine. Terry stepped forward, but he wasn't quick enough.

In one resolute slash, her blade cut across the strained throat. Bright red blood spurted out with every beat of the heart. Terry pressed a handkerchief onto the severed carotid artery, knowing there was no hope. Seconds later, she had already gone into hemorrhagic shock and died in Terry's arms.

CHAPTER FOURTEEN

THE ROOM SMELLED OF disinfectant and was lit by a small bedside lamp. Cece's frizzy curls stood out in stark contrast against the paleness of her face and the starched, white pillow. Her closed lids gave her a relaxed, peaceful look. Gingerly, Terry kissed her forehead.

"I love her so," he said with a catch in his throat.

Alan put a steadying hand on his shoulder. "They've given her something really strong so that she can sleep."

Alan had remained with Cece when she was taken to hospital. Terry couldn't stay by her side because his duties as a detective required his presence at the scene of the crime. Now, five long hours later, he could finally slip into his role as uncle and surrogate father. He still wore the suit that was stained with Joy Canova's blood.

"I've never seen a throat being cut," Alan said. "For a moment I thought it was just a horror movie. It couldn't be real."

Terry had never seen it before, either. He had seen victims with cut throats, but not the act itself. It had all happened quick as lightning, but in his mind the scene was replayed in slow motion and every detail was branded on his memory.

When Terry had raised the handcuffs and had said Joy's name, Shadoe had let go of Cece. The hand with the scalpel was lowered, just for a fraction of a second. Alan had grabbed Cece and had pulled her out of the danger zone.

"I'm glad you held Cece's face close to your chest, so she didn't see it happen," Terry said.

"How can someone cut his own throat? What a dreadful way of committing suicide."

A quick flash of the blade, accompanied by a sound like tearing paper—there had been no time for Terry to stop Joy. "It wasn't suicide, but an act of self-defense. Joy killed Shadoe."

Victor Canova had collapsed over his daughter's body. Terry doubted that the man would ever be able to reconstruct his facade of mental sanity.

And all the time, Angus Fenning had made little animal-like sounds and wrestled with his bonds.

"Angus was here," Alan said, as if he had read Terry's thoughts. "They stitched him up and he sat with me by Cece's bed for an hour before the nurse came to accompany him back to his room. Cece had a hard time convincing him that it wasn't his fault her life had been in danger."

Terry got up and flexed his shoulder muscles. "I wish I had become a pianist. I think I'm cured of stage fright for good."

"Fine. You can play at our wedding, then."

"You mean you proposed to Cece in a hospital of all places? How very romantic."

"Of course not. I proposed to her in the ambulance."

Terry grinned and went over to the window. "Alan," he said softly to the other man's reflection in the pane. "You must promise me something." He turned around and smiled at his ex-lover. "When you're my nephew-in-law, don't call me Uncle."